EL GAVILAN

Craig McDonald

TYRUS
BOOKS

a division of F+W Crime

Published by
TYRUS BOOKS
an imprint of F+W Media, Inc.
4700 East Galbraith Road
Cincinnati, Ohio 45236
www.tyrusbooks.com

ISBN 10: 1-4405-3194-3 (Hardcover)
ISBN 13: 978-1-4405-3194-1 (Hardcover)
ISBN 10: 1-4405-3191-9 (Paperback)
ISBN 13: 978-1-4405-3191-0 (Paperback)
eISBN 10: 1-4405-3192-7
eISBN 13: 978-1-4405-3192-7

Printed in the United States of America.

10   9   8   7   6   5   4   3   2   1

Library of Congress Cataloging-in-Publication Data
is available from the publisher.

This book is available at quantity discounts for bulk purchases.
For information, please call 1-800-289-0963.

THIS NOVEL IS FOR ALISON JANSSEN.

"*NEVER ATTACH MORE FEELING TO A THING THAN GOD DOES.*"

—ORIGIN UNKNOWN

THEN

Her grandmother was the first to die of thirst crossing the Sonoran Desert.

Holding her hand as the old woman passed, little Thalia looked across the heat-shimmering sand and wondered again why they had left home.

Thalia's family went back seven generations in Veracruz.

Veracruz was lushly tropical and sodden with rain. There the Gómez family lived close by the Gulf Coast beaches—palm trees and fruit to pick and eat; the Atlantic Ocean, full of fish. At least, her mother said, they could never starve there.

Though they were getting along, they had no prospects for more.

After much arguing, the Gómez family set out for the distant border.

The farther north they trekked, the uglier and emptier Mexico became for Thalia.

Her grandfather had been a Zapatista when he was only twelve. Consequently, Alfredo Gómez fancied himself more the *vaquero* than he had right to claim. Still, Alfredo had a plan. They invested a portion of their meager funds in two old horses and a mule. Alfredo loaded the mounts with jugs of water.

The unsuccessful crossers set out with too little water. That's what everyone always said. Alfredo meant to see his family well supplied for their border crossing. Thalia's grandfather set off a day's ride ahead of his family with the notion of depositing the water jugs at strategic points to see his family safely across the desert.

The money might have been better spent on professional *guías*. Thalia's father, Francisco, did meet with a couple of guides, what would now be called Coyotes feigning interest in their services, but really only fishing for free tips.

Papa learned from the *guías* that they fed their clients, or "chickens," cocaine to make them walk longer distances . . . and to make them walk faster.

After buying the horses, Alfredo and son Francisco bought some white powder.

All of them, Thalia, her mother and father and four siblings, her aunt and uncle and two cousins and her grandparents, took the cocaine and set off on foot a day behind her grandfather, aiming for the distant Arizona border.

For the first two days, Thalia brought up the rear, walking backward, waving a tree branch across their dusty path to erase signs of their passage, anything that might tip the Border Patrol. The cocaine made the little girl approach her task with furious intensity.

Long after, Thalia would wonder if the cocaine hadn't been their undoing, clouding her father's and grandfather's minds from seeing the more sensible plan of her grandfather walking alongside them, keeping the mounts loaded down with water close at hand.

And she would later wonder if the drug-induced exhilaration had spurred her grandfather on to riding greater and greater distances out there alone and euphoric in the desert, the critical water jugs being dropped farther and farther apart by the old, wired Zapatista.

And if Alfredo was less the *vaquero* than he fancied himself, her father Francisco was even less the guide.

A two-day crossing stretched into four.

They found less than a third of the water jugs left behind by Grandfather.

Sister turned against brother for want of water. Husband and brother-in-law were crazed by the blow and the thirst and out of their heads from the heat.

The two men came to a knife fight over a jug of water.

Their horrified, dizzy and drugged children looked on as they slashed at one another.

Thalia, only seven, sat with her grandmother as the old woman died from dehydration and heat exhaustion, her lips and tongue black. Her eyes were shrunken back into her head. *Abuela's* voice was a dry whisper. Sonya Gómez told her granddaughter, "You'll see it for me, Thalia. *El Norte*, it will be paradise. Your life there will be like a dream, darling."

They abandoned her *abuela* on the desert floor, already a mummy. They left Grandmother Sonya in the desert with Thalia's gutted uncle, then, days deeper into their death march, they left behind a cousin, a younger brother and Thalia's baby sister. The ground was too dry and hard to bury any of them.

When they reached the other side, it took two days to find Grandfather.

Alfredo at once set off with his horses and mule, headed back across the border to find and recover his wife's and grandchildren's bodies.

They never saw Grandfather again.

Chasing work and opportunity, the survivors of the Gómez clan kept drifting north across the decades. They became legalized citizens, picking fruit for stingy pay and cleaning hotel toilets and the houses of rich gringos.

Eventually they reached Ohio.

EL NORTE

ONE

Tell Lyon let himself in with the keys given him by the mayor of New Austin and flipped on the lights. Tell's first notion was that the place was oppressively tiny. A tight vestibule fronted a bulletproof-glass, teller-style window behind which the receptionist/dispatcher sat.

Between one A.M. and seven in the morning, all local 911 calls defaulted by relay to the Horton County Sheriff's Office.

Tell's first personal priority was to reexamine existing work schedules to see if with some overlapping shift rotations—combined with two additional full-time officers he planned to petition the administration and town council for—he could bring his force up to operational autonomy.

He checked his watch against the clock on the wall. It was early, five thirty A.M.—he wanted to be there when his crew arrived.

His last stint as a Border Patrol night-side sector chief had concluded one week earlier along the California borderlands. Tell was still most comfortable staying up nights—his lonely bed something to be avoided.

The new New Austin chief of police keyed himself through the second security door to the squad room. He had no office of his own, just a corner desk hidden behind two, seventy-two-inch upholstered fiberboard dividers.

Tell tossed his keys on his desk. His predecessor had left a Snap-On Tools calendar thumbtacked to the front fiberboard divider. An

7

oiled, pneumatic blonde in a hardhat and string bikini straddled an enormous chrome lug wrench. Tell took the calendar down and tossed it in the trash can.

* * *

He was going through the work logs and week's duty reports when the first of his crew came through the door. She was petite. Her fine, mouse-brown hair was scraped back in a limp ponytail. Tell thought, *Ditzy, but driven*. And she was the first in. She smiled uncertainly and said, "I'm Julie . . . Julie Dexter."

Tell put out a hand. "Tell Lyon. Glad to meet you, Julie."

She smiled. "Cool, but unusual. 'Tell,' I mean."

"Western novel character," Tell said. "Daddy was a huge Louis L'Amour fan. Tell Sackett was his favorite character."

Julie nodded like she understood. She said, "I was named after that cruise director on *The Love Boat*. The one who got caught up with cocaine. The actress, I mean, not the character."

"I remember." Tell said, "So, predictions: Four full-time officers here, not counting you and me. Bet you a Starbucks. Who'll be first in?"

Julie smiled uncertainly. "I'm always first in. Until today, anyway."

Tell said, "I'd have guessed that. But our uniforms—who'll be first to arrive?"

"Billy Davis," she said with a shrug and a head tilt. "And he'll bring doughnuts. Krispy Kremes . . ." Julie faltered.

Tell smiled. "Go on. We're off the record. And you're really helping me find my feet and get my bearings. I won't forget that."

She nodded, pressed a hand to her flat belly. "Billy has weight issues. Chief Sloan, *former* Police Chief Sloan, he had given Billy an ultimatum about his diet."

Tell thought about that. He asked, "How tall is Billy would you say?"

"Five-ten. Maybe five-ten-and-a-half on a good day."

"How much would you guess our Billy weighs?"

Julie hesitated again. Tell looked at her, smiling, eyebrows raised. "Two-twenty," she said.

Tell had expected worse. He said, "Julie, when was the last time one of ours had to pursue a perp on foot?"

She thought about that, screwing up her face. "Frankly?"

"Always frankly," Tell said. "That's our pact, you and me—the truth always."

"The answer is never."

Tell smiled. "Fine. I'm more interested in brains than wasp waists for my officers. And I'm not one to issue ultimatums. Any prodding I might or might not give Billy about dieting goes to concerns for his health. I'm not going to threaten his job with it." He paused. "Billy, he has good taste in doughnuts, does he?"

"Few too many things with chopped nuts, but mostly, yeah." Julie smiled uncertainly. He sensed she wanted to say more.

Tell said, "You can tell Billy all that I told you."

She was still lingering, on the edge of something. She was toying with her nails. They were blue with yellow smiley faces.

"Something else on your mind, Julie?"

"My work schedule, sir."

"Tell. My name is Tell."

Julie said, "*Chief Lyon*." She smiled. "The old chief insisted I be in at seven A.M."

"Got a conflict?"

"By minutes," she said. "My daughter has to be at school by seven forty-five, but can't go inside before seven thirty. My mother's just had cataract surgery and her driving . . . ?"

Tell waved a hand. "I get up early. I'm used to working nights and like the quiet in the morning. I'll cover the radios until you get in. Your shift now starts at eight A.M. That going to jam you up on the other end, picking your daughter up?"

"I usually take a late lunch so I can pick her up and drop her off at Mom's before I come back for my final hour." Tell had passed the school complex on his drive in—less than three minutes from the police headquarters.

"Then it sounds like we're all set," he said.

Julie said, "Thank you so much, Chief Lyon."

"What's your daughter's name?"

"Tiffany."

"Pretty."

"Thanks, Chief Lyon." Julie looked at her new boss like she was seeing him for the first time. She was emboldened by their small talk to give him a good once-over. He stood six feet, maybe six-one. Good build. He had hazel eyes and auburn hair that was graying at the temples. She guessed he was cusping forty. She smiled and said, "You have any children, Chief Lyon?" Then she remembered to check his left ring finger: bare.

Tell said, "Not anymore."

TWO

Sheriff Able Hawk lifted the dead bird by the neck and shook it in the elderly Mexican's face. "Blood sports in Horton County, Luis? Not gonna fly in my corner of Ohio, *amigo*."

Luis Lopez raised his hands, searching for words. His supply of English was wicked sparse.

The sheriff's reputation, and his harrowing image on county-line billboards, preceded him. Luis recognized Hawk from those glowering roadside portraits. Luis's legs were shaking, and that hadn't gone unnoticed by Able.

The two men were standing in the shadow of a big, buckling barn at the back of an egg farm complex.

Able cast down the dead fighting cock and spat on it. A dislodged steel gaff bounced across the gravel. The big cop stooped down and scooped up the spur. He held the bloodied spur up close to Luis's right eye.

"I don't want you feeling singled out, *amigo*," the sheriff said, waving the gaff in front of Luis's face. The old Mexican saw an expanse of grayness in Able: gray hair, at least what Luis could see of it under the sheriff's gray Stetson; gray walrus mustache and penetrating gray eyes. Able wore a dark gray uniform. The sheriff's tunic strained against his swollen gut.

"Few years back," Able continued, "had us some unwanted crackers come up from Georgia. Old boys raised pit bulls and fought 'em. You'd drive by their house and it looked like dogs had been hanged from their trees. Those Georgia boys would tie big knots in the ends of the ropes and have their dogs latch onto them. Then they'd hoist the dogs off the ground and make them hang there to strengthen their jaw muscles. Clever, huh? We cleared 'em out, though it took some time. Then we passed a slew of laws making it impossible to own one of those nasty hounds here in Horton County. Levied us some stiff and crazy penalties for violators. 'Course, before all that, one of those old boy's dogs got loose and mauled little three-year-old Sydney Adler. Pretty little thing the sweetie was." Able shook his head and spat into the dust. "*Before* the bastard's dog got at her."

The sheriff slapped Luis's arm and smiled. "Good news here is your fighting cocks ain't mauled none of my citizens yet."

Able pulled the arm of his sunglasses from his shirt collar where they dangled, flipped open the remaining closed arm and slipped the glasses on, hiding his strange gray eyes. "But that's about all the good news there's to be had this day, Luis. See, we're sending you back South, pronto, if those papers of yours come back queer."

Able ambled over to his command cruiser. Deputy Troy Marshall, thin, fit and one year back from Iraq, smiled at the sheriff and said, "Surprise. Luis here is illegal."

Deputy Marshall held up the Mexican's hand-tooled leather wallet and pulled out a driver's license and Social Security card. "I've seen better fake IDs on high school kids. Where do you think they're getting these things, boss?"

"Suppose we should just be cow-simple pleased the workmanship's so shitty," Able said, "don't you think?" Able nodded at Luis Lopez. "Book the son of a bitch, Troy. Slap him in county and get the damned paperwork started."

"Usual drill?"

Able nodded. "Sure. Feds still ain't enforcing our immigration laws. So we'll bill the federal government for Luis's room and board, since they let him stray across the border and all the way up here into Ohio to fight his fucking birds. "

Deputy Marshall nodded. "And the birds, Sheriff? Destroy 'em?"

An epiphany seized Able, and he liked the attendant spin. "Nah, don't kill 'em just yet. Call PETA and those tight-ass bastards from the Prevention of Cruelty to Animals or whatnot. Let 'em come out and shoot some footage of those birds for some of their propaganda films. We might could use those bleeding hearts to *our* ends, eh? We'll stir up those left-leaning animal lovers and maybe get 'em to put backward pressure on those ACLU-types trying to bust my balls for our tough policies on illegals here in Horton County."

The sheriff paused, then said, "Later, after, quiet-like, you kill those damn birds and drive 'em over to the food pantry and let 'em freeze 'em for our *legal* poor for Thanksgiving. They're wiry, but I 'spect they'll cook like any other bird."

Able swung into his command cruiser and headed out to the south corporation line. He pulled onto the berm across from the newly posted billboard. Able had allocated money for the billboard from a slice of post-9/11 federal grants. In theory, the funds were supposed to be used to buy new radios or to obtain and train bomb-sniffing dogs and similar policing tools that might be useful to thwart or stave off the next terrorist attack.

But Able tended to have a more rabbinical interpretation of the guidelines set forth with the federal grants. A key, stated component of Homeland Security and the federal assistance sent Able's way was border security and enforcement of immigration laws. To Able's mind, he was well within the spirit of the law with his new billboards.

Able sat in his cruiser and appraised the sign:

Notice to Horton County Employers:

Hiring illegal immigrants or those with false identifications
is a federal crime! It's the law!

—Sheriff Able Hawk

Three similar billboards had already been posted at the north, east and west county lines.

A middle-aged man on a bicycle coasted to a stop alongside the sheriff's dusty cruiser. "She's a beaut', Sheriff Hawk," the cyclist said, nodding with his helmeted head at the new billboard.

Able nodded. "So you support me, then?"

Balanced on the toe of one sneaker, fists still tight on the handlebars, the man shrugged. "Why not? It's not like Mexico's sending us her best or brightest, right?"

Able gave the cyclist a thumbs-up and got his cruiser in gear.

Radio crackle, then DeeDee said, "Sheriff Hawk? Sheriffs Denton and Pierce wanna know if you're up for a coffee out to Big G's along I-70?"

The sheriff sniffled with allergies—something new was abloom—and clicked the mic. "Headed that way anyways. Tell 'em to give me a bit to get over there, Double D."

Able hooked a U-turn on the two-lane and doubled back north. Two miles from the destination truck stop, the sheriff of Horton County saw a new message posted on the marquee above Jay Richmond's used car lot:

Spanish Spoken Here!

Stop in new Mexican Friends!

We're doin' deals!

The sheriff smiled crookedly. Well, that wetback-loving cocksucker.

Able shook his head. At least dumbass "Dealin' Jay" lacked the brains to post his message in Spanish so its intended recipients could maybe read the boldface bastard.

THREE

Shawn O'Hara took a last scan of the week's police blotter.

There were plenty of DWIs—never a shortage of drunk drivers.

There were several stops of speeders in school zones. Lots of Hispanic-sounding names attached to those. The local cops had a new acronym, DWM: Driving While Mexican.

Smash-and-grabs and purse-snatchings abounded on the West Side. The victims and witnesses of these all described suspected perpetrators as "looking Mexican."

Shawn, two weeks shy of his second anniversary as editor of the *New Austin Recorder*, executed a find/replace to swap out "Mexican" for the politically correct "Latino."

The journalist selected one nugget from the blotter to develop as a headline item.

The old-timers and retired cops Shawn had consulted swore that the last Horton County sporting house in memory had been closed down in the early seventies.

Of course there were always some straying housewives and drug-addicted young single women who'd put out for cash or a fix here and there, but Horton County, and its county seat of New Austin, hadn't had a working whorehouse in more than forty years.

But a few days back, Sheriff Able Hawk and his crew had busted up a ring of working girls operating out of a slab, run-down ranch house in a former blue-collar working tract gone mostly Mexican—make that *Latino*—on the city's West Side.

The houses were built in the 1950s for factory families of three or four.

Now each of those dilapidated houses was home to two or three families of four or more. The driveways and sidewalks of the neighborhood were lined with rusted old Astrovans and Aerostars . . . two or three antiquated vans to every dilapidated house.

The sheriff's boys arrested six women—all Hispanic—most of whom spoke little to no English.

The sheriff's boys had booked the women for prostitution.

More striking: the women were catering almost exclusively to a "Mexican clientele."

According to the last census, the West Side of New Austin was 45 percent Latino. And that census was already a few years old. The previous census had found the neighborhood was then 85 percent white, 14 percent African-American and 1 percent "other."

Call it "sea change" stuff.

The parking lots in the strip malls around the West End were lately crammed with *taqueria* trailers.

The signage for the West Side check-cashing businesses, cigarette outlets and beer and wine drive-thrus all read in Spanish now.

Shawn's desk phone rang. He scooped up the receiver and said, "Shawn O'Hara. May I help you, please?"

"You could get back here, Shawn," a silky voice said. "It's your day off, Shawn, you know? Our promised day together? And it's late afternoon. You still taking me to dinner?"

A just detectable Latin inflection—the echo of her aging parents' authentic, still-strong accents. She said, "We haven't known each other long enough to give you the right to neglect me yet."

He said, "Just shutting down the computer now. Give me five minutes."

Shawn saved his changes to the police blotter and shut down his iMac. He slapped around on his desktop until he found his keys under a pile of faxed police reports. He switched off the police-band radio, shut off the lights and locked the door behind himself.

The newspaper's office was located on New Austin's main street, between the bakery and a tax-preparation storefront that was all but dormant six months of the year.

The newspaper editor, the youngest in the *Recorder*'s history, strode down Main Street, waving at the working barbers and druggists and butchers who waved or nodded back at Shawn from behind stenciled storefront windows.

His apartment, a shotgun loft above a bar spread along the length of a city block, was three blocks from the newspaper office. Shawn climbed the fire escape that trailed up the back of the building. Patricia Maldonado met him at the door and handed him a cold Corona with a slice of lime wedged in the lip.

Patricia, forehead and bare arms and legs glistening, was wearing one of Shawn's T-shirts and nothing else.

He could hear the window air conditioners running, but with the summer swelter and heat rising from the business below it was a losing battle.

Patricia kissed him, her mouth tasting of lime and beer, and he squeezed her bare ass with his free hand, kicking the door closed behind him with his shoe. "Got lonely, huh, Patty?"

"Patricia," she said. "And 'lonely' is one word for it." She toyed with the snaps of his untucked denim shirt.

Patricia was a student at the vocational college in Vale County, where she was wrapping up a major in restaurant science and marketing. Her parents—two of Horton County's rare documented, naturalized Latinos—owned Señor Augustin's, an upscale Mexican restaurant they had launched in the mid-1990s.

Patricia was lately spooking Shawn with her frequent hints about wanting children . . . with stubborn marriage talk.

Now Patricia walked backward, leading Shawn deeper into his own apartment, room by room, French kissing and helping him shed his clothes along the way.

When they reached the bedroom, Shawn was naked.

The light through tall windows on two sides of the bedroom glowed amber in Patricia's raven hair and black bedroom eyes.

She pulled off the T-shirt and drew Shawn down onto the bed atop her.

They had been dating for three weeks.

* * *

Sprawling together on the damp comforter and sheets, bathed in sweat, they stroked one another's skin, hearts still not settled. His hand was down there. He'd been trying to talk Patricia into waxing her pubic hair. So far, she had been resistant . . . and annoyed.

Shawn told her about the short piece he'd just written on the prostitution bust. When he told Patricia the names of the women arrested, she jerked her head up sharply and searched his face. "Oh God," she said. "*That's* what happened to Luz?"

Shawn frowned. "You know her?"

"She is a hostess weeknights at my folks' place," Patricia said. "Luz didn't show up for work the past two nights. We've been trying to reach her. Mother even called the hospitals."

"She's still in county lock-up, I suppose," Shawn said. "Probably couldn't make bail, so there she sits." He stroked the lank hair back from Patricia's damp forehead. "Couldn't look good for your folks anyway, right? I mean, being linked to a hooker?"

Patricia shot him a look, café au lait cheeks running to red. "Jesus, she's not a *whore*, Shawn. She must be more desperate for money than I knew. Luz's mother, Severina, and her daughter, Elizabeth, are back in Matamoros, living in poverty I doubt you can fathom. Her mother is very sick and there is nobody else to care for Liz, who is three. Time is short. If Luz truly was sleeping with those men, I'm sure it was to make more money to bring her family here where they can have a life, Shawn. I mean, well, *Jesus* . . ."

Shawn kissed her forehead; it tasted salty. "I'm sorry," he said. "That is terrible."

Patricia sat up. "I need to let my folks know what's happened to Luz."

Shawn ran his fingernails down her long back, tracing down to her tailbone. "Use the phone there," he said. It was sitting on the nightstand by the bed. He was watching her ass.

"No," she said, slipping on black panties. "I'll call from the kitchen. Be right back."

Shawn propped up his pillow and sat up, watching her walk nearly naked through the rooms of his apartment to the kitchen, which opened onto his fire escape. Downstairs, from the bar below, he heard someone break a rack of balls. He heard billiard balls drop and roll in the coin-operated pool table.

He slid off the limp condom and knotted it off and tossed it atop a copy of his own discarded newspaper. He reached across the bed and picked up Patricia's pack of Merits and butane lighter and fired one up, balancing a promotional ashtray for the film *The Man Who Wasn't There* on his belly. He couldn't hear Patricia's words, but he watched her pacing back and forth, gesturing vigorously with her right hand while holding the phone to her ear with her left. Her big, small-nippled breasts—the real things—swayed with each emphatic hand thrust. Her tangled black hair, flat belly and shapely hips . . .

Shawn felt himself getting hard again. He thought he'd keep pressing her to go bald down there.

Patricia hung up his phone and walked back through his shotgun apartment, frowning.

She sat down on the bed next to him, one leg tucked up under her, and he stroked her left breast with his fingernails. Still frowning, she grabbed his cigarette from him, took a long draw and said, "Damn that Able Hawk, anyway. Usually I'm on the page with him, but this time . . . ?"

Shawn scowled. "Are you joking? *You* support our sheriff? Son of a bitch is like some fascist with all these raids and billboards and that damned blog of his."

"You're such an absolutist, Shawn. Always black and white with you. You're maybe too certain of things."

Patricia took another deep drag on the cigarette, stubbed it out and moved the ashtray to the side table. "Hawk is a realist. Look around. This can't continue, Shawn. The town is collapsing around us. Neighborhoods are overrun with too many people. There's crime like this area hasn't seen. Our schools can't begin to keep up. Test scores are falling and state funding with them. Most of the illegals come across from Mexico with the equivalent of an eighth-grade education—the adults, I mean. So you can imagine the level their kids are at in comparison with the ones already here."

Shawn was shaking his head. Patricia narrowed her eyes. "I know exactly what you're thinking, Shawn O'Hara, and step careful now, because it's close to racist thinking on your part. Don't even say it."

"What?"

"You're thinking that I'm some kind of traitor to Hispanics and Latinos because I support much of what Hawk does. My family played by the rules, Shawn. My mother and father are legally here. I was born here. We spent years legally getting my grandmother and grandfather here. This stuff of sneaking across the border and making money and sending money back to Mexico and then expecting some kind of amnesty, it isn't fair. Sixteen billion dollars earned by underpaid illegals and sucked out of our own economy and funneled to Mexico. It's criminal."

Shawn shook his head. "Big so what? And where'd you get that stuff? Hawk's blog?"

She bit her lip. "Maybe . . . But it's a thing we all *know*. And it isn't just my family who's worried, Shawn. Other legals feel the same about Able Hawk. He's a hero to many in the Latino community, hard as that might be for you to grasp. Friends and enemies, they have a name for him, *El Gavilan*. It's Spanish for the Hawk."

Shawn smiled crookedly. "God, Able must love that dumbass nickname."

Patricia shook her head. "Hawk's a realist, like I said. We love this country too, Shawn. I don't want to see it wrecked or crippled by presumed compassion or wrong-headed charity."

Shawn didn't know where to begin to rebut that one. He leaned forward and kissed her mouth, his hand squeezing Patricia's breast. "I can see that. That makes sense."

He sounded insincere to his own ears.

Patricia shifted her arm, felt Shawn's erection. She said with a frown, "So much for conversation."

THEN

Not long after crossing the border, Thalia's mother and father came to see that immigration worked best when one already had family in the North. Better still if that family was established and best of all if some of those family members had become U.S. citizens. Then a kind of Jacob's Ladder could establish itself, hastening ascension and assimilation of ensuing waves of clan members who made it across.

But that wisdom came too late for the Gómez clan.

They had no such foothold.

They were the first of their family to cross, spoke no English and so had to find their own way.

Young as she was, Thalia tried hard to see what advantage they had gained coming to America.

What had been the lure?

The trip across the desert to Arizona had been a nightmare that cost them *everything*. Mothers, fathers, brothers, sisters, daughters and sons had been lost.

For what?

In Veracruz, in the manner of all young children with reasonably good parents, Thalia had thought her father some kind of lesser God. Crossing the desert, she'd seen Francisco crazed and crying and helpless to save the lives of his own children.

She had seen her father become a wild-eyed madman who gutted her uncle as she and her mother looked on.

On their third day in Arizona, her father had bought a dilapidated '68 Falcon that could barely hold his surviving family. He'd bought the car from a fat bald man with gold front teeth who ran a used car lot on a gravel strip by an all-night truck stop.

The man spoke badly accented Spanish and was willing to sell a car to an obvious illegal immigrant with no insurance and no operator's license.

A handwritten sign behind the cash register cautioned in English:

Cash ONLY!

All Sales Are FINAL!

Absolutely NO Refunds

&

NO Returns!

That last line might have been the car salesman's notion of a grim joke. He never explained to the Gómez family—not in Spanish— what the sales policy was.

Francisco Gómez paid two hundred seventy-five of the one thousand American dollars they'd brought across the border for the Falcon that had thrown a rod and couldn't go much faster than a bone-shaking fifty mph. It had a leak that required the Gómez family to carry several jugs of water in the already crowded car—to make frequent stops to refill the damaged radiator.

The sloshing water jugs and the need to keep them at hand and filled were a bitter reminder of the jugs they had banked their lives on making their ill-fated border crossing.

By the time Francisco realized what a lemon he had bought, they were deep into northeastern Arizona with no way to turn back.

FOUR

Thalia Ruiz freshened the three sheriffs' coffees. The tallest of the lawmen—a very slender man—didn't hand Thalia his cup, so she had to reach over the shorter, huskier sheriff to reach the mug. Her breast accidentally brushed the shorter sheriff's arm. The man, Sheriff Walt Pierce, gave her a smile that Thalia didn't return. She felt his gaze on her hips as she moved to the next table.

"The ass on that one, huh?" Sheriff Pierce smiled meanly at Able Hawk.

Sheriff Hawk said, "Enough of that shit, Pierce. Thalia's one of *my* legals. And she's a good kid. So just let it be, cocksucker."

Hawk examined Pierce over the rim of his coffee cup. Pierce was what you'd call a sometimes "useful idiot" to Hawk's mind. Pierce was a flavor of tool about half the time at any rate.

The other half?

Sometimes Pierce was strangely effective in getting results, if one construed arrest rates and resulting convictions as "getting results." Hawk was dubious that many of Pierce's arrests were righteous collars. Even across county lines, Hawk had heard rumblings of Pierce massaging evidence and suborning witnesses to firm cases.

But Hawk didn't have the luxury of choosing his peers; the voters in the adjacent county decided Pierce's fate every four years, just as Hawk was beholden to his Horton County constituents for his own continued employment.

The one thing Walt consistently struck Able as being was a potentially dangerous enemy.

The tall sheriff—Jim Denton of neighboring Phipps County— said, "Speaking of ass, as in taking it up same, you're fuckin' killing me, Able. I mean all the pressure you're putting on your illegals. They're goddamn *running* to my county now."

"Mine too," Walt said sourly. Walt was something of a dandy. He wore gold chains. He also had rings on most every finger. Fraternity rings; lodge and service organization rings. Able thought Walt looked like a short white pimp with a buzz cut.

"That's why we need to be in lockstep," Able said. "United front's what's called for. We implement the same protocols and follow the same strategies. We make them illegals someone else's problem farther out to other compass points."

"That'll endear us to our neighbors for sure," Jim said.

Able smiled at her as Thalia brought him a slice of banana cream pie. He received a smile back. After she was gone, talking around a mouthful, Able said, "That's why, in turn, you two'll have a talk with your neighbors, just as I'm having with you now. Then they, in turn, can do the same with some others."

Another forkful of pie was poised at his mouth. Able smiled and said, "As that repeats, we'll push them illegals over the northern border into the welcoming arms of our compassionate Canadian brothers. Serves those Canuck bastards right, after that millennium bomber ass-fucking they nearly dealt us with their own lax border security."

"S'pose that's one way of lookin' at it," Jim said. He brought a fist up to suppress a belch. "Goddamn coffee," he said. "My stomach don't process this shit no more." He belched again, said, "How in hell are you keeping on top of all this, Able? I can't even get a rough estimate of my own illegals, let alone collar 'em with the ferocity you are."

Able shrugged. "Just good intelligence. He shrugged again. "You know, boys—our bread and butter. Snitches and whatnot."

Walt said, "How's that billing the feds for your jail costs goin' for you, Able?"

"I have four lawyers tell me my foundation is firm," Able said. "But if you two would do the same, and if we were to form a regional coalition, so to speak, we'd be more the force for those federal cocksuckers to reckon with. Maybe get ourselves national profile as hardliners."

Walt watched Thalia serving truckers and tourists on the other side of the diner. He stared at her ass again. "Nice notion, Able," Walt said, distracted. "But we've got to make the arrests first in order to bill the feds for our costs. We don't have the 'good intelligence' you seem to."

There it was: Able's opening.

Sheriff Hawk cleared his throat. He pulled his briefcase from under the table. He plopped it on the empty seat next to himself and flicked the latches. He pulled out two manila file folders thick with photocopies. He checked the contents of the top file then chucked one to Jim. He passed the other folder to Walt.

"These are photocopies of forged driver's licenses and Social Security cards," Able said. "All of these were issued to illegals living in your respective counties. Sorry bastards used their real addresses for obvious reasons. So now you know where to go to arrest 'em, don't you?"

Jim whistled. "Where do you come by this stuff, Able?"

"That's not talking to the goddamn point," Able said. He forked in another bite of pie. "Thing is to use what I've given you. Make your arrests, then, using the invoice samples I've given you there with the rest, you two do just like me. You bill the fucking federal government your costs for jailing your illegals."

Jim said, "Again I ask, Able: How'd you come to get these?"

"Sources," Able said. "Snitches and the like. Now, anything for me?"

Walt, sorting sheets of photocopied licenses said, "My personal goddamn priest—his church is on your side of the county line, Able—is gonna start offering Spanish-language Mass Saturday afternoons. Guess my priest did a missionary stint in El Salvador back-when and he speaks good Mex'." Walt waved a hand, muttered, "I mean fuckin' Spanish."

Able grunted, shaking his head. He looked at his half-eaten slice of pie. "I'll talk to your misguided padre about that, as he's in my county. I'll steer him straight again." He said, "Jim, you got anything for me?"

"I've got nothin'," Jim said.

The other sheriffs left and Able watched them walking out together, the one tall and thin, the other short and fat, like Laurel and Hardy with badges.

"More coffee, Sheriff?"

Able smiled at Thalia. "Always. You're about owed a break, aren't you, darlin'? Why don't you sit down and take a load off?"

Thalia freshened Able's coffee and said, "Just let me pass the pot off to Betty and tell 'em I'm going on that break."

While he waited, Able stirred cream and sugar into his coffee. He looked up and smiled as Thalia slid into the booth across from him.

Since he'd lost his own daughter, Able had taken to talking to Thalia each morning after breakfast rush—in the half-hour lull before the lunch crowd packed the place. It was all small talk directed toward no unsavory end. Able's interest in Thalia wasn't like that, although he was certainly aware of her quiet, understated beauty.

Able missed being someone's father. When Thalia's husband died, widowed Able felt himself strongly drawn to her. He found himself pulled toward her by the loss they had in common. Able believed, or had at least convinced himself, that Thalia looked forward to their morning chats as much as he did.

Able said, "The weekend looms. Big plans, or a quiet weekend with Evelia?"

Thalia sipped her coffee, then said, "I wish tonight was a quiet night with Eve. But I've begged off on Carmelita for too many nights. So we're going out for drinks. Hope to still make it an early evening. Nothing too rowdy. Not like last time."

Hawk frowned. "What happened last time?"

Thalia shrugged. "Too many drinks. I hardly ever drink, so two or three is too many. It wasn't long after the accident—just days, really—and I was lonely. Lost track of myself. Next thing I know, I'm getting a tattoo."

He winced. "Ah, Thalia . . ." Able shook his head. "Can't fault yourself for that, not going through what you were back then."

She held up a hand, looking at her coffee cup to avoid his strange, penetrating eyes. "I know, Able. I *know*. I beat myself up for it, still. At least it's on the small of my back, where I don't have to see it. And I keep it covered so Evelia never sees it. Don't want her thinking when she's older I won't mind if she gets one. 'Cause I would *so* mind."

Able smiled. "How is that little girl of yours?"

"Good. Doing good in school. *She* is, I mean. But overall, the school's test scores are very bad. Too many illegals. I don't see it getting any better."

Able said, "Yep, my grandson got out of public school just in time. Though I'm sure feeling his college tuition payments. Maybe you should look at that—some parochial school for Evelia."

"I could never afford it," Thalia said. "I'm barely making ends meet now."

Able thought about that. He said, "Seeing myself a priest soon about another matter. Maybe I'll talk to him. See if there isn't some special program or sponsorship kind of thing we can get going to get Evelia into the school tied to his church. Let me look into that."

Before she could object, Able said, "Oh, here. Something for you." He pulled a folder out of his briefcase and rooted through papers. He handed her a certificate. "I'm in a club—just had my tenth oil change and so they kick me back a free oil change and tire rotation. You take it and keep that jalopy of yours running." He smiled and said, "Don't even try to refuse. You'll insult me, and it's a dangerous thing, bein' on my bad side."

Able pulled out another slip of paper. "And I got an invitation for me and a guest to the new steakhouse opening up over to Market Street. I can't make it, so you take it. You and your mother can have a free night out. Take Evelia. I don't think they'll object. Not like she'll be at their free hooch." He forced the invitation on Thalia along with sundry coupons for free colas and burgers from various fast food operations. His badge was forever reaping him freebies.

Thalia quietly said, "Thank you so much," still unable to meet his eyes.

"Nothing. It's *nothing*. Is there anything I can do for you that counts for something? Anything I can help you with?"

Thalia hesitated, then said, "No, I don't think so."

"What is it?"

"Well, it's a breakfast thing they do once a year at school. You know, fathers, grandfathers, or even uncles if they have to dig down that deep, go in and sit with the girls for a breakfast." Thalia's surviving brother and sister had drifted away years ago; moved West. Her siblings sent Christmas cards, but usually forgot birthdays. It was just Thalia, her daughter, her mother, and a girl cousin, now.

"I'll do it," Able said quickly. "Give me the time and the place and I'll play grandpa." He smiled. "And I'll go out of uniform."

"Thank you so much," Thalia said, finally meeting his gaze. She smiled. "It'll mean the world to Evelia—to have a man there for her." He could tell she meant it.

"It's nothing," Able said. He sipped his coffee again, said, "Anything for me today? Anything I should know?"

Thalia bit her lip, then said, "I don't know what you can do about this, or if you'd even want to try. But word is there is a gang of white men, teenage boys, really, who are targeting the illegals on the West Side. Home invasions, purse-snatchings and parking lot robberies. They prey on the illegals because they can't report the crimes. You know, for fear that you or your people will deport them."

Able nodded. "You get any sense of who these white boys are, I do want to know. I'll see they're punished, all the way up."

"I will." Thalia paused, then said, "How is your grandson? How is Amos doing?"

Able shrugged. "Good. He's doin' good."

Thalia raised her coffee cup, but stopped short of her lips. "Anything exciting in his life?"

"No, I don't think so. He's just studying hard so I don't kick his ass. Seems to have some new girlfriend he never talks about." Able shrugged. "Same old, same old."

He sensed Thalia wanted to say more. He said, "Somethin' else you want to tell me?"

The moment still didn't seem right. Thalia smiled and shook her head. *Tomorrow,* she promised herself. *Tomorrow for certain.*

THEN

Thalia's family was two miles out of the Painted Desert when the radiator sprang a catastrophic leak.

Sofia was furious at her husband for the side trip. The park was supposed to be a scenic attraction, but it terrified their surviving children, stirring memories of their desert crossing.

Thalia clung sobbing to her mother, her head ducked down so she didn't have to look at the "scenery" and arresting terrain that overtaxed their beater car.

Finally, a chicken farmer took pity on them and pulled over.

The farmer quickly realized communication was out of the question and shouldered Francisco Gómez aside to check under the hood.

The chicken farmer was fiftyish; skinny and burned brown by the sun. He ambled back to his truck and fetched a crate of eggs. He pointed at himself, then the engine. The farmer cracked an eggshell and emptied its contents into the radiator.

He waited and then checked to see that the egg had fried itself over the hole, creating a membrane that temporarily closed over the radiator's puncture. He poured in more water from one of their jugs, then used a rag to replace the radiator's cap and closed the hood.

The farmer handed the crate of eleven remaining eggs to Sofia, who curtsied and said "*Gracias.*" Thalia, a little linguistic sponge, told the farmer, "Thank you."

The remaining eggs carried them to Santa Fe, where their car finally overheated and the radiator ruptured, its capacity fatally compromised by the glut of fried eggs inside.

They broke down in a run-down, Spanish-speaking neighborhood and stayed there two years.

Her parents were comfortable ensconced in the squalid, Spanish-speaking pocket universe, which kept them poor and slowed their assimilation.

Nevertheless, Thalia learned creditable English from American cartoons and the children of underprivileged gringos.

Thalia soon began tutoring her mother in English.

FIVE

Tell Lyon sat in the corner booth at the rear of Señor Augustin's, his back to the wall. His plates had been cleared but the empty glasses from his first two Texas margaritas on the rocks had been left uncollected. Tell was halfway through his third drink.

"Is everything all right? Would you like something more?"

Tell checked his watch: eight P.M. He smiled up at the young woman and said, "No, I've had enough, thanks. It was wonderful. This place is great." He looked at the three glasses and realized then that he was still in uniform.

Jesus, too sloppy. Great way to make an impression first night in town, genius.

The young woman—twenty-three, twenty-four?—smiled. She stroked black hair behind an ear. She was very pretty; personable. She had dark hair and eyes—very much to Tell's ideal. She said, "You have to be our new police chief. Saw an article about your hiring in the *Recorder*."

He put out a hand and nodded. "Tell Lyon."

Her hand was warm in his and she squeezed back firmly. "Patricia Maldonado. My parents are Kathleen and Augustin, the owners." The appraising look she gave him delighted Tell.

"Your family's restaurant is truly excellent," Tell said.

"And you'd be a great judge," Patricia said. "The newspaper article said you were a Border Patrol commander before coming here to be our chief." She spoke with a just detectable Spanish accent. "This is about as real as Mexican food gets in these parts."

"I'm sure that's true," Tell said.

"Celebrating the new job?" Her dark eyes checked his hands—his naked fingers.

"Sure," he said. "Sorry about the uniform. Makes some people uncomfortable. It's just that it's my first full night in town and I stayed late at headquarters. Had to eat before I called it a night and didn't want to lose more time changing. Everyone said this is the place to come for great Mexican food, and they were right. I'll make it plainclothes from here on out, I swear."

Patricia smiled. "Either way. We'll just be happy to have you here and often." She hesitated, then said, "Father would like to comp your meal."

That was another downside of wearing the uniform in commerce situations. Tell didn't use to be so careless. He said, "No. I appreciate it very much, Patricia, but no thank you. Please bring me the check."

"It's a one-time thing. A welcome-to-town thing, Chief Lyon," Patricia said.

"I'm off duty, and it's Tell. And, please, Patricia, I really need to pay."

She smiled. "Suit yourself. I'll have your server bring it." She hesitated again. He was aware of her checking his left hand once more. "Do you have any friends in town, Tell?"

"Just you," Tell said, not sure why he was flirting with her like this.

Turning, she bumped into someone. She said, "Shawn!" The youngish, sandy-haired stranger moved to kiss Patricia and she turned her head so he caught her cheek. Tell smiled, guessing she was embarrassed by her boyfriend's public display of affection. And "boyfriend" he surely was. Shawn slipped his arm around Patricia, his left hand settling familiarly on her shapely hip.

Disappointed, Tell thought to himself, *Just a callow young dude marking territory.* The stranger seemed boyish. Patricia seemed an old soul. Tell scented an uneasy match.

"Shawn, this is Chief Tell Lyon," Patricia said. "Chief, this is Shawn O'Hara. Shawn is editor of the *New Austin Recorder*, the weekly newspaper here in town,"

"Right, your favorite newspaper," Tell said to Patricia.

Shawn scowled. "You two know one another?"

"For all of a minute," Tell said. "Met Patricia just before I met you."

Shawn offered a hand. "Didn't realize you were in town yet, Chief."

"Got in last night," Tell said, shaking Shawn's hand. "Today was the first day on the job, and a long one." *Not much of a handshake there,* Tell thought. He let go of Shawn's hand and said, "Editor, huh?"

"Yeah, but also reporter," Shawn said. "Photographer . . . Hell, layout artist. That's the way with weeklies. It's a small operation. Could you make some time for me tomorrow, Chief? Like to interview you now that you're on the job."

"Sure, if I can't talk you out of that, Shawn. I'm no publicity seeker."

"New chief of police, well, people are going to want to know more about you."

Tell said, "Any preview questions you can share with me so I can mull answers overnight?"

"Only one: The big issue in New Austin and greater Horton County these days is immigration, immigration and immigration.

So you being an ex-Border Patrol agent makes it more interesting for my readers, right?"

Tell said, "Suppose it could look like that."

Patricia patted Tell's shoulder; Shawn frowned. She said, "Uh oh, here comes trouble."

Tell saw a husky, gray-haired man in gray slacks and a sports jacket headed their way. Patricia whispered to Tell, "That's Horton County Sheriff Able Hawk."

Hawk slapped Shawn's back and said, "My favorite New Austin reporter. How you doin', kiddo?"

Shawn introduced Patricia as his "girlfriend" and Tell saw her flinch at the term. The editor was about to introduce Tell when Hawk stepped around Shawn and extended a big hand. Tell slid out of his booth and took Able's hand. "I know this one," Able said, grinning. "Or I know *about* this one. I've been reading up on you since Shawn's article about your hiring, Chief Lyon."

"Call me Tell," Lyon said.

"Only if you call me Able."

"My pleasure to meet you, Sheriff," Tell said. Tell was amused—Able was squeezing hard, trying to outgrip him. Tell squeezed back just enough to keep it even. They broke off the childish handshake. Tell sat back down, then resisted squirming as a half-smiling Able Hawk eyed those three large margarita glasses, his light gray eyes then shifting focus to Tell's uniform. *Goddamn it.*

A busboy was a booth back, cleaning up the table behind Tell's. The chief sensed Patricia sensing his own discomfort. She picked up his two empty glasses and passed them to the busboy. She said, "*Raoul, uno Texas margarita on the rocks, por favor.*" Then she squeezed into the booth next to Tell and started sipping from his half-finished third margarita.

Tell resisted scooting over to make more room and thus under-cutting Patricia's welcome subterfuge. But he watched Shawn O'Hara's cheeks redden.

Able Hawk slid onto the bench across from Tell and slapped the empty space by his side for Shawn to sit down. "Don't wanna talk shop your first night in town, Tell," Able said. "But if you can make time for me tomorrow, I'll stand you lunch out to Big G's truck stop by the interstate. Say, noon? We'll talk about overlap and regional issues that pain both our asses, right?"

"It's a date," Tell said, watching the editor's cheeks redden more. Stupid to bait the reporter, but for some reason Tell felt impelled to do it. Probably it was the liquor. And Tell was too aware of the heat and firmness of Patricia's hip and thigh tight against his. It was the closest he'd been to another woman since his wife. Tell said to Shawn, "Maybe we could meet up there at the same place, about one thirty, for our interview?"

"Sounds fine," Shawn said.

Able Hawk nodded at Shawn. "You and Tell here should get on real good. In my research I learned Tell has a reporter in his family. Pretty famous one. Ex-reporter, anyhow. And maybe *infamous* is the word I should have used."

• That got under Tell's skin, as Able probably intended. And it got Shawn's attention, as it was also surely intended to. The journalist asked, "Anyone I might know?"

"Probably," Able said. "Kind of infamous reporter-turned-novel-ist who lives out to Cedartown lately, counties away. Fella name of Chris Lyon." The name clearly rang bells for Shawn O'Hara.

Tell met Shawn's inquiring gaze and confirmed, "Chris is my cousin. We were close as kids, then kind of drifted apart as maturity too often does to you." But Tell had stayed with Chris and his fam-ily for a couple of nights before driving west to New Austin. Such as they were, Chris Lyon, and his wife, Salome, were as close to real family as remained for Tell.

"Your cousin has built quite a reputation for himself, for better or worse," Shawn said.

Patricia drained the dregs of Tell's margarita, watching him. The waiter brought Patricia another and she handed the waiter the empty glass. She stirred her drink with its two straws and sipped. Her dark eyes were still focused on Tell.

He said, "Chris tends toward mythologizing himself. Unfortunately, so do a lot of his critics and fans. When it comes to Chris, it's best to believe half of what you hear, and less than that of what you read. And that last is true regardless of whether Chris is or isn't the author."

"Same be said for you, Tell Lyon?" Able Hawk arched a bushy eyebrow.

Tell searched the sheriff's strange eyes. He had never seen anything like them. In the right light, they were so pale that Tell could imagine Able's irises blending into the whites from a distance. They were eyes that could break a suspect just by boring into him, Tell guessed.

"No, I'm not like Chris," Tell said.

"All the same," Able said with a sad smile, those terrible eyes searching Tell's face, "I'm very sorry for the loss of your family, son."

"Thanks," Tell said evenly. "But I don't talk about that." Tell felt Patricia sizing him up again. He thought he felt her leg pressing harder against his. It was probably just his imagination. Or maybe it was the tequila.

Able said, "I really don't wanna talk shop tonight, just like I said a bit ago. But you should probably know, Chief, that I made a collar out front a few minutes ago."

"Yeah?" Tell said. "What happened?"

"Young man was weaving," Able said. "I figured him for DWI and sure enough, the boy, one Miguel Sanchez, *maybe* age eighteen, he failed the Breathalyzer, big time. He was carrying false paper. He's bein' booked at county by now."

"Thanks for catching him, Sheriff," Tell said. "Thanks for taking him down before someone got hurt in my city." New Austin was mostly located within Horton County. Getting along with Able Hawk was going to be a necessity, Tell knew.

"We're seeing a lot of these fake licenses and Social Security cards lately," Able said. "Best estimate is that 70 percent of Horton County's Hispanic population came illegally across the border."

Tell said, "Maybe you could bring some samples of those bogus identifications to lunch tomorrow. Maybe some samples I could hold on to for a time. Help me get my people up to speed."

"Happy as hell to do that," Able said, smiling. "Your predecessor, he weren't too aggressive on this subject. Good to know I've got a man with a pair here in town now who has my back. Now I should leave you two— er, three?—to your dinner and your drinks."

Shawn, red-faced again, slid out of the booth to let Able Hawk out.

Patricia slid out too. Leaning over, she said softly to Tell, "I'll have your check sent over directly, Chief Lyon."

Handshakes all around, then Tell was alone again.

He looked at Patricia's half-full margarita, traces of her lipstick still on the twin straws. Tell picked up the drink and drank it dry through the lipstick-stained straws.

SIX

"So you had to share a drink with him," Shawn said. "Why'd you do that, Pat?"

It was half an hour since they'd left Patricia's family's restaurant, leaving Tell Lyon there alone in his booth. Patricia had been inclined to stay. Now Patricia and Shawn were in another booth, seated across from one another at the back of Fusion, New Austin's sorry excuse for a hot nightspot, yet still the town's trendiest club.

Patricia had picked their table—just as far from the dance floor and speakers as she could find. She was sick of the club scene and had told Shawn so several times since they'd become lovers. Yet here they were again.

"Wasn't like it looked," Patricia said.

Shawn snagged her pack of cigarettes and fired one up. "You should buy your own, Shawn," she said, gesturing at the pack of Merits on the table between them. "I mean, rather than always bumming mine and then bitching about my brand after."

The journalist shrugged. "I only smoke in clubs and bars, you know that."

And after sex.

Patricia said, "You best cut back, Shawn, because I'm seriously thinking of quitting." It was a relatively new habit of Patricia's—the potentially deadly echo of a previous relationship with another boyish younger man who too soon rubbed Patricia wrong.

Nate had lasted just long enough to make Patricia a smoker. She said, "And anyway, it wasn't what it looked like." She appraised him: Blue eyes, sandy blond hair in need of cutting. An angular face and a too-ready smile. He was proud of his smile. She could see that. He used it to ends. But Shawn wasn't smiling now.

"I know how it looked, Patty."

"I hate Patty," she said. "Keep it Patricia."

"I know how it looked, Patricia," Shawn said, looking scolded. "And I know what it was. I saw Able Hawk notice too. All those drinks while Lyon was on duty. You were covering for him, Patricia. Trying to help him save face with Able Hawk. I'm just wondering why you did that."

"He was off duty, Shawn, but in uniform," Patricia said. "Tell seems like a nice and decent man, and he's lonely. Cut him some slack."

Shawn blew a smoke ring. She decided Shawn figured it probably made him look tough. He said, "Lots of people are lonely, Patricia."

"That is true. Sometimes even when they're not alone." She hesitated, then said, "But there's something else there. Can't put my finger on it, exactly. There's a tension in the man. And a sadness like I've never seen. Maybe that's what made me help him out with Able Hawk. The sheriff said something had happened to Chief Lyon's family. What was that? Do you know?"

Shawn blew more smoke from both nostrils, watching distant dancers. "Did some research on him. Tell Lyon's wife and daughter, a toddler, if I remember right, were killed in a firebombing of their house while he was on duty. Authorities in California concluded it might have been a ring of Coyotes or maybe some cartel chief seeking some kind of revenge against our new chief. So they snuffed his family."

Patricia shuddered. Shawn's casualness in breaking the news appalled her. She was further offended by his off-hand manner describing their deaths. Hearing the anger in her voice, Patricia asked, "And when did this happen to Tell, Shawn?"

"Late last year," he said, still watching the dancers. "Suppose that's how New Austin landed Lyon as chief. He probably just wanted the hell away from California and the West."

"Lord," Patricia said. "If I lost my family like Tell did, I'd have wiped out our stock of tequila tonight. That poor man."

Shawn drained his Corona. "These Lyons seem to attract that kind of bullshit. Almost like they court it. On that note, you oughta study up on the chief's cousin, Chris Lyon. It's all craziness. And the guy's a poster child for gone-wrong reporters."

He stubbed out his cigarette. "Let's hit the floor, 'Tricia."

"Patricia." She picked up her pack of cigarettes and lighter and put them in her purse. "Not tonight, Shawn. And I told you, the night we met was a fluke. I don't like the club scene. And I truly hate dancing. I'm a stay-at-home kind of girl. Maybe more so all the time."

Patricia tried to think of the right word for Shawn's expression as she said that to him. She settled on "pouting." Not a becoming look on Shawn, or on any man.

Shawn said, "So whose place is it going to be tonight?" She heard a tone of annoyance in his voice.

"How about neutral corners for tonight," Patricia said.

They'd driven to the club in separate cars. Standing, Patricia slung her purse over one shoulder. "You leaving too, Shawn?"

He shook his head, watching the dance floor. "Think I'll stay on a while. I'll call you."

So, it was like that.

Patricia left without saying goodbye.

On the way out, she opened her purse and pulled out her pack of cigarettes and lighter and tossed them in the trash can.

She drove to her apartment in a soft, fragrant summer rain, listening to an oldie station. Patti Scialfa's "Spanish Dancer": *A red dress of temptation over a long black slip of fear.*

Along the way, she passed a New Austin police cruiser pulled diagonally behind a beater, red pickup truck. The cruiser's lights twirled red and blue, flashing on the wet pavement. Two New Austin cops were patting down two short and husky Mexican boys. Both had red bandanas tied around their heads. Gang colors.

Mexican gangs fueled more and more of the rising violent crime in and around Horton County. Patricia was glad she didn't have a younger brother to get sucked in. Hardly any Latino males under the age of twenty were not affiliated with one or another of the new Mexican gangs.

When she got home, Patricia locked the door, threw the deadbolt and stuck a rubber wedge in the bottom crack of the door. Her neighborhood, located on the fringe of the West Side, had been relatively safe until the past year or so. Now it was a haven for home invasions, rapes and robberies.

She brushed her teeth, washed her face, and pulled on a pair of blue sweats emblazoned in white letters with the phrase "Just do it!" and a big gray sweatshirt with her college's logo across the chest. She pushed up her sleeves, pulled on a pair of reading glasses and booted up her computer. Patricia called up Google and in quotes typed, "Tell Lyon."

* * *

Killing time. Tell, slightly buzzed, was driving around aimlessly—getting lost in his new city. He was rambling to avoid going home to his too-quiet, anonymous apartment.

In retrospect, he wouldn't be able to decide if it was the smell of the fire or the guttering glow on the horizon that caught his attention. Tell knew the smell well enough. He remembered the orange light and its flicker through twirling plumes of black smoke as they rose from his own burning home.

Tell palmed the wheel, driving toward the fire and the sound of the sirens. As he drew closer he could see the true scope of the blaze and gunned his SUV into the townhouse parking lot. Unable to find a proper parking space, Tell steered around behind a fire truck and drove over the curbstone, bringing his SUV to a stop on a common lawn.

At least three of the rental units were what firefighters termed "fully involved," and smoke poured from the attic ventilation slats of several surrounding townhouses.

Nauseous, crazed, Tell fumbled with the door handle of his truck, hands shaking.

Once out of the SUV, the fire's heat on his face set Tell's legs to shaking. He thought he could smell charred flesh and hear screams other than those of the women and children gathered out on the lawn, watching their homes and possessions burn.

Tell's eyes were already watering from the stinging and stinking noxious exhaust of burning plastic, textiles and vinyl siding.

Tell took slow, deep breaths, tamping down his revulsion at the familiar stench. He was bent over, hands on his knees, trying hard to breathe only through his mouth to suppress the memories triggered by the smell of the fire.

Steadier, he looked around and saw three hook-and-ladder trucks, a couple of smaller pumpers and two EMT units. A couple of overweight medics with bushy brown moustaches were working on an old Mexican woman.

Tell searched the crowd of dispossessed townhouse dwellers and gawkers and realized they were all Latinos. The only English being spoken was that exchanged between the emergency medical technicians and firefighters yelling to one another over the sound of the fire and the white noise of the water gushing from their hoses.

Tell heard more sirens and saw several Horton County sheriff's cruisers turning into the crowded parking lot.

One of the firefighters—evidently the chief—saw Tell, noted his uniform and nodded. Tell nodded back. He looked around for something to do and saw that a crowd of Mexicans was blocking the parking lot and the sheriff's cruisers couldn't find parking.

The cruisers in turn were blocking the path of a squad waiting to drive to the hospital with two young burn victims.

Tell moved to undertake some crowd control, but the sheriff's deputies hit their sirens and engaged their speakers. In English, they ordered the crowd to disperse. The lights and the sound seemed to do the trick even if most in the crowd—as Tell suspected—were too fresh to American soil to speak much, if any, English.

A toddler girl, perhaps four or five, was being given oxygen. Her right arm was heat blistered and the EMT was applying salve. She looked terrified and confused. Tell squatted down next to her and smiled. In Spanish he said, "It's okay, honey. It's not a bad burn and the medicine will help. Don't be scared, darling. You're going to be fine."

She nodded, her dark eyes glistening. She tugged the oxygen mask aside and said in Spanish, "Antonio's still inside. He's one and can't walk yet. Will you go and get my brother for me?"

Tell felt his skin crawl. His heart kicked. Wild-eyed, he said to the EMT, "She says her baby brother is still inside one of the units."

Tell was already up as the EMT called to his chief. The firefighter Tell had exchanged nods with hurried over, soaked from the back spray of the hoses. A command radio was gripped in his gloved right hand. Tell said, "This little girl says her baby brother is inside. Or she thinks so. She says his name is Antonio and—"

A screaming woman suddenly threw herself between them and gathered up the little girl with the burned arm. In Spanish she said over and over "Thank God," then she said, still speaking Spanish, "My family—the rest are still in there! My mother and father . . . my brother and my baby boy!"

The fire chief and EMT looked bewildered. The EMT nodded at Tell and said, "This cop here speaks Mex', Chief."

Frowning, sickened now, Tell said to the firefighters, "None of you speak Spanish?"

The fire chief glowered. "*No . . .*"

"With this growing constituency, you better fucking learn." He grabbed the Mexican woman by both arms and asked in Spanish, "Which one? Which apartment do you live in?"

Sobbing, with a shaking hand, the young Mexican woman pointed at the center unit. Most of its roof was gone. Tell said, "She says her baby, her parents and a brother are still in that townhouse."

The fire chief shook his head, the fire flickering across the plastic shield of the helmet that obscured his face. "Christ, I'm sorry, then. It's too far gone, pal. I can't send my men in and there's no way anyone can be alive in there now. If she'd told us fifteen, even ten minutes ago, there might have been a chance."

Tell snarled, "How the fuck was she supposed to do that when she can't speak our fucking language? None of these people living here can speak English."

The EMT said, "And so now we see what that gets them, packed into these places like sardines and not talkin' English. Fuckin' illegals."

Tell was on the technician before he realized he had thrown himself at the man. Tell was trying to get his hands around the medical technician's throat when he felt the first kick to his ribs. The fire chief was yelling at him and kicking Tell.

Tell felt other hands on him and thought he recognized a voice: "Easy now. Easy, Tell. It's okay, son. I'll make this okay."

He struggled up to his feet, his ribs aching. He turned and saw Able Hawk. Able stepped between Tell and the technician still sprawled on the ground. The prone EMT pointed at Tell and said, "He stinks of alcohol. Fucker's drunk, I think. I want you to fucking arrest him, Sheriff!"

"I'm not drunk," Tell said.

"No, you're not," Able said. He turned to the fire chief and said, "Kenny, give this man a pass. He's our new chief of police. His own family was lost in a fire just a few months back. His little girl, about this one's age," Able said, rubbing the head of the little girl with the burned arm, "died in that fire. Mexican drug cartel set it. So you can see how this would play with Chief Lyon's mind in ugly ways, yeah?"

The fire chief shook his head. "It's my man's decision whether to press charges or not. Tommy's the aggrieved party."

"Not tonight he fucking isn't," Able said sternly. He put out a hand and helped the technician to his feet. Able said to the man, "I heard that last crack of yours. I'd have hit you too, asswipe. Only difference is, you wouldn't be getting back up after I came at you, you sorry son of a bitch. I don't pull my punches."

The fire chief started to object and Able said, "Tell Lyon here is *chief* of police of New Austin. So you can't expect him to arrest himself. I'm county sheriff, and I say this citizen of mine was justified in his desire to kick your man's ass. You should fire this cocksucker, and you may do just that soon to cover your own ass. My man Tell is right about what we all have to do with these Mexicans overrunning us. I've got me some Spanish language tapes in my cruiser. Listen to 'em all day, to teach myself Mex'. You best get to doing it too, for nights like this one. Because I'm here to tell you, when word gets out to the media that a baby and a family burned to death because your boys don't speak Spanish, you're gonna be toast yourself."

Hawk was just getting started. "And if your boy here and his dumbass statement about them 'deserving' their fate for not speakin' English goes public? Best grab your ankles now for the lawsuits coming your way, cocksucker."

Able squeezed Tell's arm. "Now, you use this man here while there's maybe still time—time to find out if anyone else is burning to death in those townhouses while you sit around jawing in the wrong language."

Tell said to the fire chief, "Just please promise you'll call me, day or night, next time you come into this neighborhood with a fire or emergency. That's all I ask. I'll translate. And I'm very sorry for attacking your man."

The fire chief said, "Anyone still left in any of those units is dead. I can't use you anymore tonight, *Chief*." He looked around and then nodded at the sobbing woman. "Well, there *is* one thing you'll do for me. You give the bad news to that poor Mexican bitch there. Tell her in her own language, so she'll understand. Then you can go home and crawl back into your bottle, asshole."

Able Hawk wrapped an arm around Tell's shoulders. "I'll help you with delivering that bad news, Tell. Well, you do the talking, Tell, and I'll see to the aftermath. Then you best get along home, Chief. Tomorrow we start fresh. Maybe get us some ideas together for bringing these kinds of backward bastards behind us up to snuff for dealing with our crazy West Side."

Tell and Able squatted down next to the Mexican woman who was crying and holding her young daughter.

The woman looked up at Tell. His eyes had already told her all that he was just beginning to explain to her in Spanish.

THEN

In Ohio, Thalia's father developed a cough that worsened.

Sofia and Francisco had yet to become citizens, so Thalia's father resisted seeing a doctor.

Lack of insurance kept Francisco from seeking treatment as his cough became deep and wet; as the coughing made him see black spots and he couldn't lie down without feeling as though he was suffocating.

Sofia was less than a week from taking her citizenship exam. She was much more fluent in English than her husband and making the better wage, so they had decided it made sense for her to be the one to become a citizen first. But as capable of communication in English as she was, Sofia was still nowhere near as bilingual as Thalia or her other two children.

Sofia saw it as a grim race now. She needed to become a legal U.S. citizen to secure insurance at work so that Francisco could be treated.

Two days before her scheduled test, Francisco collapsed on a public street. He was dead before Sofia could be notified.

An emergency room nurse tried to comfort her. The nurse listened in horror as Sofia talked of trying to become naturalized in time to save her husband.

"Oh, honey," the nurse said, "illegal or not, we would have *had* to treat him anyway."

"Don't say that," Sofia said, stricken, "please don't say that!"

Thalia looked on, confused and crying.

Francisco had died of pneumonia.

The man who had survived the so-called "Devil's Highway"—who had staved off fatal dehydration by drinking his own urine—had drowned in his own tissue fluid. Sofia thought that must be what the whites called "irony."

They buried Francisco in a potter's grave, sealed up in a box constructed of materials just a grade or two above the sheetrock that Francisco spent the last year of his life hanging for half minimum wage.

SEVEN

Tell awakened early, reaching again for his wife. He hated waking up alone.

He started coffee, showered, then dressed. He'd showered twice, but could still smell the stench of the fire in his hair and on his skin. Or at least he thought he could smell it.

He made eggs and bacon and toast and watched cable news while he ate his lonely breakfast. He came across yet another feature on Mexican border security. Some heartland politician was calling for a fence along the entire expanse of the border—a multi-billion-dollar proposition. "Better to spend the money there than trying to prop up a sinking Louisiana," the senator said. Smiling, he'd said, "Tell me I'm wrong."

Tell switched over to a music video. Shakira, enticingly shaking it.

Sipping his coffee, Tell continued to channel surf, settling on Country Music Television. Billy Joe Shaver was singing "Live Forever." The sentiment was lost on Tell, but he liked the Mexican visuals well enough.

The eggs, surprisingly, weren't bad. Tell had asked his cousin's wife, Salome—a black haired, black-eyed gypsy beauty whose coloring reminded Tell more than a little of Marita—to teach him how to make some basic meals for himself.

Tell had never learned to cook: He'd gone straight from his parents' home to school and then on into police work that started early each day and ended late. After he left home, it had been a steady diet of school cafeteria and then take-home meals and fast food until he married Marita. Salome spent two days teaching Tell to fend for himself in the kitchen and gave him a notebook filled with handwritten recipes. Tell had found himself spending most of his daylight hours with Salome and with his cousin's pretty daughters. Tell and Chris tended to catch up in the late evenings.

While sitting together a night or two before on the back porch of his cousin's cabin, Chris Lyon, five years older than Tell, had urged his cousin, "Get back out there as soon as you can, Tell. It's not a betrayal, though I know you're going to think of it like that. But the sad fact is, us Lyons, we don't do that well without a woman in our life. We just aren't built for solitude, my brother." Chris hadn't been the first male Lyon whom Tell had heard make that assertion.

Tell had paraphrased the lyrics of a song back to Chris, "Mom always said don't fall in love too quickly . . . you know—before you know your own mind."

But Chris shook his head. He'd said, "Huh-uh. Our kind? We've likely got more days behind than ahead of us. We maybe don't have the luxury of time."

Tell sipped some more coffee and stared up at the mantle. Pictures of black-eyed, black-haired Marita and their baby girl, Claudia, stared back at him, smiling forever in the only pictures he had left. The rest had perished in the fire that killed them.

*   *   *

The city fathers hadn't stipulated that Tell live in New Austin. But Tell thought it bad form to live outside the community he was sworn to protect and serve. He hadn't yet found a house to his liking, and he hadn't really settled on exactly how much house he wanted or needed. And his cousin's cautions kept eating at solitary Tell.

So as a stopgap, Tell had settled on a temporary apartment near the West Side.

Tell locked up, toting his sack lunch—something he'd made to Salome Lyon's specifications—and a metallic flask of coffee. The thermos, brushed chrome with black highlights, had been his last Father's Day gift.

He walked out to his civilian wheels, a 2000-model Suburban, and pressed the fob to disarm the alarm.

"Hey you!"

He turned as Patricia Maldonado trotted up next to his truck. She brushed damp strands of hair from her forehead. She was panting; her chest heaving. She wore sneakers, black shorts and a damp, maroon sports bra. Her long black hair was pulled back in a thick ponytail. She glistened with sweat. Tell made a conscious effort to keep his focus on her face.

"You're up early, Chief," she said.

"It's when I like to go to work," Tell said. "Get more done in an hour or two when I'm alone than I do the rest of the day once the others come in with their distractions and the phones start going. And you should talk about being out early."

"It's when I run," Patricia said. "You know, before the heat sets in. What are you doing here, Chief?"

"Tell."

"Sorry, right. *Tell*. What are you doing here, Tell?"

"I live here. In 308."

She smiled, hands on hips and chest still heaving. "How strange! Me too—304. You're just down the hall. At least I feel safe now." She drew an arm across her forehead. "Maybe it's an omen."

"Actually, it's probably not the safest thing for you to be jogging on this side of town, Patricia."

It was particularly not safe for a striking and voluptuous young woman like Patricia. Tell had been reviewing weekly crime logs going back four months. Tuesdays through Sundays in their neighborhood seemed especially treacherous. "No kidding," he said, "you really ought not to be running alone."

"I can believe that," Patricia said. "Do you run, Tell?"

"I used to, back in the day. But it's been a good long while."

"So start again. Run with me tomorrow?"

He could spare an hour or so for a morning run.

But hell, what was Patricia? Maybe twenty-four or twenty-five?

Marita had been twenty-seven to Tell's thirty-seven when she died. Somehow that didn't seem quite the age gulf it should have been.

But this was just a jog.

Yet it smacked of a mistake . . . and certainly an excellent way of getting on the wrong side of the local press.

He said, "Patricia . . ."

"It's not safe for me to run alone, Chief. You said so yourself."

"And that's true. But I don't think your boyfriend—who is scheduled to interview me in a few hours—would take it real well."

"Not my boyfriend. I'm well past boyfriends."

"Begging your pardon," Tell said, "but last night Shawn said—"

"We're not seeing each other anymore."

"He know that, Patricia?"

"Shawn will know soon."

"Okay. Maybe when he knows how it is, you'll ask me again?"

"It's just a jog, Tell. Not a date."

"Absolutely. But all the same."

"Tell, I'm just asking for you to go out running with me. To get all sweaty and out of breath *protecting* me. That's all."

"You're relentless, Patricia." He smiled. "Okay, sure. Tomorrow morning, this time, let's go for a run. But only if you lay back. Like I said, it's been a good while and I'm apt to lose my legs, fast." He smiled. "You know CPR in case this goes really south for an old man like me?"

"Sure, *old man*. And great—great you'll do it." Patricia smiled and brushed more hair back from her face. "You're on my way so I'll knock on your door."

"Perfect," Tell said, half looking forward to Saturday morning, and already half regretting it.

*   *   *

Able Hawk sat at the breakfast table with his grandson, Amos, who was in his second year of studying criminology in neighboring Vale County. Able was frustrated he couldn't find more time to help the boy, who he sensed was struggling with his studies.

Amos—Amos Tudor Sharp—had been living with his lawman grandfather since his junior year of high school. Able's wife, Katy, had died after a swift but brutal bout with cervical cancer several years before. Their daughter, Nancy, driven by her mother's sharp decline and death, had gone in for her own testing, fearing there might be something genetic at work. Nancy had checked out fine in that area, but the doctors had found a lump in her right breast. Turned out it was indeed cancer, and it had already spread to Able's daughter's lungs and lymph nodes. Nancy was dead in less than three months. Little better than a bald skeleton when they buried her, Able's daughter was wasted by the disease and weeks of aggressive chemo and radiation therapy that doctors later admitted probably hastened her decline and did flat nothing to stop the course of the cancer raging through her body.

Nancy had been deserted by Amos's father when their boy was only two months old. So Able had, in every sense, been Amos's father for the boy's entire life.

Chip Sharp was so long missing and presumed dead by most around Horton County that no one bothered looking when Amos was orphaned. It was a presumed thing that Able would take the boy in after the cancer killed his mother.

Amos looked like his father's side: tall and slender with natural muscle tone, not big-boned and husky like the Hawks tended to run. But Amos Sharp shared his grandfather's law enforcement career ambitions. And Amos had a slightly darker, mistier shade of his grandfather Able's strange gray eyes.

"You still seein' improvement this quarter?" Able asked around a mouthful of cornflakes.

"Think I'm gonna be okay," Amos said.

"Good. That's good, Amos. I'm proud of you. You know that, don't you?"

"I know you are, Grandpa."

"Met the new chief of police of New Austin last night," Able said. "I'm having lunch with him later today. Seems a solid sort. Former Border Patrol agent who paid a terrible price for doing the job. Fella name of Tell Lyon. New Austin's police department has always run internships for up-and-comers like you. I'll see if maybe he'll consider taking you on come winter, if you keep your grades up."

"Sounds great," Amos said.

"Tomorrow's Saturday," the old man said. "Want to head out to the cabin for the weekend, Aim?"

Able owned a small piece of property on a private pond on the far side of Vale County, a stocked pond with a small cabin built on the pond's wooded northern rim. It was about forty-five minutes' drive from Horton County.

Amos said, "Maybe for the morning into afternoon? Kind of have plans for tomorrow night, Gramps."

Able shook his head, talking with his mouth full. "The mystery girl again, huh? Gonna have to let me meet her soon, Amos. Or am I gonna have to go sleuth on your ass?"

Amos smiled and said, "Soon, Grandpa, if it looks like it'll last. Your time's too valuable to waste." Amos tried to sound casual about it—not tip the old man that there might be something there that Amos thought would be an issue for Sheriff Able Hawk.

The old lawman said, "Okay. Let's plan on bein' up extra early then. We'll hit the road at four thirty so we can be there just after five, when they start biting. You can do that, lazybones?"

"Hell yeah, I can do that, Grandpa," Amos said.

*   *   *

Shawn O'Hara awakened to snoring from someone other than the woman who was jammed up bare-assed against him.

He awakened realizing he was in a strange bed—too short and narrow to be his own. He realized he was naked next to the woman he'd met the night before. In the dim light, Shawn could see that her hair was dark, like he always liked them, and her skin darker than his own.

Shawn had been more attracted to her friend, Carmelita Martinez . . . yeah, that was her friend's name. As to the name of the woman Shawn had fucked in a drunken stupor—the one sprawled naked next to him now—he couldn't recall *her* name just yet.

And for his part, Shawn had been cagey; he'd never gotten beyond "Shawn."

And thank God he'd had the good sense not to take her back to his own place.

Shawn slid quietly from the bed and lifted the sheet to take another look at her bare brown body. Jesus—she was a bit heavier than he would ever go for sober. Big breasts . . . thick ankles. She was already showing signs of being one of those Mexican women who'd run a bit more to fat with each passing year. Stretch marks! Christ, she probably had a kid somewhere. Maybe she was sleeping around in search of a father for her child. He eyed the red and blue butterfly tattooed on the small of her back. Shawn remembered staring at it while he was doing her doggie style.

The snoring was louder down the hall. Carmelita, maybe? Drunk as they all were, why the hell hadn't he pressed for a three-way?

The reporter didn't want to risk waking anyone, so he slipped on his underwear and jeans, then picked up his socks, shoes and shirt and slid out the front door, leaving it unlocked behind him.

He threw his clothes over his shoulder and quietly let himself into his car. He was parked on a sloped driveway in front of a string of West Side townhouses. Shawn knew the neighborhood from dozens of crime reports. He was damned lucky his car hadn't been broken into overnight.

Shawn held the door with his left hand, steadying it so he wouldn't have to slam it and maybe awaken anyone in the apartment he'd just snuck out of. He turned the ignition to Auxiliary but didn't start the car—just engaged the electrical system enough so he could put it in gear and let it coast backward down the driveway onto the sloping street with the engine off.

Shawn backed onto the street, shifted into Drive and let it roll a few dozen yards from the apartment he'd snuck out of. Then he started his car and drove away fast with the lights off so nobody could get a look at his license plates.

The journalist checked the dashboard clock—time enough to go home, shower and grab a breakfast at McDonald's. Then he'd maybe see about smoothing things over with prettier and skinnier Patricia Maldonado so he wouldn't be forced back into the clubs next Friday night.

* * *

Thalia stood naked in her girlfriend's bathroom, surveying the ruin of her face. She frowned at the marks on her neck and breasts from his "kisses." Felt the soreness between her legs and in her ass.

Sweet Jesus, what had she *done*?

Down the hall, Carm was snoring up a storm. Carmelita had allowed Thalia to borrow her vacationing roommate's room.

But Thalia couldn't believe she'd accepted the offer—the man's or Carmelita's. What was the guy's name? John? Maybe John.

Jesus. At least he looked clean. Maybe he hadn't given her anything.

She desperately wanted a shower, but she was already in danger of being late for work. She felt nauseous, hung-over and dizzy. But not like any of the rare hangovers she had suffered before. She felt drugged. Had John . . . ? *er*, Tom . . . ? put something in her drink?

Thalia dressed and phoned her mother from downstairs. Her mother promised to see that Thalia's daughter, Evelia, would get to school on time. Thalia cringed again, thinking of the tone of bitter disapproval in her mother's voice. It was gratuitous—Thalia was already disgusted with herself . . . angry enough for both of them.

She let herself out of the apartment and then realized she left her car at the club where she'd met John . . . Tom . . . Ron?

Cursing, Thalia dialed for a cab.

Her cell phone died just as the dispatcher picked up.

Damn it!

She started walking toward the bus stop three blocks distant, already anticipating the hell she'd catch from her boss. Dreading the grief she'd get from her mother. She cursed the burning ache between her legs as she walked in the muggy morning heat.

Goddamn him! Goddamn John . . . Tom . . . Ron . . . *Shawn!*

That was his name. *Shawn!*

And Thalia knew that she knew his face from somewhere, if he could just place it. She saw a coin box for newspapers when she reached the corner and the bus stop. She indulged a hunch and dug out a couple of quarters and bought a copy of the *New Austin Recorder*. She flipped through the paper until she hit the editorial page. There he was—blond and blandly good-looking. Smiling at her from the little picture that ran each week with his column. Shawn O'Hara.

Thalia folded the paper so she could look at the picture while she sat on the bus. She looked down the road, but saw no sign of the bus.

The streets were still dead; just a lonely red pickup truck approaching slowly from a distance.

THEN

Thalia met her husband at a work-sponsored picnic. Both worked in a hospital serving the greater Dayton area. Thalia was employed as a cook in the hospital's cafeteria. Rafael was a parking lot attendant.

Sofia Gómez wasn't pleased by the relationship; she'd hoped her daughter would find a white man. The fact that Rafael's family was also originally from Southern Mexico didn't endear him to Sofia as Thalia had hoped.

Despite her mother's misgivings, Thalia and Rafael were married six months after their first date. They were expectant parents three months after that. In between those two landmarks, the hospital where they worked was bought out by an HMO that promptly shut it down for cynical tax purposes.

Thalia, Rafael and Sofia moved on to Horton County, where Rafael found work at a propane plant.

Their baby, Evelia, was born in a hospital other than the one where her parents had met—a sentimental letdown for the first-time mother and father. Their wedding too, had been a bittersweet experience, particularly for Thalia. Throughout the ceremony, the bride couldn't keep from thinking of the family who should be there sharing the day with her: her grandparents, her dead father, Francisco . . . her surviving but now distant brother and sister. Another parking lot attendant gave the bride away.

All her dead.

Standing there in church, Thalia vowed to herself that her own child would never know such loss.

EIGHT

Tell arrived twenty minutes early for lunch, thinking he'd squeeze in some paperwork while he waited for Sheriff Hawk, but Able was already sitting there in a big wrap-around booth, holding court with a bunch of codgers who were laughing and slapping the tabletop at some joke. Tell was pretty sure the half-overheard punch line involved the word "tits."

Able spotted the New Austin chief of police approaching and said, "Duty calls, boys!"

The old men dispersed quickly and Tell took a seat. The peace officers shook hands across the Formica-top table.

"You doin' okay, Chief?"

"Yeah," Tell said, feeling ashamed. "Sorry about last night. Sorry you saw me that way."

"Like I said at the scene, you had good reason. That's all we'll say on that subject ever again, 'cept, have you seen the daily paper?"

"No."

Able smiled. "That EMT you rightly clocked has been suspended. Fire chief may not be far behind. Paper's editorial is calling for sweeping reforms. Fucking newspaper's honchos insisting all Horton County civil servants be given mandatory Spanish language instruction. There's a photograph too. Guess we'll have to wait and see how the weekly newspaper treats it all. With Shawn, hell, it could go either way."

Able passed Tell a copy of the daily newspaper. The Mexican woman was photographed holding her surviving toddler daughter to her chest, crying as she was comforted by Tell and Able. Able said, "We two at least come off as sympathetic. Not that that matters. But, of course, we both know it matters."

Tell nodded and smiled faintly as the waitress brought him a plastic glass of water with a lemon wedge. She tossed a paper-wrapped plastic straw in front of Tell. Able Hawk was working on a piping hot cup of black coffee.

"Sure was a pretty girl you were with last night, Chief," Able said.

Tell shook his head, tearing the top off the straw wrapper. "She's Shawn O'Hara's girlfriend. Or so I gathered. Her folks own the restaurant. She was just being hospitable while she waited for Shawn to get there."

"But she is attractive."

"She is certainly that."

"Sorry for touching a nerve last night, my friend. I am so sorry for your loss, Tell. God knows, I know what that's like. But I should have known better than to stupidly raise the issue of your family in that setting and that company. Particularly when it's so damned raw. Jesus H. Christ, less than a year . . ."

Tell nodded. "I'll confess that I've been researching *you* since last night, Able. Read some archived articles from the *Recorder's* Web site. So I know that you know plenty about loss yourself. You know what it's like—losing your wife and your child, almost all at once."

That set Able back, but he covered it well enough. He said, "So maybe we're sorry kindred, Lyon."

Tell said, "We sure seem to share the same flavor of loss."

Able nodded. "Suspect that bloody business with your family impelled you to leave the Border Patrol and try to get distance from all that Mexican shit by comin' up here," Able said, talking fast before Tell could get his back up or maybe interrupt. "But surely you see, Tell, just looking around here now that you've arrived, and after last night, that even out here in the sticks of Ohio now-a-days, the goddamn border is nearly every-fucking-where."

"Too true, in every sense, I guess," Tell said.

"What do you think about this wall they want to build along the border?"

"I think they better have the illegals build it before they kick them out," Tell said. "Only way that damned wall will be anything like affordable."

Able laughed and rummaged through the open briefcase on the bench next to him and pulled out a yellow envelope. He tossed it on the table between them. "The copies of fake operator's licenses and Social Security cards you requested," Able said. "These are your copies to keep, Tell. And there are a couple of originals in there from some of the illegal ones we've already sent back across the border. You can keep those too—to help train your folks."

"Really appreciate it," Tell said. He slipped them out of the envelope and gave them a quick look. "Hell, Able, these aren't even that good."

"Nah, but that makes it easier for us, right? We deserve to catch a break, standing against this wicked tide like we are."

"On that note, I hear the ACLU is after your tail in a big way," Tell said. "You actually get any compensation back from the federal government yet for all the bills you sent them for your jail costs?"

Able smiled. "*Nah*. Hell no. Lawyers tell me I'm on solid ground with that gambit, but they also say my successor's successor will likely be the one to cash *that* fuckin' check. It's really about principle, though. And it's gotten me *muy* regional press. I expect my neighbors to the south and east will soon follow suit. Here's my dream. I'd like to get all eighty-eight county sheriffs on board, and I don't think it's much a reach I'll see that happen before long. Well, except maybe in goddamn Cleveland. That fucking shithole is full of Democrats who look at these hordes of undocumented Mexicans and scent votes. Traitorous assholes."

Tell let that conversational strand peter out. He said, "I wanted to give you a heads-up, Able, because I know there's some money coming Horton County's way for the interim service, but I'm wanting to take my force around the clock before the New Year."

"Good," Able said. "Good. I do mean that, Tell—better for all of us. A town the size of New Austin should be served by a full-time police force. I don't mind losing the fill-in stipend."

That was a load off—the hurdle Tell had guessed might be the hardest to clear.

The waitress came to take Tell's order. Able recommended the meatloaf and mashed potatoes with a side of buttered green beans. Sounded like 1960s-style food at twenty-first century prices. But Tell bit his lip and went along. As she moved to leave, Able Hawk said to the waitress, "Hey, where's Thalia? She's not come down ill has she?"

"She ain't called in," Betty said, "and Lou's fit to be tied. May fire her when she shows up. But it ain't like Thale. I'm worried. Tried to call her on my own during my cigarette break, but . . ."

Able nodded. "'Spect it's just car trouble or something. That jalopy of hers . . . ?"

Tell asked, "Thalia? She another waitress?"

"Yeah, real sweet girl . . . single mother, don't you know," Able said. "One of my—our—increasingly rare legals. Her husband died in a propane tank explosion time back. The fireball blew out half the windows in Horton County. She and her daughter live with her mother and younger cousin now. Suspect the cousin's another illegal, but I've givin' her a pass because of Thalia and all the trouble she's had of late. I try to help her out, quiet-like, where I can."

"You mentioned overlap," Tell said. "You and my predecessor working on anything together that we need to reevaluate or discuss?"

"No, not at all like we should have been," Able said. "The polite way to describe the former New Austin police chief would be 'maverick.' But a realist like you or me would term the cocksucker who preceded you a turf-conscience prick a hell of a lot more interested in self-advancement and job security than law enforcement. He was a weak-chinned coward."

"But you scored some big arrests in my town recently, Sheriff," Tell said. "The prostitution bust a few weeks back. A cockfighting ring. And I get the sense from reading my boys' duty reports that you're maybe working on something involving meth my way too."

"Jesus, you're sharp, Tell. Regarding the hookers and the birds, you'll notice I waited until New Austin was between chiefs to move on those messes, so as not to step on toes. And the meth traffic in Horton County, you're right, it's centered in New Austin. Out in your rural south end, but radiating out all over Horton County and beyond. I expect news maybe before week's end on that front. My folks did the heavy lifting and took the risks, but I'm happy to have your crew, and you, come along and share credit. For the sake of the media, we'll make it look like a long-term, joint operation if you're okay with that."

"Sounds great to me . . . sounds like a *gift*," Tell said. "And why would you do that?"

Able waved a hand. "It ain't an act of charity on my part, or indication I'm fucking Santa Claus, Tell. I'd do it to inspire some of the other police chiefs around Horton County to cooperate more with the sheriff's department. Stakes are too high for this balkanization and 'little kingdoms' crap that's currently too much the damned norm."

"Then let's do that," Tell said.

The old lawman smiled broadly. "Great. We will. And you're a real important symbol to me going along, Tell. I mean with your Border Patrol background and all."

Tell rubbed the back of his neck. He said softly, "Suppose that's so."

Able sipped his coffee, then said, "Anything else I can do for you, Chief?"

Tell shrugged his shoulders. "Possibly something I haven't thought of yet. Frankly, I'm still finding my feet, Able. And my bench isn't that deep. I've got some solid people, but . . ."

"But no stars," Able said. "You've got no strong right hand, right? No consigliere?"

"Not so far as I've detected yet," Tell said.

"Wish to Christ I could boast that my bench was deeper than yours in that sense," Able said. "But it so ain't. Sadly, I can't yet clone myself." Able sat back and smiled. "So, us lacking strong lieutenants, you and me, I guess we'll just have to content ourselves with the knowledge we have one another's backs, am I right, Tell?"

"Looks as though it's apt to be that way, Able." Tell paused. "You really listening to Spanish language tapes?"

"Really am," Able said. "For all the good it's doing me. I'm beginning by learning how to curse in Spanish." He raised his hand. "No, don't smile like that—I'm serious. If I can curse a blue streak in their own language, it cuts through a lot. I've concluded it's the most useful Spanish for a gringo cop."

* * *

Tell's ass was getting sore. He'd been sitting in the goddamn booth too long.

Able Hawk had no sooner hauled up his bulk and left after a firm handshake than a haggard and hung-over Shawn O'Hara shambled in and parked his skinny butt in Able's seat.

The reporter had plunked a tape recorder down on the tabletop between them. Then he'd broken out a long and slender notebook, and set off on a disjointed and rambling series of questions that veered between sophomoric, intrusive, and, in the case of the murder of Tell's wife and child, insulting—even provocative. Or Tell thought so.

Tell bit his lip and gave straight answers to matters involving his vision for the force, his priorities and his policing techniques. He indulged a few questions about his individual views on border security and immigration issues. He issued several "no comments" regarding his personal life, and, when Shawn stubbornly pushed a little too far, Tell said, "You ask me one more question about my wife and child and I'm going to shove that pen up your ass, sonny."

That had flustered Shawn—made him flinch. But then the reporter had dug his hole deeper trying to change tack and justify his intrusiveness. "You know, Chief, I just figured that you being relations to Chris Lyon and all, you'd know and understand that we reporters—"

But Tell had swiftly stepped back into Shawn for invoking his "notorious" cousin's name. "Chris was the journalist, not me. But since you raise the subject of Chris, maybe the only man who has less regard for sloppy and intrusive reporters than me, is my cousin. I suspect he'd have some definite opinions about you, if this is always the way you go about your job."

After that exchange, Shawn had fallen back to mundane questions about staffing levels, budgets and reorganizational issues. Tell fielded those questions tersely, but professionally.

Tell checked his watch. The interview had already dragged on twenty minutes longer than he had intended to allot. He said, "I've got to end this, Shawn. It's early days yet and I'm still scrambling to make up for the gap between me and the last chief."

"Sure," Shawn said coolly. "Thanks for your time. And sorry I hit so many no-go areas."

Tell looked at him a time. He shook his head and stuck out his hand. "It's early days for us too, Shawn," Tell said. "Let's neither of us take today as some hint of conversations to come."

NINE

Miguel and Candelario were playing catch at the back of the New Austin Kid's Association ball diamonds. Several organized games played by white kids were underway, so the boys had settled on the unmowed field behind the diamonds.

It had rained for at least an hour total nearly every day for a week, and that had set to bloom something that Candelario, only six months out of Mexico, had no resistance against.

The boy fresh from Sinaloa sneezed, just as Miguel let fling. Candelario brought his glove up to his screwed-up face, doubling over with the ferocity of his sneeze.

The ball flew high over Candelario's head.

The boy wiped his nose with the back of his arm, sniffled, pivoted, then set heel down the hill to a copse of evergreens to fetch the baseball—a lost ball they had found behind a dugout three days earlier. The boys had had a fistfight over who got to keep it in their home. Their gloves were cast-offs the boys had found in the dugouts and repaired with duct tape and shoelaces.

As he ran down the hill, Candelario kept his eye on the baseball, watching it part the high grass as it rolled swiftly on. The ball bumped up against something pink at the base of a thicket of trees—something Candelario at first mistook for a rock of some kind.

The boy reached for the ball and saw pink toes.

His gaze trailed up the leg and he saw hair in an unfamiliar place—curly short black hair that was matted with blood.

Candelario began screaming, running back up the hill, pointing behind himself, yelling in Spanish all the way back up to Miguel.

THEN

Thalia had known what had happened the moment she saw the rising, swelling fireball through the front windows of the diner.

The propane plant was too far away for the blast's concussion to break the windows of the diner, but she was unsteadied—Thalia felt the ground tremble even at three miles' distance.

Her husband had told Thalia about the dangers of a plant explosion—a catastrophe that could be triggered by something as small as a bit of static electricity from fabrics brushing together. He told her how devastating it could be for those at the scene of the explosion, as well as for those within a mile or so radius—the danger of the imploding windows and flying glass. He told her that those outside and close by might suffer perforated eardrums from the blast's concussion.

Flaming debris might be tossed thousands of feet into the air and could fall thousands of feet from its source, depending on wind conditions. All that falling, fiery wreckage could trigger a second round of house and brush fires around the plant.

Thalia had regained her footing and stared at the rising ball of flame; saw bits of something cascading down from its plume. Not looking back to see if her co-workers were seeing what she was seeing, or if they heard what she said, Thalia had screamed, "I have to go!"

Then she'd run out to her old truck.

* * *

Thalia got as close as the southern corporation line, where a barricade had been set up. She was still four hundred yards from the plant and her husband, yet she could feel the intense heat of the raging fire.

She grabbed the arms of anyone who looked like a plant worker or emergency technician—anyone who might help her through the barricades and take her to her husband. But nobody would do that, and city cops and county sheriff's deputies kept turning her away or asking her to leave.

She was sitting on the bumper of a Horton County sheriff's SUV, head in hands and racked with sobs when she felt a hand on her shoulder. A man said, "Ma'am, do you have family at the plant?"

Thalia looked up and saw a big, older man in a gray uniform. The sun glinted on his badge and dark sunglasses. He said carefully, "They tell me anyone in the loading area at the time of the first explosion couldn't have made it out. That they would have been vaporized—*instantly*, if that's a comfort. I have a list, honey, a list of the men who were known to be in that loading area. Who are you looking for?"

Thalia told him her husband's name.

The older, husky cop didn't tell her anything back. He looked at the list and then opened his arms.

He held her tightly to him as she sobbed and beat on his back with her fists, soaking his uniform's shirt through between the collar and epaulet with her tears.

That was how Thalia met Able Hawk.

TEN

The chief hadn't been two minutes out of the booth when Able Hawk slid into Tell Lyon's vacated seat across from Shawn.

"Had other business across the way," Able said. "Supposed to be meeting Sheriff Walt Pierce, but the bastard stood me up and his own people can't seem to find the cocksucker. Buy you another coffee, Shawn?"

The journalist shrugged. "Why not?" He stuck his notepad in his pocket. "But if you're thinking I might preview my profile of Lyon for you . . ."

Able's gray eyes narrowed. Not "Tell." Not "Chief Lyon" or "Tell Lyon," but simply, tersely, "Lyon." That was telling, so to speak.

"I'll wait to read that profile," Able said, "just like all the other rubes. That said, I was sitting just across the dining room and I do have eyes, Shawn, nearsighted though they may be. I sensed a charged exchange, even from a distance."

Shawn shook his head. "Sure you're not farsighted, Sheriff Hawk?"

The old cop smiled back. He said, "I'll confess that I thought for a second there I might have to step between you two tough guys. Am I wrong?"

"Came pretty close, I guess." Shawn surprised himself by admitting it. Then the encounter tumbled from him. He ended with, "And I think the bastard's cost me my girlfriend."

Able smiled and sipped his coffee. "Venturing out where I have no business, I will volunteer my perception the young lady was all

73

eyes for Lyon last night, and he for her." Able sipped more coffee, made a face, then tore open a packet of sugar and stirred it in. "But looking at it from a different angle, I'll only observe that Chief Lyon's late wife was Hispanic. Marita was her name, and she was twenty-seven when she was killed. Only two years older than Patricia. So you can see where she must push Lyon's buttons. Your Patricia, I mean."

Shawn opened his mouth to speak, but Able charged on, anticipating Shawn's next remark. "Your girlfriend," Able said, "well, she frankly interested me too. As a friction point between you and Lyon, if you see what I mean. So I looked Patricia up on the BMV computer. That's how I know her age, Shawn. I like to know the key players, best I can."

"So you did see it too—their infatuation with one another," Shawn shook his head.

"Maybe saw even more than you," Able said.

The journalist looked up sharply, cheeks reddening.

"That didn't come out quite right," Able said. "What I fuckin' meant was, my perception is, Patricia, she's the marrying kind, and you sure ain't. Stories get around these parts outside the stories you circulate for a livin', Shawn. About conquests and the like. Pretty clearly, you're not lookin' to settle down anytime soon, but it strikes me that Patricia is. That bein' an accurate assessment on my part, and I believe it is with all my dark heart, you're perhaps well shed of the gal."

The sheriff ran a rough hand through his close-cropped gray hair. "Jesus, Horton County's lousy with pretty Spanish tail now. Ask my advice, I'd say drive on, lad."

"Lyon's nearly thirteen years older than Patty," Shawn said. "Nearly old enough to be her father."

Able snorted. "Maybe in certain backward and backwoods parts that'd be true," the sheriff said with a lopsided grin. "Least ways in some lingering backwaters where the generations grow increasingly shorter and their eyes get wider apart. Places where the definition of a virgin is any young gal that can outrun her uncle or brother. But not in these environs. Here it's what you call a 'May-December romance.' Tell had a few years on his late wife too. 'Sides, my dispatcher, DeeDee—who reads *Cosmopolitan* and *Vogue* magazines like the old folks around the county read the Bible—DeeDee, she says that 'forty is the new thirty,' whatever to Christ that fucking means."

Shawn shook his head again. "Yeah. Whatever."

Able said, "So, should I brace for another rough and leftward-leaning editorial about my recent policies, Mild-Mannered? Been nearly two months since you took me back of the woodshed for some ACLU-hand-wringing-inducing gaffe or policing policy on my part."

Shawn said, "*No*. Readers are pretty clearly on your side now, Sheriff. Certainly the *Recorder* subscribers are. And so is my publisher. And it's hard to deny the effect that this illegal immigration is having on the school system and social services."

"Indeed," Able said, searching Shawn's face.

"You know that Patricia is one of your greatest fans, except for this latest thing you did," Shawn said, staring down into his coffee.

Able scowled. "What latest thing that I did?"

Shawn told the sheriff the story of the hostess from Patricia's parents' restaurant—the one arrested by Able Hawk and his men for prostitution. Shawn told Able of Luz's situation and Luz's ailing mother and her little girl back in Mexico.

"Deeply moving," Able said, his voice raw. "Sincerely, Shawn, I feel for her, this Luz. That's no bullshit, son. I'd help her out financially myself, if I could, knowing her story now. I think I might even remember her. There was about ten we arrested. I remember one that seemed a bit different from the rest of the pack. Either way, I'm truly sorry and heartbroken for her. And for her kid. But you see, Shawn, *every* life is a story. Every hurt is someone's personal tragedy. Your day job is taking the general and making it particular. Your mission is to humanize the news. So you look for sad examples like Luz. You write stories about people like Luz to bring the news down to human-scale. That's what you do and you do it well enough. My job requires me not to be bogged down by individual circumstances. I apply the law equally and dispassionately. I can't afford the luxury of trying to see in shades of gray, Shawn. It's one law for the lion and the lamb. That's my job. There's an old saying I favor: 'Never attach more feeling to a thing than God does.'"

Shawn scowled. "You really think like that?"

Able nodded. "I try to."

ELEVEN

Tell picked up his cruiser's radio and clicked. "Go ahead?"

"Chief Lyon? It's Julie."

"Hey, Julie. What's up?"

"It's an emergency. I'm going to call you on your cell phone, Chief Lyon. Thing like this, well, Chief Sloan insisted I keep it off the police band. Keeps the press off-footing," she said.

"Do that. Oh, and Julie, next time, I want you to know you can call me on my cell phone from the get-go." Reporters and their goddamn scanners—truly a pain in the ass, to be sure.

"Okay, Chief Lyon."

Tell racked his radio mic and picked up his cell phone, waiting. Two long minutes later, the phone rang.

"Chief Lyon, it's Julie."

Tell rolled his eyes. "Hey, Julie. It's Tell. What's up?"

"Do you know the Kid's Association ball diamonds, Chief Lyon?"

On his drive around town the night he'd gotten in, Tell had passed a sign for the ballpark But he couldn't place it. He said, "I'll need directions, Julie. Why am I going there?"

"In a field that runs behind the ball diamonds, two little Mexican boys found a body. Looks like she's been murdered. She's naked and badly beaten."

"Give me those directions, Julie."

The distances were short, so Tell took the directions in real time.

Julie said, "Best to park in the Association's parking lot and walk across the ball fields, Chief Lyon. There's no other good way back there."

Tell drifted into the Kid's Association's parking lot, spewing gravel. Julie was hedging again. Tell said, "Just tell me what you're thinking, Julie."

"This field, Chief Lyon, it's in what's called the 'Three Corners.' The jurisdictions and boundaries are a little bit blurry out there, Chief. This might not even be our crime scene."

"Let's assume that it is and stick hard to that notion, Julie. Coroner on the way?"

"He's already there, Chief. So are Billy and Rick."

"Thanks, Julie."

"Good luck, Chief Lyon."

"Thanks again, Julie."

* * *

Able Hawk held up a meaty hand to shush the reporter. He dipped his other hand in the left breast pocket of his uniform and plucked out his cell phone. He said, smiling, "Hey, DeeDee."

"Sheriff, we got a body in the Three Corners spotted by a couple of illegal juveniles. Latino female, age thirty to thirty-five. Nude and badly beaten. Signs of repeated rape according to Coroner Parks."

"Got it. Thanks, Double-Dee."

Horton County's sheriff slid out of the booth. He said to Shawn, "Okay, hands-across-the-water stuff, Mild-Mannered. We've got us a body over to the Three Corners, Shawn. I'm gonna let you ride with me, if you're game."

Shawn slid out of the booth, excited but pissed off he hadn't brought a camera. "Let's do it."

* * *

Vale County Sheriff Walt Pierce stopped scratching his crotch and scooped up his cell phone from the console between the seats of his command cruiser. He said, "Roxie, what's the story?"

"Two spic snot-noses found a naked and dead beaner bitch out to the Three Corners, Sheriff. Two or three yards either way, I hear, and it could be ours."

The Vale County sheriff closed his cell phone and checked the mirror—smoothing his bristly hair back with his right hand, rings catching sunlight. He frowned at something on one ring and held it up close to his face. He rubbed it clean, then switched on his sirens and gunned her—ninety miles an hour through a New Austin school zone.

Jaywalking Mexican kids scattered from his path.

* * *

Tell skidded into a vacant space between two of his officers' cruisers. He stepped out into the still-settling dust. One of Tell's officers, Rick Keaton, was leaning over a chain-link fence, ashen, trying to compose himself.

Rick saw his chief approaching and straightened up. Still looking shaken, Rick saluted. Tell resisted the impulse to return the absurd gesture. He said, "You were here first?"

"Yeah. Sorry, Chief. I'll get right back there in just a few minutes."

"When you can will be fine, Rick," Tell said.

The ball games underway were distracting the civilians from the crime scene developing behind them. Well, that wouldn't be true much longer, Tell thought. He said, "Rick, go over and start talking to folks around those ball diamonds. See if anyone saw anybody, any strange cars or that sort of thing. You know the drill."

Tell walked on until the parents' cheers were a dim hum. He waded into waist-high weeds.

* * *

Able Hawk skidded into the slot next to Tell Lyon's command car. He said to the reporter by his side, "Chief Lyon, he's fast. I'll give him that much. "

* * *

Tell saw his other officer, big Billy Davis, standing grim-faced by County Coroner Casey Parks, who was squatting over the body.

Tell squeezed Billy's beefy arm. "You okay, brother?"

"Fine, Chief. Thanks for askin' though. Rick, he okay?"

"He'll be fine. Guess you two don't get many like this?"

"No, Chief. This is more a Vale County-style crime."

The coroner nodded. "You must be Tell Lyon." Doc Parks held up a latex-gloved hand and said, "I'd shake, but . . ."

"Hell of a way to meet," Tell said.

"Where else to do it, with our jobs?"

"Guess that's so," Tell muttered, squatting down on his hams next to the coroner.

As a Border Patrol agent, before he'd been kicked upstairs, Tell had paid his dues, cruising the lonely roads in the no-man's land between Mexico and California, hours out of sight of anyone else. He'd go out there, armed with sack lunches and dinners, jugs of water and a roll of toilet paper, listening to CDs sent to him by his cousin. Lots of country, folk . . . vintage rock and the cream of seventies songwriters' works. And his personal favorite, Mickey Newbury.

Tell went out there looking for illegal crossers. Alive or dead, the Border Patrol lingo was such the agents called the Mexicans "bodies." But Tell had seen his share of actual corpses. He'd seen pregnant women who had delivered on the desert floor—mother and child soon after dead from exposure and dehydration. He'd found at least a dozen dead elderly couples who had frozen in the cold night or cooked in the afternoon sun. He'd found young men who'd set off from Mexico lugging two jugs of water that weighed them down; slowed them to their deaths. But they had set off with fewer gallons than the trip demanded. Hot and thirsty, they'd go off their heads, shedding shoes and clothing under the sun, hastening their own deaths by exposure. Tell had found them on their backs or bellies, dead and dusted in the alkali, faces frozen in death-rictus grimaces, curled up in fetal positions. Their skin was like leather.

The dead woman lying before him now wasn't wizened. Her body was ripe and raw and bruised; not yet mottling from the settling blood. Bruises and deep lacerations covered her torso and breasts. The woman's face was all but obliterated. Deep cuts crisscrossed her cheeks and forehead. Her lips were shredded and her nose nearly flattened from repeated blows.

Her mouth gaped and her front teeth were broken or missing. The woman's dark eyes were still open, already filming over. Her head rested in a bed of ivy. One bruised arm was crooked over her head.

"Rape, clearly," Doc Parks said. "And clearly she's been beaten. One thing for certain, the bad bastard who did this was wearing rings or brass knuckles. He was into cutting her."

"We'll never get an identification on that ruined face," Tell said. "I wouldn't even put a possible witness through trying. Jesus, but she's been torn to pieces by the son of a bitch."

The coroner offered Tell a pair of latex gloves. "You have the stomach to assist me, Chief? It'd be a great help. I'm woefully underfunded."

Tell reluctantly took the gloves. "Okay." Billy Davis turned his back. But he stayed alongside them—Tell respected the big cop for that.

A new voice behind them said, "Jesus and Mary, that luckless woman."

Tell nodded at Able Hawk. Shawn O'Hara, looking vaguely sick, was hard on the sheriff's heels.

He pulled on his latex gloves, then Tell said, "No offense on this Shawn, but, Able, you sure this is a good idea, letting press this close, this early?"

"I'd do it," Able said. "And I know you're new to these parts. So you couldn't know that this place, it's—"

Bless Julie, Tell thought. He said, "I do know, Able. This is Three Corners. Suspect if you and I and Walt Pierce don't see eye to eye on this in the next few hours, we'll be calling in surveyors and cartographers to determine whose headache this woman's murder really is. Better, absent that kind of turf war, that you and I share this one, don't you think, Sheriff?"

"Right." Able stooped down, stoic, searching the dead woman's devastated face. "He said softly, "Oh, Jesus no . . . *no*." He brushed some bloodied hair back from the woman's forehead and said, "I think this is a friend goddamn it."

Tell thought Shawn O'Hara might soon pass out. He was leagues out of his depth, but too prideful to turn away.

Coroner Parks said, "Here we go now, Chief Lyon. You get a grip on her shoulders, and I'll get her thighs. Let's roll her on over."

*　*　*

Shawn took in the body with sidelong glances. Alive, and a bit skinnier, the woman might have been hot enough to do. She was busty. Long dark hair and dark eyes. Good thighs. She was Shawn's type, okay. But then there was the gaping, destroyed mouth. The stubs and shards of broken teeth. Those cuts across her fine breasts—the cuts long and deep, but no longer bleeding. The woman's face was hamburger. Shawn couldn't believe what fists could do to a human face.

The New Austin chief of police and Horton County coroner took hold of the woman's body, then rolled her over.

The tall grass was matted and bloody where she'd been dumped. Except for the blood, the grass was dry.

Coroner Parks said, "She was dumped here post-dew fall and dew burn-off. Hell, I doubt she's been dead less than two hours. And I seriously doubt that she was out here more than an hour before she was found."

Shawn's gaze was drawn to the small of the dead woman's back. Spread across her lower back, just above her tailbone, was a tattoo—a too-familiar red and blue butterfly. It was the third time in twenty-four hours that Shawn had seen the tattoo. The first time had been the night before, when he'd been taking the murdered woman from behind. The second time was at sunrise, when he'd raised the sheet to get a better look at what he'd fucked the night before.

Shawn staggered backward and fell on his ass, vomiting uncontrollably.

The journalist heard Tell Lyon say, "Oh, Jesus Christ, Shawn!"

Shawn heard Able Hawk say, "For Christ's sake, Shawn! Scoot the hell back from the crime scene if you're going to keep puking, goddamn you."

A raspy, grating snort from behind Shawn: "Holy fuck, this is how you two do business around these parts? You assholes invite weak-stomached reporters to come and puke all over and fuck up my crime scene?"

* * *

Able turned. Short, fat Vale County sheriff Walt Pierce waddled toward them, his hands shoved down into his pockets. Able extended a hand to shake; saw his hand was trembling. Walt, hands still in pockets, came on strong. "Take your pussy reporter friend, boys, and get out of here. I'm taking custody of the scene. My jurisdiction, boys, so she's my meat."

Able stood up, shaken and red-faced and put his hands on his hips. "Chief Lyon and me have this well in hand, Walt. 'Tween us, she'd have to be two hundred, maybe two hundred and fifty yards yonder to fall in your shithole county. She's ours. And may be a friend of mine. Don't fuck with me on this, W. Don't show me your balls on this one."

"Bullshit." Sheriff Pierce looked at the dead woman and said, "Your coroner can stay, of course. At least 'til I can scare up my own."

"This one is ours," Able said again. "Victim, near as I can tell from what's left of her face, is likely Thalia Ruiz. She's one of *my* legals. And my friend. Like I pointed out to you the other day, Walt. You remember, that waitress serving us at Big G's you were all eyes for. She's also a New Austin citizen. So Tell and me have this one, Walt. This one is *ours*."

"I dispute that," Pierce said, hands still in his pockets. Shawn was on his hands and knees, dry-heaving. Walt said, "This is clearly in my county. I know my own boundaries."

"You're just plumb wrong," Able said. "Now get your ass out of here if you don't want to cooperate."

Walt said, "Gonna file me some papers on you assholes. Get me a judge to set a fire under your asses."

Able Hawk showed Pierce his broad, gray back. "Yeah, yeah, fine," Able said. "You do all that, cocksucker. Chief Lyon and me will counter file. Now get your fat ass off our crime scene before *you* foul it further."

Walt spat again, missing Shawn's vomit by inches. He said, turning, "This ain't anywhere near over, Hawk."

Tell watched the fat little sheriff trudge off through the high grass. He said, "Thanks, Able. Thanks so much for having my back."

Able said, "Screw that. I just eliminated half my competition for this collar." He frowned, stooping down again next to New Austin's chief of police. "Damn truth be told, this might well be Vale County acreage, Tell. It's a question of feet if not inches. If we're gonna make this one ours, we best be damned quick about it. And Thalia? I liked her like one of my own. If this is her, well, I want to go to the wall on this one. Lethal injection for the cocksucker that did this to her. I won't stop short of an execution for this son of a bitch. "

Tell looked at the woman's body. "I couldn't blame you."

Able gripped Tell's shoulder. "You pro-death penalty, Chief?"

"I'm not anti-death penalty," Tell said. "Put it that way."

"Subtle distinction," Able said. "Why do I have dark visions of that hair-splitting maybe biting me in the ass later?" Then Able said, "No, don't turn her back over quite yet, fellas." He fished out his cell phone. "Going to see if I can get her mother's number. Maybe get an ID via that tattoo. 'Cause I'm a sad son of a bitch if I don't think that's Thalia Ruiz there." He paused and said to Tell, "If I'm right about this being Thalia, she's leaving behind a little girl." Able searched Tell's face. He said, "That's another reason I want someone to die for this."

Behind them, Shawn gagged again.

*   *   *

Sofia Gómez frowned at the red and blue lights swirling across the walls of her living room. The knock at the door was like a punch to the stomach. She shooed her granddaughter into the next room to watch Nickelodeon, then flipped on the front porch light.

Moths beat at the light outside.

The man on the other side of the door was husky and older, and dressed all in gray. The lawman was holding a cell phone. Behind him stood more uniformed officers. The stricken look on the man's face set Sofia's heart beating faster.

He said through the screen door between them, "My name is Able Hawk. We need to speak, *señora.*"

TWELVE

Tell pulled into his apartment complex's parking lot at half past eight. The lot was nearly deserted. The chief of police wondered whether there could be such a thing as a hopping Friday night in New Austin.

He hauled himself out of his SUV and stretched. His back cracked. He'd spent hours with his men talking to young ball players and their parents and coaches. Fruitless legwork: nobody had seen anything.

Tell's apartment complex backed up to a wooded creek. He wasn't quite ready to lock himself away in some tight and lonely little apartment that didn't feel anything like home. He strode down the sloping hill to the creek side. He stood there for a while, watching the fading sunlight on the ripples over a bed of white rocks.

A voice behind and above him said, "Rough day, huh?"

Patricia was sitting on a small, bleached deck—its floor about three feet above Tell's head. He said, "Long day, anyway."

"Saw it on the six o'clock news," she said. "Sounds nasty bad."

"Terrible," Tell said. "Would've expected you'd be at work, it being Friday night rush and all."

"It's a loose thing, my schedule," she said. "Advantage of a family-owned business, I guess." Patricia stood up and leaned over the railing, her arms crossed on the rough-cut wood. "Confession, Tell. I recklessly made a pitcher of margaritas a few minutes ago. Not a smart thing when a woman's alone and in a dark study. And here at home, I don't pour 'em like I own 'em. Or maybe I do. What I mean is, the suckers are *muy* potent. Save me from getting smashed alone, Chief?"

Tell rested his hands on his hips. His gun's butt was hard under his right hand. Again, it felt like a mistake. But the coolness of the night and the sound of the creek water . . . the prospect of good drinks with a pretty, sensual young woman? How to say no to that after a day passed coping with a raped, beaten and murdered single mother? After jousting with the likes of Able Hawk and Patricia's (ex-?) boyfriend Shawn O'Hara? Tomorrow he planned to be back in the office early, despite the weekend, combing through files and checking arrest records for similar crimes or beatings that might portend what had happened to Thalia Ruiz.

Tell said, "A drink sounds real good. Just give me a few minutes to wash up and change. Anything I can bring?"

"Just yourself, Chief."

Tell keyed himself in, locked his service weapon in his gun safe, hung up his uniform and took a quick shower. He dressed in jeans, a worn, loose-fitting black Polo shirt and battered boots. He brushed his teeth and grabbed a fresh bag of tortilla chips and a jar of Newman's Own pineapple-flavored salsa.

Patricia met him at the door. Her black hair was loose and wavy. No makeup. She wore faded jeans and she was barefoot, her toenails unpainted. The T-shirt she'd been wearing a few minutes before had been discarded in favor of a white peasant blouse that bared her brown shoulders. Tell felt stricken.

He hoisted the bag of chips and jar of salsa. "Provisions."

Patricia smiled and said, "Perfect. We'll burn it off in the morning with our run." She smiled and dipped her head. "We are still on for that run, aren't we?"

He'd forgotten his promise. "Sure," Tell said. "I mean, barring still more pressing developments at work. As it is, I'll definitely be putting in some weekend hours because of today."

Patricia pulled a big plastic bowl and a small, matching soup-size bowl from her cupboards. She emptied all of the chips and salsa into the bowls. "Now we're committed to finishing," she said. Patricia looked him up and down and smiled. "Gotta say, I like this look best of all. Hate to inform you—those black uniforms you and your people wear, well, they're a little menacing."

"I didn't pick 'em," Tell said. But he agreed with Patricia; they were particularly unsettling against the surrounding sheriff's departments' muted grays and tans. Tell said, "Uniforms are a little jackboot here in New Austin. But they're more to my liking than the Border Patrol uniforms. Those are a kind of off-hunter green. You look more like a park ranger than a cop."

She said, "Sorry, I wasn't necessarily expecting company. Afraid I'm kind of—"

"Natural," he finished for her. "I love natural. Prefer it, really, to painted-up."

Patricia opened the door to her deck and he followed her out. A small table was positioned between two padded lounge chairs. A sweating pitcher of margaritas and an ice bucket sat on the table. Two glasses with salted rims were waiting.

She poured their drinks and offered her glass for Tell to tap.

He raised his glass, poised to click it against hers. "What are we toasting, Patricia?"

"How about to quieter and sweeter days in New Austin?"

"Definitely to that."

Patricia surprised herself, saying it so early, "Just to get it out of the way forever, Tell. Shawn knows that he and I are over."

Tell nodded, sipping his drink. *Okay.* That was just putting it out there. Tell took a deep breath, said, "How'd he take that?"

"You truly care?"

"Like you said, Patricia, it's just a run in the morning. This is just a drink or two tonight. Right?" He searched her dark eyes.

Patricia turned around in her chair and leaned forward, arms resting on her knees, forearms crossed. She wore no rings and her nails were cut short. "No games, not this time," she said. "Here's where maybe I scare you away, like that." She snapped her fingers. "I'm tired to death of the dance. I'm not looking for boyfriends anymore. I just want a good and decent man to be with. Whatever happens beyond that, happens." She arched a dark eyebrow. "Too direct?"

Tell smiled.

Actually, Patricia reminded him a bit of his cousin's wife, Salome: sultry, blunt and good-humored. Salome had sparked something in Tell. He sensed that his cousin Chris had caught it and had given Tell and Salome some room so Tell could harmlessly indulge it. His last day in Cedartown, Tell had taken Salome and his cousin's youngest daughter, Vesper, to the zoo. Chris had begged off, citing looming deadlines on owed revisions for his next novel.

It was vintage Chris, the calculating, self-righteous bastard: not thinking that time with sexy, dark Salome and little Vesper would remind Tell of what he'd lost, but instead remind him of what he could have again . . . and maybe spark some other, primal impulses in Tell.

And damned if Chris hadn't been right.

Tell said, "Direct is good, Patricia. Thing is, you're what, twenty-four? Maybe twenty-five? Here's where I maybe scare *you* away. I'm hard up against forty."

"They say forty is the new thirty," she said, smiling. "Read that in *Vogue* or *Cosmo* or somewhere while standing in the grocery." She took his hand. He liked the way that felt. She said, "You're a young near-forty. And you know what? I'm a world-weary twenty-five. I'll have my degree in a month and I don't find I have much ambition to use it beyond the family business. I'm ready for a lot of nights like this one, Tell."

"Fourteen years between us," he said.

"Irrelevant," Patricia said, shrugging. "But it's not been a year since . . . Well, I confess I've been reading a few items about you on the Net."

"Makes sense," Tell said.

"So I know about your family."

"Sure," Tell said. "After Able's remark the other night, I'd have researched me too."

"So it's too soon for me to be talking with you like this?"

Again, not subtle. "It's fine," he said. "But we should take our time for other reasons."

"So you don't rule out the prospect of us maybe spending time together?"

Tell smiled and squeezed her hand harder. "Think I'd like that very much, Patricia."

She smiled back and said, "I like that—that you call me by my proper name. It always seems to get shortened to 'Tricia,' or 'Tish,' or worst of all, 'Patty.' *Ugh.*"

Tell stroked the back of her hand with his thumb. "You're very much a Patricia."

A mourning dove cooed from inside the drape of a weeping willow. The tree's drooping branches brushed the banister of Patricia's small deck.

"I love the sound of mourning doves," Tell said, retreating a bit. "Used to sit out under the trees at my grandparents' home with Granddad after he retired. Those birds always nested in their trees. I hear one now, I always think of Paw-Paw."

"It's a family of birds that's nested here for the four years I've rented this place," Patricia said. "I think they sound sad. But they mate for life." She hesitated. "You're right about the neighborhood and how it's becoming dangerous. I'll hate leaving this place, but I'll need to do it soon if things continue to deteriorate around here like they are now."

"They're apt to do just that," Tell said. "Hell of a note for your chief of police to sound, huh? But it's the stark truth. Force as small as mine, and a tide of undocumented migrants as this town's getting? My force can't make a dent in a neighborhood like this one you and I are living up against."

"I'm kind of surprised you settled for an apartment, Tell," she said.

"Haven't really had time yet to scout around for houses to my liking," he said.

"Neighborhood, you're thinking? Community?"

"Acreage, I'm thinking," Tell said, smiling and sipping his drink. "Solitude."

She tipped her head to one side. "How much solitude?"

"Just me and mine."

Patricia smiled. "Sounds wonderful." She shivered.

"We can go in if you're cold," he said.

"No, I'll just slip in and grab a throw."

Patricia came back with a Navaho-pattern blanket. She freshened both their drinks. "You cold too, Tell?"

"I'm just fine." It was the first time in memory he could say that with conviction.

"You're supposed to say that you're cold, Tell."

He searched her dark eyes again. "It *is* a little brisk, Patricia."

She smiled and pulled her chair alongside his and closed the blanket over them. The sun was nearly down and the first fireflies flitted in the branches of the softly moving willow.

"I'm going to be direct one more time," Patricia said.

Tell's right arm was wrapped around her shoulders. "Sure, do that," he said. He said it with stomach flutters. This was all a little fast for his taste. And so soon after . . . ?

Patricia said, "A man loses as much as you did, he might not want to put himself at risk for that kind of hurt again." She hesitated, said, "Could you imagine yourself maybe wanting family again someday?"

He hugged her closer. "Family is very important to you, isn't it, Patricia?"

"Very much. I want my own family to be just as strong and safe-feeling as what I grew up with."

That was a kind of gut shot. But at the same time, Tell had tried to keep his family safe, and he'd sworn to himself he'd never repeat any of the mistakes that had cost him his first wife and child. Tell took his left hand from under the blanket and stroked Patricia's hair behind her ear. "Me too," he said, leaning in to a kiss.

* * *

Across town, Shawn lay in his bed, bathed in sweat, his mind racing. The murdered woman's roommate, Carmelita, knew Shawn's first name.

They'd left Shawn's ill-fated lover's own car back at the club. It was just a matter of time until cops positively identified her and started asking questions that would lead to Shawn.

If he ran tonight, he could be in Windsor within four or five hours, be safely across the Canadian border before dawn.

Did Canada have extradition agreements with the States?

Mexico didn't, Shawn was pretty sure of that. But it would take days of nonstop driving to reach and cross *that* border.

Shawn hadn't worn a condom, drunk as he was; drunk as the woman had been. What the fuck was her name? Thalia? Could the cops compel Shawn to give them a DNA sample to compare against whatever they found inside Thalia's dead body? Might they go back and draw some sample from his stale vomit back at the crime scene once they'd identified him as a suspect?

Shawn got out of bed and flipped on his computer, intent on searching for information on extradition laws, DNA tests.

Cursing, Shawn shut down his computer before logging on, realizing how such searches could be made to look later in court, if it came to that.

Frantic, pacing naked now, he punched the numbers for Patricia's home phone. Patricia had called him on his phone earlier Friday morning—just a few minutes after he'd arrived back to shower and change following his night with the murdered woman. She had said she was no longer interested in seeing him; Shawn hadn't put up much of a fight then. But he didn't need Patricia then like he felt he did now. Now Shawn figured maybe he could smooth things over from their last conversation. Maybe Patricia could at least be persuaded to say they'd been together for a few crucial hours.

No answer. He checked the clock: one A.M. She must have the ringers off. But her answering machine hadn't kicked on, either.

Jesus. Patricia had moved on quickly, the bitch.

Shawn surveyed his options.

Wait?

Run?

Maybe take himself out before they put him in jail?

THIRTEEN

Tell was bent over, his hands on his knees, panting.

"It'll come back," Patricia said. "You've just been a while away from it. This is only day three."

But Tell's lungs were on fire. He had stitches in his sides. He stood up, heart pounding and sides aching. He squinted up at a billboard planted on New Austin's western-most borderline. Arresting gray eyes stared off across the Horton County landfill above a warning:

Beware Illegals!
El Gavilan
is watching you!

Bathed in sweat, ripe and dark and beautiful to Tell's eyes, her hand still resting on his shoulder, Patricia said, "Suppose someone had to take that space after old Doc Eckleburg finally officially turned up his toes."

* * *

Shawn paced his room again. He was going to have to cover the story of the woman's death for the next edition of his own weekly. No way around that as a one-man band at the *New Austin Recorder*.

But what might that trumped-up, loaded story mean for him later? What could it cost him—writing a news story about a woman brutally attacked and murdered probably just minutes after Shawn had left her bed? After he had left his DNA sprayed inside her most private places?

* * *

Able called the county coroner and leaned hard into the old man again.

"I get first word, right, Doc?"

"Begging your pardon, Sheriff, but it was a New Austin crime, according to all paperwork sent me," Casey Parks said.

"That's an open question, Doc," Able said. "This happened at the Three Corners. Hell, Chief Lyon agreed with me at the scene we'd have to hire a fucking surveyor to determine precisely whose jurisdiction this fucking abominable discovery was made in. For all I can tell, this case may really belong to Sheriff Walt Pierce and Vale County."

"Perhaps Pierce should get first call then?"

"Don't play games, Doc. Start of business day, when you know, *I* get that first call. Otherwise, I remind you that I have a long memory and a wicked imagination."

EL GAVILAN

THEN

Tell, barely two weeks on the border and already deeply disturbed by what he was seeing, was in a south-of-the-border bar with Seth Alvin the night that Tell met the woman he'd marry.

Seth was a Bush One–era veteran . . . "Desert fucking Storm" as Seth was given to putting it.

The cantina they'd selected for their post-shift drinking that night was stocked with familiar faces—ones who'd tried to bribe "cherry" Tell and Seth to allow them across. More of those whom the pair of Border Patrol agents had caught and sent back, and some of those more than twice. There was already enough of the latter ilk that Tell was beginning to think it was high time to commence confining after-hours carousing to the other, safer side of the border.

About the time he was contemplating that, a covey of comely Latinas drifted in, setting heads to turning. There were three of them, all young and pretty. They looked like college girls who'd decided to stray across the line for a look at wicked old *Meh-hi-co* . . . at the distant homeland that was in their genes but far from their actual experience. They struck Tell as treacherously fetching prey for a certain kind of man.

Seth whistled low and stood and cracked his back. He said, "The one in the little black dress, with her hair up? She needs to meet me, *now*."

Tell shook his head, tearing at the damp label on his sweating bottle of Modelo Negro. He watched Seth make his approach on the young woman and her slumming friends.

Willie Nelson on the jukebox: "Across the Borderline."

The girl in the little black dress seemed all too receptive to Seth's company. One of the other young women, one with a tattooed rose on her ankle, was soon enough talking with another off-duty border patrolman. That left the last of the trio—by far the prettiest to Tell's mind, and certainly the most reserved—standing between her flirting friends, looking alone and very uneasy. A target of opportunity for every man in the place.

She saw Tell watching her and frowned. He held up a hand and smiled. Tell came out of his chair as he saw two hard-looking men starting to drift her way. He scooped up his white Stetson from beside his beer bottle and placed it on the seat of his chair to hold his place.

Tell approached her, smiling. He said, "Listen, ma'am, this bar—this town—is not the best place for tourists. You should talk your friends into leaving, right now. Failing that, if you need quiet, secure company until your friends are, er, free? Well, I've got plenty of room at my table. Might at least spare you some approaches from those others."

Those others: more Border Patrol agents and feral civilians. Men waiting to see if she'd shoot Tell down and so give *them* an opening. Tell could see she was thinking the same thing.

He hesitated and said, "My name's Tell Lyon. I'm only offering some company and conversation until your friends are ready to push on. If you'd prefer an escort back to the other side right now, I can get you back there too. Just a friendly offer . . . with no strings."

Tell smiled again and returned to his seat.

The young woman took another look to either side, evidently decided her friends were committed, and sighed. Shaking her head, she approached Tell's table and said, "I think I'd better take you up on that offer for a place to sit."

Tell rose and half bowed. "Absolutely. What are you drinking?"

She thought about it, looked at his beer, and said, "How about a tequila sunrise?"

He called out her order and they sat back down. She said, "You said your name is Tell?"

"That's right."

"Is that short for something?"

"Nah, just some character in a series of Western novels my old man favored."

"I'm Marita Delgado." She hesitated and said, "How'd you know I'm not native Mexican?"

"The sense I had. And nobody dresses like you and your friends are dressed to come to places like this one. You're all dolled up for a Saturday night in Austin, or San Diego or someplace like that. Not for this dive, and not even for this corner of Mexico."

"Good point. We crossed on a silly whim. Never have seen it, though I'm first-generation American. You're Border Patrol?"

"Yeah, coming off duty."

Marita nodded at their server and combed a wave of black hair behind one ear. She sipped her drink and said, "And how is that work?"

Tell didn't hesitate and he didn't couch it. "Mostly brutal. I'm fairly new to it, but feel like I've been here for years already. Hard to see some of the things we do. And, hell, if I lived here, in these conditions, I'd want to run North too. There are at least seven in here tonight I've sent back across the line in the past week."

Marita looked around, bit her bottom lip. "Yes, it's not like back home at all, is it?"

"Nothing at all like home," Tell said.

* * *

The wooing of Marita's friends was continuing apace—looked headed to some certain end. Blushing, and appearing a bit put out by what she was seeing, Marita squeezed the bridge of her nose and sighed. She said, "Think I might need that escort back across you offered. We left a bachelorette party that was going nowhere fast." She nodded at the two young women she'd come in with. "They're from out of state. I hardly know them. Sorry I let myself be dragged along, now."

Tell said, "I'm ready to head back across too. You should tell your friends, such as they are, that you're leaving. Then I'll see you across the border."

Marita nodded, managed a half smile. "The line going both ways is a pretty long one tonight. Will your uniform help speed that crossing?"

Tell smiled, said, "Like nobody's business."

She nodded at the two women she'd come in with. "Will they be safe?"

"They're with armed American law enforcement officers," Tell said evenly. "In that sense, anyway, they'll be safe enough." That was about as good a way as he could put it, he figured.

* * *

The walk back toward the border checkpoint stretched into a dinner invitation: Marita asked Tell if he was hungry.

They stopped in an Americanized version of a Mexican restaurant. Lowly lit, it provided maybe more the romantic atmosphere than

Marita had bargained for. Tell took it easy, until, emboldened by a couple of Texas margaritas on the rocks, he let his hand drift, closing over the back of hers. Her silky skin was two shades darker than Tell's own tanned hand. Marita's black eyes searched his, then she smiled and turned her hand under Tell's hand so their palms were touching. She squeezed his hand back and began moving them in time to the music: Marianne Faithful's cover of Kristofferson's "The Hawk."

Marita's parents, she confessed, were both teachers; became legal in the early 1970s. Marita was close to completing her own degree in English literature and, "Trying for the life of me to figure out what on earth I'll do with that."

A bit tipsy, Marita scooped up Tell's white straw Stetson and put it on; the tips of her ears kept the cowboy hat from falling down over her eyes. She pushed it back a bit on her head and said, "What do you think?"

Tell reached across and tilted it to a slightly more rakish angle and said, "I think anything would look perfect on you."

She smirked and took a last sip from her straw. "It's getting late, Tell Lyon. We should cross that line now, don't you think?" Her voice was naturally husky; he couldn't tell yet if she meant it in more than one way.

"Sure we should." Tell settled up and took her arm. They were hardly twenty paces out the front door when the man with the knife fell upon them.

* * *

Later, Tell would learn the man was named Enrique Zambada, a Lerdo-born scrap of nastiness suspected in the death of at least two Mexico City whores.

The bastard hadn't asked them for money, hadn't asked them even to raise their hands.

No, Enrique had just come at them, taking a slashing pass at Tell's throat with a fearsome buck knife while reaching for Marita's purse with his other hand.

Tell fell back, reaching for his gun and knowing a positive shitstorm would ensue if he shot a Mexican national on the south side of the border. Tell's being off duty and greased with tequila wouldn't help matters any.

Thinking all that in an instant, Tell stopped reaching for his gun and instead drove his boot's toe deep and hard into the fat man's crotch. As Enrique doubled over, gasping, Tell got a handful of hair and drove his knee up into the man's face once, twice, a third time. Each time, Tell heard bones or cartilage crunch.

Gawking passers-by kept moving; knew better than to get dragged into *this* scene.

Tell bent over the unconscious man, took his wallet out and grabbed a couple of cards that carried their attacker's name. He slid those in his pocket, then got out plastic handcuffs and secured the man's wrists around a rusting, old iron light fixture.

Marita was still wide-eyed. She said, "He might have killed us!"

"Don't think he'd have given it much thought otherwise," Tell admitted. "Are you okay?"

"Let's just get out of here," Marita said. She took his hand and pulled him up to her.

* * *

She was still shaking when they reached the lobby of her hotel. "I think I need a last drink," Marita said.

Tell looked toward the hotel lounge. A woman was closing out the register; a waiter was setting chairs up on tables to clear the floor for the cleaners. It was past midnight. It was raining.

"Looks like we just missed last call," he said.

"Why God invented room service," Marita said, studying his face. "Do you have an early day tomorrow, Tell?"

"It's my day off," he said softly. "That's why I was able to drink earlier this evening."

Marita nodded slowly, then reached for his hand. "Let's talk more upstairs."

FOURTEEN

Wednesday morning. Tell logged off Able Hawk's blog. He said, "Damn. Why not just post a bounty on the bastard's head for Thalia Ruiz's murder? I had no idea that Hawk was running his own blog."

Patricia shut down her computer. "This entry is relatively tame in some ways," she said. "Hawk's usually much more political. More divisive. So, Chief Lyon, when are you going to launch your blog?"

"Never." He accepted her offered cup of black coffee. "I can't conceive of doing what Hawk and I do and writing a blog."

"Too bad about your ankle," she said. "I feel stir crazy."

Tell had wrenched his leg running with Patricia. Patricia said, "Any news yet on Thalia Ruiz's murder?"

He was about to answer when his cell phone rang. Tell checked the caller ID panel: the coroner's office. Tell flipped open the phone and said, "Casey? You have something for me?"

"You called me, Chief, if this comes up later, you got that? If it becomes an issue, I'm saying. You pressed me for these results. Are we agreed on that point?"

"We are, Doc. But hell, I'm *owed* those results."

"There are two county sheriffs who'd strongly beg to differ. At least in terms of you getting first peek."

Tell held up a finger at Patricia and limped out into the common hall of their apartment complex. "What's this cryptic stuff about, Doc?"

"Able Hawk has pressed me for first word on the DNA results," Parks said. "I'm going to follow his instructions to the letter. The business day doesn't start for a few more minutes. I'm giving you *that* much head start, Chief. You should also know that I released the victim's name to the press late last night—I did that well past print deadlines."

Tell said, "Much appreciated—this 'head start,' Casey. What have you found?"

"The semen is from one man. But we also found traces of condom lubricant and latex in her mouth, vagina and rectum. As to which came first, the naked shooter or the one wearing the rubber, I can't definitively say. Oh, and someone slipped her some flunitrazepam."

"Help me out, Doc. What the hell is *that*?"

"Trade name is Rohypnol. You know, the date rape drug."

"That name I know. Okay. So to the DNA match—that's fast matching. Who is it?"

"Crazy thing," the old doctor said. "This guy was doing a story on DNA and talked your predecessor and me into typing him for background to his piece. Only way he's in the system. You know us with stuff like that—we never throw it away. We logged the luckless bastard—filed him with CODIS."

"So who the hell is he, Doc?"

"The reporter—editor—of the *New Austin Recorder*, Shawn O'Hara."

Tell nearly fell back against the wall. *Jesus!* Of all people—*Jesus Christ!*

Tell could just duck his head back inside Patricia's apartment and ask for Shawn's address. But that would likely spiral in so many potentially treacherous directions that he couldn't tally them all. He said, "Don't suppose you know where O'Hara lives?"

"Anticipated that," the coroner said. "I have it."

Tell scribbled down Shawn's address on his service notepad. He checked his watch. Getting closer to "start of business day." Normally, Tell would already be in the office, but he'd accepted Patricia's invitation for breakfast.

He said, "Thanks very much for the heads-up, Doc. I'll remember this. And I owe you."

Tell closed his phone and slipped back through Patricia's door, red-faced and uncomfortable. "Something's come up and I'm really racing the clock," he said.

Patricia kissed him. He kissed her back, then dipped his head, ashamed. She maybe confused his shame for shyness, because she tipped his head up, pressing her closed fist to his chin and handing him a brown paper bag with the other hand.

"Made you lunch, Tell. In case you don't have time to get something later."

"Thanks very much. It does look like that kind of day." She kissed him again and he felt his body responding. He said, "A man could get used to this."

"A man better," Patricia said, leaning in for a last kiss.

Tell wondered if they'd still be talking by day's end.

FIFTEEN

An emphatic banging on his door startled him.

The only people who ever knocked on Shawn's door were his women.

But Shawn was between bedmates. No way was it going to be Patricia.

And it sure wasn't going to be Thalia Ruiz. Her ruined face dogged his dreams.

The journalist pulled back the mini-blind from his storm door's window and slid straight into panic.

There he stood: Tell Lyon, looming outside, grim-faced in his black uniform. Tell said loudly through the glass, "I'm giving you a break, Shawn. Come away with me now, just us, and tell me about Thalia Ruiz. Otherwise, in about fifteen minutes, a mountain of grief is going to fall on you, and I won't be in any position to maybe help you anymore."

* * *

Shawn's stomach churned and his hands and legs were shaking. Tell stopped for two coffees at the Tim Horton's on the edge of town and thrust a cup into Shawn's trembling hands. When Shawn tried to talk, the New Austin chief of police simply cut him off. "Not yet."

They drove in silence to the southern border of New Austin, out into the undeveloped wooded area where the New Austin Police

Department's shooting range was located. Shawn slid closer to panic as the chief turned onto the rough-cut road back into the dense woods.

"Stay here," Tell said.

The cop got out of his SUV and opened the padlock securing the chain that bound two tubular-steel fence arms. Tell pushed back the metal gate halves, got back into his truck and drove through the gate. Then he got out and locked up behind himself.

They bumped along perhaps two hundred yards into the woods before they came to a clearing. The ground was littered with shining and rusted metal jacket casings. In the distance, Shawn saw wooden boards, some with bullet-riddled paper silhouettes of men still secured to them.

Now Shawn was truly close to losing it. If the police chief shot Shawn and buried him out here, Shawn figured he'd never be found. He fidgeted with a cigarette pack—finally stressed enough to break down and buy his own smokes.

Shawn was near manic. Tell said, "Shawn, you're not going to believe it, but right now, I'm about the best friend you have on earth."

Tell shut off the engine and they got out of the truck with their coffees. He told Shawn to go ahead and light one up if it might calm him. Tell held the journalist's coffee while Shawn fired up a cigarette with trembling hands.

They leaned against the front of Tell's truck, staring off across the shooting range at the bullet-pocked paper silhouettes. "Before this day is over, you're going to end up arrested and probably charged for rape and murder, Shawn," Tell said. "There's no way around that." Tell looked at him, measuring his reaction. Shawn looked like he might throw up at any second.

"No way to gloss this," Tell continued. "The county coroner's office has a positive match on your DNA. The murder victim's name is Thalia Ruiz—a friend of Able Hawk's. They found your semen in Thalia's vagina, rectum and mouth. Coroner asserts you came at least three times inside Thalia. *Once* is more than enough to take you down all the way, depending on who ends up with you and how hard they press it. And Able? He's bent on seeking the death penalty for Thalia's killer. Hell, you heard that straight from Able's mouth."

"My DNA?" Shawn was stricken. "How do they know it's mine? I haven't given any samples to check against."

"Actually, you have done just that, Shawn. You can't get out from under the DNA evidence. A while back, you wrote a story about DNA and its uses in criminal investigations. For your sidebar you let them sample your own. Stuff like that gets in the hands of investigative officials, well, they're real zealous about keeping it on file. They put you in the CODIS database, Shawn. And that story and your archived sample led straight back to you."

Shawn was furious. He could feel the heat in his cheeks. His head hurt from the pounding and his jaws were starting to hurt already from gritting his teeth. "Jesus Christ," he muttered over and over. After a while he said, "Why aren't we downtown now, Chief? Why aren't you and your people booking me?"

"Because I have my own questions first, Shawn. And because there is a lot of friction and angling going on behind the scenes regarding jurisdictions and who owns this crime scene and the eventual collar. Able Hawk was friends with this dead woman. He's hellbent for leather on a death penalty collar. This other sheriff in Vale County, Pierce, he strikes me as even more bloodthirsty. And there's a third sheriff, Denton—he could as easily as make claims on you because of where the body was found. Only thing stopping Denton, near as I can tell, is a lack of ambition. I'm not looking to kill anyone, Shawn. But I'm dubious I end up being the one who gets to arrest you or charge you on the murder. All this jockeying to claim the crime scene sets off all kinds of alarms in my head. And it should worry the hell out of you, particularly, Shawn. I'm telling you, you'll get your fairest shake from me."

"That DNA evidence," Shawn said. "You think I'm guilty too. You have to. That being so, how can you arresting me be better than someone else doing it?"

"Oh, you had yourself quite a time with Thalia, Shawn. No denying that. But the coroner also found Rohypnol in her system. Did you slip her the Rope, Shawn?"

"Fuck no! I don't need that stuff. We were both drunk. Me maybe most of all to sleep with *that*—reason I didn't wear a rubber and took her up the ass like that."

Tell narrowed his eyes.

Shawn sensed Tell's skepticism and said, "We were all over each other, Chief. Obviously you know that from the coroner. But it was all consensual. I didn't drug her." He cast down his cigarette butt, stamped it out, then fired up another. "Fuck, you hadn't gotten between me and Patricia, I wouldn't have been there with Thalia. I'd have gone home with my girl."

Shawn didn't like the look on Tell Lyon's face after that admission. The journalist said, "Look, Chief, I'm sorry. Patricia and me were at Fusion and things got . . . prickly. So I picked up this other woman. Truth is, I had the sense even before you two hit if off that Patty and me weren't going to last. Had the sense she was getting ready to dump me anyway. You just made it easier for her, more enticing to do it now." He shook his head. "Too bad it was that night, is all. Fuck me harder, huh?"

"I don't want to talk about that," Tell said. "This is about you and that dead woman. You were at the club together, drinking for a while?"

"With her and her roommate, Carmelita, yeah."

"So there are witnesses who will testify you were drinking together," Tell said. "Thalia's drunkenness can be made to look like the effects of the Rope by an attorney. That means DNA and likely the Rohypnol will go against you with a jury. Did you know Thalia Ruiz before the night you met and bedded her?"

Shawn looked at his feet. "No. Like I said, I met her, and her friend. I really wanted the other woman. The girls had come over in Thalia's car and both were too drunk to drive. We all went back to this apartment in my car. I left her there the next morning, still asleep."

"Real nice, kid. You took her in every orifice, then slipped off on Thalia without talking, without even a goodbye?"

Shawn looked away from Tell, said raw-voiced, "Yeah. I did that."

Tell said, "You sure she was alive when you left her, Shawn? After her night with you she hadn't choked on her own vomit or something?"

Shawn's eyes flared. "She was fucking fine."

"Her friend see you leave?"

"No."

Tell nodded. "That checks with what she told my people," he said. "She said she never saw you leave. Bad news is, she also didn't see Thalia leave. For all this Carmelita knows, you and Thalia left together. Few hours later, Thalia's dead. So you see, you're an easy lock to buy this one, all the way up, Shawn. I'd be lying if I said otherwise."

Shawn snarled, "Jesus, shouldn't I have a lawyer here for this?"

"Actually, I'm the one should have a lawyer here," Tell said. "I'm taking some real risks here for you." He shook his head, sipped some more coffee. "You will need a lawyer eventually. Say, by lunchtime.

But we're not having this conversation now, Shawn. This is off the record. We didn't ever see each other this morning."

Shawn scowled. "You're kicking me loose?"

"Not the gift it sounds," Tell said. "And don't get stupid ideas about running. A couple of sheriffs who want Thalia's killer's collar, they could fall on you big time. And they might issue shoot-to-kill orders if you make them. With the DNA stuff standing against you, and Thalia's friend's testimony, bringing you in dead saves court costs. I'm pretty sure Walt Pierce would see it that way."

Shawn felt freshly sick.

Tell said, "When you had sex with her, did you start out with a condom on? Did you put one on at any point with Thalia?"

"No, we were both drunk, like I said. It was urgent."

"Sure. Urgent." Tell said, "Put out your hands, Shawn."

"I thought you weren't arresting me."

"I'm not handcuffing you," Tell said sourly. "I just want to see your damned hands."

Shawn held them out. Tell said, "No rings. You ever wear rings?"

"Never."

"Didn't expect so. Shawn, this is important. If someone other than me arrests you, you be extra careful not to resist in any way. In anger, don't go punching any walls. You keep those city hands of yours nice and pink and healthy-looking like they are right now. They take you into custody, you insist that they photograph you naked. And that they get close-ups of your hands."

"Why?"

"I've already said too much."

"Why are you doing this, Chief?"

"Because I don't think you killed this woman, Shawn. Partly it's the way you reacted seeing her body. You'd never have been able to transport her to that field. But I expect I'm going to be nearly alone in that belief. You're an easy, *easy* solution for a vicious and terrible crime. You are a convenient—hell, a *perfect*—scapegoat."

"Again I ask, Chief, why are we here?"

"Because I'm trying to get at the truth and arrest the right bastard for murdering this woman. This was overkill, Shawn. Thalia was beaten to death. Kind of thing someone will likely do again, given the chance. The man who killed Thalia hates women."

"Beaten . . . that's why I should protect my hands," Shawn said, getting it.

Tell said, "Summarizing, here: You were angry at your girlfriend. You figured you two were history, so you decided to ease your disappointment by losing yourself in the arms of another woman. You and Thalia, already both drunk, met and clicked. You took her back to the place of her choosing, fucked her ten ways from Tuesday—all of it unprotected, but mutually enthusiastic sex—then you ungallantly snuck out on her while she was asleep. Left her in her own bed. Alive and unbeaten."

"That's it," Shawn said. "That's actually the truth."

Tell said, "Then that *is* it so far as what you should say. Makes you a heel, but not a killer. Stay to that story, whoever's custody you end up in. I'll move ahead looking for an alternative suspect. And yeah, you should find yourself an attorney, Shawn, and I mean now. Given the crime, I'd get myself a woman lawyer if I could find one. Might help you with a jury."

Shawn stared at the shot-up targets on the other side of the field. "I'm a small-town newspaperman, Lyon. I'm underpaid. What kind of decent counsel can I afford? And I'm probably going to be fired by day's end. No cash flow at all then."

Tell said, "On my way over to pick you up, I called my so-called infamous cousin. I asked him to formulate a strategy that would maybe tie his hands if you were his newspaper employee—short-circuit his ability as a manger to terminate you."

"Yeah? What'd your cousin say?"

"Chris's first question was whether you've drafted a story about Thalia's murder. Have you?"

"To get it in this Thursday's paper, I'd need to do that by day's end."

"That wasn't my question, Shawn."

"I haven't written a story yet."

"Were you going to?"

"That wasn't your question, Tell."

"I'm just curious."

"I didn't know what to do." Shawn looked down at his feet again. "So I've done nothing. What was your cousin's advice?"

"That you draft a letter to your publisher. Chris says you should tell him or her that you were intimate with a woman who became a murder victim, and, because you had unprotected sex, your DNA links you to her. You should admit that you're almost certainly apt to become a near-term person of interest and you're therefore requesting a leave of absence. Use your owed personal, sick and vacation time as you have to, then go on unpaid leave if you're not yet out from under. You need to do this in the next hour before you can be terminated."

"Jesus," Shawn said. "And hell, I can't go home and do this. I can't go to my office. Those are the first two places anyone will look for me. How—where—do I write this note?"

Tell said, "I'm going to drop you in front of the public library, Shawn. You use their computers and printers to put your note together. Then you fax and e-mail it from there before you're picked up. Those time imprints may be important later, Chris said."

"I'll be picked up by your force? By you?"

"If you want to go that way, I'll make my run at being the one to take you into custody, Shawn. Thing to remember is, even if nobody takes you away from me, I can only hold you in city jail for seventy-two hours. Then you go to county jail, under Able Hawk's watch. Unless we can get you out on bail, first. But I'm not sure that's the way to go, either."

"I didn't kill that woman, Tell."

"I don't think you *killed* her, Shawn. It's the reason we're having this discussion that we're not having."

* * *

Time was getting on. Tell was still skeptical on the question of rape. He increasingly suspected Shawn had slipped Thalia the drug. But that was for later.

Tell said, "Get in now. I'm going to drive you to the library. Take care of your note and get it off to your publisher. Then sit down with a phone book and start thinking about attorneys. At ten fifteen A.M., I'll come to the library and quietly escort you out and we'll take you and book you, kid. Then we'll let you call that lawyer you'll have lined up. Not that I'd let him or her press for bail, were I you. Just remember, when I see you again, it's for the first time this morning. Agreed?"

The journalist nodded, looking like a lost kid. "Thanks for helping me like this, Tell."

Tell opened the passenger door. He said to Shawn, "Like I said, this vicious bastard who killed Thalia will likely do it again. I need to focus on catching *him*. You're no more than a goddamn distraction."

Tell started the engine and got his truck in gear, driving back out toward the gate.

Shawn gestured at the paper sack on the seat between them. "She made a couple of those for me a time back," he said.

Not quite so much bitterness in his voice, now, Tell thought.

Shawn asked, "Patricia put you up to this? To helping me, I mean?"

"She doesn't even know you're about to be a suspect," Tell said. "I told you, this meeting between us is secret."

When Tell got out of his truck this time to open and reshut the gate, he took his car keys with him—worried Shawn might panic and try to run.

As they pulled back onto the road, they drove past a billboard dominated by two narrowed, piercing gray eyes: "*El Gavilan* is watching!"

SIXTEEN

Tell received double takes from the librarians. One of them—forty-ish, slender and handsome—said, "Is there some trouble, Officer?"

"No trouble," Tell said, smiling. "I'm new to town and a reader. Actually have a crime novelist in the family. You have a pretty good crime fiction section?"

The librarian smiled back. "Pretty good. I handle acquisitions, and it's nearly all that I read."

"Then I'll try to get back in a day or so to get a card," he said. "For now I'll look around."

Tell strode toward the computer carousels at the back of the library, behind the stacks. Shawn was sitting in a corner stall. He appeared a short step from slipping into a fugue state. He looked up at Tell with wide, wild eyes. Shawn's hands fidgeted with an empty cigarette pack. Tell asked, "You doing okay?"

Shawn said, "Guess it's time, huh?"

"It is." Tell sat down beside the flustered reporter. "You get your letters off okay?"

"Yeah. Publisher sent me back an e-mail receipt. No answer, but at least I know he's seen my note and I'm not fired yet."

The publisher was probably busy calling *his* lawyer. Tell said, "We should get going now, Shawn. Get you in my custody before someone else can lay hands on you."

Shawn sighed and stood, looking pale. "You going to handcuff me, Chief?"

"No," Tell said. "We walk out of here together, like we're going to a late breakfast or something. You got any pets or anything like that needs looking after back at your place, Shawn?"

"Uh, *no.*"

"Got an attorney in mind?"

"Yeah."

"You can call him, or her, from my office."

"*Her.*" Shawn had decided Lyon was right about the importance of having a woman represent him in court if it came to that. "And thanks for doing it this way, Chief." Shawn tossed his empty cigarette pack in the trash receptacle on the way out the library door. "Think we could stop and get a carton of cigarettes on the way? Maybe something to read?"

Tell looked at him sourly and said, "Why not?" They'd do their shopping, Tell figured, then he'd read the kid his rights.

* * *

A shadow fell across Tell's desk. Able Hawk was looming over him.

Tell said, "Hey, Able."

"Hey there, Tell." Able took off his mirrored sunglasses. He nodded at Tell. "You take a walk with me?"

"Surely."

On his way out, Tell paused at Billy Davis's desk. Billy was dunking a Bismarck in his coffee. Tell said, "Any trouble, I'm on my cell phone—stay off the damn radios."

Able Hawk nodded approvingly. "I'm the same way. Especially with anything related to this case. Damned police scanners are the bane of my existence."

"We'll go out the back way into the alley," Tell said.

"Just in case some flunky of Walt Pierce's is watching out front?"

"You called it."

The sheriff said, smiling crookedly, "How'd you get first word on that DNA?"

Tell shrugged. "I leaned hard on the coroner, so don't blame him. I really stepped into him, Able."

"I guess to save face I'll choose to believe your kind damn lie, Tell. So far as Shawn goes for the killing, I'm not buyin' that poon-hound scribbler for the murder. Not even a little," Able said. "He was tied up with us all morning. He couldn't have dumped her body. And not weak-stomached as he is, either."

"Agreed," Tell said. "He couldn't hope for better alibis than the likes of us."

"Unless of course someone tries to argue Shawn had an accomplice. But then we'd have to expect his DNA to be all over Thalia's insides like Shawn's was." The sheriff pushed his hat back on his head. "You can only hold him so long, Tell."

"And I aim to hold Shawn here in my jail just as long as I can," Tell said. "Then I mean to charge him for rape and move him to county. Give him over to you. Then it's up to you to hold him for as long as you can. Try and stall out Walt Pierce on charging him for murder."

"Then you've heard?"

"That Walt Pierce has determined Thalia Ruiz's body was found in his county? Yeah. Not a happy development."

"Old Walt, he'd eat Shawn alive, he got hold of him in his jail," Able said.

"You'd know better than me," Tell said. "So far as Walt goes, I just know the fat son of a bitch rubbed me wrong from the get-go."

"So you're a solid judge of character too." Able stopped walking and put his broad back to the wall of the New Austin police

HQ. He stared down the alley. A rat scuttled from a drainpipe and scampered under a dumpster. "Tell, I'm talkin' out of school confiding this next, but, well, a number of folks have perished in Walt's custody over the years. Most of those lost souls looked real good for the crimes they were collared for, but they didn't ever get to trial. Some hanged themselves. Some choked on their own vomit. One or two somehow smuggled in pills and OD'd. Or so the coroner found later." Able looked at his own feet. "Did I mention that the Vale County coroner is Walt's brother-in-law?"

Tell leaned a hand against the brick wall above Able's shoulder. "Not as I recall, Able."

"Well, you see how cozy that is. That DNA of Shawn's is going to be a tough thing for Walt to walk away from. And maybe for a jury out this way too. Especially Shawn's sperm being found in Thalia where it was. That doesn't exactly say, 'consensual,' to conservative minds out this way. *I'm* more broadminded—different strokes, so to speak, and all that. Old Shawn's a wild one. I didn't know Thalia was." Able hesitated. "I'm gonna need to talk to Shawn's girlfriend I met that night I met you the first time. Need to know some things about Shawn's bedroom predilections. I'm not sure I don't think he drugged my Thalia."

"Can see why you might think so," Tell said evenly. "You'll have to handle that interview, although I think it's a waste of time. That was a different kind of relationship. Be obliged if you and your folks concentrated on clearing Shawn. I'll focus, personally, on finding the real killer."

Able smiled. "Can't promise you an exclusive on that, brother. I've got a far bigger force and we can multi-task just fine. But you share and I'll share, and we'll share the collar, it comes time. Yeah?"

Tell shook Able's hand. "Right. Let's just be quick about it."

"About that," Able said. "You should know, the past three years, there have been three pretty similar crimes—all of them rape-murders. All three were committed in Vale County."

"Send me the files?"

"What I've got, sure," Able said. "But it's precious little. They were Walt's cases."

"Appreciate anything you can dig up on them, all the same."

"I should go in and see Shawn now, if you'll let me."

Tell nodded. "*Mi casa es su casa*, Able."

Able slapped Tell's arm. "Doesn't help our cause a lick that Shawn diddled Thalia so down and dirty like he did. Like I said, this is a conservative county, most ways."

"Yeah, I can see it. And, like you, I'm not sure Shawn didn't drug Thalia."

Able nodded. "He'll be sorry if I find out he did that to her. I'd be sorely tempted to kill him myself, that being the fact. Now, no more tricks, right, Tell? No more stuff like finessing Doc Parks into givin' you DNA results first?"

"I wasn't trying to screw you, Able. I just wanted to stay out in front of your neighbor—Walt Pierce."

Those strange gray eyes assessed him. Able finally said, "Again, I elect to believe you. Now I'm gonna go talk to that miserable young bastard."

"Be my guest. They should be done with the photos just about now."

Able scowled. "You're just now getting around to a mug shot?"

"I hired a photographer to shoot Shawn naked, head to toe."

Able smiled. "With concentration on the hands, no doubt."

Tell said, "Yeah."

Able said, "You and me, we're really gonna get on fine together, I think."

THEN

Tell awakened in Marita's arms; the mostly full pitcher of margaritas was still there on the bedside table. They'd shared a couple of drinks, some deep talk, then Marita had fingered the buttons on his uniform, looked up into his eyes, and holding his gaze, kissed him.

From there, it was a loving frenzy.

Marita stirred and said, "It's morning?"

"Late morning," he said. "I'm sorry if—"

She pressed dusky fingers to his lips. "Are you *really* sorry? I ask because if you aren't, you shouldn't fill the silence with words like that."

Tell took her hand from his cheek; squeezed it. "I'm not sorry at all. And you?"

She kissed his chest. "Far from sorry as I can be."

SEVENTEEN

Tell palmed into a slot in his apartment complex's lot, shut down the engine and tossed his sunglasses on the dashboard. He rubbed his eyes and squeezed the bridge of his nose. He massaged his temples, then sighed and hauled himself out.

He got out and stretched, then walked down the creek bank and stood under the willow. After a time, the crickets quieted by Tell's passage started up again. The mourning doves nesting above Patricia's deck cooed softly.

A voice behind him said, "Really, Chief Lyon? Suspicion of rape? Honestly?"

Patricia stood on the bank above him, arms crossed. Frowning, she said, "Shawn wouldn't do that. Whatever else he might do, he's no rapist, Tell."

"He's no killer, I know that." Tell trudged back up the embankment to Patricia. She turned and began walking along the creek side. Tell fell into stride alongside her, hands in his pockets.

"If you don't think Shawn raped that murdered woman, then why are you still holding him, Tell?"

"Because legally, I can hold Shawn for a period of time before I formally charge him."

Patricia scowled at him. "But if you don't believe he did it, *why* would you hold him? Why would you consider charging him for something you don't believe he did?"

"To help protect him, Patricia. To run out the clock before some or another sheriff can arrest his ass, if I can."

Accusation in her black eyes: "But you intend to maybe still charge Shawn, knowing he didn't do this?"

"*Yeah*. And I'd do it with his consent, Patricia," Tell said. "I've also persuaded Shawn not to seek bail when he is charged and arraigned. *If* we even get that far."

"Again . . . *Why*, Tell?"

"For Shawn's own protection, Patricia, just like I said before. Shawn has a pretty good alibi in some respects. When that woman's body was theoretically dumped, Shawn was variously with me and with Sheriff Hawk."

"Then I ask again, why would you hold him?"

"Because Sheriff Pierce has determined Thalia Ruiz's body was dumped in his county. It's Pierce's murder case now and he's spoiling to hang it on Shawn. And forensic evidence, a big damned chunk of it, is squarely on Pierce's side. Or at least it could be made to look as though it is in court."

"But with you and Able as witnesses for Shawn . . ."

"Eventually, yes, in a hypothetical trial, we'd be there for Shawn," Tell said. "If he ever got to trial. But I'm told a number of murder suspects have died in Walt Pierce's jail. Suspicious suicides, almost all of them. If you put Able's and my potential testimony aside, then in a certain light, Shawn's a slam-dunk for conviction for murdering this Ruiz woman. He spent the night with her. He wasn't seen leaving her place alone as he claims. Last time she was seen alive was going into a bedroom with him. The next time anyone saw her, she was raped, beaten and dead in that field in Pierce's county. And Shawn's DNA is throughout Thalia's corpse. Nobody else's is."

Patricia scowled at Tell. He pressed on.

"Someone also fed that woman a date rape drug. I don't know yet whether Shawn did that to her. But for now, I choose to think he did, and, at least publicly, to act accordingly."

"Why?"

"Because Shawn slept with Thalia in New Austin. So the rape aspect of this case is mine until proven otherwise. I can maybe make Pierce wait in line for a time. I can maybe force Pierce to jump through hoops to take custody of Shawn on suspicion of murder. I can buy Able and me time to find the one who really did this and clear Shawn of the killing."

"At the expense of Shawn's reputation? His job?"

"He's already through in this town, Patricia," Tell said. "Believe me, he'll want to be out of here once his fellow press members out him as a person of interest. Sheriff Pierce has already issued a statement naming Shawn as his prime suspect in Thalia's murder and accusing me of impeding his homicide investigation. It'll hit the eleven o'clock news tonight and the papers in the morning. Shawn wandered into a real tight frame, sleeping with that woman the reckless and wanton way that he did." That TV attention wasn't going to do wonders for Tell's reputation.

"Oh my God, poor Shawn."

Poor Shawn? "Yeah," Tell said, sour voiced. "He's in it real deep. Stuck his foot in it, but good."

"What a nightmare for him."

Tell said, "He put himself in that nightmare, picking that woman up. Doing what he did with her, then sneaking out on her. Leaving her alone to walk into the arms of her killer. Shawn damned near perfectly framed himself for her murder."

Patricia searched Tell's face. "You said the police have his DNA on her?"

Tell said, "*In* her. Everywhere." He immediately regretted the way he'd said it.

Patricia shot Tell a look. "I'm only going to say this once, Tell, and only to you. That can't be. Shawn, well, he always used condoms."

"We two are the last ones who should be having this conversation," Tell said, queasy now. Patricia and Tell hadn't yet crossed that last and most profound line of intimacy.

"But it's a fact. He did use protection."

Looking at his own feet, Tell said, "At your request, Patricia?"

Her cheeks were flushed. "Yes."

"Well, Thalia must not have asked. And left to his own devices, a man's not often going to volunteer that *protection*. Not going to opt for that dulling of the experience. And they were both extremely drunk."

"So he came inside her." Patricia shook her head.

"Orally, vaginally and anally. I don't know in what order." Tell also immediately hated himself for that last. It was an exceptionally cheap shot, and at Thalia's expense too.

Patricia said, "Jesus Christ . . . *Shawn* . . ."

"He never tried to hit you, did he, Patricia?"

Patricia's voice went cold. "No."

"Didn't expect so. You're right. We don't talk about this part of it again."

Patricia stopped walking and turned to face Tell. She said, "Do you have your own real 'person of interest,' Chief Lyon?"

"Not yet. Not even close."

"And El Gavilan?"

"Not Hawk, either."

Patricia said, "You know, tonight I don't think . . ."

Tell held up a hand. "You're right. And I need to make myself a quick dinner and grab a shower and get back out there. I don't have much time, and neither does Shawn."

EIGHTEEN

Amos Sharp held Luisa tightly to him. Her body quaked and her tears sogged the shoulder of his shirt.

He couldn't find worthy words to comfort her, so Amos rubbed her back and kissed her forehead, shushing her and hoping she would soon catch her breath. At a loss to say anything comforting, Amos instead started volunteering what he knew.

"Granddad says this one who's been arrested, he probably didn't do it."

Luisa drew back and looked him in the eye. Her own eyes were bloodshot from days of crying. She said, "Are you sure it's not just whites protecting whites, Amos? Maybe your *abuelo, El Gavilan,* and these other cops, that damned border patrolman you want to work for. Maybe they just can't stand to see this other white, this reporter, punished for what he did to my cousin. They'll put it off on some *cholo.*"

"He's not like that, my granddad," Amos said. "It's not like that at all. This reporter—" He hesitated.

Luisa, eight months pregnant with their child, said, "*What?* Tell me, Amos."

"It's . . . confidential," Amos said. "I've said too much already. It's an ongoing case."

"You're not police yourself yet, Amos. You don't have a badge to hide behind."

"I can't betray a trust."

"You're betraying me and our family, Amos. And, please, all the secrets you keep from that old man? About us? And about our child? You said we'd be married already. You said we'd be living together. We made this baby now because it could save me being sent back to Juarez. Yet still you live in that house with that old man, with *El Gavilan*." It sounded like an obscenity the way she said it. "I'm at least eight months pregnant. What if the baby comes early? Our time is so short now." She had no pediatrician . . . hell, no insurance. When the time came, she was going to be at the mercy of the emergency room to deliver her baby.

"I'll tell him soon," Amos said.

"We don't have time," Luisa said.

"Then we'll marry this weekend. Once we've done that, and he knows about our baby, it'll be over and he'll accept it. He'll have to."

"While they investigate Thalia's murder, they may learn that I'm illegal, Amos. We may not have even days."

"Then we'll do it tomorrow night—get married, I mean."

She shook her head, staring down at her swollen belly. "I don't know how we got to this place," she said. "Talking marriage again and about doing it so quickly, like this. I was just asking about Thalia, and about this reporter and what you know of him."

Amos stared at his hands, at his own fidgeting fingers. "The reporter met her in a bar and spent the night with Thalia at the apartment of a friend of your cousin's. What happened to Thalia— her being attacked and murdered—that happened after the reporter left her. Shawn O'Hara was with my grandfather and with Chief Lyon when her body was being put in that field."

"Convenient for the reporter it's those two who were with him, no?" She was red-faced, her eyes filled with hate.

"No, it's not like that, Luisa," Amos insisted. "The reporter was interviewing them for stories for the paper. He was doing that in front of the wait staff, other diners. A bunch of people saw him there. There is no way he could have done it."

"Who then?"

"I haven't heard more than that," Amos said. "Except that, well, whoever did this to Thalia, he wore rings that cut her when he hit her." Amos held up his own hands. He wore a bulbous high school class ring, a silver ring with skull and crossbones, and a ring that Luisa had given him. "The man's hands should be badly bruised," Amos said. "O'Hara's aren't."

Luisa dipped her head, her hand resting on her swollen belly. She wore no rings, fearing they might get stuck from the swelling in her hands and feet and ankles as she moved into her last weeks. "I miss Thal so much," she said. "The funeral home man says we can't have an open casket. They won't even let my aunt see her a last time. They won't let her see Thalia, her own daughter, for 'her own good' they said."

"That was a favor. It was very bad, Granddad told me." Amos put his hand on her belly; felt motion under there. He cupped Luisa's chin in his hand and tilted her face up to his. "I mean it. Let's do it tomorrow. Let's get married."

"Amos, I didn't mean to—I wasn't trying to back you into this . . . marrying me. Not like that."

"Doesn't matter, either way. I want to."

"Really?"

"I do," Amos said. "Tomorrow."

"Tomorrow we bury Thalia."

"Then the day after."

She gazed up at him wonderingly. "Yes, then." She stroked his cheek. "Your grandfather—he'll really keep looking for the man who killed my cousin? He won't let this pass?"

Now Amos felt a little anger. "He told me your cousin was his friend, Luisa. Granddad, well, despite what was done to your cousin, it was Granddad who first identified her. That's how well he knew her. Granddad takes this real personal, Luisa. He's not ever going to let this go until he solves it. He's angry in a way I've never seen him. It's tamped down on the outside, but I see it. I do."

"Will he be angry like that when he knows about us? About our baby?"

"He'll be happy," Amos said. "He'll be happy for me. Happy for *us*. It's his great-grandchild, you know?"

NINETEEN

Tell had just finished his quick dinner and was dressed to go back out. There was a knock at the door. Tell opened it, half expecting Patricia to be standing there.

Sheriff Hawk gave the New Austin chief an up-and-down look. He fingered Tell's badge and said, "I guess you weren't goddamn kidding about a working night."

"No, Able, I meant it well enough. What's up?"

"I think my crew and I have hauled that damned reporter's sorry ass clear of the fire, Tell."

Tell narrowed his eyes. "How so?"

"I questioned our friend Shawn pretty close back at your jail and jogged his memory," Able said. "Young man stopped for some smokes on his way back to his apartment after banging and then sneaking out on my poor Thalia. My boys screened the surveillance tape at the fillin' station where Shawn stopped. Time imprint on the film says he was there at seven fifteen A.M. Coroner Parks puts time of death at ten A.M. or eleven A.M. at the latest."

Tell gestured Able inside. Able took a seat on a stool by the breakfast bar. Tell said, "Something to drink?"

"I'm never truly at rest," Able said. "But official hours are over, so yeah, a beer would be good."

Tell opened the refrigerator. He pulled out a Sam Adams and twisted the lid. "You want a glass, Able?"

"Fuck that."

Tell slid the bottle across the bar. He said, "Some might argue back—Sheriff Walt Pierce, for instance—that Shawn had time to return to rape and kill Thalia and still make our respective interviews . . . assuming someone else dumped the body for him in that field."

Able savored the peaty Scotch ale. "But it gets better, Tell. Shawn's apartment's outside staircase backs up to the bank's drive-through windows. Turns out that the ATM security camera is aimed right at the back of Shawn's building. The camera caught Shawn arriving at his apartment—time imprint again—at eight ten A.M. He doesn't leave the building again until twelve fifty P.M., leaving him just enough time to get to Big G's to hook up with us."

"Impressive," Tell said. "And enough to do the trick for any honest and sane lawman." Tell smiled. "But do you think Walt Pierce will go for it?"

Able looked at his beer bottle. "Already broke the news to Walt. He's upset, but, I think, stymied."

"So we should go kick Shawn loose?"

Able lowered the bottle from his lips, shaking his head. "Oh, hell no. Not quite yet. My inclination is to paint the bastard—Walt—into a tighter corner. Let Shawn spend a bit longer in your jail. Hell, way he did Thalia, I'd make him do six months if we could, for doing her like he did. On that note, we may yet get back to him on that date rape drug. And if we kick Shawn loose tonight, Old Walt might pick him up and put him through a hard and wet interrogation just to soothe his own shitty ego. He might do that all right. He's the type."

"So what do you propose?"

"I've already done my media interviews and pointed the news crews your way, Tell. You give 'em some interviews. Reinforce what I've told you. Maybe indicate you've got a better suspect for Thalia's murder. Convince them you've got a real and viable suspect, even if you don't. Do that, and our combined quotes will shut Walt's business down for keeps, so far as Shawn is concerned."

"I'll do it." Tell nodded at Able. "You and your folks did great work, and fast. You delivered your end and cleared Shawn."

"Sure. Cocksucker's life is trashed though," Able said. "Shawn's media confreres in the daily papers and local TV stations will likely roast his nuts, and I mean good."

"Expect so," Tell agreed. He checked his watch. "I've gotta get out there and deliver my end now, Able."

Hawk nodded. "On that note, no hard feelings, but as Shawn's out of Walt's clutches, come morning, I'm going to focus on getting my gal Thalia some true justice."

"Exactly," Tell said. "Whoever did that to her, he'll do it again. I've combed all my department's files looking at wife-beaters and male-on-female assault victims going back ten years in this town. But there's nothing in the New Austin records that approaches what happened to Thalia. My guys and I have spoken with every coach, parent and kid who was out at those ball fields. Nobody saw anything. It's frustrating as hell."

"Yeah," Able said. "That's not how we're going to get there; that's pretty clear at this point. Thanks for the beer." He drained the dregs and slammed the bottle down, smacking his lips. "Tasty stuff. Now I gotta go visit your neighbor."

Tell hesitated, his hand clutching Able's empty bottle, poised over the trash basket. "Yeah? Why would you do that, Able? You've cleared Shawn. Why question Patricia?"

"Just dottin' the damned i's, Tell. Crossin' them fuckin' t's."

"It's irrelevant now, their relationship. Why don't you give her a pass, Able?"

"Because that's not my way, Tell. You be sure to be available to the goddamn reporters tonight now, you hear?"

TWENTY

Walt Pierce sat in Big G's diner with three of his deputies. Harry Moffatt and Luke Strider were veterans, each about four years younger than Sheriff Pierce. Tom Winch was a new recruit, still baby-faced, despite his recently cultivated mustache.

Pierce said, "So the reporter's cleared, nearly as I can tell. Hawk found an ass-load of camera evidence at filling stations and banks. Airtight stuff. Meddling fat-ass cocksucker."

Harry had a big gut. Harry had gin blossoms at his cheeks and a veined, red, swollen and several-times-broken nose. He said, "So what's the next move, W.P.?"

"Search warrant," Sheriff Pierce said. "Dead girl's mother wouldn't cooperate with me, so I got me a judge for that warrant. Should have it soon. We'll go tonight and search this Ruiz cunt's home. Hawk was through there, but didn't do anything forensically. Just looked for letters, diaries . . . anything that might refer to some man. *We'll* comb her bedroom. *We'll* get this cocksucker, sure enough. Or we'll get someone. And we'll do it first. If Hawk's right about this reporter being innocent, then we need fresh clues." He scratched his head and said, "On the other hand, maybe Hawk is wrong about this reporter, and we'll yet find something on that journalist Hawk missed. Maybe we'll do that."

Pierce kneaded his swollen hands; his knuckles were split. He wrenched loose one of his less ostentatious rings—his wedding band—and massaged his left ring finger. Harry smiled at his chief's hands. They were always like that—barked and swollen and bloodied . . . the legacy of hard interrogations and bar fights that the chief favored wading into rather than diffusing. Walt was short and fat, but deadly in close combat, even at the age of fifty-seven.

Young Tom Winch sipped his coffee, uncomfortable, taking it all in. He wanted to be home with his wife of three months, Cheryl-Ann. But Sheriff Pierce was an avid proponent of after-hours fraternization amongst his deputies. Tom had begged off once . . . and he had learned his lesson.

He looked again at Pierce; pressed his legs harder against the legs of his chair to stop their trembling. Walt fucking Pierce—what was *his* story?

THEN

"*La frontera, amigos*! We're headed way down south, out past where you've dared to go before!"

The blast-furnace wind almost stirred Buddy Troy's butch-waxed flattop. They were six in all, piled into Buddy's ragtop Bonneville. Navy boys straying across the line from San Diego to old *Meh-hi-co* to TJ for a three-day-pass blowout.

Buddy drained his longneck, bellowed back over the wind shear, "We all know that you can leave Brownsville, but you can never get Matamoros outta your soul!"

Walt Pierce, a shade thick around the middle and just-this-side of asocial, crowded into the rear corner of the passenger side's backseat, yelled back, "We're in San Diego, not Texas, Buddy."

Buddy belched, yelled back, "What the fuck ever. It's the goddamn spirit of the thing that matters, dipshit. I aim to misbehave!"

Walt had heard the stories from pretty much the day he'd arrived at base: Cherry boys with butterflies in their bellies stealing across the border to get laid. To drink rum at TJ's infamous "longest bar in the world" and to try to find out exactly what the hell a "Donkey Show" is.

Pretty clearly, Walt figured, his road mates had made more than one trip across that borderline. It was obvious the boys had *been with* women.

And they were *always* riding Walt for *something*.

Walt? He *was* cherry, and how.

139

His tendency to run to fat, what his mother excused as a genetic lean toward being "big-boned,"—coupled with Walt's dental and acne issues—had contributed to his goddamn "cherry" state. So he'd lied. He made claims about myriad conquests. He figured they believed him. He *had* to believe they would.

Walt had bought a jug of rum and a six-pack of Coca-Cola to provision himself for the border run. He'd been mixing half-assed Cuba libras in a Styrofoam cup to steel himself for what was to come.

Thank God, Walt thought, *the other boys don't suspect I'm a fucking virgin.* Those last two words made him smile. Feeling the rum, he laughed at his own accidental word joke.

Then the one sitting next to him, Lyle Porter—tall, thin and bookish . . . yet worldly, in his way—disabused Walt of that comforting illusion. Lyle drawled, "Go easy on that rum there, Walt. You'll want to be a bit sharper than you're looking to go into tonight, *hombre*. Rum and first sex can be a treacherous mix."

Walt ground his teeth. He decided if he could get Lyle alone in some TJ alley, he'd make the cocksucker regret that remark. Walt twisted rings on his fat fingers, imagining Lyle on his back, bleeding and spitting out teeth.

From up front, Buddy yelled back, "Matamoros? Tijuana? What the fuck difference does it make? Either way, the *señoritas* are there and waiting all wet and ready. Gut-shoot me or break my heart, because, tonight, I just want to *feel* somethin'!"

* * *

Maybe it was the lowest-rung whorehouse in Tijuana. Certainly it struck Walt that way, though admittedly, he had nothing to measure it against.

They stumbled out of the Pontiac into the dusty parking lot at the back of the bordello. They were already sweating from the booze and the desert swelter. The night was heavy with heat lightning and the scent of rain; all that only made the heat seem somehow fiercer.

Walt steadied himself against the rear fender. He closed his eyes and the world began to spin. He thought he might vomit. Walt opened his eyes and the world steadied a shade.

Buddy cast another empty bottle into the dust and said, "Ya'll got cash right, 'cause these spic cunts inside, they don't give it away, you know."

Dragging an arm across his damp forehead, Walt concentrated, feeling his roll in his tube sock. He'd left only a few token dollars tucked in his wallet in case he fell prey to a pickpocket or treacherous whore who might try to rob him after. He'd heard plenty bad about Mexico; and worse about those low ones who chose to live in it.

"Let's just get to it," Walt said. "I'm fuckin' tired to death of waiting."

He could have added: *Tired of imagining.*

* * *

The girls were lined up for their choosing.

The whorehouse smelled of something Walt couldn't put a name to.

He looked around, afraid to focus on the women. Joint was a dive all right: faltering overhead light bulbs; peeling paint and wallpaper. Sagging sofas and Naugehyde chairs were held together with duct tape.

Eventually, Walt *had* to look at the girls; had to make his choice.

He was getting leftovers; the other boys had already made their selections.

The ones who remained were either too fat or too skinny. Most were topless; their bare breasts fascinated Walt. They were slick with sweat and he had a strong temptation to taste them. Well, that's the way it was supposed to be, right?

Right?

How could he know how this was supposed to be? How it was supposed to go?

Walt walked the line, end to end; once, twice.

He finally settled on some dark-haired, dark-eyed skinny girl who looked sadder than the rest. Walt figured maybe that sadness would make her nice. Nicer than the fatter ones who dared Walt with their eyes, or the one with the gold front tooth who'd said something in Spanish to him and then laughed. Said something Walt just *knew* must have been a dig of some kind. *Bitch.*

He looked at the skinny one again. Said, "I think this one. She speak English?"

The boss whore—three hundred pounds if she went two-fifty—a one-eyed hag, said, "She knows all the gringo words you'll need, *niño.*"

Walt grunted, listened to the terms, then skidded off two tens.

He didn't think he needed to pay for anything . . . *exotic.*

Not for his first time.

The girl looked him over . . . pulled her open blouse closer around her breasts. The boss whore snarled and tore the blouse off the girl. She said, "Go with him, *rápidamente.*"

TWENTY ONE

Tell drove aimlessly around New Austin in his SUV, trying to think of other investigative avenues to pursue Thalia Ruiz's killer now that he had exhausted all the paper trails and obvious investigative paths. He shook his head, thinking of the sorry parade of men who'd beaten Latinas in the past few years whom he'd spoken with over the past several hours. Tell walked out of every interview with trembling fists and the taste of his own blood in his mouth from biting his lip.

In the early going, his job with the Border Patrol had found Tell driving, day and night, alone and looking for men and women whose greatest crimes consisted mostly of crossing an invisible line in the dust.

Later, after he had risen to a supervisory post, he spent his hours coordinating the efforts of others who drove through the desert looking for bodies. In the end, during that last terrible year in California, Tell had drifted into a whole new level of policing and promptly gotten crosswise with the Rios cartel. He lost his family for his trouble playing detective.

Tell had taken the New Austin chief's post thinking it would be relatively light duty.

New Austin hadn't suffered a murder or violent crime in three years. But now Tell was confronted with a rape-murder less than one week in. More of his good luck . . .

Returning to old habits, Tell drove on through the night, roaming the blackened back roads again just like the old days, trying to think of fresh moves. Hell, he'd even plunked on his old white Border Patrol hat for some reason.

A jacked-up Nova whipped by Tell's SUV doing sixty-five, seventy, *easy*, in a forty-five-mile-per-hour zone.

Tell had loaded a portable, magnetic cherry light in his SUV. He rolled down his window, slapped the light on the roof and flipped it on, giving chase.

Some circumspect part of Tell knew that it was a reckless, stupid thing to do. He had not equipped his personal vehicle with a radio, or even a walkie-talkie, so he had no prospect of securing backup if needed.

And a late-night, high-speed pursuit often as not ended with some civilian—some mother and a toddler daughter, for instance—slaughtered, T-boned while innocently attempting to negotiate some crossroads.

Tell was about to break off the chase when the Nova's brake lights flared and drifted right.

To his surprise, the Nova was slowing, eventually rolling to a stop on the shoulder.

Tell cruised to an angled halt behind the Chevy. The car was clearly some kid's vanity project: air shocks and a license plate frame composed of entwined, busty, golden nude silhouettes. Lots of flat-black primer patch gave the mostly faded yellow Nova a leopard-spot appearance. The kid was probably still saving money for the cherry paint job he envisioned.

Because Tell had no police radio, he couldn't run a check on the plate.

He got out warily, hearing his boot falls on crunching berm gravel, his flashlight held out to his side to draw any potential fire, his right hand on the butt of his gun. He saw four heads bobbing inside the Chevy.

The driver wisely turned on the interior lights as Tell approached, so he could see inside. It was four kids—two couples. Guy and girl up front, and girl and guy in back. They couldn't be more than seventeen, any of them. Hispanic. Too-new clothes on the girls, which meant they'd likely just come across and drifted northeast to Ohio. They all looked terrified.

Tell's adrenaline kicked down several notches. He said, "License and registration."

The driver, clean cut, subservient, handed over a driver's license. He said, his accent still relatively heavy, "Sir, my r-registra-tion, uh, I do have it, but I bought this car a few days ago. I think that it's in my jacket at home, Officer, sir."

Tell believed him. The kid was too scared and too green at dealing with American cops to lie. Tell didn't believe the license he held in his hand, however. The thickness of the plastic was astonishingly slight. The background color in the photo was wrong. The holographic elements were badly blurred. Tell half smiled: the fake driver's license was exactly like the sorry samples given him by Able Hawk.

Extending his hand palm up, Tell said, "I want all your IDs, now." The girls, pretty despite their yet-to-wane baby fat, looked confused. The driver spoke to them in Spanish, evidently confident that Tell wasn't a Spanish speaker. The boy told his riders to pull out their licenses. "He needs to see them," he told them in Spanish. "Just stay cool, it'll be all right. Jerry said these licenses always stand up to scrutiny by these town cops. It's the sheriff's boys we have to worry about, Jerry said. We'll be fine."

Purses opened and were rummaged through. The young dude in the backseat leaned left to pry his wallet out of the ass pocket of his low-rider jeans.

The kids passed three more operator's licenses out the window to Tell. He shone his flashlight on the plastic cards—three more dismal fakes. The boy in back was allegedly named Magdaleno Ortiz.

Tell slid all four bogus licenses into his breast pocket.

The driver—Richie Huerta, if his own bogus license was to be believed that far—frowned. He said, "Officer? Sir?"

"Police Chief Lyon," Tell said. "Chief of the *town cops* here in New Austin." Tell stepped back from the Nova. "Step out of your car, would you Rich?"

The young man got out uncertainly, maybe expecting a beating.

"Walk around the back of your car with me and over to my SUV," Tell told Richie in Spanish. Now the boy looked truly scared.

"Don't sweat it yet, kid, I just want a private word with you." Tell said that in Spanish too. Then, in English, he said, "Rich, I could run you all in and charge you for speeding, false IDs, endangering the public. Probably many other things too. I should impound your sweet car here. I'm frankly figuring you for having no insurance, and that's a state violation that could send you away for a while. Let alone your lack of a valid license. I should call the county and turn you and your friends over to Able Hawk—*El Gavilan*—which I hope you know, Rich, would be a real dark prospect for you and your friends. Particularly given all the charges that could come your way from that man. You kids could go away for a long, long time."

The boy, trembling, said, "What could I do to—"

Tell quickly held up a hand—not even wanting to contemplate what the kid might be prepared to offer of himself or of the girls to get out from under. The other three Mexican kids were twisted around in their seats, watching. The breath of the two in the backseat had fogged the rear window of the Nova. The girls were clearly terrified; afraid, probably, that at any minute Tell would swing on Richie. Or maybe that Richie would commit them to something.

Tell said, "I'm going to make you and your friends an offer."

The kid swallowed hard, watching Tell watching the girls. Richie said, "What do you want?"

"Not much, kid. And it's between you and me, and stays that way. I'm prepared to believe that is your car, Rich. I'm prepared to take your promise that you're going to drive the speed limit in my town, here on out. Because if you don't, if your name comes across my desk in some complaint or report, I'm going to personally land on you and send you back to Mexico, and much the worse for wear."

"What do you want from me, sir?"

"I want you to swear to obey the law in my town, Rich. And your friends in that car—their behavior is on your head now too—from now to forever. I want you to promise me you're going to get some kind of proof of insurance for that spanking sled of yours. Failing to become legal citizens in the next few weeks, I want you all to find better false identifications, and you're going to need to do that damned fast, because I'm keeping these phony ones in my pocket. And that brings us to the heart of our deal. I forget tonight, and you all do that too. In return, I just want the name and location of the man who got you these false identifications."

"I do that, he'll kill me and rape my sisters," Richie said. "He swore to me he would do that."

"He'll never know who sent me, Rich. You have my word as *jefe* and as your new best friend on that."

Richie looked skeptical.

Tell said in Spanish, "I promise you on the soul of my dead baby daughter. I was Border Patrol and a Mexican drug cartel burned her and my wife alive in our home. I swear to you, I won't let anything like that happen to you or to yours, Rich."

Richie nodded, wild-eyed.

Tell pulled out his pen and notebook. "Shoot me a name, Rich."

THEN

Walt had sensed it was the girl's first time doing it for money as he made his selection. She struck him as a bit shy; half-innocent, really. It was a large part of the reason he'd chosen her from among the remaining whores.

When they reached her room, Walt saw how wrong he was. Playing the tyro, it soon became obvious, was a kind of strategy on her part. A timeworn ploy.

In her dank room, stripping, her demeanor changed. She laughed at his shyness undressing.

The girl was still laughing at Walt. She was speaking in Spanish and pointing between his legs. What was that Mex' word she kept repeating as she laughed and pointed?

Poco?

Something like that. She kept laughing at his inability to get it up.

Too scared? Not sure what to do? Maybe it was the fact he felt the clock; he'd only paid for half an hour.

Her laughing grew meaner, a grating bray.

She'd pushed him too far, whatever she was gibbering on about.

Walt hit her with the back of his hand and sent her sprawling. When she looked up at him, scared and holding her own hand to her mouth, he saw he'd drawn blood.

He felt this stirring—looked down and sucked in his gut; saw he was finally getting hard.

Walt forced his bulk on the skinny Mexican girl, closing a hand over her mouth to keep her from screaming and alerting the big boss whore.

He slid inside her, nearly coming at once. Well, she wasn't laughing now, was she?

TWENTY TWO

Shawn lay on his cot, deep into his second pack of cigarettes, feeling lightheaded and nauseous from all the smoking; from too much coffee. Too many Krispy Kreme doughnuts the fat cop kept spotting him.

His hands were shaking and he was already stir-crazy.

Stir-crazy.

He understood that term too well now. Shawn felt like banging his head bloody against the walls or bars until he fell unconscious or died.

The New Austin police headquarters was nearly empty. It was just Shawn and the obese cop who sat outside his cell, on guard. "You're our first all-nighter," the fat-assed cop, Billy, had confided to Shawn.

Shawn had finally reached some kind of rapport with the bloated son of a bitch, though—at least persuading Billy to step outside so Shawn could take a dump in private.

The weekly newspaper reporter who had never covered a murder or seen a violent crime scene before standing over Thalia's body, nevertheless had always fancied himself a hard-liner when it came to crime and punishment. But incarcerated now, Shawn was reassessing past positions. This was hell. Shawn chaffed in the too-tight space. He cursed the hard and narrow cot, too stingy blankets and especially that fucking toilet with no privacy.

But Billy wasn't so bad. He'd even brought the portable TV into the jail area and angled the thing so they could watch a *Hunter* rerun together.

Shawn said, "You got cable, right?"

Billy said, "Yeah . . . you got a show this hour?"

"*The Shield*, on FX," Shawn said. "Or *Nip-Tuck* . . . they show tits and ass on those."

"And it isn't a premium channel?" Billy, sucking the filling from a jelly-filled doughnut, seemed incredulous.

"No shit, they do. Lots of righteous nudity. And it's basic cable," Shawn said.

Billy wiped his hands down on his socks and picked up the remote. "Which channel?"

THEN

Patricia was fourteen when her parents flew the family to Texas to cross the borderline *back*.

All the blood relatives the Maldonados had left were still down there in Mexico. It was time, Kathleen and Augustin said, that Patricia met them. Time for her to see what her parents had felt so necessary to flee in order to build this new life in *El Norte*.

Her mother had another, unstated motive too, Patricia rightly sensed.

Kathleen had begun to worry about how thoroughly Americanized Patricia seemed. She felt Patricia had begun to acquire a certain kind of gringo's entitlement mentality.

For his part, Augustin was abraded by his daughter's increasingly romantic wonderings about the country her parents had deserted years before things truly began to go to pieces back home.

Initially, the trip to the border had done to nothing to further Kathleen's and Augustin's agendas.

The dry heat and desert—the strange plants that stubbornly thrived there—captivated Patricia. The terrain further sparked her imagination. She picked up a novel about the life of Pancho Villa, the Mexican peasant-turned-self-styled Revolutionary general, and became lost in its pages.

But then they'd finally left Texas—crossed over to the other side.

Squalor . . . strange smells. The sounds of distant gunfire, and, too often, of sirens.

Patricia's cousin, Yolanda, was about her same age. But the boys who interested Yolanda horrified Patricia. They had gang tattoos and hid guns in their pants under their shirttails. They all smoked and they blasted *narcocorridos* from beater cars and trucks.

Yolanda's house was a rotting pueblo with no reliable plumbing—but had a giant satellite dish up top that was probably their most expensive possession.

The neighbors incessantly screamed at one another, issued threats and ultimatums.

After the first of three planned nights sleeping over, Patricia awakened to find a cockroach crawling across her bed sheets. She begged her parents to let them return to spend nights in the hotel in El Paso. The hotel wasn't wonderful—it wasn't as good as the Holiday Inns they'd visited on trips for cheap family get-aways to Gatlinburg, Tennessee. But it was comparatively clean and something like heaven compared to her cousin's home.

And she didn't have to plug her ears against the blasting "music" of Valentín Elizalde and Sergio Vega.

When they were seated on the plane back to Ohio, squeezed in between her parents, Patricia said, "It's good you left there. Thank you for doing that."

Her parents took Patricia's hands in theirs and squeezed hard as the jet taxied down the runway. As the plane dipped its wing for a turn before beginning its steep ascent, Patricia never looked down . . . never looked back.

TWENTY THREE

Tell returned home at eleven thirty P.M. He parked next to Patricia's Honda—the only available slot in the parking lot. He sat in his car, finishing a song: Springsteen's "I Wish I Were Blind."

He locked up his SUV and stared off across the creek at the last, straggling fireflies. Frogs croaked in the high weeds.

Tell had talked to two TV reporters by cell phone on the drive home. He'd toed up to the hint of having his own person of interest for the murder of Thalia Ruiz. He hated to lie about the case, but he'd done it anyway, thinking perhaps the publicity would spark the real killer to some stupid act of reckless and attention-getting rabbiting. Or perhaps Tell's hints about a suspect would provoke the killer into surrendering himself in time to cut a deal and escape the wrath of Able Hawk. The sheriff was frequently on television and in the newspapers too, making rumblings about a "slam-dunk, death penalty bounce."

Tell had decided to release Shawn when he got into the HQ in the morning. He had already concluded that his morning run with Patricia was probably off, so he figured for another early morning at the station house.

A note was taped to the door of Tell's apartment. The handwriting was feminine:

Whatever the hour, please knock.—P.

Tell thought about ignoring it. She'd probably be asleep at this hour. And some time to think more overnight about things regarding Shawn and his sorry actions with Thalia might mellow Patricia's attitude toward him. Tell hoped so, anyway. Then Tell heard a hinge squeak. Patricia stepped out onto the shaft of light from her opening door. She whispered, "Tell? Can we please talk?"

He doffed his hat, said, "Surely." He nodded at his door. "Mine or yours?"

Patricia smiled and shrugged. She wore sweats and a T-shirt cut short to expose her midriff. Bare feet. He wanted to pull her close; to undress her tonight and never let go. This time, he wanted to spend the night; to love her and hold her all night long. "My door's open, Tell."

"So it is."

Patricia stepped back to let Tell in. She locked the door behind him. She reached out and took his white hat. "This what you wore on the Border Patrol? It's kind of high contrast with that black uniform."

She put his hat on her head, just like Marita used to do. Looking at Patricia standing there—with her black hair and eyes, wearing his hat as his wife had in playful moments, dark eyes looking up teasingly from under the shadow of its brim—it was far too much. Tell lifted the hat from her head and tossed it on the breakfast counter to try to make the memory go away. He kissed her forehead through her hair. "Yeah," he said. "It's my hat from back then. Not sure why I wore it tonight."

Patricia shrugged, her arms around his waist now, pulling him close. "It's a white hat. You're a good man. The hero, right? Maybe you're just reminding yourself of that."

"I'm no *white hat*, Patricia. No hero like that."

"Beg to differ, Tell." She hesitated, then said, "If you'd let me, I'd like to visit Shawn tomorrow. He must be scared there and he doesn't have many, if any, friends, you know. Some people just stay back from him because of what he does. And he works crazy hours since he's about the only staff at that paper. When he's not writing or designing pages, he's cruising bars. I really think I'm probably as close to a friend as Shawn's got in this town, especially now, God help him."

"Visit him if you like," Tell said, stepping from her embrace. He walked over to her sliding glass door and looked out at the wind-stirred willow—its draped branches pushed around by the warm night wind. "You can visit him at his place, if that's what you want. Come morning, I'm kicking the sorry son of a bitch loose."

"Really?"

Tell shrugged. "Able Hawk—*El Gavilan*—amassed scads of exculpatory evidence. So, Shawn will walk. At least on the murder rap. Though I think he's pretty well through in this town. I also sincerely doubt Shawn's denials about having slipped that dead woman the Rohypnol. Hawk doubts it too, and he's driven to pursue it. If Shawn did drug Thalia—even if it had nothing to do with her getting herself murdered later—it's still a terrible crime."

Patricia stepped up behind Tell and wrapped her arms around his waist again, her cheek pressed to his back. "You're right. In that light, I'll keep some distance from Shawn for now. You're right, of course too, that he's ruined in this town. I just hope Shawn has the good sense to cut his losses and move on fast. Find himself a good position elsewhere and grow the hell up. Maybe even clean up his act."

"That may be asking a lot of that one," Tell said. "He has a tendency to follow his dick around. Or so Able says." Tell hated the taint of jealousy in his voice.

"I really didn't ask you in to talk about Shawn," Patricia said, pulling Tell closer.

"You brought him up, Patricia."

She released her grip and walked into the kitchen. She opened the refrigerator and rummaged. She said, "Maybe I did it because he was on my mind. A few hours ago, Hawk—*El Gavilan*—came and tried to ask me a lot of very personal, very invasive questions about Shawn and what he liked to do in bed."

"I didn't send Able to talk to you, Patricia. And I don't want to talk about any of this."

"Did you know he was coming, Tell?"

"I tried to talk him out of it."

"Then you did know."

"I tried to stop Able, Patricia."

"You might have warned me."

"Yeah. I might have with more time. But Hawk walked out of my place, straight down the hall, and knocked on your door. There was simply no time to give you that heads-up. I'm sorry you had to go through it."

"I really didn't . . . didn't give him his answers. I showed Hawk the door. I think he hates me now."

"Good for you," Tell said. "And good on you." He picked up his hat. "I should let you sleep. Hell, I'm exhausted myself."

"*I'm* wide awake," Patricia said.

She pulled a small bowl of sliced limes from the refrigerator and tugged off the bowl's plastic lid. She opened the cupboard and pulled out a saltshaker. "Drink with me, Tell."

She poured two waiting shot glasses full of tequila.

Tell tossed his hat back on the counter.

Patricia squeezed lime juice on both of their hands—on the space between their thumbs and index fingers—and then sprinkled salt on the wet spots. They hoisted their shot glasses, entwining arms, licking one another's hands, then downing their shots.

She said, "That's one." Patricia poured a second round.

"Go easy there, we both have work tomorrow," Tell said.

"Yes, we do." She picked up a remote control and pressed a button. Gordon Lightfoot on the stereo: "If You Could Read My Mind." Melancholy stuff and very much his kind of music.

They downed their second tequila shots and Patricia pushed her shot glass aside. She began fumbling with the buckle of his gun belt. "Let's finally get you out of this uniform tonight," she said.

Tell took her hand from his gun belt. "Patricia . . ."

She looked up at him from beneath careless black bangs with dark bedroom eyes. For a moment, she reminded Tell of his cousin's wife. It didn't unsettle him. And he found that . . . unsettling. She said, "Tell, I want this. Don't you want it too?"

He started to answer, but then her mouth was pressed to his mouth, her salty tongue tangling with his own. Her hands began fumbling with his gun belt again. He moved her hands and unbuckled his gun belt and placed it on the counter by the discarded shot glasses. Patricia was already working on his tunic's buttons.

She pushed his shirt over his shoulders and it fell with a thunk to the floor—drawn down by the weight of his badge. Patricia slipped off her own T-shirt, naked underneath. Her hands went to Tell's neck, urging his mouth to her breast. He sucked on her nipple and felt her knees tremble. She moaned softly. Long as it had been since he had been with a woman, Tell felt weak in the knees too. He said, "I should go to a store, get something." God, he felt like a kid. It had been so long since the last time, and thinking about buying rubbers? *God's sake.*

"We don't need anything," Patricia said, her mouth hungry against his. "I have all we need."

Then it was a feverish tangle, backing to her bedroom, shedding shoes and pants along the way; a wild, desperate coupling. Her kisses drew blood, her teeth nicked his bottom lip. Her short nails dug into the small of his back and his ass. She wrapped her legs tightly around him, refusing to let him pull out when it was on him. She screamed, coming with him, coaxing his body with hidden muscles.

After, tangled up and damp in one another's arms and legs and in the half-kicked-off comforter and twisted sheets, Patricia said, "Oh God, Tell . . . oh God."

She must have set the song on a loop, because "If You Could Read My Mind" was still playing, just as it had been through their fumbling, hungry lovemaking. *Heroes often fail.*

He asked, "What have we done, Patricia?"

She smiled, her lips still swollen from their hard kisses. Her black, moist eyes glistened. "We know exactly what we've done—just what we wanted to."

TWENTY FOUR

Able collapsed into his favorite armchair, barefoot, still dressed in his gray uniform pants, but stripped down to a Fraternal Order of Police T-shirt up top. He'd taken a beer from the refrigerator—Pabst—and had snagged a bag of Eagle pretzels. The beer tasted of aluminum. Able thought that Tell Lyon might be onto something with his pricier, glass-bottle Samuel Adams brews.

Able sorted stacks of newspapers he hadn't gotten to yet; found a copy of the daily with a photo of Thalia on the cover. It was a hastily cropped version of an engagement photograph. Newspaper bastards never discarded any fucking thing. And now they kept it all archived on the damned Web. Nothing ever went away anymore, *not ever*.

Well, not what you wanted to be gone, anyway. The stuff that mattered? That was lost all too easily.

Already, Able's late mornings seemed empty.

He cast down the newspaper. No, goddamit, this wasn't about him or anything he'd lately lost.

Thalia's little girl, her mother—they were the real *living* victims.

That was what this was all about now. Finding the one who killed Thalia wouldn't give the mother and daughter anything back, but they might rest a shade easier knowing the cocksucker who killed theirs no longer breathed their same sweet air.

Able could avenge Thalia's killing. He could find her killer and kill that son of a bitch back. Hell, it wasn't even a decision. His commitment to putting the slayer down like a mad dog was a given.

But to see to the mother's keeping? To give Thalia's little girl a worthy future? A different fucking challenge. One maybe beyond Able's grasp; beyond his talents if he truly had any.

He thought again of all those late morning cups of coffee across the counter or table with Thalia.

Well, Able's mornings were just going to be a sorry and dire fucking prospect. Christ knew Able was acquainted with the like.

He flicked on the television and found he had no patience for Leno's or Letterman's Bush-bashing monologues. Not that Able was a W. fan. He found the president woefully lacking stones on the immigration front. Able figured W.'s perspective on illegals had been fundamentally warped from his time playing Texas governor. And Bush had that Mexican nephew in the mix. Able finally settled on his man Lou Dobb's rerun report—another hard-edged piece on illegal immigration and its monetary effect on the southwestern American working poor. Grist for Able's blog.

Amos ambled out—shorts and a T-shirt. "I left the computer on and ready for you in the morning, Granddad. Type it all in, then when I get up, I'll upload it to your blog for you."

"Appreciate it, Amos."

"It's late, Gramps. You should go to bed. Try to get eight hours for once."

"Been a bastard of a day, Amos, make no mistake on that count. Just need to unwind a bit first. You want a beer?"

"No thanks. I hate the taste from the cans."

"Me too, lately. Remind me of that, next store trip. We'll get some of that Sam Adams ale. It comes in glass bottles. Hi-tone stuff."

Amos smiled. "Sure, Gramps." He sat down on a short sofa that was starting to look a bit worn. If his grandmother had still been around, Amos knew there would have been new furniture in the house by now. He looked around, remembering the way his grandmother kept things and decided he'd sweep the carpet in the morning. And dust . . . especially the TV screen. The old man wasn't good at fending for himself. Amos didn't know what would happen to his grandfather if he moved out. Amos's unformed plan was that Able might let Luisa and their child move in with them. The house was big enough. And God knew that it needed a woman's touch. Amos said, "Anything new on the murder, Granddad?"

Able was pleased his grandson was taking a real interest in his work. He told Amos about how he and his deputies had cleared Shawn O'Hara of suspicion.

Amos nodded, taking it in, proud of the old lawman. "So, you have someone else in your sights? Some other suspect in Thalia's murder?"

Able grunted, suppressing a belch. In his sheriff's voice he said, "'Thalia'? You knew her?"

Amos said, "Her name, it's all over the news." At least it wasn't a direct lie.

"Yeah." Able took another sip of beer and made a sour face. "No, I got nobody else yet. No other person of fuckin' interest, to use the jargon of the day." He hefted his beer can. "But 'tween me and Chief Lyon, we'll get my Thalia justice. Lyon, *heh*. I suspect that bastard Lyon's sharper than even he knows. You could do a hell of a lot worse than him for a first skipper."

Amos's cell phone rang.

"Your mystery girl?" Able arched an eyebrow.

"That's right," Amos said, backing toward his room.

"Tellin' you, Amos, you don't introduce me soon, boy, I'm gonna sleuth your ass come the weekend."

Amos smiled, backing into his bedroom. He closed the door and said, "Luisa? What's wrong? Are you sick?"

"Amos! Sheriff Pierce is here!"

"What?"

"Sheriff Walt Pierce, he came with a . . . a . . ."

"Subpoena? A search warrant?"

"*Sí. Yes.* A search warrant."

"Where are you now, Luisa?"

"Outside, at the corner, by the mailbox."

"Good. Stay out of their way, Lu. Just stay out of their way, and maybe you'll get by."

"They're in her bedroom now. They put Thalia's sheets and pillowcases in bags. They're searching her drawers now. Took her unwashed laundry."

"Trace evidence search," Amos said. "Looking for clues that might identify who killed her."

"She never had a man in this house!" He could hear Luisa's anger in her voice.

"I'm just saying what they're looking for—Pierce, I mean."

"And his men, about six of them," Luisa said. "And the corner."

"*Coroner*," Amos corrected her. "Just stay out of their way and they may not think to ask you for papers. Maybe not figure out you're not legal."

"I will. I'm scared, Amos."

"Call me when they leave, Luisa." He set his cell phone to "vibrate" so his grandfather wouldn't hear when she called back.

THEN

Marita proposed marriage to Tell. And she didn't want to wait.

Tell didn't require much thought before saying yes.

His superior had already told Tell that he'd identified him as "a comer." Said he'd be recommending Tell for promotion at the first opportunity. Professionally, Tell's future seemed assured.

Except:

Tell said, "I don't qualify for vacation yet, so any honeymoon . . ."

"We'll squeeze it in on a weekend," Marita said, looking up into his eyes. "Then we'll do it right, *bigger*, later."

TWENTY FIVE

Half awake, Tell had a sense of Patricia leaving, then returning. Then her mouth was on his mouth again, but minty. Opening his eyes, he said, "You cheated, woman."

"So go brush your teeth, Tell. I won't peek at you getting there." Her bedroom was already flooded with morning light. He wished it were darker.

"My toothbrush is several doors down," he said, propping himself up on one elbow. She had brushed the tangles from her black hair. He stroked her bare shoulder. He said, "My God, you wake up beautiful."

She smiled and said, "Use my toothbrush, Tell. And don't play squeamish at that prospect, not after the things we did last night."

She smiled again, watching as he padded to the bathroom.

He heard music. He called from the bathroom, "What's that song, Patricia?"

"You had your tunes last night. My music this time. 'Calling All Angels,' by Jane Siberry."

"I like it."

"Good answer."

"Patricia—eyes elsewhere," he said, but she watched him return naked to her bed.

"Six A.M.," she said. "Still early. Still enough time." She lifted the blankets and he slid in next to her. Smiling, moving half-atop him, she closed the covers over them. Her hair tickled his chest as she kissed his breastbone . . . his neck and then chin. His mouth. "*Mm, minty*," she said.

She straddled him, breasts firm against his chest and her black hair a curtain around his face. She said, "I hope you're not sorry for last night."

"Not a bit."

Her mouth was on his again. He could hear the mourning doves outside, their cooing some strange counterpoint to Jane Siberry's song. He felt her hand on him, guiding him; her weight settling on him. "You better not have other plans tonight," she said breathily, moaning as their bodies were joined.

"I don't have other plans any night," he said.

* * *

They were still languishing naked in bed. Jane was now singing, "Love is Everything." It was nearly seven; another late start for Tell. He said, "I'm running out of avenues, Patricia. Able, too. It's going to take an accident or a fluke to bring this guy in, short of another killing and more clues left. That is, short of some sideways inspiration." Tell smiled and shook his head. "My cousin, Chris, he has a natural facility for this kind of thing. He'd probably have a suspect already."

"I thought Chris is a writer."

"He is, but he tends to run afoul of these things. Then he uses it for source material. He'd be a hell of a cop. Though it's half-instinctual with him. It's like he can just seize *the* thread and run it to its end. He has a gift for detecting human weakness. Chris can always suss out the worst or weakest in a man or woman and see how it drives them. It's a hell of gift. Or curse. When he's really on, he's like a force of nature. Of course he's not moving under color of authority, and so not bound by evidentiary stipulations. He doesn't have to act with an eye toward the courts."

"You sound jealous of him."

"Mostly of his latitude," Tell said.

"So call him, maybe. Ask for Chris's advice?"

Tell couldn't confide to Patricia he'd already consulted Chris for strategies to help Shawn O'Hara keep his newspaper job. He said, "Chris has a gift for getting justice, but he doesn't do it by the book. So he's not going to be much help to me in this case."

Patricia rolled over on her belly, her right breast pillowed against his chest, her head propped up on one hand. She stroked his lips with her right hand, her fingers softly tracing his mouth and jaw-line. "A lot of murders go unsolved, Tell, all over the place. Don't take it personally. And you say Able Hawk is just as stymied as you think you are."

Tell loved her for that phrasing. He said, "Sure. But Able was also focused on trying to pull Shawn's ass out of the fire." Saying Shawn's name, lying naked in her bed, Tell felt guilty. He checked the clock. Every moment spent in Patricia's bed was another minute her ex had to spend in jail.

He thought of the Mexican kids he had stopped the night before, the name and phone number that he'd been given by young, scared Richie. Tell said, "You could help me with something else, Patricia. It could be big in its own respect. Or at least useful."

"Sure, anything. What?"

"Be my operative?"

"Maybe. Sure." She smiled crookedly. "But I don't have to dress as a hooker or something, do I?"

He smiled. "No, just make a phone call. But when you do, try to come on more . . . well, Mexican."

She narrowed her eyes. "You mean, like, fresher to the soil this side? Pidgin English?"

"Yeah, like that."

"I can do that. Funny, you know, it's only the past year or so I've encountered real racism here. I mean, before I open my mouth, I suppose I look Mexican enough, so I'm a target for it."

"I'm sorry."

"I can handle it. It's just strange coming this late, is all. What do you need me to do?"

Tell said, "We'll use my cell phone. It's blocked so it can't be traced. You'll call and ask for a new fake driver's license. You'll probably have to promise to pay three hundred dollars. And you'll agree to meet wherever the man on the other end of the line suggests."

Now Patricia was a little nervous. "Do I have to keep that meeting?"

"Not at all. God, no. I'll keep your appointment for you. That's the whole point."

"This dangerous? Not to me—I mean to you?"

"No, probably not." His fingers combed through her raven hair. "But as you mention it, we're early days yet as lovers"—he smiled at her smile when he used the term—"and I'm a cop. You go into this knowing what I do to make my living, right, Patricia? You can't spend all your time worrying about me every time I go out the door."

"The job is you, Tell. I can see that." She stretched up and kissed him again, slowly, using her tongue. She pulled away, eyes already open, searching his face. "Where'd you leave your cell phone?"

TWENTY SIX

Able sipped his coffee: *Not that good.*

Father Anthony Ruscilli said, "Why are you here, Sheriff? If memory and rumor serve, you're a Presbyterian."

Able frowned. He hadn't found much use for religion since he lost his wife and daughter. It had been years since he last ventured inside a church. "What I am, is peeved, Father," Able said.

"Peeved? At what? At whom?"

"Why, at you, Father."

"Whatever for?"

"These Spanish sermons—they piss me off."

The priest wagged a finger. "You, of all people, know the situation, Sheriff—the throngs of Spanish-only-speaking immigrants among us. More come every day. Most, perhaps 85 percent, are Catholic. This is *outreach*. They're owed the services of the church too."

Able sighed. "Yeah. I'm sure that's so, Padre. But they're not 'immigrants,' to use your word. They're illegals."

"But they are here, Sheriff."

"And they should at very least try to assimilate, Father. *Muy pronto*. You offerin' these well-meaning but misguided Spanish-only sermons, it's cosseting their weakness."

"I'm not sure I understand, Sheriff Hawk."

"Then I'll spell it out for you, Padre, in English. You mollycoddle them, Father. You undercut their assimilation by giving 'em a little piece of home here. Better to teach them English. Tough love. Tend to their souls in *our* lingo. These little Mexican environs are poppin' up all over my county and I hate it. It's especially true on the West Side of New Austin. Little Mexican worlds where the signage is in Spanish. Where Spanish is the dominant language. Hell, it's the only language. The McDonald's on the West Side has a fucking menu in Spanish. There's a Spanish-language shelf in the library now. And Spanish-only story hours offered for illegal tykes. And now we have these 'English-as-second-a-language' standards foisted on us by bleeding-heart school honchos. That's dragging down our test scores and threatening to push our school district into state receivership. And not speakin' English is actually getting these poor bastards killed these days."

"Yes, Sheriff," Fr. Ruscilli said, impatience in his voice. "I've read your blog. I read about the recent fire."

"Count yourself lucky you can read it, Father. Unlike these illegals you're catering to."

The priest shrugged and smiled. "I'm simply easing their transition, Sheriff."

"Bullshit. You're slowing that transition, Father. More likely, *aborting* it."

"I think we're finished here now, Sheriff Hawk. I will continue to do what I should do—what I'm charged with doing. We both have our obligations."

Able Hawk stared at the bleary eyed priest. Able had already concluded the priest was a profound alcoholic. Able said, "Well, Father, then in the same spirit, I'm going to do what *I* should do—what *I'm* charged with doing."

"And what is that, Sheriff?"

"I'm going to take advantage of your convenient consolidation of all these Spanish-only-speaking illegals and stage a mass arrest. No fuckin' pun intended."

The priest exploded. "The church is sanctuary! What you threaten is monstrous!"

"What I *propose* is the law," Able said. "And your sanctuary doesn't extend to your parking lot, or to your city- and TIF-funded fucking access road back to the rest of my county. Coming or going, I'll arrest 'em just fine along that path, Father. And rest easy—I'll recognize your cooperation in said 'mass arrest' on my blog, which is now up to fifteen hundred hits a day, and thank you, or your absentee landlord, very much." Able gestured at the empty cavern around them.

Able pushed his coffee cup aside and stood up. He smiled and said, "Sanctuary sure enough ain't what it used to be. But then what is, these days, eh?"

The Horton County sheriff picked up his hat and put it on; fished his sunglasses from his breast pocket. "Now you best try and stay off my radar, you fucking degenerate," Able said. "I've been researching you, Padre. You try anything on the kids here like you did in your past post, and I get wind of it, well, I'm going to go medieval on your ass—Spanish Inquisition-style, if you get my drift. And that vow doesn't preclude me 'outing' you on my Web site in advance of any possible sin, should I stray into a dark and heady mood. I've found retaliating first to pay dividends, more often than not."

THEN

Military brat.

A time-worn phrase, Shawn balked at the term. Military brat conjured images of baby boomers—sons and daughters of World War II– and Korea-era vets. But Shawn's father's age was such he had no war to claim as his own. He never served "in country," if that was the right dumb-ass phrase for it. Jeff O'Hara was one of those lucky few who floated a military career without ever facing combat. Too young for Vietnam and too old for Desert Storm. Jeff had never faced fire outside of training exercises.

Still, with Jeff being career military, the O'Hara family moved, *a lot*.

The best posting to Shawn's mind was San Diego. His father's stationing came just as Shawn was coming of age.

Shawn and his slightly older fellow "brats" would stray across that borderline on weekend tears.

The girls south of the border were easier—everyone said so.

Shawn lost his virginity on his first Friday-night trip across.

The girl was a pretty young Latina; a *chica* named, no kidding, Rosalita. Shawn and his friends met Rosie and her slumming friends in a bar in TJ. Shawn found the Springsteen song of the same name on the jukebox and fed coins to play it twice. Finding that song with her name there in the jukebox made it seem something like fate.

They danced to "her song," both times. It was a long piece of music and by the end of the second rendition, they were both winded, a sheen on her arms and forehead. Shawn kissed Rosalita's neck; it was salty. He kissed it again when they were back at the table. He chased her taste with tequila. Then he dared to kiss her on the mouth. He felt her tongue pressing his mouth open, searching for his tongue.

From there, Rosalita took the lead. Shawn wasn't her first; he hoped she didn't guess she was his.

They made love in the backseat of a Ford Mustang of undistinguished vintage.

And right there, Rosalita became Shawn's template, his ideal for a lover: dusky, Latin and lusty.

Their feelings caught fire too. Weekend runs to TJ to spend nights with one another became the norm. As the young lovers' zeal for one another grew, Shawn was oblivious to the fact that his parents' passion was ebbing; their marriage cooling, fast.

He got his first and most potent inkling one Monday night, sacked out in his bed, unable to sleep, lusting for his girl across the border in Tijuana.

Shawn heard his mother snarl something about another woman. Something about a "Mexican whore." Then there was the sound of something thrown breaking.

His father denied it all, his voice getting louder to be heard over Moira O'Hara's screamed accusations and denunciations.

Friday found Moira and a shattered Shawn on a plane back to the Midwest—his mother had family there. They didn't talk once during the long flight east. Shawn thought he loathed his mother now.

He'd asked to stay with his father—gave some excuse about wanting to follow in his father's footsteps . . . be career military. He said he wanted to finish school with friends. To do that, he must stay on base with his dad. His mother and father both rejected a military career as a credible option; Shawn had writing talent, and they both saw it. Since he was a child, Shawn had talked of writing as a career. As to friends, well, leaving for the next place had always been the norm. What was different now? Shawn was not yet eighteen; he couldn't declare for himself.

So Shawn argued *harder* to stay with his old man. He said if it came down to a choice, this was his. "I want to stay with Dad."

His mother slapped Shawn, hard, then said he had no voice in the matter.

Shawn begged, tears burning his eyes. But his father caved in to Moira. Jeff said it was best he leave with his mother. Jeff hugged Shawn tight; his son didn't hug back.

Pouting, Shawn stormed to his room. He never got to say goodbye to Rosie. He never got to cross that borderline again. Never got to taste her mouth; to again taste Rosie there and kiss her with that taste on both their lips. Never again got to comb his fingers through her long, glistening black hair.

His mother found a lawyer and filed for divorce within six hours of their plane hitting the tarmac back there in the flatlands.

A couple of days later, she learned it was a moot point.

Sometime between Sunday evening and Monday morning, Jeff O'Hara had put the snout of a .45 in his mouth and pulled the trigger. They found him with a framed family photograph clutched in his other hand.

TWENTY SEVEN

Shawn looked up. Tell Lyon, crisp and refreshed-looking, was standing outside his cell. Lyon's black uniform was pressed and still reminded Shawn of some Nazi storm trooper's togs. But now Lyon was wearing black cowboy boots in lieu of the standard black, high-polish dress shoes his deputies wore.

"Least someone got some sleep, from the looks of it," Shawn said. His mouth tasted like someone else's ashtray.

Tell said, "I hear Able already phoned you and gave you a heads-up on your status. As I'm sure Hawk told you, we're kicking you loose shortly."

"Can't say I'm sorry to go, but I am surprised," Shawn said. "I mean, a few hours ago, the worry from you two seemed to be protecting me from Walt Pierce."

"It was a real concern for a time," Tell said. "You can thank Able Hawk. He and his men found enough irrefutable evidence of your innocence in Thalia Ruiz's murder to placate even Sheriff Pierce. I think you're okay now on that front—the homicide."

"You say that like maybe there's some other front where I'm not so fine," Shawn said, forehead wrinkled.

Tell shrugged and handed Shawn a bag edgewise through the bars. "Your personal effects. And some clippings from the area news-papers. You might as well read them now, Shawn. Digest them and prepare yourself. See what your fourth estate brethren have been saying about you. Or conjecturing, in some cases."

Shawn scowled. "Pretty bad?"

"Sucks to be you. New Austin, in most ways that count, is still a small town, Shawn. Was me, I'd cut my losses and get out of this part of Ohio. The reach on these articles, fortunately for you, can't be far. The local papers—other than your own, which is silent on this story for obvious reasons—they don't even have proper Web sites yet, so this episode shouldn't dog you in terms of eventual Google searches kicking up old bad press."

Tell stepped back from Shawn's cell. "Another twenty minutes or so, we'll have the paperwork wrapped up and you'll be free to go home. At least for the present time."

"Present time?"

"I haven't cleared you in my own mind of suspicion of rape. That Rope."

Frowning, Shawn said, "You really ought to think about putting up walls or stalls around the toilets, Chief."

Tell shook his head. "We did, we'd have the only jail on earth with them. This is supposed to be hell, Shawn. Just be glad you get to walk out of it. At least for a time."

The reporter nodded. "Thanks for what you did, Tell. What you tried to do for me . . . what you protected me from."

Tell said, "Billy's stuck around an extra hour before going off shift. He's volunteered to drop you at your place. You should take him up on that offer."

"Thanks, but Christ, it's only two blocks' walk," Shawn said. "I'll hoof it. Need the air after this shitty night."

"There are a couple of newspaper photographers and reporters camped out front," Tell said. "One TV news crew too. And some demonstrators—about twelve Latinos out there, marching with signs and calling for your head. They look pissed." Tell didn't like the way he was riding Shawn.

"Shit."

Tell said, "So Billy will take you out back and get you in a cruiser inside the sally port. You duck down when he drives outside and you'll get away clean. For now. But tensions are running high in the Latino community right now. Time-bomb stuff. If I was you, Shawn, I'd think hard about leaving the state of Ohio. At least for a while." Tell was still weighing Shawn's likelihood to have committed rape.

"I'll think about that," Shawn said sourly. "Thanks again, Chief."

* * *

Billy swung into the lot behind Shawn's building. He gestured at the ATM mounted on the wall of the bank across the parking lot. "If I was you," Billy said, "I'd plant a kiss on that camera on that gizmo. Sucker saved you from Walt Pierce, you know, you lucky friggin' Mick."

"I may do that," Shawn said. "Thanks for everything, Billy. You made it bearable, buddy."

"No sweat, Shawn. Stay in touch, brother."

Shawn got out, stretched in the sunlight, then trotted up the fire escape, invigorated—acutely exhilarated to be free.

He unlocked his back door, then frowned when the door stalled against something inside—banging up against some barricade. Like that, his good mood vanished.

Shawn carefully reached around the door, groping. He felt a chair leg and moved it back, at the same time pushing the door further open.

Broken dishes and drinking glasses were strewn everywhere. His kitchen sink reeked of piss and all of the cabinet doors had been torn off.

His sofa and matching chair had been sliced open; stuffing and batting were scooped out and strewn around the room.

A word was spray-painted on the wall above the ruins of his couch: *Violador.*

The carnage went all the way back to the bedroom. And some items were missing: his television and DVD players, many DVDs. His stereo, armfuls of CDs and his personal computer were gone too.

The sheets and mattresses on his bed were sliced to ribbons.

A pile of shit lay on one of his pillows.

A scrawled note lay on the foot of his ruined bed. "Be glad you weren't here, cocksucker. Not after the way you *joder* that sister, *pendejo*. Even if you didn't kill her, if you treat her better, she be alive still, maybe. This no over, asshole."

Illiterate cocksuckers.

Shawn cursed and went back to his kitchen. His phone had been ripped from the wall. The receiver evidently had been used to smash the glass front of his oven door, as it lay broken across the top of his gas range.

He fished out his cell phone, then saw that it had died without a charge while he had been in jail. Cursing again, Shawn slipped out the back door and clanged down the fire escape, headed back to the police station to file a report.

An old red Isuzu pickup truck rolled by. Two young Latino men sat up front. Three more were sitting in the truck's bed, leaning over the side and gesturing at Shawn. The ones in back wore muscle shirts and matching red bandanas. The driver honked the horn and the Latinos waved at him, screaming things at him in Spanish. A *narcocorrido* blasted from the car stereo. One of the teens raised a baseball bat, pointing at the bat and then pointing at Shawn's head.

The journalist sprinted toward the police station.

TWENTY EIGHT

Tell hauled himself out his command cruiser and locked it up. The ball fields were to be used for the coming Latino Festival, so the teams were crowding in extra summer games.

It was already muggy and it wasn't yet ten A.M. Tell walked over toward the ball diamonds. He looked around again, searching for fresh inspiration. Far off, down the unmowed hill, he could see the tree where Thalia Ruiz's body had been found. A few strands of broken crime scene tape were twisted in the twigs there, twirling in the muggy wind.

The backs of houses fronted the parking lot, but high hedgerows and privacy fences had been positioned to obscure the view of the gravel lot. There would be no helpful hints or clues coming from the homeowners.

Tell wandered over to the biggest of the ball diamonds. A mosquito league game was underway. Some screaming parents sat fanning themselves in the stands. A few solitary old men sipped Coca-Cola from waxed paper cups, watching the game. The bleachers' backs were to the distant field where Thalia's body had been dropped, so no sports spectators were going to be of likely use to Tell.

Apart from the bleachers and backstops—the dingy little dugouts—the only structure on the sports field was a small, cinderblock concession stand. Tell leaned against a fence next to a youngish man who held what looked to Tell to be a fairly high-end video camera with a directional mic mount.

The players went back to their respective dugouts between innings and the man turned off his camera, lowered it and massaged his neck and shoulder.

Tell said, "That looks like too much rig for you to be just a proud parent."

The man glanced over, saw Tell's uniform, and straightened.

"Right. I'm with Sports Images," the stranger said. "Well, I *am* Sports Images. Kind of a one-man band. I record youth sports matches and games on spec. Work with the Kid's Association and local schools' athletic boosters. I burn the games onto DVDs, then sell 'em to proud parents who can't afford a rig like mine. Or I try to sell them. High school and college scouters come around for them once in a while too."

"Making a living?"

"Not bad."

"You usually shoot from this angle?"

"Mostly," the man said, looking curious. "You get each kid's turn at bat . . . maybe grab a few reaction shots of parents in the bleachers behind the batters. And damn few of the kids drive one low and fast and over the head of the pitcher. You know, where they could drive one right into my lens before I could duck."

"Digital camera?"

"Oh yeah."

Tell said, "Can you let me stand there a moment?"

The sports photographer stepped aside. Tell moved into his place. The angle was right. When the batter was absent and the catcher in motion, Thalia's "death tree" was in line of sight, as well as some buildings far behind the tree.

Tell moved back and said, "Please tell me you were standing just there last Friday, late morning."

"I was."

"What time would you say?"

"Oh, maybe ten A.M. to half past noon."

"I need a copy of everything that you shot. It could be evidence in a murder case."

The photographer said, "Oh, *that* case. Sure." He paused. "Usually I get paid thirty bucks a disc."

"I'll pay you. When can I pick it up?"

The man handed Tell a business card with his address. "Drop by anytime after one. I'll have it for you, Chief."

TWENTY NINE

Shawn didn't have the stomach to clean his place, so he got a couple of garbage bags and stuffed them full with the clothes the vandals hadn't slashed, painted or pissed on. He gathered other mementos that survived their raid. He moved them into the newspaper office, along with his one, untouched pillow and a big old ugly afghan that his long-dead grandmother had knitted.

He cleared his desk, and, starved for sleep, climbed atop it and pulled the blanket over himself. The newspaper's only advertising rep—the only other employee who regularly visited the office—might venture in at some point, but likely not for several more hours. Shawn promised himself a couple of hours' sleep, then he'd tackle his apartment. Call a locksmith . . . get his place better secured.

He was stretched out on his hard desk, feet dangling off the end, uncomfortable, but still close to sleep, when the phone rang.

"Yeah?"

"Shawn? Jesus, but you're the scarce one. It's Able Hawk. As you're in the office, I take it that for at least the moment you're still fucking working press?"

"For the moment, yeah, Sheriff. Or I think so."

"Well, get your ass to where I am, kid. This is either one to rebuild your godless career, or one to go out on. In other words, a hot fucking scoop."

"What's going on?"

"Mexican meth lab raid. Come on by my HQ, pronto. We're suiting up now and we'll roll without you. Make it here in ten, and you can go in with me and the second wave."

"On my way."

* * *

The lot was full of trucks, sheriff's cruisers and Scioto County squad cars and vans.

Able Hawk was stepping into a white plastic hazmat suit. "Shawn!" He waved and said, "Scioto County, they're the quadrant specialists in meth lab cleanups." Able winked at Shawn. "Hot as can be, these fuckin' suits, but what can you do? These meth sites, they're like fuckin' Love Canal, like Chernobyl." He checked his watch. "Where the hell is Lyon?"

Shawn accepted a white hazmat suit. "Tell's in on this too?"

"Interagency cooperation, for the record," Able said. "Presupposing the fucking knight errant arrives in time."

Shawn got both legs in the suit and started hiking it up around his torso. "So this stuff is as dangerous as they say?"

"Worse, Shawn. My grandson, he was showin' me this Web site the other night called 'Faces of Meth.' Auschwitz-thin twenty-year-olds with no teeth. They look sixty. Depending on the mix, this shit can contain stuff taken from lithium batteries, rubbing alcohol, lighter fluid, road flare scrapings, phosphorus, kitchen match scrapings, ammonia, gasoline, Drano, peroxide, battery acid, hydrochloric acid and sulfuric acid, among other rancid shit never meant to eat."

Shawn zipped up his protective suit. "Really? All that crap?"

"First wave of cops who dealt with these shit piles?" Able waved a hand and wrinkled his nose. "Unlucky bastards went in with nothing more than rubber gloves." Able Hawk pulled on a big pair of white gloves that went up past his elbows. "Those bastards are now dying in droves from hideous kinds of cancer and lung diseases. Taking these Morales brothers down is doing God's work."

Tell Lyon skidded into the parking lot, his command cruiser kicking up a cloud of dust.

Able Hawk waved. "Get your suit on, Tell. We need to haul ass out of here."

Tell shook his head. "Can't, Able. I really want to, and I appreciate the interagency nod. I really do. But something else is up."

Able scowled. "Thalia?"

"Tenuous, but a possible lead, yes."

"You'll keep me on the page, Lyon?"

"Absolutely."

Able said, "Loan me your notepad and pen." He scrawled down an address. "Let's not bag that interagency beard, huh, Lyon? I still want that cozy patina of New Austin and Horton County law enforcement cooperation on this meth bust. Just to motivate the other municipal chiefs, like I told you a while back. Send one of your brightest lesser lights to that address. Do it in say, thirty minutes so he don't beat us there and get in over his head. Whoever you send can be your proxy. Just don't send that fat one, yeah? Billy? We don't have spare suits that big."

THEN

It was the day Tell had about decided to seek promotion. All he needed was that extra push.

The day seemed determined to give him a shove with both hands.

The morning brought a grisly discovery: a family dead a mile off the roadside.

A man—boy, really—*maybe* nineteen. The young woman found with him might not even be eighteen. A child of perhaps two was with them. Their second child looked newborn, probably out there in the desert scrub. After, the girl would have been in no condition to move, let alone to hike across that alkali wasteland. So they'd all died out there together, lost in the sand and saguaro no man's land between North and South. There was really no saying how long they'd been there, either. The desert too often made casual calculations of time of death . . . treacherous.

Tell radioed in his find. The others wondered how he'd found the bodies so far off the road. He told them the truth; he had indulged a hunch and driven out to see what all those big-winged, desert carrion birds were circling out there in the dust.

Later that afternoon, Tell made another grim discovery. He found a dead man and woman—two elderly Mexicans who died in one another's arms.

The day ended with Tell and Seth getting shot at by some wannabe *narcotrafficantes*.

185

Over shots of tequila, the two Border Patrol agents wondered aloud to one another what brought them back to work each day.

Later, a bit buzzed, Tell palmed into his driveway, pulling his duty SUV into the shade of their rental's attached awning. A jackrabbit scampered off in the glare before he doused the headlights.

In twelve hours, he'd have to be up and behind this same steering wheel, headed back the other direction for another potentially hellish day in the desert.

At the moment, that seemed unthinkable.

He saw two distinct paths before him: quit before he burned out far too early, or let himself be bumped upstairs.

Marita met him at the door. She kissed him hard.

He said, "That's quite a welcome."

Taking his hat from his head and putting it on her own, Marita held up the home pregnancy test, still in its shrink-wrap.

THIRTY

"Thanks for letting me use your DVD player," Tell said. "We don't have one at the station—hell, I'm beginning to think cable TV there is a mistake—and I never got 'round to replacing my own."

Patricia moved on fast from that last admission—not wanting to dwell on the fire that cost Tell his possessions and so much more. She said, trying for a light tone, "So, it's a movie matinee. What's your pleasure? This isn't porn, is it?"

Tell smiled. Patricia, back from morning classes, was wearing a black T-shirt and black sweats. Her hair was drawn back in a pony-tail. He said, "You said that with an air of hopefulness."

"I like some of Vivid's product," she said. "You?"

"I don't know what you're talking about," Tell said.

She smirked. "Sure. So what are we watching instead?"

"A little league game."

"*Ooh, ah!* I'll pop some popcorn, maybe."

"Sounds good."

"I was being sarcastic."

"Oh."

"You said that with an air of disappointment, Tell."

"Sincere disappointment."

Patricia rolled her eyes. "You have beer back at your place?"

"Yeah, but I'm on duty."

"I'm not. So go grab me a beer. I'll make the damned popcorn."

"Sounds good."

Patricia said, "This really a little league game we're going to watch?"

"Afraid so."

"Why?"

"Clues, I hope."

"So go get my beer."

*　*　*

"I never dreamed baseball could be more boring than I already imagined it to be," Patricia said. "But I was so wrong." She was sitting with her legs tucked up under her, an arm resting on his thigh and her head on Tell's shoulder, munching occasionally on popcorn scooped from the big plastic bowl balanced on his lap.

"I'm watching the background," Tell said.

"Hard to focus on that this long in," Patricia said. "How far into this damned game are we?"

"About thirty minutes," Tell said. He sat up suddenly. "Whoa! Go back."

Patricia fiddled with the remote control. She rolled the DVD back several frames, then hit Forward, slowing down the speed. "There," Tell said. "See?"

"Not much."

"Give me the remote."

Patricia scowled. "Already we've come to this—fights over the TV remote."

"Please?"

Tell hit Freeze Frame, then Zoom. He pushed arrows on the remote until the portion of the frame he wanted was centered on the television screen. The portion that interested him was badly pixelated.

"Going to have to get the original from the sports photographer, I guess," he said. "See if some lab can enhance that patch."

Patricia said, "Whatever kind of truck that is, it's red. But that's about all I'm sure of."

"It's a Dodge Ram," Tell said. "Those front ends are very distinctive. And they're big . . . a short man's truck. You know—store-bought muscle. And you'd *need* four-wheel drive to come across that back way."

"Looks like two men," she said. "One skinny, and one short and fat. That thing they're lugging between them," Patricia said, "the body, you think? That's Thalia Ruiz they're carrying?"

"I do think so," Tell said. "And by my estimates, the timing is just what it should be in terms of the body dump."

The blurry figures—with the blocky pixelation-distortion they looked like little murderous Lego men—hauled their load straight to the tree under which Thalia Ruiz had been found. Together, they let something roll out of the black blanket or tarp they'd used for transport.

Afterward, one looked as if he slapped the other on the back. They set back off together toward the red Dodge Ram pickup.

Tell felt Patricia shudder next to him. "My God, how callous they were," she said, disbelieving. "Almost casual. Like business as usual. I'm going to have nightmares tonight."

"If this is the third or fourth woman to die like that, this is as routine as that sort of thing can ever be," Tell said. "And sorry I let you see that."

"It's very disturbing," Patricia said. "But at least not graphic. And I'm sorry for that in a way. I mean, unless you find some CSI-level tech wizard, you're never going to get much identification from that DVD. If it was me on some jury, I'd have a very hard time convicting anyone on the basis of that blurry thing."

"It's a start, though," Tell said. "See those buildings back there, the ones the truck is driving back toward now? There's a nine-foot security fence that runs along the backs of those buildings and right on around them to their fronts. We never really bothered exploring much on that side back there because of the fences. Conventional wisdom on the part of some uniforms at the crime scene was that the killers more likely came in as we had—across the ball diamonds."

"While games were underway?" Patricia shook her head. "No way. And that'd be a hell of a long way to carry a body."

Tell said, "Where were you last Friday morning, Sherlock, when we were bumbling around out there? You up to a trip out to that industrial site, Patricia?"

"I can think of sexier things I'd rather us be doing," she said. "But okay. I get to be an operative again?"

"More like sidekick."

"Is that a promotion?"

"I'd call it that."

* * *

"Outside of going to and from campus, I haven't driven around much in Vale County," Patricia said. "If it's all like this, I guess I haven't missed much."

"This is just the industrial quadrant," Tell said. "It looks like all these sorts of industrial parks look—squalid and weedy."

Tell badged an elderly security guard loafing in a booth at the front entrance of the industrial park. He quizzed the old guard and learned that each of the industrial installations had a back fence that slid open to afford forklift access to the railroad spur for offloading freight cars.

"And the owners of the installations hold the only keys, I'd guess," Tell said.

The codger guard shook his head. "No, also the fire department in case of some explosion or fire or rail derailment or the like. Called a key-holder provision. The Vale County Sheriff's Department also holds sets for other emergency situations."

Tell nodded. "You have security cameras arrayed around the exterior, I take it?"

"'Course."

"You recycle those tapes?"

"Once a week or so."

"Well don't this time, okay? I need access to those tapes from last Friday."

The old guard smiled and pointed a bony finger. "Been wondering when someone would get around to that after that body was dumped out back. But you're kind of out of your jurisdiction, ain'tcha?"

Tell said, "I'll get the proper court orders, don't sweat that. Just don't scrub those tapes for reuse."

"See what I can do," the old guard said. Tell wasn't sure he believed him.

Tell said, "You have keypad codes or some security-card means of monitoring who comes and goes through those gates out back?"

The guard shrugged. "Theoretically, yes. But fact is, we never really figured out how to individually code those cards. So they all have the same access code . . . same identification signature. No way to tell them apart."

"I'll be back with court papers for those tapes," Tell said.

*   *   *

"Going to take at least a couple of hours to get those orders from the judge," Tell said, closing his cell phone.

Patricia squeezed his thigh. "This could solve it all, don't you think?"

"Don't want to jinx it," Tell said. He checked his watch. "I'll drop you off, then I need to go see your friend about the false driver's license you're contracting him for."

"You up for dinner tonight after, Tell? Figured we could eat at my folks' place. The restaurant, I mean. Not their house. They both want to meet you, to spend an evening together."

"Meet the parents already, huh? Okay . . . but let's keep it as tentative as we can, Patricia. Way things are moving right now, this day could get away from me in some crazy ways."

Tell's cell phone buzzed. He checked the caller ID, then opened it and said, "Julie?"

His dispatcher said, "Hi, Chief Lyon? It's Julie."

"What's up, Julie?"

"I have Sheriff Walt Pierce on the other line. He's pretty mad. He insisted I give him your cell number, but I didn't want to do that without your permission."

"I appreciate it, Julie. Patch him through, can you?"

"Will do, Chief Lyon."

Walt Pierce said, "You back-stabbing son of a bitch! Courtesy is you contact me, you come nosing around my county."

"How you doin', Walt?"

"'Cause I'm still focused on protocol, Lyon, I'm lettin' you know to ease back on writs and the like. I got them tapes myself, already. I'll take it from here."

Tell, trying hard to tamp down his anger, said, "Security guard tipped you, did he?"

Walt said, "He's retired sheriff's department. Retired Vale County Sheriff's Department. And he's real loyal. A rarer and rarer fuckin' trait in men."

He cleared his throat, then Tell said, evenly as he could, "Then you'll let me know what you find?"

"What the fuck gave you that idea, Lyon?"

Tell closed his phone without saying good-bye. Then he said, "I fucked that up."

Patricia said, "His voice carried. What an asshole." She reached across the seat and stroked his cheek. "I'm so sorry, Tell."

THEN

They celebrated with dinner out: a little family-owned-and-operated Mexican joint on their own side of the border.

Tell had a margarita on the rocks; Marita allowed herself a virgin daiquiri.

After they thought they'd talked out the baby who'd soon be joining them, they talked about Tell's hellish day. Marita looked stricken when she heard about the shots fired at him.

She made the case for staying and for Tell's seeking promotion.

Many were the nights later when Tell wished he'd dared to muddy the waters as she argued her position. If he'd only played devil's advocate, how else might it have played out?

Tell would eventually come to regret not winning a debate he'd never attempted to start.

Marita switched them back to the earlier topic. "A girl or a boy?"

Tell ran his index finger along the rim of his glass, licked salt off his fingertip. He sipped his drink, weighing his answer, and said, "Honestly? I have no preference."

Marita raised her glass, the straw close to her lips. "None?"

"None whatsoever." He sipped from his glass again. "You?"

She smiled. "Either way it goes, it'll be perfect."

THIRTY ONE

Able had done Shawn a favor when they were talking after the meth-lab raid, jawing as they stripped down and washed off following their tour of the drug shack.

Able told Shawn about a couple of middle-aged Mexican women trained in "custodial rehabilitation" of crime scenes. The Horton County Sheriff's Department hired the women frequently for cleansing publicly owned crime scenes. The department also recommended them to private parties. When some unfortunate ended up murdered, overdosed, "or otherwise suicided"—as Able had put it—in hotel and motel rooms, they were the ones called. When someone died or got themselves killed in rental units or homes that realtors thought they might still move despite the shadow of violent crime looming over their latest "location, location, location" listing, they called in the Mexican women.

Shawn contacted the specialized cleaning crew, opened his place up to them, then sprinted down the back alleys to the newspaper office to write up his account of the raid of the Morales brothers' meth-cookery farmhouse while it was all still fresh in his mind.

After he had filed his report with the police regarding the destruction at his apartment, Shawn had sent his publisher an e-mail indicating his exoneration in the Ruiz murder. He'd never received any word back from corporate. Shawn figured, then, he was still on the payroll and free to resume reporting.

Shawn finished his story, read it over once on screen, then printed a hard copy and read it again, finding four more typos. He saved his changes and shut down his computer.

The phone rang and Shawn made the mistake of answering. It was the newspaper chain's human resources specialist. She wished Shawn well on his release from jail. Then she reminded Shawn—informed him, really, because he didn't remember it in his contract—of a morals clause. Because of the "licentious nature" of his "recent personal publicity," he was being placed on a ninety-day probation. "Any similar violation or other performance issues" would result in his immediate termination. It felt to Shawn like a first feint toward inevitable firing.

Shawn thanked her as cordially as he could manage, and hung up.

Maybe his meth-raid package would win him back some face with his employers.

He locked up the newspaper office and walked back to his home to see how the Mexican women had done cleaning his apartment.

As he walked along Main Street back to his loft, nobody waved back at Shawn. None of the barbers, the butchers or the hardware store staff as much as nodded at him as he passed by their storefronts. Shawn felt stomach acid burning the back of his throat. Maybe Lyon was right; maybe he needed to get the hell out of town. Out of the goddamn *state*.

At least his loft was neat and orderly. It smelled strongly of bleach and ammonia—the smell so intense it burned Shawn's eyes and nose. It stank of chemicals, but of the kind his brain had been trained to think of as "clean." He found comfort in that.

Shawn called a locksmith and had a new deadbolt installed. When the locksmith left, Shawn manhandled his ruined mattress to the fire escape and tipped it over the handrail into the dumpster below.

Then he locked up with his new set of keys and padded down the fire escape, planning a run to the Walmart to buy a new mattress, sheets and pillows. Between those new bedding accessories, the locksmith's and cleaner's fees—not to mention his lawyer's bill for consultation via phone—it was going to be a tight rest of the year, Shawn figured. And that was another reason, to his mind, to take extra pains to retain his current job as long as possible.

As he stormed down the fire escape, Shawn thought about calling Patricia, then decided against it. The fickle bitch hadn't reached out to him when he was in jail and facing possible rape and murder charges. So fuck Patricia.

Shawn sensed motion under the fire escape stairs. It was probably a cat, he thought. Then something grabbed his ankles through the spaces between the lower steps and sent Shaw toppling onto the hood of his car.

Hands gripped his arms and fingers knotted in his hair. His face was slammed against the hot metal of his car's hood. Shawn's nose broke and began streaming blood. Then he was lifted up and thrown down again. His hands were held behind him so he couldn't cushion his own impact.

Latino voices snarled words at Shawn: *violador*, *cabrón* and *pendejo*.

A leg swept behind Shawn's legs, hitting the backs of his knees. That sent Shawn sprawling backward onto his ass.

There were five of them, each wearing identical red bandanas—some dumb-ass gang colors, Shawn guessed. None of them could be older than twenty-two or twenty-three. They circled around Shawn and one said, "This is for Thalia Ruiz, cocksucker."

Then they began kicking Shawn, and pummeling him with their fists.

Shawn tasted blood. The cartilage in his nose crunched again and he gagged on his own blood. Ribs cracked and he tried to roll tight into a ball, torn between using his hands to protect his head or his genitals. He settled on his head after their kicks to his crotch stopped registering.

Shawn surrendered, collapsing onto his back, spread-eagle and defenseless. One of the gangbangers kicked him hard in the crotch again, and Shawn felt like he might have a heart attack. Two more lifted Shawn, leaned him up against his car. Shawn saw one lift a ball bat. He thought, *I'm going to end up brain damaged or dead from that fucking bat.*

Shawn's field of vision was narrowed now, blocked on one side by the intrusion of his broken, swollen nose. His eyes and eyebrows were similarly swollen. There was a gust of air. His teeth cracked and splintered as the bat struck him in the mouth. Something in Shawn's jaw popped. Instinctively, afraid he might choke on them, Shawn began spitting out teeth and teeth fragments.

His attackers let him go and he fell back onto the pavement, still spitting out teeth.

One of them said in English, "Get his teeth and pitch 'em. Don't want the *pendejo* finding some dentist to save them."

One stooped down and began plucking teeth off Shawn's bloodied shirt. Shawn couldn't raise his own arms to try to stop them. He heard the one close to him say, "*Guácala*," then heard small things fall distantly across the parking lot. He was still gagging on his own blood as it gushed down the back of his throat from his flattened and ruptured nasal passages and the holes where his teeth had been.

The attacker who'd spoken English squatted down next to Shawn and whispered into his bloody, torn ear, "My brother, he worked for the Morales brothers, so you fucked him *too*." He spit in Shawn's face. He snarled, "*This* is for Javier." Then he slammed the bat down on Shawn's right kneecap.

THIRTY TWO

Tell changed into jeans and a polo shirt. He drove out in his SUV to keep Patricia's appointment with the man paid to fashion her false ID. Robbie Robertson on the car stereo: "Somewhere Down the Crazy River."

The stipulated rendezvous site was a Chipotle on New Austin's east side. Patricia had been instructed to look for a young man with a red and blue backpack.

Slipping off his sunglasses, Tell stepped out of the afternoon heat into the headache-inducing cold of the darkened restaurant, his eyes slow to adjust to the dimmer light. The smell of seasoned meat and chicken reminded Tell he hadn't eaten since early morning.

A young man, maybe twenty-two or twenty-three, sat eating an overstuffed burrito and sipping from a sweating bottle of Negra Modelo. A red and blue backpack was positioned on the chrome table in front of his food basket.

Tell approached casually then sat down across from the young man, who looked up, startled.

"Easy," Tell said. He flashed his badge. "Go ahead and eat up. We'll just have a chat. But I would like to see some identification."

The young man put down his sauce-dripping burrito. Looking sick, he leaned onto his left butt cheek and pulled his wallet out of his right rear pocket. He slid out a plastic card and held it between thumb and forefinger.

Tell glanced the card over, then slipped it into his wallet. "That thing's as bad as the ones you sell to the undocumented workers. Let me see your *real* driver's license."

Frowning, the stranger passed Tell another wafer of plastic. This one was properly thick and rigid. Tell read aloud, "Trent Paris, age twenty-two." He whistled low. "Okay, Trent, how many illegals you suppose you've sold fake driver's licenses to this year?"

"This isn't what it looks like, Officer."

"It's exactly what it looks like, Trent. So let's not piss away one another's time with the lame dodges. You making these pieces of crap out of your own home? What've you got, a home computer, some special printer and a lamination machine? What's the cheap machinery behind these things?"

That question drew a stare.

Tell leaned across the table. "I asked you a fucking question, Trent. You best answer me. What you're involved in could cost you ten, twenty years in prison and fines you can't fathom or pay in this lifetime. Faking social security cards is a federal offense, and with the new terrorism laws, a very high-end felony. Time you got out of jail, you'd qualify for AARP and Golden Buckeye cards. I might be persuaded to treat this as something less than a major crime. But I'll only do that, Trent, if I'm satisfied that your cooperation is full and cheerful. I put it to you again: Are you making these in your home?"

"I don't make them. I'm, like, the middleman, yeah? I take the meetings, take the cash and pass along the product."

"Even you must see how shitty these things are," Tell said. "Your 'product' sucks."

Trent went silent again. He mustered up some courage and drank deeply of his Mexican beer. Tell snagged a couple of stray tortilla chips from Trent's plastic food basket.

Talking while munching the chips, Tell said, "You're just hell-bent on making me charge you all the way up, aren't you, Trent? You want to leave jail a fifty-year-old man?"

The younger man continued to sit silently, staring at his food basket, playing stoic.

Tell kicked Trent's foot under the table, getting his attention again. He said, "Do I need to enumerate for you, Trent, all the charges I can lay against you, state and federal? It's not like you're selling these things so kids can buy beer. You're faking national residency qualification. Homeland Security and the FBI are all over that kind of shit."

Trent just looked back at him—scared, but silent.

Now Tell was getting pissed off. He said, "Okay, Trent. Put your fucking hands flat on the table. I'm going to cuff you, and then I'm going to parade you out of here like the world's lowest child molester. Now stand the fuck up."

"No, I—"

"What did you say?"

"Someone else makes the fake licenses," Trent said softly.

"Who? Give me a name that checks out and I'll see you walk on a misdemeanor."

"Amos Sharp." Trent sat back, staring at his lap. "Amos Sharp makes them."

The name mildly resonated for Tell, but he couldn't yet put it in context. He said, "I'm going to need more from you, Trent. I'm going to need much more."

THIRTY THREE

Patricia sat in the emergency room, waiting for the promised doctor who would update her on Shawn's condition.

She heard a clearing of a throat and looked up, expecting a physician.

Able Hawk said, "Don't expect you want much to lay eyes on me after the other night. But that was business, *señorita*."

Nodding, she scooted over and Able sat down on the couch beside her. "A doctor is supposed to be by soon to talk about Shawn's condition," Patricia said.

Able nodded. He hesitated, then said, "I . . . well, I actually just left Shawn's room. I've seen him."

Patricia said, "They wouldn't let me in."

"I had to question Shawn before they put him under. Try to get some information so we can catch the vicious bastards who did this to him." Able leaned over a little closer toward Patricia. "Chief Lyon been by? By rights, this'd really be his case."

Patricia looked at the floor, feeling her own blush. "I'm not sure he even knows yet. One of his men was by earlier. At least, I saw him go in, but then he left very quickly."

Able grunted. "Was it Billy Davis? I mean, was it a big boy?"

"Heavy-set, yes," Patricia said. "How is Shawn, Sheriff? They won't tell me anything."

"He'll live, thank Christ. But he's got a long, hard road ahead. And a brand new face. No concussion, which is a miracle given the beating he sustained. So no brain damage, probably. But he's got two fractured eye sockets. His palate is fractured and his jaw might be broken. He lost most of his teeth. And they shattered his kneecap. Docs seem to think he'll need a leg brace from now on. Maybe a cane, or even a walker. And he's got a shitload of broken ribs."

"Oh my God! And his teeth? What happened to his teeth?"

"They hit him in the mouth with a baseball bat. That's likely as not what broke his jaw and cracked his palate."

"But he can talk?"

"Not so good now. And when I left they were getting ready to wire his mouth shut. Once it heals, they said they can fit him for dentures or bridges or implants. Whatever the guy's insurance will cover. I'm just sick for Shawn. They fucked him up and I mean good."

"Who did it, Sheriff? Who are 'they'?"

"At least five young Mexican males. Shawn indicated they drove by him earlier today, after they trashed his place. They drove by him in a red Isuzu pickup, waving the bat they beat him with later."

"But why?"

"They told Shawn they were avenging Thalia Ruiz. That was part of it. But one of them was also stupid enough to mention a brother. This Mexican said his brother, 'Javier,' worked for the Morales brothers. The Morales clan, well, they are meth cookers. Or they used to be. We raided their place a few hours back. Shawn went along to cover the raid. He wrote a story for next week's paper just before he was beaten. Seems the Moraleses, or their cronies, spotted Shawn at the raid. Just one more stick in their eye, I guess. At the end of the day, I think these animals just love hurting people and any excuse will do."

Patricia heard footfalls on tile. A thirtyish-looking doctor took a seat next to her. He said, "You're a friend of Shawn O'Hara's?"

She nodded, twisting around to face the doctor and showing Able Hawk her back. "Yes. Can I please see him?"

"Not today," the doctor said. "We've just put Mr. O'Hara into an induced coma. There's been some swelling of his brain in the past half hour. Nothing life threatening at this point, but given his other traumas, it's kindest and prudent to keep him under for now."

Patricia felt queasy. She tried to imagine what he must look like. She said, "What are Shawn's long-term prospects?"

"Generally good. Conditionally hopeful. He may have a damaged kidney that will eventually bear extraction. There was also severe trauma to his genitals. Shawn will also require extensive oral reconstruction. I'm fairly certain his speech has been permanently impaired. It's a little too soon to tell, but we may also have to replace his right knee. Either way, running, or any kind of strenuous sports involving his legs—skating or skiing, for instance—are off the table forever."

"My God," Patricia said, unbelieving. Then she said, "Shawn's a writer. Did they hurt his hands?"

"No," the doctor said. "Some cuts and scrapes and mild bruising from where Shawn evidently tried to use his hands to protect himself, but that's all. Good thing too. With all the packing in his mouth, and with his jaw wired shut, he'll be communicating through written notes or keyboards for the next several days."

"How long will you keep him?"

"At least several weeks, I'm guessing."

"When I can see him?"

"Leave a number with the nurses at the desk. We'll call you when we bring him back around."

Able stood and offered Patricia a hand. She accepted it and he steadied her as she stood. "You going to be okay, Ms. Maldonado?"

"I'll be fine, Sheriff. It's Shawn who is suffering. Just find who did this and make them pay."

"That's my job," Able said.

THEN

Sofia Gómez and daughter Thalia drifted from the party room out onto a balcony overlooking a shaded lagoon. They were both a little tipsy.

Sophia's friend's daughter had married a white . . . one with *prospects*. The wedding reception was held at the clubhouse of a very exclusive golf club—one at which Sofia doubted she could even get a cleaning job. Sophia hated to think what Thalia must be thinking; the jealousy she must feel for this other young Latina's new life.

Neither Sofia nor Thalia had ever had much champagne and now both had sampled too much. Tongues were loosened, inhibitions lowered. Better judgment was dulled.

Searching her mother's face, Thalia said, "Was it worth it, mother? Do you still find it all was worth it? Coming here, I mean. All those we lost crossing . . . ?"

Thalia's dark eyes were smoldering, accusing. Sofia actually flinched at the edge in her daughter's voice. Thalia pressed harder. "Mother, *answer*. Is this life truly better? We barely make rent. Evelia's grades are suffering because of all the illegals coming in. My job—all that I can get—is terrible. Mother, *was* it worth it?" She reached over and squeezed Sophia's arm. *"Is it?"*

Sofia kept staring at her hands, into her drink with its rising column of bubbles.

"Mother . . ."

She shrugged, still unable to meet her daughter's eyes. "You can't remember how it was back there, Thalia. They was no money there, either."

"But was it worse? Truly worse?" Thalia sighed at her mother's silence. "Mother, stop staring at your hands. Was it worse? Is this *truly* better?"

Despite her daughter's pleas, Sofia never answered her questions.

Putting words to it, admitting all those deaths were for nothing? For Sofia, that was unthinkable.

THIRTY FOUR

He was holding Trent Paris in the cell recently vacated by Shawn. Tell hadn't yet allowed his prisoner to make a phone call, but he had offered to contact an attorney for Trent if the young man had one in mind.

Tell had been given a report of Shawn's beating and condition when he reached Billy Davis at the hospital. He'd called to order Billy back to sit as guard so Tell could go back out and find this partner of Trent's, Amos Sharp.

Julie walked back to the holding cell area and said, "Chief Lyon, you have a couple of visitors. Mrs. Sofia Gómez and Evelia Ruiz."

Tell said, "'Ruiz'? Related to Thalia?"

"Her daughter, yes, Chief Lyon. Sofia Gómez is Thalia Ruiz's mother."

"Billy here yet, Julie?"

"Just radioed that he's two minutes out."

"Great. Send him straight back here to watch our prisoner," Tell said. "And go ahead and escort our visitors to my desk, would you, Julie?"

* * *

The only picture that Tell had seen of Thalia Ruiz was an unremarkable, poorly lit driver's license photo that he'd called up from the DMV computer system. Thalia was unsmiling in that impromptu portrait. It was hard to make any judgments regarding her looks. Yet the older woman seated beside Tell's desk was unmistakably Thalia's mother. And the little girl—black hair and black eyes—was beautiful. She unsettled Tell, suggesting his dead daughter's unspoiled features just enough to hurt.

"Would you care for coffee, *señora?*"

Sofia shook her head. "I've come for a report of your progress finding the man who violated and murdered my daughter. I see you on TV talking about Thalia's murder, and making statements to the newspapers, but you've never spoken with me. Why is that?"

Her eyes came to rest on the photos of Marita and Claudia that Tell had had copied from the ones at home and had recently placed on his desk. She said, "Your family?"

"Yes."

"They are very beautiful."

"So is your granddaughter, Mrs. Gómez."

She nodded. "About this inquiry, Officer. Why have you not come to me?"

"My department is working closely with the county sheriff's department to solve this crime—combining resources so we can do more than either of our departments might working alone. I know that Able Hawk has—"

"Have you a suspect, *Jefe?*"

"Possibly." Tell said, "Listen, I'll tell you all I can, but would you mind if I asked Julie, who let you in, to distract your granddaughter? Evelia shouldn't hear this."

"That is very thoughtful of you. Yes, please."

Tell called to Julie. She turned from the radio desk. "Yes, Chief Lyon?"

Tell fished out his wallet and pulled out a ten-dollar bill.

"Julie, I need about fifteen or twenty minutes with Mrs. Gómez alone. I'll cover the radios and phone. Could you please take Evelia here next door to Graeters and buy her an ice cream cone or sundae? And treat yourself."

"Sure, Chief Lyon." Julie held out a hand and Evelia slid off her grandmother's knee and took the dispatcher's hand and waved once to her grandmother, unsmiling.

"You behave, Eve," Sofia Gómez said. She turned back to Tell and said, "I'm concerned that time has passed but there has been no word of progress, Chief Lyon. I'm worried that nothing is really being done. Perhaps this is because Thalia was Mexican."

Tell raised a hand. "No. Don't even think that, please. Your daughter was a citizen of the United States and under my protection. I'm committed to finding the ones who did this and seeing that they pay for your daughter's death."

"And what of Sheriff Hawk who you and the papers say you're working with—the one they call *El Gavilan*? He came to tell me of my daughter's death. He came to make me look at a photo of a tattoo to confirm it was Thalia who was dead. I've not seen or heard from that man since."

"Able Hawk considered Thalia to be his good friend," Tell said. "He told me he spoke to her each day before lunch. He went to the diner where she worked to visit with her. Able Hawk looked forward to seeing Thalia each morning."

"Thalia spoke of him too," Sofia said. "And yet, days have passed and I've not heard a word from this friend of my daughter's about his attempts to find her killer."

"Sheriff Hawk is taking this *very* personally," Tell said. "I can see he's sincere about that. We both mean to find who did this and make them pay."

"The reporter who was in custody—the one Thalia spent her last night with—it's been on the radio that he was beaten nearly to death. Did that have something to do with my daughter?"

"Only in so far as the ones who attacked the reporter were male Latinos. My officers report that before they beat him, his attackers told Mr. O'Hara he was going to be punished for sleeping with your daughter and then sneaking out on her the next morning. For leaving her vulnerable to what came next."

Mrs. Gómez seemed to consider that. Then she said, "I hope I'm wrong in my belief that you will devote more time—achieve faster results—in finding those that hurt that reporter than the man who killed my daughter."

"Your daughter's murder is my number one priority," Tell said. "I know it is Able Hawk's, as well."

The older woman looked again at the pictures on Tell's desk. "I'm sorry, Chief Lyon. Sorry for implying some racism on your part. Clearly that would not be so in your case. Your wife and daughter are beautiful. Where is your wife from?"

Tell smiled. "San Diego. Marita's family was originally from Veracruz."

Sofia Gómez smiled back. "So were we." Sofia told Tell the story of her family's crossing. Told him of the loss of Thalia's grandmother and the others. When she finished the tale of their ill-fated border crossing, Sofia said, "But I'm told you were Border Patrol before coming here to be *jefe*. I'm sure that story of what happened to mine is nothing particularly striking to you. I'm sure you've seen the same, perhaps worse, there in the desert doing your other job."

"It never stops affecting you," Tell said. "Not unless you are truly dead inside."

"How old is your daughter, Chief Lyon?"

"She was three when that picture was taken," Tell said. He looked at the pictures. "My family was murdered last year. Both are unsolved killings. So I take what happened to your daughter very personally. I won't let your daughter's death be like those of my family—unsolved. We *will* get these people, I promise you that."

"What happened to your family, Chief? If that is not too personal a question?"

"After the story you shared with me? No, I owe you a hard story of my own." So Tell told Sofia of the killing of his wife and daughter.

She shook her head sadly afterward. "And they were never caught—their killers?"

"No," Tell said. "It was impossible to make a case against them. They were very careful in their planning and execution to see to that. They were paid killers. Very professional."

"But you knew who they were?"

"No, not for certain."

That was a lie.

Tell had known well enough. His cousin, Chris, left his own family in Ohio and came to California alone—or *nearly* alone—for Marita's and Claudia's funerals. Chris had brought along a "special friend" . . . some dead-eyed Scots mercenary. He was another of Chris's myriad, mysterious acquaintances collected during the years that Chris and Tell had drifted apart.

The three of them, accompanied by two of Tell's Border Patrol confreres and a retired Texas Ranger, had gone out in the desert and sought out Tell's family's killers. They left the bodies of the Coyotes for the real coyotes; for the ants and big, ragged-winged desert birds.

"I'm sorry for your sake you didn't know, that you couldn't avenge your family," Sofia Gómez said, looking Tell hard in the eye. "I want my baby's killers to pay. I want them to die for what they've done."

"Able Hawk has already told me he wishes to seek the death penalty for them."

"You said something, Chief. You were speaking of my daughter's murder and you said, 'the ones' who did it. You talked as though you're sure that there is more than one who killed my Thalia. And later you vowed to me, 'We will get *these people*.'"

Tell smiled. "You're a close listener. And you're a clever woman, Mrs. Gómez."

"Do you have someone you suspect?"

"In a manner of speaking. First tell me, do you know if your daughter knew anybody who drives a big red pickup truck? A Dodge Ram, perhaps?"

"I don't. I know nobody who drives one, either." She sat forward. "Why do you ask about that car?"

"I can't speak in detail about this, even to you, Mrs. Gómez. Not until I know more. All I will say is that it's possible there were some camera images that captured the dropping of your daughter's body in that field where she was found. Two men in a big red pickup truck."

"Mexican men?"

"No. It's impossible to say for certain right now, but I think whites."

"Please tell me more."

"I can't yet. I'm sorry. I have to have the film looked at by specialists and then I may know more. And I need to talk to Sheriff Hawk. He's not aware of this development yet; I haven't had time to fill him in. But we are working closely together. We mean to bring the killers to justice, Mrs. Gómez. I swear to you we will do everything in our power to do that."

"Within the law?"

"Within the law."

"Thank you for seeing me. I'm grateful for this talk, *Jefe*."

"I wish we had more time to talk," Tell said. "But I have something else I need to be doing now."

Sofia squeezed his arm—surprising strength in that old hand of hers. "Thank you for sharing the story of your family. You're a strong man to come through and continue doing what you do. You're a good man. I'm glad you're the one working for my Thalia."

Tell offered her his arm and she slipped her arm through his. He said, "I'll walk you next door to collect your granddaughter."

"The other sheriff, Walter Pierce? I do not like him, Chief Lyon. He came to my house and searched Thalia's room. He took her sheets, her unwashed clothes."

"He was looking for DNA then." Tell wanted to kick himself. He should have taken a more active hand in terms of going over to the Gómez house the night of the murder instead of interrogating all those baseball players and fans who saw nothing. As simple procedure, he might have thought to have had Thalia's bed clothes bagged. Now more possible trace evidence was denied him and Able.

Sofia Gómez stopped and took her arm from Tell's. "My daughter did not bring men in my house. She wasn't like that. There was never a man with her in that room. But perhaps if she had done that, she'd be alive still."

"You can't think like that, Mrs. Gómez."

"I can't control my own thoughts anymore. I can't *believe* anymore. You must know what it is like. Remember when we still had God? What do we have when we no longer have Him?"

"The ones we love. The ones who matter to us."

"And the ones who killed my daughter?"

Tell took her arm again, slipped it through his own and closed his other hand over her arm. "You have that little girl to care for.

You have to protect her. Let me see to finding and punishing those men."

"Better than I did my own, one hopes. Evelia, and my niece, who might as well be a child," Sofia said. "She's twenty-two and already many months pregnant without me knowing for certain the man responsible."

"If, in the days ahead, there's anything I might do . . . ?"

"Thank you, Chief. Thank you, *Jefe*. We'll make it. But I'm not young, and Evelia is."

"And your niece? You said there is no man there to take responsibility for her condition?"

"Maybe a man," Sofia said. "A young man. Hardly more than a boy himself, really, if my suspicions are correct."

"You believe he's the father, then?"

"Possibly. Probably. He's a student. A serious boy, in that way."

"Perhaps he'll do the right thing. Perhaps I could help you by talking to him."

Sofia began walking again, headed on in the direction of the ice cream parlor. "Perhaps he will do this on his own. Perhaps Amos is Luisa's best hope."

That got Tell's attention. "Amos? That's the young man's name?"

"*Sí*. Amos Sharp," Sofia said. "He's Able Hawk's grandson. So you see, again, this Hawk, he disappoints me. With all the connections between our families, you think he could find time to tell me about what is happening with the investigation of my daughter's murder." Sofia shrugged at Tell. "You're distracted, Chief Lyon. I see it in your face. This is pointless gossip to you, I'm sure. They are discreet and only ever together at my house, but Hawk must be blind not to know what's going on between that boy and Luisa." Sofia smiled bitterly and shook her head. "And you said you have to be somewhere else. I can go the rest of the way myself."

"You're sure?"

"Of course," she said. "I trust you to do right by my Thalia. And to keep me informed as you can. But this Able Hawk? As I've said to you, more than once, if he was such a good friend of Thalia's, would he not have come to her funeral? Would there not be some discussion, or gesture, toward the resolving of this matter of his grandson, Amos, and my niece, Luisa? Amos and Able Hawk live under the same roof, after all."

"I can't speak to that, *señora*. But I do trust Hawk and I believe your daughter mattered to him. That she still matters."

"I really don't expect you to speak to any of that, *Jefe*."

"When you see Julie, my dispatcher, please tell her the radios and phones are unmanned back at headquarters."

Sofia Gómez watched, curious as Tell Lyon ran back toward the police station.

THIRTY FIVE

Tell got out onto the road, then called back to the station house on his cell phone. "Julie, I need Able Hawk's home phone number and address."

Julie said, "I have Sheriff Hawk's cell phone number, Chief Lyon."

"Right. Good. But I need his home number, Julie. And I need it right now."

* * *

Tell rolled to a stop in front of Able Hawk's house. He pulled curbside and looked it over. It was a widower's house: a sprawling, two-story wood structure at least a year past a needed painting. And it was too big for two people. A deep front porch was cluttered with wicker chairs. The chair pads were faded and rotting from not having been stored for winter. There looked to be another living quarters sitting atop the too-large, unattached garage.

Tell punched in Able's home phone number then looked back up at the house. Three rings, then a pickup. The voice was a young male's. "Yeah?"

Tell said, "This Amos Sharp?"

"Yeah. Who's this?"

"New Austin police chief Tell Lyon—"

"My grandfather said you might take me on as an intern," Amos said, cutting Tell off. "But that's a few months out. My break from school, I mean."

"It's not like that, Amos," Tell said. "This is official business. I need to talk to you. This is about the bogus documents you're manufacturing and selling to undocumented workers. I'm parked in front of your place. This could go a lot of different ways, son. And your being Able Hawk's grandson makes it all the more complicated. We need to talk this out. See where we end up. Like I said, I'm parked out front. I want you to hang up the phone and come straight out here. Don't get ideas about calling your grandfather first. Nothing cute like that."

Tell hesitated, then said, "Just to underscore how bad an idea trying to tip Able would be, I'm going to tell you I know about Luisa and her baby. And I suspect, in that, I'm way ahead of your grandfather. Now come on out and let's take a ride together, Amos. Just to talk."

"Be right there," Amos said. Like Shawn before him, he sounded like a scared little boy.

* * *

"Amos, I'm going to be honest with you," Tell said, "and I hope you'll be just as honest back. I don't know what I want to do here. I know what I should do, up to a point, but even that leaves me uncertain in some key ways. Why are you making these false identification cards? Is it for the money?"

Amos Sharp looked out the window. He seemed fascinated by a barley field whipping by on his side. "Sure," Amos said. "For the money. Yeah, it was for the money."

"You're a lousy liar, Amos. You said your grandfather mentioned something about interning with me. You really want to be a cop?"

"More than anything."

"You're never going to get there if I press this with the cards. That's a career killer, son, and that's on the light side. What you're doing is a felony . . . a two-decade bounce, minimum, if you're convicted." Tell's stomach growled; he checked his watch. "You hungry, Amos?"

"I was until you called," Amos said. "But not now."

"Me neither, I guess. Your grandfather, Able—you're doing this for him, aren't you?"

"Best just arrest me, Chief Lyon. Charge me."

"I'm not sure I want to do that, Amos. Maybe I want answers more than an arrest. My notion is that your grandfather hit on this brilliant, if misdirected, Machiavellian and *very* illegal notion of providing the false IDs to Horton County's illegals. Able set up a low-cost and wicked way to control his own undocumented workers problem. And damned if it's not working like a charm."

"Not from where I sit," Amos said.

"No," Tell said. "Not since I know now."

"So what do you want to do to me, Chief Lyon?"

"Stop it, Amos. Just stop it cold. I'll talk to your grandfather and persuade him that he needs to go along. I know what it's going to cost him, and a dark part of me actually admires his cleverness. But this is very wrong. And just as I did, someone will eventually figure it out and they'll act on it. Say, the INS, or maybe some American Civil Liberties Union lawyer. The ACLU is hot to burn your granddad down for his treatment of illegals. If the ACLU got wind of this, you and your grandfather would be destroyed by those bastards. You'll both go to prison if anyone catches you and prosecutes. Prison for a cop is a place worse than hell."

"I'm not sure Granddad will be able to accept this. He doesn't like being ordered to do anything."

Tell shook his head. "He has no choice, this time. Fact is, if I figured it out, and did it after just a few days in town, it's just a matter of time—and not much time, I'm afraid—until someone else does too."

"You'd really let me walk on this?"

"I want a promise from you you'll stop," Tell said. "Promise you'll stop *now*."

Amos put out a hand. "I promise."

Tell hesitated, then shook Amos's hand. He palmed the wheel, making a U-turn and heading back toward town. They were in Vale County now, and Tell didn't want to further provoke Walt Pierce by driving around the bastard's county in a New Austin cruiser. He said, "There's this other thing. You *are* the father of Luisa's baby?"

Amos couldn't look at Tell again. He stared out the window at the industrial park this time.

"Luisa is illegal," Amos said. "She came over from Juarez like so many do now—moved in with family that's legal to buy time to get herself set up here. The quickest way to do that, is, well, if she's pregnant with my baby . . ."

"I get the logic—and the law—so far as it goes," Tell said. "Able doesn't know? Doesn't know about the baby? Doesn't know about Luisa?"

"No."

"You need to tell him about that too," Tell said. "From what I understand, Luisa's not too long away from delivering."

"No, a few more weeks, maybe."

Tell said, "Did Thalia know about you two? About you and her cousin?"

"She knew. She was the only one who knew."

"No, Luisa's aunt knows too. What was Thalia like?"

"Nice. I liked her a lot. But it was hard for her, with the little girl and not much money. And she never really got over her husband dying like he did. He was blown to pieces in an explosion at the propane plant. Static electricity, they said. One spark while he was filling a container. Gone."

Tell said, "There's no good way to put this, and with your career ambitions, I'm going to trust you'll take this question in the spirit of investigation: Thalia, did she spend the night with a lot of men?"

"God, no," Amos said. "That thing with the reporter, so far as I know from things Granddad said and shared, that was a fluke. I think she was out alone, she was drinking, and maybe she thought this reporter was a better guy than he turned out to be. It was a fluke." Amos hesitated, then said, "Wouldn't surprise me if Shawn O'Hara was the first man Thalia had sex with since her husband got blown up."

"Okay then," Tell said. "Thanks for the fill. I think we're through here. Just need to decide between us which one of us is going to talk to Able about this identification card mess. And about Luisa."

"You really going to let me walk on this thing with the cards?"

"Keep your promise and, yeah, I mean to." Tell's cell phone rang. He checked the caller ID panel: it was the number for the Horton County coroner. The coroner had keyed in "911." Code for an emergency.

Tell said, "I have to return a call." He pulled curbside in case he needed to take down any notes and called up Doctor Parks.

Parks said, "Thank God you're prompt, Lyon. This is another thing I'm not giving you, Tell. You alone? Nobody else in earshot?"

"One second."

Tell said to Amos, "Stay here, son. I need to take this in private." Tell got out and parked his ass on the hood. "Go ahead, Doc."

"Some information leaked my way. A couple flunkies were having conversation over handball with some opposite numbers in Vale County's coroner's office. Seems Walt Pierce conducted a search of Thalia Ruiz's bedroom. They've got some DNA from her sheets. Semen, hairs. So Pierce is getting a warrant. Like Shawn O'Hara, it's another screwball thing. The suspect Pierce has identified is not a repeat offender, so the DNA isn't in the system that way. Pierce's suspect went through a Junior Police Academy camp a couple of summers ago. Something Vale County runs for aspiring young cop-hopefuls. The participants all got typed and their DNA samples just never quite got tossed."

Tell's mouth was dry. His hands were moist. He could already see where this was going. Parks said, "You're not going to fucking believe who Walt Pierce is about to arrest and question in the murder of Thalia Ruiz."

Tell knew. But it was better to let Parks say it, in case it became an issue later. Parks said, "Pierce is going after Amos Sharp. He's Able Hawk's grandson. Hawk is going to go apeshit, Lyon. This is going to be fucking Armageddon."

Tell said, "We need to move fast, then. You going to break the news to Hawk, or should I?"

Parks said, "I think it could cause trouble for me later if I'm not the one to give Hawk the heads-up on this."

"Good thinking," Tell said. "Do it *now*. Thanks for the tip, Doc."

Tell closed his phone. *Jesus Christ.*

He walked around and slipped back behind the wheel of his cruiser. He said, "Amos, I've got another personal question for you." Tell's voice sounded strange to himself. He could tell it unsettled Amos too. Tell said, "You and Luisa made a decision to have a baby to enhance her prospects of dodging deportation. You must love her very much to do that. Have you two ever used condoms?"

"Not in at least nine months," Amos said, red-faced.

"Right. Anyway, you obviously couldn't risk being alone with her at your place. They don't make many cars big enough to have sex in anymore. Where'd you two go to be alone? It's important kid, or I wouldn't ask you a question like this. Where'd you go to have sex with Luisa?"

Amos said, "Her aunt works three days a week. So did Thalia. Luisa sleeps on a cot." He looked at his rings. "We used Thalia's bed."

"Thalia know?"

Amos looked ashamed. "Not unless Luisa told her."

"Did Luisa tell you that Sheriff Pierce has recently searched Thalia's room . . . took away her bedding?"

Tell saw it in Amos's face when it clicked. "Oh, God."

"Warrant's being issued now, Amos. Get out of the car, son."

Amos hauled himself out. "What are you going to do? Hold me for fucking Pierce to come and get?" The boy looked crazed.

"No, Amos," Tell said, a hand on his shoulder. "I'm going to arrest you for manufacturing and selling fraudulent identification cards. I'm sorry for what this is going to do to you, kid. Sorry for what it's going to do to your ambitions. But you, of all people, in the hands of Walt Pierce? That's too much potential leverage over your grandfather. Get in the backseat, Amos. I'm not going to cuff you, but get in the backseat, son."

THEN

It was the night before his last day in the field as a Border Patrol agent. Monday morning would find him starting his new desk position.

Tell had cranked up the AC in the house—the new position came with a significant raise, so they could splurge a little at last. The summer heat was unbearable, the humidity insane as the clouds were swollen with threatened rain that wasn't yet falling. All that heat and humidity was hardest on Marita, now eight months pregnant. The heat had been making the nights even longer for his wife as she struggled to find a way to position herself in their bed, wrapped around a long, puffy pregnancy pillow.

Marita shivered and snuggled in tighter against Tell. She pulled the covers up snug around her chin. "It'll be safer, won't it? No more Coyotes or drug traffickers to take shots at you? No more having to look for bodies out there? *God*, it *has* to be better, right?"

"Yes," Tell said, one hand on her swollen belly. He believed his answer to be an honest one. "It'll be much safer."

THIRTY SIX

Tell heard Able arrive. There was a bellow at Julie Dexter. "Let me the fuck back there, now, or so help me . . . !"

Tell called, "Let Able come, Julie." He nodded at Billy Davis—increasingly looking to be, to Tell's pleasant surprise, his most dependable right hand. Tell said, "Sit with Amos and Trent here, Billy, while I talk to Hawk."

Billy looked worried. "'Talk'? You going to be okay with him, skipper?"

"Sure. I'll be fine." As he left, Tell heard Billy say, "Either of you boys want a doughnut?"

Tell intercepted Able Hawk at his desk. "Steady, Able," Tell said. "Let's go out back again."

Able bit his mustache with his bottom teeth and said, "Tell Lyon, don't you dare treat me like some hotheaded civilian who's apt to go pugilist on your ass, or else I'll do just that." The sheriff looked around. He saw wide-eyed Julie Dexter; saw Billy in the doorway, his back to the holding cells, one fat hand on the butt of his gun. Able said, "Out back'll do." Then he led the way to Tell's own back door.

They stepped into the alley and Tell pulled the door shut tight behind them. He said, "You know what was about to go down concerning your grandson."

"Parks called me to give me the heads-up," Able said. "So, yeah. I'm going to assume he called you too. Hence us bein' here like this now. Because I don't want to be more pissed off at you than I am at this moment, I'm not going to explore the question of which of us got called first."

Able took off his mirrored sunglasses and looked at Tell with his unsettling eyes. "I appreciate you getting Amos out of the line of fire of that cocksucker Walt Pierce. I'm trying, for the life of me, to figure out how Walt and his crew fucked up this one. This DNA shit is some wild kind of mistake. Has to be. Thalia was a middle-aged Mexican woman. You've seen Amos. Idea of them together is crazy. And the idea that I wouldn't know if they had somehow ended up together? That's crazier still."

Tell said, "Amos should probably be the one to tell you this, but as we're here and Christ knows what comes next—maybe Walt Pierce with an arrest and extradition warrant—you need to know it all. Amos *was* in Thalia's bed. But he wasn't in bed with Thalia. Thalia has a younger cousin, Luisa, who's twenty-two. She's an illegal. Your grandson Amos is in love with her. They've been together for nearly a year now. And they've been together in Thalia's bed many times when Thalia and her mother were out of the house."

"Oh, Jesus," Able said. "Boy's fucked up by half this time."

"There's more," Tell said. "They were afraid you or one of yours might figure out about Luisa. Maybe try to deport her. So, in love as they think they are, and naïve as they are—"

"Amos fucking knocked her up to stay my hand," Able said sourly. "Hence the DNA from the fucking resultant wet spots in Thalia's bed, after. *Jesus.*"

Tell said nothing, just watched those arresting gray eyes. There was a strange new expression there.

"How far along is this girl?"

"Much too far along for an abortion," Tell said. "If that's what you're thinking."

Able said, "Ain't saying I was or wasn't, Lyon. How far along?"

"At least seven, maybe eight months."

"Fuck." Able put back on his sunglasses. "Well, turn him on over to me. I'll get this worked out with Walt Pierce somehow. Then I'm going to kick Amos's ass so hard his next five children will stutter."

Tell said evenly, "I mean to charge Amos and hold him. For protection."

"He don't need no fuckin' protection now that I'm here," Able said. He took off his glasses. He was using his eyes for effect again. "What exactly did you mean to charge Amos with, Lyon?"

"Something big enough to justify my holding Amos in the face of Sheriff Pierce's suspicion of murder charges."

"You fucking intended *what?*"

"I'm holding Trent Paris too. I stumbled onto your false identification 'sting,' Able. I'd call it clever if it weren't so damned illegal. You have to know the fire you're playing with. Christ's sake, that's a federal felony with Homeland Security considerations. You'd die in jail."

"You'll excuse me not thanking you for your fucking disingenuous compliment. And I know the law. Please fucking tell me you haven't filed paper on Amos yet. On either of them."

"Minutes away from that," Tell said. "Or I was."

"Good thing that you didn't, or I'd be kicking your ass along with Amos's." Able lowered his voice. "Look, Tell, this identification sting, it's a gray thing. They're going to try and secure these fake papers anyway. This way, at least, I know who's who and where to find the worst of them. Know where to find the real criminals among the illegals."

Tell said, "The trouble is, your cover is too thin. And your exposure far too great. You could be burned down for this—do decades in jail." Tell narrowed his eyes. "Where are the proceeds going?"

"What's not used to cover costs? Benevolence fund for the families of fallen cops. How'd you crack it? How'd you trace it back to me?"

"I wish I could say it was something ingenious I did, but this should *scare* you: I picked up a couple of speeding Mexican kids the other night and noticed their fake operator's licenses were the same as the samples you gave me," Tell said. "The kids gave up Trent. Trent rolled over on Amos, just like that." Tell snapped his fingers. "I confronted Trent in a Chipotle. Maybe he was afraid I'd try to take his big-ass burrito. Either way, he caved fast. Gave me Amos off the bat."

"And Amos handed me up?"

"No, Able. He didn't have to. Amos was determined to fall on his sword for you."

"Faint comfort, Lyon. You realize, if you charged Amos for that—charged him in the well-meaning but infinitely misguided notion of protecting him—you realize what that would have resulted in for me?"

"I know. That's why I'd initially told Amos to simply desist. I urged him to walk away from this mess and get you to quit too. I told him I'd drop the whole thing if you two shut it down immediately. And I pointed out to Amos that if I stumbled upon your scam this easily and as quickly as I did, it's inevitable your ACLU enemies will do the same. And they'll run it through you like a harpoon. They'll burn you down with it."

Able nodded. "When did you decide to charge Amos despite all that? When did you decide to renege on your amnesty offer?"

"When he was sitting next to me in my cruiser and I took a call warning me Amos was about to be arrested on suspicion of Thalia Ruiz's murder . . . arrested by *Walt*."

"Well, like I said, I'm here now, Tell. So go back to your original plan. Let Amos and Trent walk."

"You'll stop this bogus ID scheme if I do?"

"Sort of. I was getting antsy myself," Able said. "So I'm turning over the franchise to two guinea hoodlums based a couple of county's south of here. I'm giving the business over to them. In return, they'll float me copies of all the fake papers they sell to Horton County Mexicans. We'll call them dagos 'informants,' at that point. That'll make it all four-square."

Tell said, "You're sure you can cool Pierce's jets? I want to know if you're sure you can do that before I commit to anything, Able. Because if you're wrong, you and Amos are going to pay a terrible price."

"Let me have my boys back, Tell. Please. I'll take care of Walt. No sweat there."

Tell opened the door and held it for Able. He called, "Billy, let Amos and Trent out and give 'em back their stuff. We're kicking them loose."

Julie Dexter came around the corner then. Behind her trailed Sofia Gómez. Sofia held the hand of Evelia. Behind them was a pretty, very pregnant young girl, about a half a head taller than Sofia.

Mrs. Gómez nodded at Tell. "I can't believe after our talk this afternoon you used what I told you to do this to Amos Sharp. Could I have so badly misjudged you, Chief Lyon?"

"No," Tell said. "You didn't. I didn't do what you suggest, *señora*. This isn't how it must appear to you. But I'll leave Amos to explain."

Then Tell said, "Sofia Gómez, I believe you know Sheriff Able Hawk." Tell stroked the hair of the little girl. "This is Thalia's daughter, Evelia. And this," he gestured at the pregnant young girl, "must be Luisa. You all have a lot to talk about. Please use this area as long as you need." Tell said, "Billy, bring Trent. We'll show him out and then keep Julie company up front."

THIRTY SEVEN

"I should fucking kill you, boy."

It was hours since they'd left the New Austin Police HQ. Amos now sat across the dusty kitchen table from his grandfather, trying hard to meet the old man's angry glare. Able said, "I don't have to tell you how close you came today to losing any shot you have at a law enforcement career. If Tell Lyon had really booked you, if he'd filed any paper whatsoever, you'd be fucked on that dream, boy. And I mean forever."

"I know."

"Then we'll talk no more about that," Able said. "But when were you going to tell me about Luisa? When were you going to clue me in about her?"

"Soon," Amos said. "Real, real soon."

"And only because time was running out for you two. Luisa is about to drop that baby inside her. That's why you say that."

"Luisa's also illegal," Amos said. "She's illegal and you're *El Gavilan.*"

"I know that," Able said. "I knew she was illegal before I knew of any ties she had to you. I knew from Thalia. And I did nothing about Luisa in deference to Thalia. And drop that *El Gavilan,* shit, Amos. Under this roof, I'm your fucking grandfather. That's true out on the streets too."

"So what now, Grandpa?"

"So now I damn well don't do anything on that front," Able said. "But you should have trusted me, Amos. That's all I'm saying."

"I should have, I know," Amos said. "I'm sorry."

Able stared at his coffee cup. "You love this girl?" He looked up and searched his grandson's darker eyes. "I mean, you're sure—*really* sure—you really love this girl?"

"Yes," Amos said. "I really do."

"Then you need to marry her, Amos. Now. Do it before that baby gets here. At least bring that baby into this fucking black world with a proper name."

"I want to do that. I want to do that now."

"Then that's just what you will do," Able said. "Where did you two figure on living, after? You can't spend money you don't have on rent or a mortgage. You have to finish school first. That's all I'm requiring of you. That you finish school so you can join me on the job and support this girl and your baby. You have to finish your studies, Amos. Get that degree."

"I'd thought about us maybe being here," Amos said carefully. "At least to start. We have plenty of room, you know? If you'd let us, I thought maybe we could be here for a while. Place could use a woman's touch, don't you think?"

"Sure, a *woman's* touch," Able said, trying hard to reign in the mocking smile he could feel on his own face. "Impossible to deny that. But this girl of yours is just that—a girl. She's young. And with her condition, it's going to be a good while before she can do much to whip this sorry-ass place back in shape. And things are different now than they were even a week ago. I mean different for Luisa's family. Thalia was helping pay for that shitty apartment that she and her mother and her daughter and Luisa are living in. With Thalia gone, money will be tight for all of them. Vicious tight. They might not make it."

Amos wasn't sure where his grandfather was headed with that thought so he said nothing.

Finally, Able said, "See if you can find out what Sofia's paying each month for that apartment they're all crowded into. We'll halve that, and Sofia can move in with her granddaughter over top the garage if she wants."

Amos was pole-armed. "That's great! Really? You're sure, Grandpa?"

"I am for now," Able said. "So you best move on this fast, Amos, 'fore I come to my goddamn ebbing senses."

THEN

"Got a minute?"

Nothing good ever started with that question.

Tell took his feet off his desk and tipped his chair down. He scooted in behind his desk and said to his superior, "Surely."

A file folder tossed in front of him. "A project for you, Tell. His name is Angel Valenzuela. A long-standing problem. He's running a very effective smuggling operation, Tell. One with two prongs—smuggling illegals, of course. But he requires each illegal his team leads across to carry a load of drugs on their backs. Kind of taking the concept of drug mules to literal lengths, you might say."

His superior smiled and winked at his own joke.

Tell just picked up the folder with a sinking *sense;* touched it like it was a rattlesnake.

THIRTY EIGHT

Sympathetic music played as Tell pulled into the lot of his apartment, his long day over. Bob Dylan was singing "Knockin' on Heaven's Door." He again waited for the song to finish, then turned off his engine.

Patricia was again on her porch, waiting for him to come home. She leaned over the deck rail and said, "Based on radio and local TV news, I've given my folks the brush-off for tonight, Tell. That said, I'm hoping your Hell Day is over and you're home to stay now."

He smiled. "It *is*. And I am. Just let me shower and change."

But Patricia was waiting by his door when Tell stepped into their common corridor. She kissed him and said, "You didn't say anything about wanting to shower alone, Tell."

* * *

Patricia had gotten out of their shared shower first. She was dressed and her back was to Tell as he stepped into the living room, pulling on a blue Polo shirt. It was the first time that Patricia had been in his apartment and she was looking at the photos of Marita and Claudia.

She heard Tell behind her and said, "They're beautiful, Tell. Your wife was very beautiful. And your daughter—she was remarkable."

"Thank you," Tell said softly, taking her hand. He squeezed her hand and turned her face from the pictures toward his own. "If not dinner with your folks, then . . . ?"

"I've made our dinner," Patricia said. "Let's go back to my place."

"Let's do that," Tell said.

* * *

Tell drained his drink and then nodded as Patricia offered a refill. "Your margarita skills begin to scare me," he said. "Your cooking skills too. I mean that in the best way."

Dinner was chicken *carnitas* with fresh-diced tomatoes, red onions, avocado and lime slices, cilantro, saffron rice and salted black beans. They ate by candlelight on her deck. The mourning doves were cooing in the willow again.

Patricia and Tell had found a common, favored recording artist in Lucinda Williams. "Ventura," one of the saddest songs of loss and longing ever written to Tell's mind, was playing on the stereo.

Her fingers stroked the back of his hand. "Hell of a day, huh, Chief?"

Tell sipped his margarita and ran his fingers through his hair. "It's sure been some kind of watermark day. I'm afraid high or low is still to be determined." Tell sipped his freshened drink then rolled the dice. "Able Hawk mentioned seeing you at the hospital today, Patricia."

She shrugged. "Don't read much into that, Tell. Like I told you before, who else was there to visit Shawn? His mother lives in Illinois. Able said he would see to contacting them. Did *you* make it over to the hospital to see Shawn?"

"No," Tell said. "There wasn't any time. And if there had been, it would have been a hollow gesture. Hear they put Shawn under while you were there. Hear they mean to keep him that way a few days."

"His brain was swelling," Patricia said, shuddering. "*Jesus*. They were mulling removing part of his skull for a time. Doctors think his knee is ruined and he'll need a cane. And they said Shawn could lose a kidney."

Tell had also heard from Able that Shawn's nose would require bone grafts to restore it to some vague semblance of a nose. Able Hawk, characteristically, had probably put it best, if bluntly: "Shawn," Able said, "is going to end up looking like some loser rummy middleweight 'fore this is all over. And that's *if* he's fucking goddamn lucky. Bet he winds up a pain pill junkie too."

Patricia said, "Able told me the ones who beat Shawn were driving a red pickup truck. That made me think of that recording we watched together of Thalia's body being dumped."

Tell paused, a fork-full of *carnitas* halfway to his mouth. "Did you mention that recording to Able?" He hadn't had a chance to share that tidbit yet with Sheriff Hawk—hadn't found the right opening. Tell braced for Patricia's answer. Able learning through a second party could be a terrible thing. It was already clear to Tell that Hawk only half trusted him now.

"I didn't think it was my place to do that," Patricia said.

"I know that footage is blurry," Tell said, "but the ones who attacked Shawn were riding in an Isuzu. The difference between an Isuzu and a Dodge Ram is the difference between a lap dog and a Great Dane, Patricia."

"How many Rams are there in Horton County? Can't be that many, right?"

"In *this* county? It's a muscle truck and appeals to a certain kind of car-poor half-wit. Two hundred and fifty Rams in Horton County, and one hundred and sixty-seven of those are red."

Tell reached across the table and took her left hand. "I've gotten another copy of the footage we watched and I've turned it over to the criminology department at your university. They're going to take the sports photographer back over to the ballpark tomorrow morning—same time and position as the last time. Then they are going to go out in the field to the approximate location of the truck on the tape. They're going to position various license plates on a stand of the same height of a Dodge Ram's bumper. They'll see how the various numbers and letters on the plates pixelate. Then they'll try to use that information to extrapolate backward—see if they can give me a reading on the plate on that tape we watched earlier."

Patricia, beaming, said, "That's brilliant. How long will it take?"

"Days . . . maybe a week," Tell said. He nodded at his plate. "Lord, this is really delicious. You should open your own restaurant."

Patricia smiled. "No. Not here in New Austin, anyway. Although my mom and dad have talked about maybe branching out to other communities or counties." She squeezed his hand harder and then let go. "Semi-related topic—I'm reminded because my parents operate a food tent there—the Latino Festival is coming up. You going to squire me, Chief?"

"I'd love to do that," Tell said. "But is that a good idea for you? I have to work it, so I'll be there in an official capacity off and on. In uniform, I mean. I don't want 'us' to hurt you in any way."

"Your point, Tell?"

"Being seen with the law isn't going to hurt you? Stigmatize you?"

"Hurt me? What do you mean? In 'my community'? Is that what you mean? I'm American, Tell. I was born here, just like you. Hell, your Spanish is better than mine."

"Sorry," Tell said. "I just meant charged as things are now, after Thalia's murder and after Shawn's beating, we may be on the edge of some ugly racial tension if things keep going like they have. Wouldn't want to hurt your folks' business."

"I don't accept your premise," she said.

Tell shook his head. "All right then. I'd be happy to squire you, Patricia."

"Good." She smiled. "Now, big day tomorrow, Chief?"

"Not like today I hope," Tell said. "Come morning, I'll start looking for Shawn's attackers. Though I suspect Able might get there first. He's had a day's start and one of the suspects ties back to those meth-cooking brothers whose farm Able and Shawn raided earlier today."

"No more shoptalk," Patricia said. "I know I kind of started it, Tell, so I'm stopping it, right now."

"Suits me." Tell started gathering up empty plates. They carried in the dirty dishes and pans. Patricia blew out the candles and locked up the back door. "I know this day knocked the hell out of you, Tell." Her fingers traced his chin. She said, "But you will stay the night, won't you?"

* * *

She had been astride him. Patricia straightened her legs, stretching out half-atop Tell. Her breasts were pressed to his chest; she was moving carefully so that they remained joined.

Tell stroked her back. Patricia said, "Your wife and daughter were beautiful, Tell."

"So you said." He combed her damp hair back behind her ear. He cupped her chin in his hand and lifted her face up to where he could see her eyes. "Why do you say that again, Patricia? Particularly now, just after . . . ? While we're like this?"

"I was thinking of their pictures, Tell. Especially the one of your little girl." She pressed her hand to his temple. "How are you about all that now? Up here, I mean."

"Holding on," he said after some reflection. "Getting stronger, I think. It was terrible at first. All but insupportable. My wife was dead when the emergency crews reached what was left of our house. Claudia was badly burned. She was already mortally wounded although the doctors wouldn't or couldn't tell me that. But she held on for four days. The misguided little fighter in her just wouldn't give up that easy." He felt the stinging in his eyes, but pushed ahead, aware Patricia saw his tears. He said, his voice thick, "My cousin Chris was there within a few hours of getting the news. Chris really kept me together for Claudia. He kept me in this world. Thanks to him, I was holding Claudia's hand when she passed. I owe him for that."

Tell felt Patricia's grip tighten on him. He took a deep breath, resisting the notion to wipe his eyes. He let out his breath and said raggedly, "Then there were the funerals to get through. Oh, God, how they nearly killed me again. Chris held me tight to him through both of them. Her parents attacked me. Blamed me. But I agreed with them. I was a goddamn wreck. But by the time the funerals were over, and they were both buried, Chris and some co-workers of mine had identified who had killed Marita and Claudia. And that handed me a new distraction."

Patricia kissed his chest, then pressed her cheek to the damp spot left by her own lips. "I don't remember any of those articles I read about you mentioning arrests, or of any trials of the ones who killed your family," she said.

Tell hesitated, then said, "That doesn't mean there wasn't a reckoning."

Patricia stretched and kissed Tell on the mouth, kissed him passionately—hard and slow. She said, "Tell Lyon, won't you make a baby with me someday?"

He shook his head. "It's very early days yet, Patricia. We hardly—"

She pressed her fingers to his lips. "I *know*. But I want to know that you want to have a baby with me someday."

Lying there in her bed, feeling Patricia stretched long and smooth and warm against him, her hand softly exploring him, urging him again to hardness inside her, Tell thought about the last time with Marita. He'd made love with his wife the night before the fire. They'd decided that night to have another child—a little brother or sister for Claudia.

The next morning, Tell had kissed his wife and left for work. He left without saying goodbye to Claudia so as not to wake her. It was a week to Christmas and Marita had given him a copy of their daughter's wish list for Santa as they kissed the last time.

Tell left his house and he never saw Marita alive again. Claudia was a tiny mummy in the hospital bed the next time that Tell saw her. His baby girl was burned so badly that she had already lost her feet and all the fingers of her left hand by the time Tell reached the hospital.

Claudia never regained consciousness.

That was a "terrible blessing" his cousin Chris had said, sitting faithless vigil all night with Tell that first night in the hospital by Claudia's bedside.

That was how it happened too fucking often: walk out a door and return to a wrecked world.

Tell had left in the morning for another routine day, so far as any of them had known. He strolled out to his SUV and lost his world, suddenly and without warning.

Shawn O'Hara snuck out a stranger's front door on a different morning and effectively burned down his own life.

Shawn bounced back from that one, in most ways—as much the result of dumb luck running the *other* direction for a short time.

But then Shawn woke up and walked out *another* door and ended up maimed; unmanned so far as children of his own were concerned. When Shawn eventually limped out of that hospital— or, more likely, when he was wheeled out—he would leave it a toothless, infertile gimp with a stranger's face, as Able had said.

One bad day.

One life-changing, five-minute delay could fuck a man over for a lifetime.

Someone else's momentary distraction in heavy traffic? It could cost you, all the way up. A stranger's eyes roam from the road to their passenger seat to seek their cell phone and the next thing you know, you or your life's one true love is being zipped into a body bag.

Chris's wife, Salome, building on her husband's urgings to Tell to get "back in the game," had bequeathed to Tell a new axiom. Salome, like Chris, had urged Tell not just to bury himself in work, as he was doing, but for Tell to lose himself in sensation, to seize life with both hands again.

Salome had tossed off a casual comment that had lodged in Tell's brain. Tell had all but decided to adopt Salome's aside as his life's new guiding principle: "All any of us has," Salome had said, "is the moment we're living in."

His cousin Chris had first met Salome while trying to climb out of his own private hell. To hear Chris tell it, he had taken Salome to his bed the first night he met her. If true, that was very *un*-Chris. But Chris also told Tell that he'd promptly made Salome pregnant, and, within a few short weeks, Chris had married her. Sixteen years later, and they were still going strong. Salome was even pressing Chris for a third child while she was still young enough to carry a baby. Certainly Tell's courtship with Marita had been equally whirlwind.

But Chris had come to Salome without the weight and history of a previous marriage. And Patricia was now about the age that Salome had been back then, when she met Chris. Tell was only a few years behind his cousin's current age.

Tell stroked Patricia's back, looking into her dark, moist eyes. She said, "What's going through that head of yours, Tell? Have I wrecked us, being honest? Was I mistaken telling you that I want so much from you?"

His fingers stroked her lips—her generous mouth. Her mouth was so gentle most times, but so hungry in passion.

Patricia was beautiful and sensual and ripe and loving. Unspoiled. Still full of at least some of her dreams. Tell felt like he was exploiting her, wanting her as he did with so many ghosts of his own crowding his heart. He said, "How sure are you of this really, Patricia?"

"I'm sure," she said, searching his eyes. She kissed him again and traced his lower lip afterward. "If every night we have in front of us is like this one, I can't imagine myself happier. We don't have to do it now, but if you're willing, we could be married soon. Married in a church, in a park. Hell, in my parents' restaurant, with a mariachi band, if you want. A mayor or a priest can perform the ceremony. I don't care. Invite your cousin and his wife. See if they'll come. If they are there, and if my parents and grandmother are there, it's all we need, isn't it?"

Tell stroked her hair behind her ear.

"That was a question, Tell. It requires an answer."

EL LÉON

Extracts from the *New Austin Recorder* social pages:

Sharp-Gómez are wed
Luisa Mary Gómez, 22, married Amos Thorpe Sharp, 23, last Saturday at the New Austin Presbyterian Church with Rev. Charles Laird officiating.

The bride is the daughter of Francisco and Inez Gómez of Juarez, Mexico. The groom is the son of the late Nancy (Hawk) Sharp of New Austin.

The bride was given in marriage by the groom's maternal grandfather, Able Grant Hawk. The bride's aunt, Sofia Gómez, served as matron of honor. The bride's cousin, Evelia Ruiz, was the ring-bearer.

The groom is currently completing his studies in criminology at Vale County Vocational Institute.

No honeymoon is planned.

Lyon-Maldonado engagement announced
Patricia Rene Maldonado, 25, has announced her engagement to Tell Mills Lyon, 39. A full church ceremony is planned in September at Our Lady of the Veil.

The bride is the daughter of Kathleen and Augustin Maldonado. The groom is the son of the late Harper (Ross) Lyon and the late Zayre Clark Lyon.

The bride-to-be is currently completing a degree in restaurant management at Vale County Vocational Institute. The groom-to-be recently accepted appointment to the position of New Austin chief of police.

A December honeymoon to the Virgin Islands is planned.

THIRTY NINE

Shawn had been awake for several hours.

The physician had brought him a laptop so he could communicate. Doctors weren't too sure how long they would be requiring his mouth to remain wired shut. It was maybe just as well, Shawn thought, because his lower face was still a zone of pain, despite the medication he was being given. Talking around all the packing, even if it was only his lips and tongue moving, was a special kind of agony.

He had cried when the doctor told him about his lost teeth—twelve of them in all, and three more that might yet be removed if they didn't tighten up in the jellied remains of his gums.

Then Shawn learned of the removal and replacement of his kneecap while he'd been under—some aluminum thing he was going to have to learn to use through six or more weeks of intense physical rehabilitation.

But he was numb to the revelation he might be infertile as a result of the attack. He'd never been convinced he wanted children. Patricia's hints that she was ready for them had appalled and unsettled Shawn. He just wanted to know if he could hope to get it up again.

When he asked for a mirror, the doctor refused. "There's still a great deal of swelling and bruising. While that is alarming in appearance for the moment, I can assure you it is transient. I don't want you further traumatized from seeing yourself in your present state, Shawn. But that's going to fix itself in a couple of days. Believe that. But we also need to reconstruct your nose and reposition your left cheekbone. We have a reconstructive surgeon coming tomorrow to do that. Your mother is in town, and at our request, she brought along a number of photos of you. We'll use those to try to come as close as we can in reconstructing your nose. Let us do that, then give it a few more days to heal. Then we'll give you a look at your face."

That scenario terrified Shawn. How bad could he look? What kind of monster had those fucking Mexicans made of him? How much could he recover of his former face?

He listened, horrified, as the doctor detailed his "extensive dental trauma." The extent of those injuries precluded dentures or bridges. Shawn was instead to be fitted with permanent implants. "There's some discomfort associated with that procedure," the doctor said. "The results more than make up for that. First we have to wait for your gums to heal a bit more before we go at them again. The good news is that an Officer Davis, who helped keep you stable until the squad arrived after your beating, he searched the lot and found several of your teeth. They couldn't be saved, but they will be used in helping to shape your replacement teeth. But as I say, there will be some discomfort associated with the procedure."

Shawn wanted to laugh at that. Could there be more pain than he was experiencing now? He typed in: *'Discomfort? Worse than this?*

The doctor smiled and patted his shoulder. "No, not like this. So you're in pain now? I'll see about increasing your pain medication. You will recover from this, Shawn. But it will take some time. Your nose may be a bit different from what you remembered. And you'll probably always have a slight limp. But you'll be yourself again. I'm sorry about your prospects for children. It's the epididymis, your 'delivery system,' so to speak, that's been compromised."

Shawn shrugged off that last again and asked for any newspapers from the time he was in his medically induced coma that the doctor could scrounge up for him.

When Shawn reached the latest copy of his own paper—assembled by some middling, fill-in reporter named Barbara Ruskin—he stalled at the engagement announcement for Patricia and Tell Lyon. He stared at it for a long time. Then, wondering again how long he had been out, he checked the paper's publication date. He looked at Patricia's picture, stunned at how quickly she had dumped him—starting his spiral, anyway you looked at it—and agreed to marry Tell Lyon.

Bitch, he thought. Mexican cunt.

* * *

There was still an exciting newness to sleeping all night in the same bed with Luisa. Now that she was so far along, the doctor had restricted sexual relations. But the novelty of being all night in bed together—naked, of course; Luisa using her hands or mouth to take off Amos's edge—the novelty of whole nights together, was enough for the young groom. In Thalia's bed, their couplings had been brief, edgy, urgent encounters—an eye always on the clock. Amos thought this was, in some ways, even better.

And as their room was so close to Able's, Amos thought it was as well for now they couldn't fully have sex. The box springs of Amos's big old bed were insanely squeaky.

"Your grandfather is already up," Luisa said in her heavily accented English. "For some long time now. I heard him moving around, heard him on the phone. Then I heard him talking to Aunt Sofia. I think they're out back now, fixing something in Sofia's and Evelia's place."

Amos traced the curve of her swollen right breast, its nipple hard as it was almost all the time now. "You've been up a long time yourself, huh? Couldn't sleep?"

"I hardly sleep at all," Luisa said. "Not for many days. I can't get comfortable, and it's hard sleeping on my side all of the time."

"Shouldn't be long now," Amos said hopefully.

Luisa pushed his hand from her breast. "No," she said. "No, not long now. Then it will be the baby waking up many times in the night, hungry."

* * *

"They're in so far over their heads," Sofia Gómez said. "Too young for this. These now, at twenty-two or twenty-three, they are what we were at fifteen or sixteen, in so many ways."

Able drove a nail, then hung up a framed photo of Thalia. It made him feel better to see the face he remembered smiling back at him. It helped to erase some of the memory of the bloody mess he'd seen behind the ball fields. He asked Sofia, "How old were you when Thalia was born?"

That segued into another recounting of the Gómez clan's border crossing. Able listened, all grave attention. When she finished, Able said, "Mine came over by boat. Four brothers, four wives and sixteen children, down in a filthy hold. There was cholera on the boat. Three brothers, two wives and nine children—several of them orphaned—came ashore."

Evelia walked up next to Able, looking up at him with big, moist black eyes. She pressed her hand to her belly and he heard her stomach growl loudly.

Able struggled down onto one knee and pulled a face at the little girl. Evelia smiled. He asked, "You ever have a Happy Meal, Evelia? Not so much real food, but it can hit the spot." The little girl looked at him, silent.

Sofia said, "Sheriff Hawk asked you a question, Evelia."

Evelia said, "I like the Burger King better."

"Let's go do that now then," Able said. "Three of us are past ready for a treat."

* * *

Patricia pulled into the lot, returning from her day's only class—an early morning session that ran from eight to nine.

As a new tenant, Tell was locked into a six-month lease. Patricia, after so many years, was granted month-to-month status. Patricia was arguing that she move into Tell's place while they looked for a house. Tell insisted that he preferred Patricia's place. He said he loved her shaded deck and the tree full of mourning doves.

Complicating things was Tell's cousin, Chris.

After their engagement announcement, Tell's cousin had invited him out to his place in Cedartown for a few days. Patricia pushed Tell to accept the invitation, intrigued to meet Chris and Salome. Insisting he couldn't leave town with the investigation underway, Chris and Salome instead came their way for an evening together—Salome armed with a DVD of their property outside Cedartown. Over dinner, Chris pulled Tell aside and made him an offer. Chris and his family lived on a wooded expanse of acreage that backed up to a historic, protected creek. Tell had told Patricia that Chris had, from time to time, joked about establishing his own compound. Chris seemed to be well on his way to doing just that. He was building a cabin for his aging parents and his single-mother sister and her children on his property. He offered another plat on his property's western edge to Tell as an eventual wedding gift—a place for Tell and Patricia to build their own cabin.

Patricia had loved the footage of their log home. She loved the old-growth trees surrounding the cabin and the constant soothing gurgle of the creek running along the back of the property line. She asked Tell, "Does it really look like that?"

"It's better in person," Tell said.

And there was more: Cedartown's longtime chief of police, a man named Roy Atchity, was to retire soon. Chris could, he said, arrange for Atchity and Tell to speak; Atchity had intimated he was in a position to stipulate his own successor to Cedartown's city fathers.

Patricia was also drawn to Salome Lyon—the two of them had hit it off immediately. Patricia could see herself and her babies and Tell living there, part of this constructed clan. Salome badly wanted another baby and spoke of the prospect of she and Patricia maybe being pregnant together.

Chris Lyon was a different matter. Chris alternately fascinated and unsettled Patricia. She found him attractive, but, at least initially, harrowingly forbidding. Chris was a couple of inches taller than Tell and darker in every sense—charismatic and intense. And a bit menacing. Then Patricia had spent some time alone with Chris. Just a few minutes really, but when they were over, Patricia felt she and Chris knew all there was worth knowing about one another.

Patricia had asked Chris, the one who knew Tell longest and best of all, how he would sum up Tell. Chris had thought about that for a few long, uncomfortable seconds. Then he'd said, "We used to play cowboys as kids. Tell never really stopped playing. I think maybe that Tell is really the last truly good man on earth, Patricia. And that makes him the most vulnerable man alive. A magnet for grief. But he's the best man I know. So I worry for him, doing what he does."

Patricia had said, "But you're offering Tell another law enforcement post in Cedartown. If you fear so much for him . . . ?"

"Yes," Chris told her. "But Roy Atchity, the man whom Tell could replace, has been on the force for thirty-five years. Roy has been chief for twenty-one years. He'll retire with a wife of thirty-six years and several grown children. It's a relatively safe post as these things go. And if Tell is in Cedartown, close by in every sense, then I can have his back like I couldn't when he was out West. Like I can't if he's living in New Austin. He's the closest thing I have to a brother. I can't risk him."

Patricia had hugged Chris hard, then. She kissed his cheek and said, "I'll see what I can do to persuade him."

Now Patricia keyed herself into her—*their*—apartment. She checked her answering machine.

A call from her mother: "It's Mom. Just calling to see how you are doing. Call me, Patricia."

A call from the hospital: "Ms. Maldonado, this is Dr. James Grier. I'm calling as promised to let you know that Shawn O'Hara is conscious now. I told him you were by and asked to see him and he asked if you could come by the hospital today. He'll be undergoing surgery again tomorrow, so it could otherwise be a few days."

FORTY

Tell sat at his desk, reviewing the thin files sent to him by Able Hawk. Each file consisted of seven or eight pages of photocopied crime reports, autopsy reports and news clippings about the three other women—all Vale County women—who had died in the previous two years. All had died in a manner very similar to the way that Thalia Ruiz had been murdered.

All three were Latino. All three, like Thalia, were in their early- to mid-thirties. One had a child. Two of the previous victims, Marisol Hernandez and Sonya Lorca, had been prostitutes—classic targets of opportunity.

The previous victims had been raped and beaten, their bodies dropped nude in fields, or, in one case, a stream in remote Vale County.

And all three cases remained unsolved.

Tell looked longest at the third file. Like Thalia, the victim was another youngish single mother, not a prostitute, who ended up violated and beaten to death six months before Thalia.

Carlita Marquez was a night clerk at a hotel located on an off-ramp of I-70. She punched out at work at six A.M.

The hotel's exterior security camera caught an image of Carlita alone, entering her green Elantra and pulling out of the lot. No indication there of any trouble ahead.

But her car was found four hours later, less than a mile from the hotel where she worked. On examination, authorities determined someone had cut halfway through her Hyundai's timing belt. Carlita had driven less than five-tenths of a mile before the timing belt snapped, effectively killing her car and trashing the engine, stalling it just where police later found it.

Seven hours later, two senior citizens were seining for crayfish for a planned fishing trip the next morning. They found Carlita face down in the stream, clouds of blood still hanging in the slow-moving water around her head and between her bruised thighs.

No persons of interest were noted in any of the files and no suspicious people or vehicles had apparently surfaced. There was no mention of a red Dodge Ram pickup truck seen in or around any of the body dump sites.

The phone rang. Patricia asked, "You foresee another long day?"

"They all seem that way now," Tell said.

And they seemed longer still, knowing that Patricia was alone all day at home. He wanted to be home with her. He told her that and she said, "You can always come home for a quickie." Her smile there in her voice, she said, "I mean, for *lunch*."

When he hung up, he saw his phone's message light was flashing. He punched in his password: it was his technical guru at the university. "We have seven possible license plate combinations, Chief. It's ten thirty A.M. I'll be in all day."

* * *

Tell handed Billy Davis the slip of paper with the license plate possibilities arrived at by the university analysts. He said, "Run these please, Billy. Results and comments to me only, and not by radio."

Billy nodded, setting chins in motion. "Heading out?"

Tell held up the file folders sent to him by Able Hawk. "Going to go look at the dump sites. Or near as I can come to them, based on what's in these. Just want to get a feel for the places. And doing that, I may get some notion of the ones who'd drop them there."

Billy paused, hand poised over the Krispy Kreme box. "That's all Vale County, skipper."

"That's why I'm taking my own SUV."

"Stay in contact then, Chief," Billy said, looking worried. "Walt Pierce is a goddamn whack job. I know one of his new deputies, fella name of Tom Winch. Bastard fills my ear with stuff about Pierce. Old Tom, he's terrified of his boss. And he says Pierce has a real hard-on for Able Hawk and you."

Tell smiled. "In that order?"

Billy selected a sugar-dusted, jelly-filled doughnut. "I'll clarify that with Winch, next time I see him."

FORTY ONE

Patricia was about to head out to the hospital when Luz called. Luz had been scarce since Patricia's mother and father had posted bail to get her out of county jail on the prostitution charges brought against her by Able Hawk. Luz said, "Could you meet me for coffee, Patricia?"

"Trouble, Luz?"

"I want to say goodbye."

* * *

"I'm so ashamed," Luz said, staring into her coffee mug. "After all you and your parents have done for me. Giving me the job at the restaurant. And then I . . ."

"I just wish you'd called me before you, well . . . before you started doing *that*," Patricia said. "I just wished you'd done that."

"I didn't know what to do," Luz said. "So I did that terrible thing. Made myself a whore."

"You're not a whore," Patricia said firmly. "For God's sake, you're not *that*."

"I am. I did it eight times. Twice, I actually loved it. They were bachelor parties. Three men there one night, all good looking. The sex was *so* hot. And I got paid for having that great time. The next night was an old man. Fat. I got paid then too."

"Oh, Luz . . ."

"I've been hiding. I didn't realize what it was like. Didn't realize how the ones who make the connections for you can be . . . possessive." Patricia nodded, only half-understanding. She presumed Luz was trying to avoid using the word "pimp." Patricia guessed that whoever had "turned her out," to use a phrase she'd learned from Tell, was now threatening Luz in some way.

"My mother's very sick now," Luz pressed on. "Worse than before. I can't get Elizabeth here. And would I if I could? Would I bring her to this place where her mother became a *puta*? Where this man, this Tomás Calderone, threatens to cut off my nose if I don't return to work for him? I'm going back to Mexico, Patricia."

"Do you know what it will take for the two of you to come back here again someday, when you're ready? Do you know how much harder it could be as things stand now? With the Minute Men? With the National Guard on the border? With that wall maybe coming?"

"I won't be coming back, Patricia. I can't make it here. There I was poor. But I was okay. I wasn't a whore. I don't want to come back here, ever."

"You're sure?"

"More than anything. But I'm pregnant, Patricia. Maybe from the party. I can't afford another child. And I can't afford to be pregnant, not now, not having to care for Mother and for Elizabeth. I'm going to the clinic now. To take care of it. I—I wondered if you'd sit with me, help to see me through it."

Patricia's hand was pressed to her own belly. "I . . . can," she said without enthusiasm, not wanting to do it. "Sure Luz. Sure. Okay."

* * *

Patricia drove Luz in silence. She stopped at the bank and withdrew a thousand dollars. She forced the money on Luz, who looked nauseous. "To get you home more quickly after," Patricia said. "Use some of it tonight for a hotel. I'll drop you there. You can't go home with this Calderone dude after you."

"But my stuff . . . ?"

"I'll pack it all for you and bring it by your hotel. If you're going to do this, you need to do it now. Right away. Get out before this bastard can hurt you."

"But you wouldn't be safe in my place, cleaning it out."

"I'll go in with Tell, or one of his people, then," Patricia said. "Maybe one of Able Hawk's deputies. Did you tell Hawk, *El Gavilan*, about Calderone?"

"No. Tomás said he would kill any of us who told. So we didn't."

"Well, plan on leaving tomorrow. I'll drive you to the airport. Do you have money for the fare?"

"I have the ticket."

"When you're back with your mother and daughter, let me know, and I'll send you another thousand."

"It's too much," Luz said.

Patricia said, "It's nothing. Really—it's not enough."

* * *

It was several hours later that Patricia drove to the hospital, depressed and shaken.

The abortion clinic had been a nightmare. Patricia had to run a gauntlet with Luz through a thicket of demonstrators. One, a preacher, had spat on Patricia. Luz wasn't yet showing, so it was any fanatic's call which of the young women was going inside to kill her baby. The demonstrators evidently decided it was Patricia. The preacher called her "*puta*," his lip curled.

They waited in a room with a mix of pregnant girls and women. Some were alone. Some were there with mothers, somber boyfriends or tight-jawed brothers. Some with other women who were there, like Patricia, for support.

Patricia sat with Luz through a brief counseling session. When they described the procedure, Patricia became nauseous and excused herself, vomiting in the sink. It was late morning, and she'd missed breakfast between her early class and her time with Luz. She returned just in time to hug Luz as she went back for "treatment." That was the term the counselor used for what Luz was to do. As though it was an illness that Luz suffered from—a condition to be corrected.

Then, after, the two of them had to again run that gauntlet of protestors to reach the car.

Alone, glad to be away from Luz, who angered Patricia now— who disgusted her even—Patricia had to drive through four levels of the hospital's parking garage before finding an empty parking space. She followed a color-coded stripe through twisting corridors that stank of medicine and turned her stomach again. She followed the red stripe to the intensive care unit. She inquired at the nurses' desk for Shawn's room number.

"Mr. O'Hara is not accepting visitors," a heavyset black nurse said, not looking up from a chart she was examining.

Patricia said, "But I came here because Shawn—because Mr. O'Hara—*asked* that I come."

The nurse held up a finger, remembering something. "You're Patricia, aren't you? Shawn asked I give you this." She handed Patricia an envelope. Patricia took it and slit it open with her index finger. She winced as the envelope's edge cut the side of her finger, blood staining the letter inside. Distractedly, Patricia said, "But Shawn did ask that I come by personally."

The nurse held out a hand, offering Patricia a Band-Aid for her paper cut. "He said you were to be given the letter," the nurse said, "but not to be allowed back. He's a mess, honey. Ask me, he wants you to see him after we make him pretty again." Patricia half heard her, concentrating on Shawn's message. The nurse paused, looking at Patricia's face. She said, "You okay, sweetie?"

Patricia's chin trembled. Her mouth was dry and her heart was pounding. She backed away, staring at the letter. She twisted her ankle as she turned and ran down the corridor to the elevator.

Shaken, she walked as fast as she could to her car, limping slightly and wincing from the pain in her ankle. She got in her car, turned the air conditioner up high and read Shawn's note again:

Patty,

Congratulations on the engagement.

Jesus, but you move on fast.

Seems like not two weeks ago you were sucking *my* cock.

Me, I won't be using my own mouth for a while, or so the doctors say.

Guess it's a good thing I'm a writer, huh?

One night. If you'd waited one more night to kick me loose, none of this would have happened to me, you know.

It's your fault, P. It's *all* your fucking fault.

So thanks, Pat. It's been a hell of a short ride, lady.

Wish I could say you were worth it.

You know, it's evidently so bad—my face I mean—that I can't even get them to let me look in a mirror. So I figure myself for a monster now.

Thanks, Patty. You changed my life, 'Tish.

Maybe someday I can return the favor. I'll be giving it a lot of thought as I'm stuck here like this.

About all I can do now is think, thanks to you.

All best,

(The former) Shawn O'Hara

Patricia wadded up his letter, then, hesitating before throwing it out the window, she unfolded it and read it again. She wondered about the last lines of the letter. She wondered if they conveyed a real threat. She smoothed the note, folded it up and slipped it into her purse. She couldn't imagine showing it to Tell with that dig about fellatio.

The bastard. The goddamn self-centered monster.

While she waited for the idle to kick down on her car, Patricia pulled out her cell phone and called information. She asked for a non-emergency number for the Horton County Sheriff's Department. She thought about asking Tell for help with Luz, but he was shorthanded and focused on the murder investigation. She jotted down the number and called the Horton County Sheriff's Office. When she identified herself, she was surprised to be passed directly along to Able Hawk.

Able said, "Patricia—a pleasure. Congratulations and my best to Tell. Have to say, the night I met you two, I was sure you two were the couple. I'm thrilled for you both."

Patricia thanked him and told him about Luz. "Could you send someone to kind of watch me while I pack her stuff, Sheriff? There isn't much there, so it shouldn't take long."

"No, Patricia, I won't do that," Able said. "Better you swing by here and drop off her keys. If that pimp of hers has threatened her he could be watching her place. Like as not, he is. I don't want him seeing you and getting focused on you as a way to get to her. I'll send a male and female deputy out to gather Luz's stuff. They can make sure they're not followed and get her belongings to her. I'll have them drive her to the airport or bus station too. See she's not followed."

Patricia said, "I can't thank you enough, Sheriff."

"*Able*. And we'd be more than even if you could get her to give me the name of this pimp of hers before she blows town. Not that I'd try to force her to testify. I just want to know myself. Can use it to start building my own case against the low bastard."

Patricia said, "You and your people won't confront Luz about it today or tomorrow? You'll just get her stuff and see her safely out of town?"

"On my soul," Able said. She could hear the excitement in his voice. "You know this son of a bitch's name?"

"I do. It's Tomás Calderone."

"I owe you a hell of a wedding present," Able said.

* * *

Patricia dropped off Luz's keys at the Horton County Sheriff's Department, then drove home, Lucinda Williams on the car stereo. She played Lucinda's moody "Minneapolis" over and over, almost calming herself from the fallout of reading Shawn's vile note.

Once home, she curled up on the couch and tried to study for a test, but found herself too distracted. Her mind kept turning back to Shawn and his last letter. Restless, she turned on her computer, pulled her glasses back on. While her computer booted up, she got some saltines and a glass of 7-Up, hoping to settle her stomach.

When her home page came up she learned she had three e-mail messages waiting. She opened the letter from Salome Lyon first, already smiling. "Just checking to see how you and your man are doing, Patricia," Salome wrote. She continued, "And Chris and I are wondering if you two have come to any decisions about the chief's job here. And about us being neighbors. And Chris says Cedartown needs a 'top-shelf Mexican restaurant.' So please call me when you get this, sister, yeah?"

The second e-mail was a spam offer for painkillers.

The third was a mystery. It was labeled "Good news, Patricia!" The sender was someone named Wendy Fahy. *Wendy?* Patricia knew nobody with that name. The message included an attached photo, a jpg titled "nuface."

Patricia clicked on the e-mail and read, "Heard you were just by, Patricia. So, like I wrote, no mirrors here, but I just conned my current nurse into loaning me her cell phone so I could check my office voicemail. Her phone is a camera phone. She was changing my bandages and was called out for a moment. Isn't that lucky? See attached jpg to see what you did to me, you Mexican cunt."

Patricia clicked on the attached photo. She looked at the ruin of Shawn's face. She held down her bile long enough to close the file completely—so she wouldn't have to confront that image ever again. Shawn had virtually no nose—just an implied cavity covered by the flap of dangling skin that had sheathed the bones and crushed cartilage of his nose. What was left looked a little like Lon Chaney Sr.'s nose in *The Phantom of the Opera*. Like what Michael Jackson was supposed to have left after all his gone-wrong plastic surgery. Shawn's mouth was sunken where his missing teeth should be, like that of an old man with his dentures out. The missing teeth shortened the appearance of Shawn's jawline and made his chin more prominent . . . even pointy. His head was swollen far beyond its normal size and his cheekbones were uneven . . . like someone had sawed his head in half vertically and misaligned the two pieces trying to put Shawn back together. His bruised and swollen eyes were hateful slits.

The file closed but the image wouldn't leave Patricia. She stumble-crawled to the kitchen sink and threw up twice. She turned on the tap, sloshing water on the mess to move it down the drain. She cupped more water into her hands and washed out the taste from her mouth.

Patricia hung over the sink, breathing deeply through her mouth until her stomach settled. She took deep breaths until her heart rate regulated itself and the black spots left her eyes. Then she pulled out a glass and a bottle of tequila. She started to unscrew the cap, then hesitated.

What if she was pregnant? It seemed a crazy thought, but it wasn't yet noon and might explain her repeated bouts of vomiting. Rattled as she was, the impetuous notion took hold in a funny way. Almost made happy by her sickness now—viewed in this new light—she sealed the bottle, and put it back under the sink. Patricia thought about Salome, who was also trying to become pregnant—despite Chris's resistance—and called her. It would be good to hear Salome's voice, to talk to her.

THEN

Sophia looked at the scraggly Christmas tree—the last on the lot and already drying out. She'd dragged the fir up four flights of steps, shedding needles all the way. They'd be finding those dried needles on the stairs well into the following summer; still tracking them into the apartment in July.

Even decorated with second-hand ornaments and handmade construction paper decorations—strings of popcorn—the tree looked . . . bare. Forlorn.

The hours dragged on; the other children fell asleep. Thalia lingered. Her little girl didn't look so little now. She was already in a training bra, already becoming more womanly.

White people's Christmas music on the radio: Bing Crosby crooning "White Christmas."

Thalia said, "Is there *really* a Santa? Really?"

Sophia, unable to fib it away this night, said, "Honey, of course there is no Santa. It's a thing we say to give children hope."

Sophia bit her lip, felt a pang as she saw the change in Thalia's expression. She'd presumed Thalia had already dispensed with Santa Claus—saw through the myth and just wanted final confirmation. It was a catastrophic deduction on Sophia's part.

Thalia twisted the knife. "Anything you want to tell me about God and Jesus, Mother?"

FORTY TWO

Able had stopped home for lunch. He'd run upstairs to make some calls away from the station. Using his home phone, *El Gavilan* had set the ball rolling against Tomás Calderone.

He'd given the name over to his new Italian cohorts. They said they didn't run women themselves anymore, but they knew some others who did. When Davey James assured Able there'd be no county expense of burying Calderone in some county-funded potter's grave, Able had said, "Huzzah."

Able walked down the stairs to the smell of bacon and eggs. Sofia was at the stove. "I hope you don't mind, Mr. Hawk," she said. "But Luisa is so useless in the kitchen at the best of times, and much less so now."

"It's *Able*," Able said. "And it smells wonderful. We should all do this every day."

"I'm sorry it's breakfast food, but it's what I could find," Sofia said.

"It smells delicious," Able said. A notion seized him. "You and me and the little one, this evening, after work, let's go to the store and do some shopping. Get these cabinets filled up proper."

Sofia smiled and handed Able a cup of coffee. He sipped it and said, "Now I know where Thalia learned to make it so good. Thought I'd never taste its like again." He looked around and said, "Where is that little girl?"

Able heard, "Boo!" and felt tiny arms squeeze his leg. He ran his hand over Evelia's head and sat his coffee cup on the counter. He realized, suddenly, he could set something on the counter. There was surface area there again. Everything was shining and orderly.

Able pretended to pluck a new quarter from behind Evelia's ear and then pressed it into her tiny hand. He said, "I'm thinking maybe Saturday we could take this little gal to the movies. Give the lovebirds some time alone before they have that little one of their own to contend with."

"That could be very nice," Sofia said.

A floorboard squeaked. Able looked over his shoulder at Amos. His grandson said, "Got the computer prepped. Just give me the word and we'll get your blog updated, Grandpop." It was a weekly routine.

Able sipped his coffee, savored it. His other hand was still combing through Evelia's shiny black hair. "Think we'll give it a rest this weekend," Able said. "Just don't have a hankering to say much right now."

Sofia, sliding the spatula around the pan of eggs said, "Have you or Chief Lyon learned anything more about that red pickup truck? The one in the film?"

Able scowled and said, "Red pickup truck? Film? What film?"

*   *   *

Tell Lyon was quizzing the manager of the hotel where one of the murder victims, Esmeralda Marquez had worked. "I'm curious about something," Tell told the manager—a smallish, bald, overweight man of perhaps sixty. He wore several rings on the fingers of his left hand including—*God*—a pinkie ring. Tell said, "The police reports indicate there was footage from your exterior security cameras that recorded Esmeralda leaving after her shift, getting in her car and driving away."

"Uh, yeah. That's right," the manager, John Rook, said. "I remember that."

"Thing is," Tell continued, "someone tampered with Esmeralda's car. They cut halfway through the timing belt. You know how those things work—they drive damn near everything in those engines. Messed with like it was, it was only going to carry her a short ways up the road, just as it did."

"I remember that too. That her belt was screwed with." Rook twisted his pinkie ring. "But I'm not seeing your point, Officer."

"Haven't made my point yet," Tell said, watching him play with his rings. "Here we go. Because of the way the belt was cut through, the sabotage to Esmeralda's car *had* to happen in your lot. The car had to be sitting just where it was when your security cameras filmed her leaving from her shift."

"Makes sense . . ."

"So your cameras had to have recorded an image of whoever it was using a shimmy to open her locked car door and popping the hood to cut that belt. Or the camera had to have recorded an image of some son of a bitch sliding under her car to do that."

John Rook chewed his lip. "Yeah. Fuck yeah! It should have."

"So why isn't that reported anywhere—what was filmed?"

Rook shrugged, looking perplexed. "That's a question for the cops. I never watched the films. They took them."

"Who took them? Which agency?"

"The Vale County Sheriff's Department. Sheriff Pierce himself came by with one of his men—skinny, mean-looking bastard—and took that tape. When I didn't hear about any arrest, I just figured there was nothing useful on the tape. You want to know more, you're going to have to talk to Walt Pierce."

"Yeah," Tell said, seething. He slammed his open hand down on the counter. "Damn it," he said, his hand stinging. He looked at the worried-looking manager. "It's not you. Thanks for your help, pal. And please forget that I was ever here."

Tell stepped out into the hot sun. His cell phone rang. He checked the number: Able Hawk was trying to reach him. Tell thought about it, then decided to ignore the call for the present time. If Able called right back, he'd answer. Otherwise Tell decided he'd get back to Able on his own timetable.

He swung into the cab of his SUV and rolled down the windows until the air kicked in.

Across the road, sitting between two big Ford pickup trucks, Vale County deputy Luke Strider sat in own pickup truck, smoking a cigarette and flicking ashes out the window, watching Tell.

* * *

The roadside dumpsites were easy to reach and uninteresting—nothing revelatory there. The only thing Tell gleaned sitting parked in his truck where he deduced the bodies had been dropped was how little traveled the roads running alongside the particular fields were. In that way, the sites made sense in terms of disposing of corpses. And they indicated that whoever did the deed knew cars passing by were damned rare. But that was hardly useful information.

The last site, the stream where Esmeralda was dropped, was harder to reach. Tell was bathed in sweat by the time he heard the gurgle of the stream. Mosquitoes had bitten his neck and arms. The way his luck was running, he figured that one of the little blood-suckers would probably be carrying West Nile Virus.

He was startled by the ringing of his cell phone again. It was made more jarring by the solitude under the shade of the trees; by the sound of the stream and the birds and the trill of crickets in the weeds by the creek. He checked the number: Able Hawk calling again.

Tell took a deep breath and said, "Hey Able."

"Hey, partner."

Uh-oh. Tell could already tell the tone was set for the call.

Able said, "What's this about a fucking surveillance film and a red truck? I thought we were sharing information, cocksucker."

"I wasn't deliberately keeping it from you, Able. Things have just been moving so fast. Every time I was about to pick up the phone to call you or tell you, something else got in the way . . . Amos's possible arrest, for instance."

"So fucking talk to me now, buddy," Able said. "Fill me in now, and all the way up."

Tell did that. Able said, "Clever find on your part. Too damned bad we didn't consult first before you saw that old guard at the industrial complex. I knew that bastard was ex-Vale County Sheriff's. We might have found a way to get those security tapes without him tipping Pierce. So how long until we get a rundown on those possible plates?"

"Should have them in a couple of hours or so," Tell said. "Meet me at my HQ in two hours and we'll look them over together."

"You just redeemed yourself, Tell. Where are you now?"

Tell told Able Hawk about his morning's investigation. He shared with Hawk the taped evidence he deduced must have existed depicting the tampering that had been done with Esmeralda Marquez's Hyundai.

Able said, "Walt does seem to be amassing himself a mess of film. We're going to have to confront him on all that eventually, just to move this thing along. But we need more to hang our hats on than we have. At this point, he can just stonewall us too easily. Presuming we don't catch some other breaks like that baseball film you found. That really was good work, Tell."

The sheriff hesitated, then said, "In the interest of full disclosure, and to encourage you in the future to reciprocate with more, you know, *alacrity*, I should tell you I did your lady a favor this morning." Able told Tell about Luz and about the pimp's name given him by Patricia. "I'll keep her out of it of course," Able said. "Patricia stays invisible through this," he said. "But old Tomás? 'Tween us, for him there'll soon be consequences."

"Don't need to hear you say it, Able. But thanks for the heads-up. I'll keep it secret. And thanks very much for helping out Patricia."

Able said, "Just repaying a favor. Now get your ass out of that godforsaken creek bed, Tell, and get back to my country. I don't like you in that other cocksucker's county alone."

Tell was soaked in sweat again when he reached his cruiser . . . and covered in fresh mosquito bites.

Deputy Luke Strider, parked in his red pickup behind a billboard, watched Tell Lyon leave, headed back toward the county line. He called Sheriff Pierce to report all that he'd seen, then drove into New Austin himself.

FORTY THREE

Patricia hung up the phone, feeling better after thirty minutes of talking with Salome.

She had told the woman she already thought of as a sister-in-law *everything*.

Salome listened and said, "It's only about two hours' drive, Patricia. If Tell's going to be long away, and you think this guy Shawn might really try something through others—because clearly in his present condition he's going nowhere himself for a long, long time—Chris'll be eager to come over and keep you company. He's having a hard time not inviting himself over there as it is. Chomping at the bit to try and nose into this investigation of Tell's."

"Will do, but for now, I'm okay," Patricia had said.

Salome had then quizzed Patricia further about her bouts of sickness. Salome asked, "Any sequels?"

"No, none," Patricia had said.

"It's after one o'clock," Salome had pressed further. "Day's gotten on into afternoon . . . morning's far over. You hungry?"

"A bit."

"What sounds good to you? What do you have a taste for?"

Patricia thought about that, then said, "Chinese. Chinese sounds real good."

She could hear Salome's resulting smile in her voice. "Tonight, when Tell finally gets home, whenever that is, you two go hit a Walgreens or CVS, yeah, Patricia? Go and get yourself a home pregnancy test."

Patricia had been delighted. "You *think?*"

Salome had hesitated, then said, "I'm not saying. I'm just . . . *saying.* You know?"

Patricia looked for a few moments at the phone she had just hung up. She took off her jeans and panties and T-shirt and bra. Naked, she walked to her bedroom, dug out her black bikini and made herself a tall glass of iced tea. She stepped out onto her deck and folded down a chaise lounge. The increasingly seedy neighborhood was quiet for the afternoon so she felt safe doing it: those who had jobs were at work; the others were probably still sleeping off hangovers and highs. She settled in with her iced tea and a copy of Tell's cousin's first novel.

The deck was in the shade of the rooftop for the first hour, so Patricia read, resting on her back. When the sun reached the back of the building, she rolled onto her belly and undid her top so there wouldn't be a tan line. She slipped on her sunglasses and sipped more tea from her sweating glass, its beaded surface slippery in her hand. She was reaching out to set her empty glass on the table, rising up a little so her breasts were exposed, when she suddenly had the sense she was being spied on. She settled back down, her breasts pressed to the lounge chair, and angled her book up and looked over its top at the parking lot.

A red Dodge Ram pickup truck was parked below, its hulking mass blocking Patricia's view of her own car parked alongside.

Tell was right; the Ram was massive. It screamed of the compensatory purchase of an insecure, self-esteem-challenged asshole.

A thin man with a shaven head sat in the pickup, trying to look as though he was reading a newspaper in his car in the 95-degree heat and 65-percent humidity. The price of gas had impelled the man to shut down the engine and he had both windows down, his sweating arm dangling out the window. Very little hair on his arm. There was no jewelry, not even a wedding band, on his long-fingered left hand.

Patricia pretended to read her book for a time, studying him, committing things to memory. She guessed he was probably in his late forties or early fifties. He had a wormy, graying mustache. Patricia could only see the last three digits of his license plate; an ornamental shrub obscured the rest. The last three digits of the Ram's plate read "3-7-8."

She waited another few minutes, turning pages she wasn't reading here and there, staring at and studying the man from behind her black sunglasses. She put down her book and reached around behind her, refastening her bikini top. She stood and stretched and collected her book and empty glass and walked back inside.

Patricia locked the sliding glass door to her deck and pulled shut the drapes, then called Tell on his cell phone. Five rings later he picked up. She told Tell about the red Dodge Ram parked outside and described the man sitting inside it in close detail. "It may be nothing," she said.

"You wouldn't have called me if you believed that," Tell said. "I was heading over to the station to meet Able Hawk. I'm five minutes from home. Stay inside and keep the doors locked. Don't answer the door except to the sound of my voice."

Patricia hung up and sat down on her couch and looked at the clock. Edgy, she turned on the stereo, settling on Lucinda William's "Sidewalks of the City." The song's refrain was a plea of assurance for the safety and sanctity of one's private world. Patricia was startled by the ring of the phone. "I'm parked in the spot where the bastard was parked," Tell said. "He's gone. Gone before I got here. Probably gave up when you went inside and closed the drapes."

She said, "You will come up a moment won't you?"

"I'm running late already, but sure. I could use a quick lunch."

She looked down at her bikini, half-smiling. "Sure. We'll keep it quick."

FORTY FOUR

Able Hawk said, "You're late, Lyon." He was sitting at Tell's desk, the chair tipped back and his feet crossed and resting on the corner of Tell's desk.

Tell strove for a nonchalant tone. "Something happened at home, Able. Had to swing by and make sure everything was okay. And I needed a shower after poking around that creek's bed."

Able pulled down his feet and leaned forward. "What was up?"

"A red Dodge Ram pickup truck was parked outside my place. It shook up Patricia. I think with good reason." Tell related Patricia's description of the man inside the truck.

Able said, "A red Ram like on the tape you told me about."

"That's right," Tell said.

"There are no coincidences," Able said.

"My thought too," Tell said.

"And the truck driver in question fled?"

"Yeah, but not because of me. I think he left when there was no more to see." Tell thought of Patricia in her black bikini. "He was gone by the time I got there. Patricia's with her parents for now. I'm thinking of sending her east to stay with my cousin. She'll be safe there."

"A fine idea," Able said. "Particularly given your cousin's spooky damned reputation. I'd urge action on that notion, Tell. At least maybe for a day or two. Until we get a firmer handle on the scale and dimensions of this thing."

"Probably will do that."

"Yeah, let that formidable cousin of yours see to her safety. Free you up to ride shotgun with me a few days. We might could wrap this damned thing up fast, working in tandem."

"I will, then."

"*Good.* Don't suppose Patricia got a license number from that truck?"

"A partial."

Able turned to Billy Davis. "What have you got for us?"

Billy said, "Shoot me what Patricia got from the plate, Chief. I'll see if it matches anything I have here." Billy was being cagey. Tell figured he either was hesitant to trust Able and share information, or shaky over something his license registration searches had turned up.

"Three-seven-eight," Tell said. "Those are the last three digits, Billy."

"It's a match," Billy said. "I have one here that's AJL-378. Registered through Vale County. Boy. I really hoped it wouldn't be that one of the eight possibles we've got here and the four that checked out as real license plate combos."

Able said, "Stop jawing, Billy. Give us the damned name that plate is registered to."

"Luke Strider," Billy said. His voice was full of tension.

"Name doesn't speak to me," Tell said.

Able whistled low. "It does to me. Volumes. Fucking hell. Luke Strider is one of Walt Pierce's veteran deputies."

Frowning, Tell took the report from Billy and looked it over. "Luke owns a 2003, red Dodge Ram pickup truck. Damn." He said to Able, "You know this Strider at all, Able?"

"Met him a few times briefly," Able said. "I have no real sense of the bastard, though. Unremarkable. Didn't impress me, but so few do. I will say that he meets the description of the man your lady said was spying on her."

Tell said, "You think he's capable of murdering these women?"

"Whoa, Tell." Able shook his head. "Let's not get ahead of our facts. I'm still trying to grasp this identification. Given the near misses with Shawn and with Amos, I don't want to go off half-cocked, you know? Don't want to tear off on some witch-hunt worthy of old Walt. I'm still trying to get my head around the fact our trail has led to Strider. He and Pierce go *way* back."

"So we do need to slow down and step careful," Tell said. "I agree with that. If this is the guy, and if the guy we saw on tape with him is another Vale County deputy, this is going to turn into something wicked."

"You're pretty grossly understating that," Able said. "And even if it's just Strider, it's already something wicked *and* thorny as all hell. The politics of this are going to be lethal."

"I'm not ready to approach this bastard yet," Tell said.

"I'd counsel against it if you thought you were," Able said. "It's not time yet. Any way we decide to go, we have to factor Pierce and his possible reactions and actions into our plans. We have to have a firm handle on what his response might be. I'd predict scorched earth."

"There's also the question of what his own culpability might be," Tell said. He was aware now of Billy's wide-eyed gaze roaming between Tell and Able. Tell said, "This has to stay between the three of us for now, right, Billy?"

"Damn better believe it, skipper," Billy said, wetting his lips. "I wish I didn't know. Way I figure it, Sheriff Pierce might try to fuck this up for us on principle. Or, angling to protect his own, he might fuck us over, whether it's the right or wrong thing to do in terms of justice for these women. He's got a reputation for an extreme temper, Chief. He comes by that rep honest enough."

"Bill's right that Walt's well capable of lashing out in pique," Able said. He smoothed his mustache over and over with his thumb and forefinger's tip. "We push ahead quietly and carefully, like you say, Tell. What we have now isn't nearly enough. All we've got is a blurry image and license plate—a half plate from Patricia and a full plate extrapolated by eggheads from that fuzzy film you found. It's all real, but it ain't nearly enough."

Tell nodded. "So we try to learn more about Luke's movements. See if we can tie him to the other killings, which I'm now convinced are linked."

"And we stay in close touch, the three of us," Able said. "This is cocksucking treacherous. I'd urge none of us to do any damned thing without consulting first with the other two. Walt or his gets wind we're looking their way, it could be a bloodbath. Us looking to Strider and leaving fingerprints of our looking? Well, Walt could misconstrue our intent. Walt might realize the fact we're looking to *him* as a suspect. That happens, I'd hate to predict his response. That's why I say you should get your lady out of town, Tell." Able looked at Billy. "You a single fella, Bill?"

"I'm not married, if that's what you mean." Billy said, ashen.

Able stood up and his knees cracked. "I gotta get on to elsewhere. Let's convene again, but not here. Let's plan on lunch tomorrow. Say Patricia's folks' place, Tell. Somethin' like sanctuary. What do you say?"

"Sounds good to me," Tell said.

"Think hard on this boys," Able said. "Let's have some ideas for action next time we meet."

THEN

A cantina they used to drink in when they were peers. Springsteen's "My Beautiful Reward" on the jukebox and sweating glasses of margaritas splashed with amaretto.

Tell had been after Seth to allow him to place Seth's name in the pool for possible promotion. Some stalwarts were retiring; opportunity, Tell said, loomed.

Seth balked.

At first Tell feared there might be jealousy or resentment bound up in Seth's resistance.

But that didn't seem right or possible. While originally insisting he had no interest in climbing the ladder himself, Seth had urged Tell into accepting a bump upstairs. Seth figured time might have changed his friend's mind about his own career path.

But Seth still insisted he had no ambitions running that way. He craved, he claimed, no more than he presently had. "I just don't want to think that hard for one thing," Seth said.

Tell persisted. Seth just shook his head. "I'm no family man like you, Tell. I like women too much and I don't like bosses, not at all. I can follow orders only up to a point and I do it best at a distance. I like being alone out there on the road. Even with all that shit we see and endure, I'd rather be out there alone with my tunes, doin' my job, than sitting behind a desk."

Despite the difference in their positions now, the two men had stayed friends. That had required a tightrope walk. Tell was just politic enough to know how things could be made to look—or how they might be perceived. You just weren't supposed to fraternize with "subordinates."

Seth got that too. At the HQ they were cordial. After hours, they still drank in the same obscure little hole-in-the-wall cantina they'd chosen when all the usual, better-known watering holes on the other side became too crowded with the too familiar faces they'd caught and sent back across the line.

The waitress plunked a bowl of oily nachos down between them. They tapped glasses and toasted Tell's pending fatherhood.

Seth scooped a heaping pile of salsa onto a sodden tortilla chip and said, "You should hand off this Angel Valenzuela thing, buddy. They don't call him *El Muerte* for no reason at all, Tell. This is a bag of shit that can bring nothin' but grief, brother. I mean it, buddy. Those assholes at the top have been after Angel for years. They call him the Angel of Death—our so-called superiors. The only one of us who ever supposedly came close to laying hands on the son of a bitch ended up getting himself killed. And it wasn't slow by all accounts. Think on that last, Tell. Think on it hard. You're the only friend I've got from the day job, and I don't want to lose you. I'm pretty sure Marita feels the same way."

Tell just smiled and shook his head. "More so, I hope."

"Anyway, even if some lucky bastard does take Angel down, it won't change anything in the long run, Tell. Not a lick."

"What do you mean?"

Seth helped himself to another chip. "The Mexicans want to be on our side of the line. Every damn one of 'em, I expect. And people on both sides want their next fix or cheap-as-dirt illegal worker. So there'll always be more of Angel's kind to see to those wrong desires. There always have been, and there always will be. Short of building a wall a hundred feet high and ten feet thick along the border, end-to-end, there always will be ones like Angel. That's just the way it is and nobody, least of all you and I, can change it."

FORTY FIVE

Patricia hugged Tell hard. "It's been *my* long day this time," she said.

Over dinner, she told him about Luz. She confessed about Shawn's note and the photo he sent her. Tell looked grave and then, to Patricia's eyes, angry.

Patricia didn't know that after she had confided Shawn's note and e-mail to Salome, and Salome had told Chris, that Chris Lyon, fearing for Patricia and afraid she might keep it from Tell, had already tipped his cousin to Shawn's threats. Tell had already promised himself a "chat" with Shawn in the morning.

Tell said, "I want you to go to Cedartown for a few days, Patricia. I'll drive you halfway. Chris will meet us in Morton Springs. He's got business there, anyway. He'll take you the rest of the way to his place."

"I'll be fine," she said. "I don't want to step on sensitive ground here, but not every case you handle is going to put me in danger, Tell."

"Stop right there," Tell said. "We had this guy parked under our window watching you today. This is a done deal. You're going to Cedartown. I'm not going to risk having happen again—" He brought himself up short.

Patricia knew where he was headed, of course. She wet her lips, nodded. "You're right," she said. "I'll go there. I just hate you being alone."

"I'll frankly be safer alone," Tell said. "You're a major distraction, Patricia."

She managed a smile. "I sure hope so."

He combed her hair with his fingers. "So that's settled. You go and hang with Salome and Chris. Take a good look at that land they offered us to build on. Think about where the rising sun might fall on windows. Bedroom windows, particularly."

She nodded, smiling. "Have you thought more about that? Because, I have. I want to do it. I want to live there."

"I haven't been here a month," Tell said. "Seems wrong to be looking for another job already."

"But think of the fringes," Patricia said. "You'd go in commanding a force that's staffed with pros, according to Chris. You've spoken with Atchity. Did he impress you?"

"Very much," Tell said. "He's like Able Hawk with a conscience."

Patricia didn't know how to respond to that, so she said, "And we'd have Chris and Salome as neighbors. I like her very much. She's like the cooler older sister I never had. Their kids are great and who better for our children to grow up around? I mean, if we have any."

Tell said, "And Chris?"

His fiancée hesitated. "He's scary in some ways. I read one of his books today."

"Yeah? Which one?"

"The first, *Parts Unknown*. How much of that one is made up?"

"He pretty much just changed some names. In terms of fiction, he didn't have to make up a lot in that one. It was all tied to stuff from his reporting days. The Occam Butcher case was all too real. The killer really came after Chris, and after the women he knew at the time."

"Oh . . ." Patricia bit her lip and stroked a wing of hair behind her ear. "Like I said, Chris is scary. But strangely appealing. And I do feel safe around him. Don't know how Salome lives with him though. The intensity that comes off the guy is exhausting."

"Salome's the same way, on her own level," Tell said. "It's good they found one another. I don't expect there are many, if any, others out there for either of them."

Patricia said, "So you're inclined to take them up on their offer?"

"Oh, I incline. But for all kinds of reasons, I need to close this case first."

"How close are you, Tell?"

"We may have turned the corner today. But I can't say more."

"I don't want to know more," Patricia said. "When are we sending me off?"

"Could do it tonight," he said.

"No, Tell. Please. It's Friday night. *Our* night. And you promised to take me to the festival tomorrow."

"Sunday, then," Tell said. "I'll stick as close to you as I can in the meantime."

Patricia squeezed his hand, then stood and started gathering dishes. He noticed she hadn't made them drinks. That was some kind of first. As if reading his mind, she said, "I'm two days late now. Did you make it to the pharmacy?"

He smiled and stood and fetched the bag with the drugstore's logo on the outside. He held up the test kit. "You ready for this?"

She said, "Better question is, are *you* ready for this, Tell Lyon? We were reckless. This wasn't planned. I mean, I want you to know now, either way this goes, I wasn't trying to get pregnant, but if I am, I'm not sorry."

"Understood. I was reckless too." He kissed her and she took the box from his hand. The familiarity of this scene—this waiting once again on the maybe life-changing verdict of a plastic stick—cut through him. It struck him again how unbalanced their experiences were. This was a moment for Patricia. For him too, of course . . . but on his side, it was one fraught with memory and loss. He hoped Patricia didn't sense it.

She pulled on her reading glasses and started reading the enclosed instructions. "You load the dishwasher," she said. "I'll go in the bathroom and see about changing our lives."

FORTY SIX

Tell awakened first, lying there in the dark, watching the light through cracks around the curtains go from blue to red and finally to soft orange-yellow. The mourning doves were calling to one another and he listened to those, his hand straying to Patricia's bare belly, stroking it.

He remembered Patricia's face as she came out of the bathroom holding the test device with the little blue minus sign. Her look of sadness pierced him. She had said, "I'm disappointed, frankly. How about you?"

Tell had responded, "Me too, a little. But it will also be good to have time together first. Time for the two of us, I mean. There'll be plenty of time for children later."

He had moved to kiss her then, but she showed him her cheek. "Better be careful," she had said, backing away. "I must really have something—flu or a virus."

"More likely just nerves," Tell said. "You've been through the ringer these past few days."

Awaiting the results, they had talked through the door about children. He wondered if it might be a son or a daughter. A son would be new territory for him. But he wasn't sure a daughter would be the mixed blessing that Patricia had feared out loud it might be. Patricia risked admitting that she feared another little girl would perpetually remind Tell of his lost Claudia. Particularly since, given Patricia's own ethnic background, the little girl Tell and

284

Patricia might make together would likely have Claudia's coloring . . . her dark hair and eyes and whatever similarity of facial features that Tell's genes mandated. Tell believed it would be okay. Their daughter, if their baby *was* a daughter, would be Patricia's and his together, apart from Claudia and what he had shared with Marita. He was certain of that and promised Patricia it was so.

But it wasn't to be, so far as the home-testing kit could be trusted.

He felt the tension of Patricia's skin change under his fingertips and he knew she had awakened.

Tell checked the clock by the bed. "Really don't want to go. But I should shower. Have to get over to the festival and walk the grounds before it opens. I'll have one of my men sit out front while I'm gone. Won't be gone more than two hours. Then I have a lunch appointment with Able Hawk at your folks' place. Thought you could ride along with me and maybe visit with your folks while Able and I hash some things out. Then we can head on over to the festival."

"Sounds good," she said, hoarse from sleep. "Better leave the bathroom door unlocked while you shower, Tell. Just in case I get sick again."

* * *

Tell waited until Officer Rick Keaton arrived in his squad car to take up post guarding Patricia. He thanked Rick and then made a quick detour to the hospital. Visiting hours hadn't started yet, but Tell's badge bought him an audience. Shawn was a pile of bandages. Most of the reporter's face was obscured by the new dressings covering his just-completed nose job.

Shawn weakly waved a hand in hello. With all the wrappings around Shawn's head wounds, Tell could really only see his eyes and not enough of the skin and eyebrows around those to know for certain whether Shawn's gaze was curious or scared or angry.

Tell said, "Hey, Shawn. I'm very sorry for what happened to you. I really am. But this isn't a social or compassionate call."

Now Tell thought he saw some uneasiness in Shawn's suddenly wider eyes. Shawn clacked on the computer keyboard resting on the tray table above his lap. Tell moved in close, crowding Shawn to read what was on the screen. Shawn had typed, *You arrest the ones who did this to me?*

"No, not yet," Tell said. "Able Hawk's on your case. I'm chasing a murderer. I'm here to be on your case in a different way, Shawn. Ignore my badge now. I'm not here under color of authority. I'm here to tell you if you threaten Patricia again, or if you send her any more notes or e-mails like the last ones, regardless of what your current condition is, I'm going to finish what those Mexican gangbangers started. Do we understand one another?"

After two long seconds of silence, of staring at Shawn's wide, unblinking, angry eyes, Tell pointed at the laptop. "Do you understand?"

Shawn typed, *Yes.*

Tell reached out for Shawn's chest and the reporter flinched. Tell patted Shawn's chest. "Hope you feel better soon, Shawn. I surely don't envy you the climb back." Tell backed away from the computer screen. "I'll be having lunch in a bit with Able Hawk, Shawn. I'll ask him how he's coming on your case. I'll tell him you'd appreciate an update on his progress. You just remember to put Patricia out of your mind, because you've clearly suffered enough."

Tell paused at the door and half turned. "One more thing, Shawn. I've decided you *did* slip Thalia that Rohypnol. That you set her up for what happened later. That last part was unwitting. But you feeding Thalia that dope, that's still rape and it's still fucking evil. That makes you a monster. I mean to see that you pay for that once you get your health back."

* * *

Tell walked the festival grounds, waving to a few carnies and food-stand operators who were still setting up. New Austin's mayor, Ernest Rice, called to him. Tell met him in the middle of the midway and shook hands.

"Life going well, Chief?"

"Could be worse," Tell said.

The mayor said, "Anything we need to talk about, Chief?"

"Not from my direction, Tell said. "From yours?"

"Just give me a quiet festival, Chief. With all the racial tension in town since the Ruiz murder, and that reporter being beaten by those Mexicans, quiet is all I ask."

"I certainly aim to deliver that, Mayor."

They shook hands again and Tell wandered the festival grounds a bit longer—the festival grounds that consisted of the ball diamonds fronting the field where Thalia Ruiz was found dead, the parking lot and a few adjacent residential streets. A mobile stage was set up in a corner of the parking lot. A mariachi band was warming up on the stage.

Tell checked his watch. It was time to get Patricia.

* * *

Tell dismissed Rick Keaton from guard duty so that Rick could commence his shift at the festival.

He keyed himself in and Patricia hugged him hard. Tell had let Patricia talk him into a trip to the uniform store a couple of days before. She had picked out khaki pants and shirts, long and short-sleeved—both kinds with epaulets. She'd sewed on the New Austin patches and he'd transferred his insignia and bars and badge from the black uniforms to the tan ones.

"At least this rig will be cooler in this damned heat," Tell said.

Patricia raised her eyebrows, disappointed. "You don't like it?"

"I look like a Texas Ranger."

"I think you look wonderful," Patricia said. "And it doesn't come off scary like those black, Nazi-style outfits your crew wears now. Any of your other folks going for the tan option now that you've offered it?"

Tell pulled on his second cowboy boot and pulled his pant leg down to cover the cuff of his boot. "All but Billy Davis. He says black is slimming."

"That's true up to a point," Patricia said. "But at some size, you just become a big, black, sweaty wall."

"You probably just described Bill later this afternoon," Tell said. "His shift at the festival runs two to ten. Oven hours."

"And your shift, Tell?"

"Once you're out of harm's way, I go all day Sunday," he said. "Wanted to give my folks at least one day off this weekend."

"So you take me to Chris for protection tonight?"

"No, still plan on that early Sunday morning," Tell said. "No way I'm letting go of you tonight. Especially not looking like you do now. I don't want to leave this room."

Patricia was wearing a white cotton dress that bared her shoulders and emphasized her dark hair, which she had gathered up.

She kissed Tell and said, "*Now* I can put on my lipstick." He kissed the back of her long, tanned neck while she did that. She said, "I'm gonna look like a clown, if you keep making me crazy doing that."

* * *

Tell, Able and Billy were gathered around a table at Señor Augustin's. Patricia was sitting across the dining room in a booth with her parents. She sensed Tell watching her and glanced over and smiled. Able said, "God, but she's lovely, your Patricia."

Billy said, "She surely is that." Then he said, "Hey, fellas, to the topic of this meeting. I'm going to say up front, I've had no great ideas about next moves on this Strider mess."

Able, sour-faced, said, "Confess that I'm similarly stymied. Tell? It's up to you, Chief."

Tell shrugged. "My nature favors rushing in where smarter angels like you two fear to tread. It's always my impulse. And sometimes my undoing. It's cost me before. And now I have something to lose again."

Able's gaze drifted back to Patricia, thinking of Tell's lost wife and child. "Yes, you surely do," Able agreed. "It's a wise man knows his weaknesses. So what then?"

Tell said, "I'm going to be alone for a couple of days starting tomorrow morning. Patricia will be safely out of the way. So I propose a two-pronged strategy."

Able—officially off duty—sipped his Texas margarita on the rocks. "Already I'm not liking the drift of this. So what's your too intrepid plan that I'm going to reject, Tell?"

"Billy here is chatting acquaintances with one of Walt Pierce's young guys—Tom Winch, a new dude with a conscience." Tell sipped his iced tea. He nodded at Billy Davis. "Billy, if you can arrange it, tonight, ideally, I'd like you to take your friend out for a drink or something. Commiserate with him. Bitch about your respective bosses. Draw Tom out on the subject of Strider. Then, if the mood seems right, confide that I'm looking at Luke Strider

Craig McDonald

for Thalia's murder. Without getting too specific about the exact nature of the evidence—because we don't want Walt or Luke going looking for their own copy of the film and learning how little we actually have—let slip about that tape I have of Luke dumping the body. We'll see if doing that we can provoke a response from Luke. Something spastic, I hope. Maybe make Luke do something archly stupid. Force him to make a mistake we can use to our advantage."

"And paint a big-ass target on your back doing it, Tell," Able said. "I don't fucking like it. Not a bit. It's sloppy and unpredictable. You can't point a snake, son."

"Patricia will be safe enough."

"But *you* won't be safe, Tell," Able said. "Just what fool morning, exactly, did you wake up and fancy yourself of a sudden bulletproof?"

"I'll be very careful," Tell said. "I really don't want to die, and particularly not now."

"I'll have every deputy I can spare having your back," Able said. "That's what's going to happen, *if* we go down this road. And my instincts are all against doing that."

Tell said, "Can you make this happen, Billy?"

"I gotta work the festival tonight," Billy said, shrugging. "Otherwise, well, Saturday nights, we have this bunch of us who get together." Billy looked a little queasy. But he was also three-quarters of the way through a "mucho grande burrito," overstuffed with *carne asada* sirloin. As tribute for finishing the out-sized entrée, Señor Augustin's awarded the successful with a complimentary serving of fried ice cream. It was a little like rewarding a binge drinker with a beer keg. Billy sipped his third Cherry Coke and said, "I'm seeing a friend of Tom's new wife Cheryl-Ann's, lately. Four of us and another couple get together Saturday nights for Pictionary."

Billy's head was down as he confessed that last and Tell was grateful that his officer missed the eye-rolling his admission prompted on

290

the part of Able Hawk. "Long about nine," Bill continued, "things kind of split off. Us guys end up on the porch with beers."

Able asked, "Who's the third man? Could he queer the conversation?"

"Funny you should say it that way," Billy said. "Fella name of Syd Cord. He's a beautician. He tends to hang in with the women to watch *Sex and the City* episodes on DVD."

Able was in danger of saying something hurtful—Tell sensed it. A mocking smile was spreading across Able's face. Tell quickly said, "Do it tonight, then, Billy. Tell them your work schedule changed. I'll be at the festival most of today, anyway, so I'll relieve Rick early this afternoon. I'll have Rick take the back half of your shift and throw him some overtime. His daughter needs braces so Rick needs the cash, anyway."

Able sipped his margarita. "I still don't like you drawing fire this way, Tell. Not a bit."

"So let's just see it doesn't stretch much beyond Monday night." Tell scooped salsa up on a chip, munched on it. "You really going to put shadows on me, Able?"

Able pointed a thick finger at him. "Don't start trying to argue me out of that, Tell."

"Wouldn't think of it. Hell, I'll be glad knowing they are there."

"That's the only reasonable fucking thing you've said this session," Able said.

Billy left them. After some more dickering on strategy, Tell confided to Able his visit to Shawn O'Hara, and its reason. Able said, "I'd have done the same. That said, if Shawn eventually goes back to work, he can be a tool for us. And he can be a dangerous enemy, pissed on. He already hates you for you and Patricia. Any objection to my staying friendly on face with Shawn—good cop to your bad cop?"

"I surely made myself bad cop with Shawn this morning," Tell said. "So why deviate now? Besides, I authentically despise the sorry bastard. I mean to charge him with rape, Able."

"Me too, particularly if you're right about him doping my girl," Able said. "But he's the reporter we've got to cope with for the moment. And I should close that case of his beating to win his short-term favor. Just got distracted with other things. I'll go close that case now."

Tell smiled. "What? Just like that?" He snapped his fingers.

Able said, "Sure. Why not? This is easy."

Tell said, "Maybe see you at the Latino Festival later, Able?"

The Horton County sheriff scoffed at that. "Hell no. Mine's the last mug them folks want to see. No, I'm going to take Thalia's mamma and little girl to the movies tonight. Figure on seein' the new Superman flick."

Smiling, Tell said, "That's a fine thing you did, taking them on, giving them a roof."

"What else was I going to do?" Able shook his head. "That girl's carrying my great-grandchild. Sofia ain't got the money to support three mouths. Someone had to do the right thing."

Tell considered that. "Word of what you've done gets out, it may wreck your wicked reputation in certain quarters of the West Side."

"I ain't that cynical," Hawk said. "Even in an election year."

"I've never thought you to be that," Tell said.

* * *

After his meeting with Able and Billy broke up, Tell drifted over to his future in-laws' booth to chat for a few minutes. He was acutely aware of how closely Patricia's parents watched the two of them together. He and her father had hit it off immediately. Augustin was also several years older than his own wife. Not quite the span that lay between Tell and Patricia, but close enough. Patricia slipped her arm through Tell's and he closed his hand over hers. Smiling, her father said, "Our Patricia will be the prettiest girl at the festival."

"Yes, she will be," Tell said.

Patricia's mother, who Tell sensed was still taking his measure, said, "Have you two given any thought to children?" She smiled at Tell. "We're not getting any younger and Augustin is very eager to be an *abuelo* . . ."

We're not getting any younger?

Red-faced, Tell smiled at Patricia. He said, "You want to field that one?"

* * *

About a dozen white demonstrators stood outside the festival grounds, waving signs that said *Go home!* and *Illegals are illegal!*

As they climbed out of his SUV, Patricia said, "Wear your hat, won't you Tell? With the boots, it makes the whole uniform work."

"No way," Tell said. "I'd really look like a Texas Ranger then."

"No, you'll look dashing," she said. "And if the sun gets too intense, I'll be borrowing that hat of yours."

He said, "Always the ulterior motive with you."

"Always." She took Tell's arm and they crossed the dusty gravel lot toward the ball diamonds. Patricia said, "Wicked hot." She pointed at a lemon-shakeup stand. "Let's get a couple of those."

"Sure." They were halfway to the concession stand when an old Mexican woman stopped them. She said in Spanish, "Is it true, *Jefe*, that you speak Spanish as good as I do?"

Tell answered in the woman's own tongue, "I'll leave you to decide how well I speak it, *señora*." He tipped his hat to her.

The old woman smiled and said, "You speak very well. I'm thanking you for what you did to help my grandson. His name is Richie Huerta."

Tell remembered the boy driving the car he had stopped for speeding. It was Richie's false identification—and those of his passengers—that had put Tell on the path to uncovering Able's false identification scheme.

"Yes. I remember Richie," Tell said. "How is he?"

"*Bueno*," the old woman said. "He's working hard to do all you asked of him. You made quite an impression on Richie and he won't ever forget it. Neither will I. Or any of those who we know. I wanted to tell you how grateful I am. How grateful I am, and many others. We are calling you *El Léon* now. The antidote, we hope maybe, for *El Gavilan*."

Nodding and smiling, Tell wondered what this elderly woman— who was presumably undocumented herself—would think if she knew that Tell had just left a lunch with *El Gavilan*. What would she think of Tell if she knew of his strategic alliance with Able Hawk? He saw that the old woman was closely studying Patricia. Tell said, still speaking in Spanish, "A thousand pardons, *señora*. This is my fiancée, Patricia."

The old woman dipped her head and smiled at Patricia. "I saw your picture and announcement in *El Pueblo*. It's a new newspaper in Spanish that commenced printing last week." She shook Patricia's hand. "You're even more beautiful than in your photo."

Tell figured the new newspaper must have picked up the engagement announcement from the *New Austin Recorder*. The old woman said, "I wish you both all happiness. But please be careful, *Jefe*. You have many friends among mine now. Many more than just a week ago. But they still watch you carefully. And a good man in your position can have just as many enemies. So be careful, *Jefe*."

"I will, thank you," Tell said. He was aware of a small crowd that had gathered around them. He was beginning to sense the old woman must be some kind of wheel in the New Austin Latino community.

The small group of Latino men and women were watching Tell speak to the old woman, who was backing away, aware now herself of the ring forming around them. The old woman suddenly smiled and held up her right fist and shouted, "*Viva Léon!*"

The call was taken up by several of those around them, and soon by others whose attention had been caught by the cheers. Tell murmured, "Oh, good Christ," and took Patricia's bare brown arm, smiling awkwardly and trying to get away from them all as quickly as he could and still remain politely respectful.

Patricia leaned in and said softly, "What exactly did you do for her grandson to merit that?"

Tell steered her toward a distant concession trailer. "I'll tell you on the way to our lemon shakeups," he said. "But let's get away from these folks first." There were still a few scattered *vivas* being shouted behind them in Tell's honor.

Patricia smiled and said, "You're actually embarrassed by that, aren't you?"

"Horribly."

"You really seem to be their hero," she said. "That's kind of strange, particularly given what you did before coming here. I mean, assuming they know you were Border Patrol."

"I think some of it probably has more to do with the fact I'm simply not Hawk."

There were quieter sequels as the day ground on. Young Mexican men and older Latino men and women greeted Tell in Spanish, "*Hola, Léon,*" or "*Hola, Jefe Léon.*"

They had lunch in a big tent set up alongside Señor Augustin's food trailer—tacos and burritos. Evading the heat, her parents had stayed to staff the restaurant, sending in the second string to work the festival.

Patricia ordered a cold Tecate in a waxed-paper cup. But she exchanged it for Tell's Sprite when they reached their table. "Need to loosen you up a bit," Patricia said. "Get you to accept these *vivas* with more grace." She sipped Tell's Sprite.

"I ever reach that point, you should decry me for a consummate ass," Tell said. "So what do you make of the event?"

Patricia shrugged. "I don't know. I'm not exactly getting the cold shoulder, but on the other hand, nobody's real friendly. Guess that's the kind of the thing I notice now, the chilliness between the legal and illegal Latinos around here. Not to say they view me as an Uncle Tom, but in a way, maybe they do."

Across the midway, a painter was displaying his works for sale. All of them were portraits painted on black velvet: Che Guevara, Pancho Villa, Emiliano Zapata . . . Antonio Banderas and Salma Hayek. And there was one of Able Hawk. Hawk was depicted full figure, holding a Mexican flag in one hand and an American flag in the other. A hawk was perched on one of black-velvet Able's shoulders. Smiling, Tell pointed out the painting to Patricia. She laughed and said, "That's so friggin' hideous!"

"Remind me before we leave to come back for it," Tell said. "I want it very much."

Patricia scowled through her smile. "Not as décor for our house . . . ?"

"No, for Able Hawk's," Tell said. "He'll *love* it."

She said, "Sad thing is, that's probably all too true." She smiled and leaning across the table, showing him the tops of her breasts and making him hard, she said, "Bet you dinner by tomorrow he's painted one of you."

Tell said, "I think you just cost me an erection." Patricia laughed and squeezed his hand.

Across the festival grounds, a band was closing with a raucous and ragged rendition of "Volver, Volver."

Tell heard a new band introduced and the lead singer said in Spanish, then in English, "My nephew was recently helped out of a jam by our new police chief, Tell Lyon. So we send this song out in tribute to *Jefe* Lyon. *Viva, Jefe Lyon!*"

Exasperated, Tell said, "Oh, for God's sake." He drained his drink as the band began a ragged and gravelly cover of Ry Cooder's beautiful and stirring "Across the Borderline." Tell tossed the cup in a nearby trash bin. His cell phone rang. It was the mayor.

"Where are you right now, Tell?"

Tell told him. "Stay there," Mayor Rice said. "Need two minutes with you."

It took less than half a minute for Mayor Ernest Rice to reach them. Tell pulled out a chair, said, "Howdy, Mayor."

Patricia said, "Good to meet you, sir."

"Truly my pleasure, miss," the mayor said, sizing her up—a look in his eyes of an idea forming.

Tell said, "What's up, Mayor?"

Ernest Rice said, "I had no idea you'd already accumulated such stature in the Latino community." The mayor was suddenly red-faced. Tell sensed it would be easier for the mayor to speak whatever was on his mind if Tell asked Patricia to give them a few moments alone. But he already didn't like the drift of the conversation, so he said nothing.

The mayor continued, "Rumor has it that you speak fluent Spanish."

"He does," Patricia said. "Like a native." Tell wanted to spank her.

"Well good!" Mayor Rice smiled. "That's *real* real good."

Frowning, Tell said, "Get you a chimichanga, Mayor? Maybe some fish tacos?"

"No thanks, Chief," Ernest Rice said. "You see, I've been asked to say a few words in a bit. I trust you know that I'm up for reelection in November, Tell. I can barely string together a sentence in English, some would say. Not a natural public speaker. Would be a great help to me if, popular as you clearly are, and speaking Spanish like you do, if you could maybe stand with me as interpreter. Maybe after that, you could say a few words yourself."

Tell suppressed a wince. He said, "I'm not really good at translating off-the-cuff, necessarily."

Mayor Rice narrowed his eyes. "Ever tried?"

"Not so much, no," Tell said, squirming. "But talking for myself, I can pick my own path, navigate to my own vocabulary, so to speak. Paraphrasing you on the fly . . . ? And for such an important speech?" Tell sensed Patricia suppressing a smile, amused by his predicament. "I'd just hate not to do you justice, Mayor."

Ernest Rice held up a hand, smiling. "I have the text of my speech here," he said. "We could adjust to your vocabulary, to borrow your phrase. Tweak the phrasing so you're comfortable."

Nodding and smiling a smile that felt sickly to himself, Tell accepted the slip of paper and read over the mayor's speech. It could have been worse. As it was, it stressed inclusion and tolerance. Nothing too wince-inducing in any of that.

Tell said, "No, I think we're okay. I can keep up with this just fine. Certainly, the sentiments are fine ones."

Crawling in bed with the man who'd gotten Tell his job—as Tell would be doing delivering his speech in tandem with Mayor Ernest Rice—he could only hope that Rice's opponent wasn't the victor in the fall election. But then, if Tell accepted the post as Cedartown chief of police, it would all be academic, anyway.

"So you'll do it, Chief?"

"Sure, Mayor."

"We're on at four P.M. at the stage in the parking lot yonder." Mayor Rice stood and folded up his speech and slipped it in his pocket. He shook Tell's hand heartily and leaned down and gave Patricia an air kiss. "Be happy to have you join your fiancé on stage, ma'am."

Patricia smiled and said, "Thanks, but I'd probably break my leg in these damned heels trying to get up on that stage."

"Thanks again, Tell," the mayor said, waving over his shoulder.

"*De nada,*" Tell said. "See you at four."

When the mayor was out of earshot, Patricia said, "That was cynical and transparent—I mean him trying to get your 'Mexican' girlfriend up there with the two of you." She smiled. "But I'm going to relish this show to come."

Tell said, "I'm going to be one hell of a lot stingier handing out my damned cell phone number."

"You'll be terrific," Patricia said. She cleared off their plates and pointed at the Ferris wheel. "Take me for a spin?"

THEN

It was some old codger who drove home for Able the realization of what was happening around him.

Oh, Able sensed it before, in his way. He knew things were changing and he was seeing a lot more Mexicans in his neck of the woods. But it took old Elmer Engles to make Able see it fully.

They were sitting in adjacent chairs in White's Barber Shop. His barber, Jim McDonald, was finishing up Able's haircut; Elmer was just settling in. The old man raised his chin to get his wattle clear as the drop cloth was clipped secure there around his throat. He said in a cracked voice, "Holy fucking Christ Sheriff Hawk, what's become of our West Side?"

Able rarely ventured that way—it was mostly city in his mind, and a part of it actually overlapped an adjacent county. He and the current chief didn't get on at all, so Able had focused his efforts on the rest of the county, thinking to outwait the chief; something about New Austin ate municipal lawmen, usually in under five years.

But then Able thought about it harder and realized it had been nearly a year since he'd even ventured into that neck of the woods for so much as an idle drive. He waited as the drop cloth was whipped off and Jim whisked him off with a small stiff-bristled brush. Able paid for his haircut and waved at the old-timer. "I'll go have a look-see now, Elmer. Do it now." He paused and smiled. "You stay away from them young women, now, you hear, Elmer? You ain't seventy no more."

* * *

Able drove slowly down the four-lane, looking at strip malls that had gone native. Spanish signage and a profusion of *taqueria* trailers littered the outlots. The Giant Eagle advertised a Latino shopping selection. The library was touting its ESL magazines and books on audio. Mexican groceries and bars proliferated.

It was like someone scooped up several blocks of Juarez and dropped it all in the middle of the Buckeye State. Able was aghast.

He drove back to headquarters; got his people pulling crime reports. By the time he finished surveying stats from this little Mexico festering in his county, Able was seething.

FORTY SEVEN

Able Hawk crammed his barrel chest into the bulletproof vest and then wedged his head into a flak helmet. Smiling, he checked his four deputies who were now similarly armored.

"Here's the rundown my lads," Able said. "One of the bastards who beat Shawn O'Hara near to death mentioned he was doing it to avenge a brother put out of work by our little raid out to the Morales brothers' shithole farm a few days back. This brother was a meth cooker, I expect. Anyway, Shawn's attacker was stupid enough to put a name to this brother of his. So we've gone back and matched that name, 'Javier,' with the cheerful assistance of some of the ones we've got in custody from the raid. We've already picked up Javier Acosta. Javier, in turn, gave us the finger on his brother, who was Shawn's lead attacker. We go to take him down, now. His name is Jésus Acosta. Figure that Jésus, in turn, will give us the names of the others who fucked up that sorry-ass reporter."

Deputy Troy Marshall looked down at his body armor. "We expecting they might have some serious firepower, Sheriff?"

"We expect, I'm afraid," Able said. "The old boy we go to see has ties to the Morales brothers. Through his sibling, we know that. But maybe, also, this Jésus has ties to that badass Mexican gang 'MS-13.' Or so I hear through the Mexican grapevine. So, as I say, our quarry today is Jésus Acosta. I want this little bastard alive and talking, boys. That said, if Jésus were to lose a few teeth—short of a broken jaw—I wouldn't look askance at the man who rendered same. As to legs, I'll only say that it would be something like a Biblical balancing of the scales if Jésus were to sustain a broken kneecap, or even two. Particularly viewed in light of what he did with a baseball bat to Shawn O'Hara's leg, I mean. Suppose what I'm saying is, if this Mexican thug's leg *was* to be broken to the far margins of medical repair, I'd shed no crocodile tears. Blows to the groin are also acceptable, given the plumbing damage he did that reporter. Old Testament, eye-for-eye balance. And frankly, we do not want Jésus spreading his evil seed. Now let's go and get this sorry cocksucker."

* * *

An hour later, Able was standing over a half snarling, half crying Jésus Acosta. The boy's front teeth were broken off at the gumline and blood trails ran down both sides of his mouth and spilled down over his pointed chin . . . drying in the sparse and curly strands of a goatee there.

Jésus's right leg was twisted at a severe right angle to his thigh. "I can't feel my fucking foot," Jésus whimpered.

"Nerve damage, likely," Able said. "Probably a permanent thing. Would have gone easier for you if you hadn't put a round in Deputy Marshall's leg, Jésus. You just better hope Deputy Marshall doesn't have nerve damage in *his* leg. Now, Jésus, I want the names of those that helped you beat Shawn O'Hara. This is my day off and I resent working on my day off."

Jésus said, "*Gordo maricón*," and spat blood clots at Able. "Fuck you, old man! *Chupa mi huevos, maricón!*"

Able said, "Hey, I know them fuckin' Mexican cuss words and I know what they mean, *cholo*. And you best be choosier with them words, 'cause without your front teeth, Jésus, you're the one talking with a fucking lisp. Provoke me and I'll go to work on your cock like you animals did to Shawn O'Hara's. Maybe put you in the 'tranny' stakes. Then who'll be the *maricón*? Will your boss back in Mexico, Guzman, want you back then?"

With the toe of his boot, Able abruptly nudged Jésus's broken leg a few inches backward and Jésus screamed, tears flowing again. "See, you can feel something after all," Able said. "Ain't that fine news for both of us? Now, names. Names right now, or I'm going to see if I can shove the toe of your numb foot into what's left of your ear."

The sheriff motioned and a deputy got down next to Jésus and started taking down names.

"He gets through giving you those," Able said, "you get him going on names connected to MS-13. About damned time we engaged those gangbanger cocksuckers. Time to shut their sorry business down in Horton County and fire a shot back across the border at the cartels."

Able nodded at a deputy. "You see to the paperwork and details here on out? My plate's still full and I've got other places to be."

* * *

Later, Able dropped by the hospital to briefly check in on Troy Marshall. The bullet had passed through his deputy's calf, just missing most of the muscle and the Achilles tendon. Troy said, "Friggin' luck ain't it, Sheriff? Did two tours of Iraq and worst I got was a cut from a jagged piece of rebar during a night operation. Had to come home to Ohio to get my ass shot. How's the one who did it to me?"

"Jésus lost most of an ear," Able said. "Four teeth knocked out and another six they may have to pull if they show no signs of tightening up. And his right leg's fucked up, but good. He may yet lose that leg above the knee. Docs say it's the worst compound fracture they've ever seen and his kneecap is like baby powder. Nerves were severed and an artery cut. Not much blood getting down there to the foot, I guess. Vicious little punk deserved much worse. But Jésus gave up his friends that helped beat Shawn O'Hara. Our Jésus proved to be a fine little Judas. They're all MS-13 members. So we've made a good first dent in that gang of Mexican cocksuckers. We'll make a bigger dent in days to come once the rest start talking. We've got 'em all in custody now. Being as they're illegals, due process is off the table to my mind."

The deputy said, "Thanks for checking in on me, Sheriff. And thanks for giving that bastard some back for me."

Able patted Troy's arm in farewell then went up a floor and dropped in on Shawn O'Hara. An overweight black nurse was just finishing a check-in and scribbled something on his chart and hung it back on its hook at the foot of Shawn's bed. Shawn still looked like a mummy. Able said to the nurse, "How's this tough guy doing?"

The nurse looked at Able's uniform and frowning said, "You're not Tell Lyon are you?"

Able sensed Shawn watching him. Able said, "Tell no! *Chief* Tell Lyon is an asshole. Jesus may love him, but I surely don't. I'm Sheriff Able Hawk. But there would be some problem if I was Lyon? That the drift of your question?"

The nurse said, "Mr. O'Hara has asked that Tell Lyon not be permitted access to Mr. O'Hara. The only New Austin policeman Mr. O'Hara will see is William Davis." The nurse, one Wendy Fahy, Able saw from her tag, walked over and patted Shawn's shoulder. "You okay alone with this one, sugar?"

Shawn winked with one black-and-purple eye—the lid still swollen and drooping. He gave her a thumbs-up.

Wendy waddled off, all ass and elbows, pushing a cart. Able took up her place by Shawn's bed and said, "We got the ones who beat you, Shawn. Every damned one of them. They're all in jail."

Shawn typed, *Tell me everything.*

As Able started to do that, Shawn began typing notes.

Scowling, Able said, "What the hell? You mean to report this yourself?"

Shawn typed, *Who else?*

* * *

Tell reached the stage at 3:55 P.M. Patricia split off from him as they approached the show trailer. She wandered into the watching crowd, moving as far to the front as she could.

A nervous Mayor Ernest Rice spotted Tell and motioned him to the back of the trailer-stage where the staircase up onto the platform was positioned.

"Cutting it close," Rice said testily, "aren't you?"

"Five minutes to spare," Tell said with a shrug. "And I am on duty, you know. Trying to keep this festival quiet and without incident, just as you asked of me. Making sure those demonstrators stay off the grounds."

"So we'll keep this short," the mayor said. "I've told the emcee to announce us together. That way, we'll step out together and you'll be on hand to translate what I say from word one. How do we best do this? Probably don't want to be talking over one another."

"No," Tell agreed, "we don't. You're reading from a prepared text. Your sentences look short. Just stop at the end of every second sentence and I'll repeat what you've said."

The mayor clapped Tell on the back. "Thanks again, *Jefe*." He said that last word with a too-strong southern Ohio accent, like some hick mocking a Mexican. Frito Bandito stuff.

Tell played along, though. He said, "You *sure* you're not fluent in Spanish, Mayor?"

The emcee introduced them and Mayor Rice grinned at being called "Ernesto." His smile disappeared as the more enthusiastic cheers and applause for Tell ensued.

Mayor Rice gave his halting speech with its awkward intermissions for Tell's translations. When it was over, there were cheers for "Ernesto" and "*El Léon.*"

At Rice's urging, Tell made a brief statement. Nothing too substantive—just his stated admiration for the town and good people of New Austin and thanking them for being so welcoming. He made a vow to concentrate efforts on stemming local drug trafficking.

Someone in the crowd yelled in Spanish, "What about Thalia Ruiz? What are you doing about that, *Jefe?*"

In Spanish, Tell said, "I'm working very hard to get Thalia justice. And I will do that, soon. I'm working with Able Hawk to do that. We have a definite suspect."

There were some boos at the mention of Able Hawk's name. Some cheers too, but mostly catcalls. Tell held up a hand for quiet. He said, "Able Hawk is working hard, hand-in-hand with me, to bring Thalia Ruiz's killer to justice. We hope to make an announcement soon about an arrest. I'll only add my personal observation that Able Hawk was friends with Thalia and he has in fact taken her family—her daughter, mother and cousin—into his own home. We will—Able and I—see justice done for Thalia, and for three other Latino women who died under similar circumstances. Women we believe were murdered by the same man or men who killed Thalia Ruiz. Hawk and I will catch this killer. This is our shared pledge."

Scattered calls of "*Viva El Léon!*" and "*Viva El Gavilan!*"

Tell held up both hands. "Enough of that," he said. "A moment of silence for Thalia Ruiz and all the other lost ones."

The silence held for a minute—just a few coughs and babies' cries.

Tell said, "Amen."

He left the stage to cheers and more *vivas*. Patricia was standing by the bottom step, awaiting him. "That was so sorry dreadful," Tell said.

Patricia was squinting up at him—squinting against the sun. She looked miserably hot. Tell put his hat on her head. She smiled, adjusting his hat, and said, "It was better than fine, Tell. It was honest and straight. Maybe not what they expected, but surely what they needed."

"You're a lovely liar, Patricia."

"That prayer at the end—I didn't know you had a religious streak," she said.

"I don't. Or haven't for some time." He ran the back of his hand across her damp cheek. "This heat is too much for you, isn't it?"

"Would be nice to find some air conditioning," she said. "Be good to relax and cool off before you hustle me off to your cousin's place."

"Restaurant?"

"Our place would be better," she said. "The AC cranked up and no clothes. If you're through here, now, I mean."

"I'm finished," Tell said, wrapping an arm around her bare shoulders, her skin hot and moist to the touch. "I think you have a little sunburn," he said.

"Nothing too bad."

"Pick up some food on the way? Belgian waffle? Maybe an elephant ear, or a funnel cake?"

"How about Italian? And wine since I can drink, again. I'm really up to here with carnival food and Latino culture."

"Italian then," Tell said. "And early to bed?"

"Very early to bed and very late to sleep," she said, smiling. She took his arm from around her shoulders and held his hand. "I'm glad you wore that uniform today, Tell. If you'd worn that black Nazi rig you usually do, and with all those cheers, well, I think watching you speak up there would have been like watching a Nuremberg rally."

* * *

Able had to carry Evelia from the theatre. They'd had to catch a later showing, and despite the blasting soundtrack, she'd fallen asleep during the last twenty minutes of the film. He got her into the car without waking her.

Sofia Gómez watched Able see to her grandchild and said, "It was her first movie. Thank you so much for taking us out. I just liked watching her face watching that big screen. Thalia always talked of taking her to a movie, but time just got away, I guess."

"It was my pleasure," Able said. Hell, he should have taken Thalia and her daughter to a movie ages ago. Hell, several of them.

He took Sofia's hand to steady her as she reclined back into the passenger seat of his car. He realized Sofia's was the first woman's hand he'd touched like that since his wife.

"First movie I've seen in a theatre in several years myself," Able said, hearing a brittleness in his voice. "Don't remember them being so damned loud back in the day."

He closed her door and walked around the rear of his car and got behind the wheel. Despite the fact the sun was down, the car was hot inside. Able started the engine, lowered the power windows and turned the air up. He backed out of the space and pulled out onto the road. The speed limit was forty-five and the wind through the windows blew out the close, hot air. Able rolled the windows up and knocked the air conditioner down a couple of notches. "Early yet," he said. "You up for a little drive?"

"That would be very nice," Sofia said. "Thank you again for all you've done for us. Without Thalia's income, I don't know what we would have done."

Able waved a hand. He smiled and said, "That's nothing. That little girl back there, losing her mother, you losing your daughter . . . *that's* the thing. How is Evelia doing? Does she grasp what's happened?"

"Of course not," Sofia said. "She thinks her mother is angry at her. Or sick. She insists her mother will return, despite everything I say to the contrary. Maybe, if we're all lucky, if Evelia is lucky, the days will stretch and Evelia will forget to remember that her mother isn't here. Maybe she'll even forget her mother. That will be terrible in its way. But easier maybe for Evelia. And the big house and you, nights like this one, they distract her."

"And you, Sofia?"

She shrugged. "You know what I feel. You know loss too, Able."

That echoed Tell. Able wondered if he wore his grief on his face in some way.

He said, "It's good to have you in the house. All of you. Hell, it's the first time in years I look forward to meals in that place."

"It's a beautiful home," Sofia said.

"You're a kind liar," Able responded. He reached over and gave her hand a fleeting squeeze. "The place is careworn, neglected. Looks like something an old cop and a young student would allow to settle around their sorry selves."

"I can see what it was," Sofia said.

"You mean when there was a woman in the house. I can too. I can *remember*. Maybe the question is, can you see what it could be again?"

"I'm not sure I understand," Sofia said.

"I'm thinking of doing some furniture shopping tomorrow," Able said. "Would you come along, Sofia? You and that angel in the backseat? I need to pick out a couch and some chairs. Sure would be nice if my selection didn't end in some expensive embarrassment."

Thirty minutes later, Able palmed into the driveway of his home. They stepped out into the muggy night. Able said, "I'm not sure I can carry her up all those steps in this humidity without stroking out. And it's brutally hot over that garage, even with the window air conditioners. My daughter's bedroom is standing empty. How about if we put you and Evelia up in the main house tonight? Turn up that air conditioner until our teeth chatter?"

* * *

Tell felt her body tauten there under his tongue, her thighs trembling and back arching. Her head thrashed side to side. Patricia gave herself over to it for as long as she could stand it. When it became too intense for her she knotted her fingers in his hair and urged him back up. "It's gone from exquisite to too much," she said huskily. "Come to me."

He settled in alongside her and she wiped his lips with both hands, then kissed him, tasting herself on his mouth and tongue. "Soon as my heart stops pounding," Patricia said, "it will be your turn."

"No, not like that," he said. "You're ready, we'll do it the old-fashioned way, together."

Patricia said, "I can't promise that." She stroked his thigh, said, "I don't want to leave tomorrow, Tell. I should be here. You shouldn't be alone."

"Able Hawk's insisting on keeping me up to my ass in deputies and electronic surveillance," Tell said. "I'll be far from alone."

She rolled onto her side, catching her breath at the spasms still seizing her body, the fluttering between her legs. Her fingers trailed through his chest hair, down across his belly and closed around him, moving gently back and forth, stroking him. Patricia said, "Seems to me, based on things read and said, that Salome never left Chris when he found himself up against it."

"Different dynamic," Tell said, voice thickening. "She was being hunted too. And Salome once had to shoot someone to save Chris a few years back. I'd never put you in that position. And I'll never risk loss again. I *can't* ever run that risk again. We'll get through this week and I'll close this case. Then I'll take that job in Cedartown, and we'll have our good life together. Maybe get to work on having that child."

He realized she was moving down the bed, her long black hair tickling his chest and then belly. He closed his eyes as he felt her mouth, warm and wet around him. She paused what she was doing to him just long enough to say, "*Children.*"

FORTY EIGHT

Shawn was awakened by a hand shaking his shoulder. He was momentarily in a panic, as he had been several times waking up since his beating. Each time, he had been awakening, trying to say something, or to scream, and found that his mouth wouldn't open. It was like those dreams he had so often as a kid—trying to run from something, but finding himself moving in slow motion. Eventually, struggling out of sleep in a panic, he'd remember he was in the hospital and what had happened to him—that his mouth wouldn't work because it was wired shut.

Squinting his eyes, Shawn tried to focus on the face pressed down close to his. In his confusion, he thought perhaps it was Patricia. Blinking through sleep, Shawn realized it was the face of a sneering Mexican kid. Shawn slid straight into panic.

"Hey, *pendejo*," the stranger said, grinning at him. "I missed the big party when my friends fucked you up so well, *hombre*. My man, Jésus, he is upstairs now. The cops fucked *him* up for what he did to you. Your cop friends knocked out all Jésus's teeth and ripped off an ear. I came to visit and the fucking nurses sent me away. Whores say the doc is going to cut off my man's leg 'cause the *maricón* pigs fucked it up so bad. So I thought I'd come down here and visit you instead."

Shawn's hand was still resting on the remote control that raised and lowered his bed, controlled the television and could summon a nurse. Shawn stabbed the nurse's call button repeatedly. The Mexican gangbanger laughed and tossed the other end of the remote control across Shawn's chest. He said, "Unplugged that before I woke you up, asshole. You're just meat here now. Waiting to be taken down. Can't walk, I see. Can't defend yourself or call for help. Next time I come back—and I *will* be back—I will bring my big knife. Take away a piece of you to give to Jésus's girl. You're a writer, right? Maybe I'll take your fingers or a whole fucking hand."

As though he suddenly remembered something, the stranger held up a finger in "Ah-hah!" fashion.

With his other hand, he pulled a switchblade from his pocket and sprung its blade. "Guess this would do the job well enough, huh, *amigo*? I mean, it'll cut through finger bones easy enough."

His eyes wide, Shawn looked at the Mexican. Shawn traced the signal cord from his heart monitor to the wall socket. He grabbed the cord and pulled it loose from the wall. Maybe the nurses would construe it as Shawn going into some kind of cardiac arrest or even flat lining. At least they would have to come to investigate why his vitals monitor that fed back to their station had gone dead. Or so Shawn hoped.

Seeing the wall plug pulled seemed to unsettle Shawn's attacker. He hid his knife in his jacket pocket and edged to the door. He leaned around and looked down the hall toward the nurses' station. He moved quickly back to Shawn's bed. "You ain't safe here, *pendejo*. You see that now. I can see it in your fucking eyes. I will be back for you. I will come back to cut you down. I will kill that fat ass *El Gavilan* and the other—Lyon—too. All of you going to die."

The Mexican *cholo*'s gaze skittered to the edge of Shawn's bed. He unhooked and lifted the renal bag fed by Shawn's catheter and pulled out his knife again. He slit the bag near its top and then sprayed the strong-smelling contents into Shawn's face.

Shawn's eyes burned with his own chemically fortified, dark-with-blood urine. The bandages absorbed much of it, but some went up his nose, almost drowning Shawn.

His attacker looked a last time over his shoulder at the door. Shawn rubbed at his burning eyes with his fingers. Through the

stinging blur he saw the Mexican grab the laptop by Shawn's bed—
the laptop containing Shawn's notes and journals and the stories
he'd composed for the paper about his own beating.

The young Mexican slid the laptop up under his shirt and held
it there with his left hand. "See what I can fence this motherfucker
for," he said to Shawn. He moved to leave, then hesitated again. He
suddenly grabbed hold of Shawn's right hand. He winnowed down to
Shawn's middle finger and jerked back hard until the bone snapped.
Shawn screamed through his wired-tight jaws and mouth packing.

"Write with that, asshole," Shawn's attacker said. "Next time
I visit, I am gonna cut off all your fucking fingers." He waved at
Shawn and slid into the hall.

Shawn heard the squeak of shoes retreating toward the nurses'
desk. But he heard no sound of footfalls coming the other way—no
indication anyone was coming to check on him—nobody rushing
to see why his vital signs had ceased registering.

Fucking incompetent cows.

His eyes burned with tears and his own urine. Shawn held his
mangled hand up to his face and saw his finger was skewed backward at a right angle to his hand. The finger was already turning
black and blue and was swollen to twice its proper size.

Sobbing now, sickened by the smell and taste of his own urine up
his nose and down his throat, Shawn looked around for something
to throw through the door—something that might make some
noise or attract attention to his room. He picked up the unplugged
remote unit thrown across his chest. With his left hand, he awkwardly slung it at his room's door. The unit hit the handle and clat-
tered to the tile floor of the common hallway.

Shawn thought, Maybe that will get that fat nigger nurse's
attention.

THEN

The Border Patrol's Christmas party had started at the HQ, but then drifted down the street to a bar as things got on and the craving for harder liquor took hold.

Tell was sitting at a corner table, a bit off to himself, watching it all. He was one of the few family men in the joint. He would have preferred to be at home, spending time playing with Claudia, watching her draw more pictures of Santa Claus and his flying reindeer.

"Not in the partying spirit?"

It was Seth Alvin. "Figure as we're soberest, it's safe to take a drink together now, eh?"

"Absolutely." Tell moved his feet from the chair across from his so Seth could sit down.

"What's Santa bringing you for Christmas, Tell?"

"An arrest, I hope. I want this stuff with Angel over. It's already costing me holiday time with my family."

Seth sipped his longneck and said, "How so?"

"Marita and Claudia are going ahead to her folks' place tomorrow for the run-up to Christmas. If things go to plan on this end, I'll figure on joining them on Christmas Eve."

A slow nod. Seth began to pick at the label on his sweating beer bottle. He stopped making eye contact with Tell. Later, Tell would remember Seth's reaction. Later still, Tell would have context for it—for Seth's demeanor.

Seth said, "Bacheloring it for the holidays? All alone?"

"*Solo lobo*," Tell confirmed.

Seth took a long breath, let it out. "That sucks large, brother."

Tell said, "Don't it?"

FORTY NINE

Tell was ten miles out of Morton Springs, bound back to Horton County, when the call came.

"Patricia?"

"Chris insisted I call," Patricia said. "But I would have anyway. We were followed out of town, Chris and I. So Chris figures you are probably being followed too."

Tell's gaze flicked from the road to the rearview mirror. It was half past eight on a Sunday morning and the roads were still relatively dead.

Yet there was an old, rusted-out Monte Carlo eight car lengths behind him. Three Latino youths wearing matching red headbands were crowded into the front seat. It was impossible to tell how many more might be seated behind them. Chris, the writer, had immediately spotted the tails. Tell, the alleged career lawman, hadn't. Tell silently cursed himself.

But Tell didn't want to worry Patricia. He said, "All clear for now." He was in his command cruiser, so he could radio for help if needed. He was also between two of the larger highway patrol barracks dotted along I-70, so help would be quick arriving. And he had a riot gun and his own backup Magnum tucked under the front seat. He asked, "You and Chris okay?"

"We're good," Patricia said, soundly strangely euphoric. Tell recognized the tone—echoing the giddy exhilaration of surviving a near miss. Her chirpy tone unsettled Tell. He said, "What happened, exactly? You two *really* okay?"

"Chris spotted them very quickly," she said. "There weren't many cars on the road and the one they were driving was a beater and really stood out. There were a lot of heads in the car, and they were all wearing what looked to be gang colors. Chris says they're probably wannabe members of MS-13, some nasty Latino gang he says is infiltrating the Midwest. So Chris slowed down. They got real close behind us, and apparently, they got *real* confused. Then Chris floored it. 'Unmanned them,' as he put it. They got caught up in the moment, I guess, because they gunned it, tried to overtake us. Chris let them pull up alongside and there were eight of them in the car, I think. They were screaming at us and waving guns and knives."

Tell could see it in his head. Chris drove a restored 1966 Chevy Impala, a real muscle car. His cousin could have easily outrun them and their beater car. But that wouldn't be like Chris.

Patricia hesitated. Some of the excitement out of her voice now, she said, "Chris shot the front tire out on their car. They went into a ditch and the car's frame broke in half. No way they could follow. We're not sure if any were hurt, or maybe even worse."

Christ. Tell said, "Let's hope for maybe *worse*. So you're really both okay?"

"Fine. We're already halfway home." Her use of "home" wasn't lost on Tell. She said, "You just be careful, Tell. I see what you're up against now. It terrifies me. I'm worried, you being alone back there."

"I'll be fine, I swear. You just be sure to call me when you get safely to Chris's place."

Tell checked his rearview again. There was no indication that the gang behind him was intent on crowding him, or provoking him. And Tell wouldn't cowboy the bastards the way his cousin had. Not that Tell could blame Chris for what he had done. Chris had his own family to protect. He couldn't expect his cousin to risk leading the likes of some Mexican drug gang back to his own family. Thank God that Chris, the lethal paranoid, had come armed to pick up Patricia.

Tell's cell phone rang again. He recognized the number. He flipped open his phone and said, "Talk to me, Billy Davis."

"Got word this morning, Chief, that some gangbanger attacked Shawn O'Hara in his hospital room."

"Goddamn it," Tell said. "How bad is it?"

"Could have been much worse," Billy said. "As it is, the bastard broke the middle finger of Shawn's right hand. He also emptied Shawn's own urine bag onto his face. Did you know urine is sterile? Good thing too," Billy said, "as Shawn's wounds from earlier are pretty bad. But with his mouth all sealed up, and all that stuff going up his nose, Shawn nearly drowned in his own piss. That'd be a hell of a way to go, wouldn't it?"

Hard to argue that. Tell said, "He give us a description of his attacker, Billy?"

"That's the problem, skipper. Shawn still can't really speak. He's also right-handed. With that busted finger, he can't write longhand with it now."

Tell said, "Shawn was using a laptop to communicate, last time I saw him."

"Appears the one who broke his finger also stole the laptop," Billy said. "Hospital isn't lousy with spare laptops, so they're trying to free one up to get Shawn back in touch with the world."

"We get anything at all useful from Shawn?"

"He tried to write me some notes with his left hand," Billy said. "Hard to do. He kept it short. Wrote 'spic,' for instance . . . I mean, 'Mexican' being so much longer a word."

"Yeah, three whole letters," Tell said. "That's a killer, for sure."

"Have to expect some bitterness on Shawn's part on that front," Billy said. "Can't say as I blame him, given what's been done to him. And now, done to him again, right here in the hospital. Those goddamn animals."

He couldn't afford to get mad at Billy. Tamping down his tone, Tell said, "You get anything else from him, B.?"

"Red bandana," Billy said. "That's all Shawn wrote before they hustled me out to go to work on his hand."

Tell said, "*Bandana*? That's a handful, writing with the wrong hand. Almost like *spic* squared."

"I wasn't defending Shawn's attitude toward the Mexicans," Billy said, "just explaining it."

"I get it," Tell said. "Best stay there with him, if you can. I'll call Able and see if he can shoulder seeing Shawn's under guard as long as he remains in the hospital. Being it's Sunday, the pawnshops are all closed. I'll get Rick to hit those hard on Monday. See if we can retrieve the hospital's laptop and get a lead on whoever worked Shawn over this time."

"You're still on all-day duty at the festival? I mean, despite me making you a target for Sheriff Pierce and Strider?"

"That's the plan, Billy," Tell said. He checked his rearview mirror again: all those gangbangers with their red bandanas bound 'round their heads were still back there. "But I've got something to take care of, first." Tell was about to say goodbye, then he remembered and said, "How'd last night go? You did deliver the news to Tom Winch?"

"I did," Billy said.

"His reaction?"

"Less surprised than I would have expected," Billy said. "Which makes me wonder if he already suspected it, or knew himself."

"He offer us anything back, Billy?"

"Tom says Luke Strider shakes down hookers."

"White, Mexican or black prostitutes?"

"Tom said race makes no difference to Strider," Billy said.

"That won't help our case," Tell said. "Does he hit them?"

"Shakes them down for money. And he often screws them, of course."

"Okay, Billy. I'll try to get you kicked loose from hospital guard duty soon. See what Able can do for us on that front."

"Calling him now, Chief?"

"Soon. First I've got to radio the highway patrol and get them to peel a tail off my ass."

"Able's folks? Pierce's?"

"I don't think either of the sheriffs would follow me out this far. No, these look like gangbangers."

* * *

"You're sure you like the pattern?" Able seemed to Sofia . . . *dubious*.

"Hell yes," Able said. "Got me an ace painter I'll be getting to lighten that sitting room with a new coat or two of color. Make it blend better. I like this earth-tone angle you got going, Sofia."

"Really?"

"Honest Injun," Able said, holding up three fingers on his right hand in a dimly remembered Boy Scout salute. Evelia giggled and held up three fingers.

"See," Able said. "Dogs and kids, they know the truth when I speak it."

"It would also help," Sofia said carefully, "if we took down those heavy drapes. Maybe put up some sheers. Let in more light, yes?"

"Let's do that," Able said. He led Sofia and Evelia from the furniture store, holding Evelia's tiny hand in his own rough right hand, and lightly holding Sofia's left arm in his left. "Dog days are upon us," he said carefully.

Sofia arched an eyebrow, made curious by his tone. "What I mean," Able said, "is the August heat's near upon us. Too hot for living above the garage. What I was thinking was, we've got that empty den on the first floor. Thought maybe I'd move down there. It's frankly cooler downstairs. And that would give you and Evelia a room in the main house."

"How much more would that cost us?" Sofia asked.

"I'm thinking, well, the house is long paid off," Able said. "You two are family. So you'd just be there, the two of you. No charge. You wouldn't pay me nothing. Put the money aside for Evelia's college fund, maybe. It would just be like you'd always been there." He stumbled. "I mean, like the family you are."

Sofia searched his eyes. "You're unexpectedly kind, Able," she said. "Big-hearted in a way maybe some more like me should see. But taking charity, that I cannot do."

She saw the flare in his eyes and winced. "Not damned charity," Able said. "This is my will, what I want for you."

Still half-uncertain, Sofia said, "If that's your position . . ."

Able said, "It is. So it's settled."

Sofia met his gaze, said, "It *is* settled."

Able smiled broadly. He tousled Evelia's glistening black hair. "Who wants ice cream?"

* * *

The highway patrol intercepted Tell's pursuers five miles short of the Horton County line. As the trio of cruisers converged, Tell slowed and walked back to meet them. The lead trooper said, "Undocumented, every one of them. Just as you predicted."

Tell said, "Thanks for the assist. They packing?"

"Oh, yeah."

"What do you do with them?"

"Deport them. We're state, so it goes quickly. And because they were all armed, that means real consequences for them back on the other side. I give the Mexicans just that much."

Tell left them there, divvying up gang members into the trio of state troopers' cruisers. Tell figured that however many he'd just gotten arrested—coupled with the number Able had taken down and his cousin Chris had killed or injured by crashing their car—should constitute a crippling blow to the Mexican gang's New Austin chapter.

Tell drove back to New Austin and into the festival lot. He cruised three rows of parking spaces before finding a slot. Tell hauled himself out of his command cruiser and locked it up. He slipped on his hat and sunglasses and began walking the grounds. A band was playing "*Flor de Mal*." Tell figured to walk laps—it took no more than seven minutes to make a circuit—until the festival closed down around eleven P.M.

To amuse himself, Tell looked for Able's tails but came up dry. He couldn't imagine they could be *that* good at surveillance, so Tell decided something was mucking up Able's promise of protection. His theory was bolstered by Able's scarcity by phone too.

But Tell detected no tails at all—no gangbangers.

No Luke Strider.

No Able-directed shadows.

Very odd.

As he wandered the festival grounds, Tell endured several sequels to his afternoon visit with Patricia—back slaps and *vivas* and thumbs-ups and high-fives.

Several young Mexican women stopped Tell throughout early afternoon, asking him to pose for pictures with them. Three of them took off his hat and asked if they could wear it in the pictures. That seemed too much; he had visions of the damned photos cropping up in some bad context on some Web site.

Confused and embarrassed, Tell did agree to be photographed a couple of times with demure women. He finally asked one woman whom he turned down—an almost too-thin, bright-eyed Chicana dressed in cut-offs and a purple tube-top, "Why the photo?"

She shrugged and smiled at Tell with crooked teeth. She said, "Everyone is talking about you. *El Léon* they call you." She frowned. "You really didn't just get engaged?"

"I really did."

"Oh. Damn."

He crossed paths with Mayor Ernest Rice. The mayor said, "Thanks again for yesterday."

"It was nothing," Tell said.

"You made some big promises," the mayor said. "You really aim to deliver on an arrest in this Ruiz murder case? I ask, because it is *the* topic in the Latino community."

"Really?"

"It is. Conventional wisdom, near as I can tell, seems to be that we'll leave this one unsolved. Sweep it under the rug, you know. Or worse, that we'll *make* it an unsolved." The mayor bit his lip. "Then you made that speech yesterday and you put the fact out there about the other three murders. Now the whole Latino community seems to believe it's the target of some serial killer. Do you really believe that to be true?"

"I do, up to a point. A serial rapist, anyway. I don't believe killing his victims is the goal. It ends up that way from time to time. That's my theory."

"And do you really have a solid suspect?"

Tell thought about Billy Davis and Billy's ordained leak of Tell's suspicions to Tom Winch.

What if Tom really was the callow and conscience-stricken good soldier that Billy had characterized him to be? If that was true, then Tell's own strategy might be fatally flawed. If things had gone to Tell's plan, then Luke or some accomplice should already be hard on Tell's heels . . . or have already taken a shot at him. But there was no indication of any of that.

So Tell was revising his theory. Tom Winch was—take your pick—too shrewd, timid or too politic to leak Tell's suspicions back to his co-workers.

But a career politician like this one standing before him?

A politician, to Tell's mind, was a sieve in a suit.

Tell said, "Can you keep a confidence, Mayor?"

Ernest Rice seemed genuinely taken aback by the implication of Tell's question—that he, the august Mayor "Ernesto" Rice of New Austin, Ohio, might not be trustworthy with a confidence.

Tell said, "I have what appears to be filmed evidence of two men dropping the body of Thalia Ruiz in that field where we found her." Tell explained about the film and the extrapolated license plate.

"And did this plate check out as real? I'm supposing it led to your suspect?"

"That's right," Tell said.

"But all you've got is dubious film and a deduced license number," the mayor said. "Begging your pardon, but this all sounds tenuous, Chief. I have a law degree. Maybe you didn't know that, Tell. Speaking as an attorney, if I were a judge, and if you brought this to me for a warrant, I'd turn it down. It screams 'insufficient' to me."

"I'd agree, circumstances being different," Tell said. "But the experts who looked at the film unanimously arrived at a single 'deduced' license plate. We ran that plate and found it was indeed registered to a red Dodge Ram pickup truck, just like the one caught on film."

Mayor Rice narrowed his eyes. "Who owns this Ram?"

Tell said, "Luke Strider. He's a Vale County sheriff's deputy."

"One of Walt Pierce's men? Holy fucking Christ."

"Exactly."

"So what do you do next?"

"It's what you do next that counts, Mayor. I want you not to keep my confidence."

"What?"

Tell steered the mayor under the shade of an exhibitor's tent. He said, "New Austin's police department making an arrest—working under the auspices of your administration—would be a huge coup for you and for me."

"You don't need to spell that out for me, Tell," Rice said. "So, again, I ask, why tell me this in confidence and then ask me to spread it around?"

"As you say, Mayor, my present evidence is too scant for prosecution. But if you were to be liberal with the information in the right quarters, in some way and company that wouldn't result in some kind of slander suit, you might enhance my case."

"I see," Rice said. "You aim to force this son of a bitch to react. To maybe incriminate himself or do something precipitous that would allow you to arrest him and build on that."

"Something like that," Tell said. "Hell, anything would do. I just want to take this bastard out before he rapes or kills again."

"Any hesitation I have about doing what you suggest stems from the fact I really like you. You're an asset to me. And having met this woman who plans to marry you . . . ?"

"She's out of harm's way," Tell said.

"But what of you?"

"I'm vigilant," Tell said.

"Right . . ." The mayor said, "You're sure? Really sure you want to me to set this in motion?"

"Dead sure."

"Wish you'd chosen your words more judiciously just there," Mayor Rice said. "Okay. I'll do it."

"Any idea who you'll tell?"

"My opposite number in Vale County, Mayor John Fitzgerald of Janssenville. He's very tight with Walt Pierce. I'll be seeing him later this evening. We're judges for the New Austin Latino 'Little Princess' contest."

* * *

Shawn pushed the power button of the new laptop the hospital had found for him. When it powered up, with his left hand, he pulled down the Applications menu and opened Microsoft Word.

Across the room, Billy Davis said, "Going okay for you, brother?"

Shawn shot him a thumbs-up with his left hand.

"Give 'em hell, Shawn," Billy said.

Shawn winked and typed: "A Portrait of Law Enforcement Incompetence."

* * *

Able pushed his new couch to its third position in the sitting room. "Better?"

"Perfect," Sofia said.

"I can see it—your vision, I mean." Able slapped Amos's back. "Once my painter here gets this room finished, it's going to look great."

Able's cell phone vibrated. Two callers were listed on his missed calls log. The first was from Tell Lyon. The other was from Walt Pierce. Pierce rarely made direct calls. Able decided to return Walt's call first, figuring to get the potentially bad news out of the way first.

* * *

Tell was watching a talent show. Eleven- to fifteen-year-old girls were taking their best swings at lip-syncing and dancing to Shakira singles. Tell told himself he wouldn't let any daughter of his participate in such a contest. He felt his cell phone vibrate in his left breast pocket.

He checked the caller ID panel: Patricia. He said, "So you're okay?"

"Wonderful," Patricia said, calmer-sounding now. "We're fine. Of course I wish you were here."

Tell said, "No more signs of gangs? I mean, apart from the ones you two cowboyed off the road?"

"*Nada*," Patricia said. "All is well. How are *you*?"

"Frustrated," Tell said. "Nothing is going to plan."

"Your voice carries," Patricia said. "Chris says he's offering a last time to come out and bunk with you. He's been reading old Louis L'Amour paperbacks in what he calls 'an unseemly spasm of sentiment.' Citing 'contrition,' he says he feels like you and he should 'do an Earp' on New Austin."

"That's Chris's synonymous terms for a 'killing floor,'" Tell said. "Let Chris know I'm going for subtle, or else I'd take him up on that offer. We haven't budgeted body bags in bulk this year."

Patricia said, "Chris says that 'subtle' would be a first from you."

"He should talk, after shooting out tires," Tell said. "But, no, I'm fine. Really. Plans aren't going right, that's all."

"I so wish you were here. Then it would be perfect."

"I wish I was too," he said.

"So you and *El Gavilan* shut this thing down, now, right? End this and get to me, Tell. Our future is right here."

* * *

Shawn typed with his left hand, picking out characters:

"It's time to take it all back from them.

"Since my last column, I've been falsely accused of a terrible crime and I've been fully exonerated.

"Upshot: The cops can't be trusted.

"Since my last column, I was nearly beaten to death by Mexicans.

"Upshot: Illegals are killing our city.

"These Mexicans beat me with impunity. Beat me so badly I can no longer speak or have children.

"As I lay in my hospital bed—missing most of my teeth, missing my kneecap and rendered infertile . . . missing most of my nose—as I lay here in bed, I was attacked by another Mexican. I was attacked in my sick bed because of the incompetence of the Horton County Sheriff's Department, and New Austin police who didn't have the brains to post a guard on me. Because of that, this Mexican strutted into my room and broke the middle finger of my right hand. So I slowly type this short column with my left hand.

"I indict Able Hawk for not seeing that I'm protected.

"I indict New Austin police chief Tell Lyon for not seeing that I'm protected.

"I live in New Austin. I edit New Austin's newspaper of record. Yet I've learned I can be attacked in my hospital bed by some illegal scum.

"With all these young illegal Mexican gang members running amok, how safe can any of you be in your own homes?

"I repudiate Able Hawk for hypocrisy; for talking a big game, then taking an illegal into his own family.

"I repudiate New Austin police chief Tell Lyon and the politician who hired a Border Patrol thug with no prior municipal policing experience or training—a vicious incompetent.

"I urge you to think hard when making your vote this November. I urge you to vote for *change*. We don't need the likes of these losers. We need change, and we need hope.

"And I say it's time to take it all back—to drive out all these illegal Mexicans. Arrest them, deport them—I don't care which. These taco munchers have to go before they foul our city further. That's the bottom line."

THEN

Bing Crosby crooning on the radio: "White Christmas," then a jaw-dropping duet with David Bowie on "The Little Drummer Boy."

Their Christmas plans had changed; Marita's mother had come down with a virus, so Marita had decided to stay home the extra couple of days. She'd wait for Tell to finish his hellish work week, then together they would drive to her folks' home for the holiday. Burl Ives on the radio now: "Holly Jolly Christmas."

"You've been parked on that station for a week," he said.

"It's wall-to-wall to Christmas music," Marita said. She stroked his cheek and said, "I love this season. *Feliz Navidad*, sweetheart."

"And to you, *mi corazón*."

Marita was finishing packing his lunch; Claudia was sleeping in. Tell said, "She's still out? She never sleeps this late."

"It was staying up late last night to watch '*Rudolph*,' I think." Marita folded down the top of the lunch bag and taped it closed.

"I hope that TV special didn't give her nightmares," Tell said, watching Marita and wishing he had an extra hour. "I was four, maybe five when I first saw *Rudolph* on TV. The Abominable Snowman terrified me." Christmas—it didn't feel that way out here in the West for a Midwest boy, not even after several years. The holiday had felt hollow since he'd left Ohio with its cold and snow and all the seasons in all their fury.

Marita bit her lip, thinking. "I don't remember that monster doing that to me. Mostly, I remember thinking Santa Claus seemed very mean in that one." She smiled. "Last night didn't change my mind about any of that."

He smiled back, shook his head. He looked up at the ceiling. "I should go up there and say good-bye. She hates it when I don't do that."

"Just try to be home early tonight instead," Marita said. "She sleeps lightly, like you. I don't want her taking a nap today or she'll be up late again tonight, and I have *other* plans for us." Marita began to fill his thermos—his most recent Father's Day gift. "You *will* be home early, won't you?"

"I aim to be." He always did *aim* for that. Maybe tonight he could really pull it off. After all, they had Angel Valenzuela on the run; his organization was in tatters.

There was already more talk of another promotion in the offing for Tell. He hadn't confided that to Marita yet; he didn't want to get her hopes up. The position also opened up the possibility of relocation. Of course none of those prospects offered the possibility of snow, either.

Tell stared at their Christmas tree—something he'd assembled a week ago. He thought again of home. Ohio, often as not, offered at least a dusting of Christmas morning snow.

Marita hoisted his thermos. "You want some cream in this?"

"Not this morning. I'll take it black, please. Going to be a long day and I need to stay sharp."

Sharp? By noon his hands would probably be shaking. His skin would be itching. He'd been running on high-test java for at least two weeks.

"Think you might have time to hit the mall? I have Claudia's Christmas list."

Marita's car was in the shop . . . and anyway, they were between babysitters.

Tell took the folded sheet of paper as she kissed him. He stuffed the letter to Santa in his shirt pocket. Later, he'd throw it away, still never having read it. He couldn't bear to see what his little girl dreamed of finding under that artificial tree.

Marita kissed him, said, "Remember, try to come home early tonight."

"I will. I swear."

Marita said, "Isn't the Christmas season wonderful?"

She had always lived in the southwest, never even seen snow in person. Little Claudia had pointed at all that white stuff on TV last night and asked, "What *is* it?"

At least he wouldn't have to try to explain to her how Santa could get into a house with no chimney.

Tell kissed Marita a last time. He said, "Please tell Claudia I wanted to say good-bye."

He let himself out quietly. The engine on the Crown Vic rolled over; he'd had to turn in the SUV for reissue to some incoming field agent. He backed out, simultaneously fiddling with the radio. He settled on Mickey Newbury's "Let Me Sleep."

His mind full of work, he missed seeing Claudia waving to him through the living room picture window.

FIFTY

It was half past nine and Tell was watching a young man trying to upend a Coke bottle by lifting it at the neck with a rubber ring secured to a string dangling from a wicker stick. It wasn't enough just to get the Coke bottle upright. The bottle also had to be brought into standing position within a circle painted on the wooden platform supporting the bottle.

The game, like most carnival games, was rigged. Tell thought about calling the operator on his scam, but decided against it. He'd chosen a bigger battle, or rather, it had chosen him.

Tell checked his watch: ten P.M. One more hour to go.

There had still been no contact with Able Hawk. That worried Tell.

He had reached one of Able's deputies and put in a request that Horton County post a guard on Shawn O'Hara. The deputy instead arranged for Shawn to be quartered with another recuperating Horton County deputy.

Shawn was moved into a shared room with Deputy Troy Marshall, who had been shot in the leg arresting Shawn's chief attacker. Marshall was already ambulatory—"Marine tough" as his co-worker put it.

And Marshall was eschewing pain medication. The deputy who spoke with Tell said he would therefore run Marshall's sidearm to the hospital. "It's win-win," he told Tell. "Who better to watch this reporter than his ex-Marine-turned-sheriff's deputy bunkmate?"

Tell agreed and asked the deputy if he had heard from his superior.

The deputy said, "Nah, Sheriff Hawk's been scarce. Kind of unusual, although since his grandson married, everything has been kind of unusual, I guess."

Tell made a last circuit of the festival grounds. As he walked around the fair, he rubbed his naked ring finger, thinking of Patricia. He imagined that she'd probably be sitting out on the back porch with Chris and Salome, talking about their hypothetical cabin's construction.

He watched the twirl and blur of the carnival. The field was full of fireflies and they looked like little bits of lights flung free from the Ferris wheel and merry-go-round. The air smelled of sugar, popcorn and sweat.

The last band was playing "*La Pistola y el Corazon.*" He checked his watch again: a quarter to eleven and everything was quiet. He headed back to his command cruiser, wary of tails. But he saw no one, friend or otherwise.

Time to bag it, he thought.

As he pulled into the parking lot of his apartment complex, Tell thought about where he would sleep. He still had his own apartment. And the prospect of sleeping alone in Patricia's place, in her bed—*their* bed—depressed him.

Tell keyed himself into his own place and cranked up the AC He stripped and showered and climbed naked into bed, tucking his gun under the adjacent pillow before quickly falling asleep.

* * *

They were parked in the back lot of the high school, up against the football field, sitting with the lights off.

Able Hawk sat in the passenger seat of Walt Pierce's cruiser, staring off into the dark. It was drizzling now and raindrops trailed down the windshield and pattered softly against the roof. The windows of the cruiser were cracked and the air smelled of rain and earthworms.

Walt said, "I've got you and your grandson nailed on manufacturing and selling false driver's licenses. That's a *federal* felony, as you well know, Hawk. A Homeland Security beef. But more than prosecuting you myself, I'll hand you up to the fucking ACLU for an ass-reaming of unending vigor. I watched your grandson play ball on that field many times, Able. Remember when we'd come and watch Friday night games? Who'd have thought I'd be the one to have to put him in prison? If you survive your sentence, you'll come out, oh, I figure about eighty. Your grandson will be long past his prime too."

Able tasted blood and realized he'd bitten through his lip. "How'd you get onto it?"

Brusquely—annoyed to be knocked off his agenda—Walt said, "You were fucking sloppy, Hawk." Walt then described a circumstance almost identical to Tell Lyon's uncovering of Able's scheme. Walt had arrested two Mexican teens. The duo had handed up Trent Paris. Just as he had with Tell Lyon, goddamn Trent had rolled over on Amos.

Able should have known to threaten Trent out of town after handing over the business to those two Italian thugs. He should have severed the only loose end that might lead back to himself.

"So what's the fucking upshot, Pierce?"

Walt smiled. "I've got me a copy of that fucking baseball film I hear Lyon is trying to use to take down my deputy, Luke Strider. I've watched that film several times with my key men. Like me, they see a fuckin' red Isuzu in that film. A red Isuzu like them spic gangbangers who beat up that reporter drove. Them spics you've already got in custody. You're going to close ranks with me, Hawk. We're going to close this case *together*. We're going to hang the murders of Thalia Ruiz and them three others on them that did it—those vicious spic gang members who you're holding. Them that ain't owed due process. God evidently don't care what happens to them, so why should we, eh?"

"But they didn't *do* it." Able licked his bloodied lip. "That's Luke Strider and his truck on that piece of film. We both know that." Able looked at Walt's hands and something clicked. He was suddenly cold all over. Able said, "And looking now at your hands and all those damned rings, I'll be a sorry son of a bitch if I don't think you're the other man on that tape. I think you're the fat main man in that film—the one who beat my Thalia to death. It's you, isn't it? It's *always* been you. I'll be a sorry son of a bitch if I'm not right."

Spraying spittle, Walt snarled obscenities and went for his gun, struggling in his seated position to draw clear, his arm bumping up against the car seat—fouling his draw. Able grabbed Walt's head with both hands and slammed his face into the steering wheel. The cruiser's horn blared and Walt screamed, tasting blood in his mouth.

Walt raised his right hand and waved it in Able's face. Able saw the can of mace in Walt's hand, but too late to try to take it from him. Able screamed as the mace hit him in the eyes and nose and sprayed into his open mouth.

Screaming himself—his own eyes burning from the mace he'd released in the tight confines of his cruiser—Walt emptied the can in Able's face.

"Jesus fuck!" Able bellowed. He got his hand on the door release and fell out of the Vale County sheriff's cruiser onto the damp pavement. It was raining steadily now and Able scooped rainwater from a chuckhole and washed his burning eyes, clearing them just enough to see Walt lumbering around the back of the cruiser, one hand working at his own eyes and the other reaching again for his gun.

Able pulled his back-up gun from his ankle holster. Waving their guns, blinking back tears and rain, the sheriffs stared one another down. "What I guess you'd call a fucking Mexican standoff," Able said, his voice raw from the mace.

"You fucking take back what you said, Able!"

"I can't do that, Walt, not thinking as I do. And I'm thinking it more with each damned second."

"You goddamn take it back, Able! Then we go before the cameras together and declare them gang members guilty."

Able sneered. "And *then* what? As you point out, they ain't legal, none of them. So we can't try them here, Walt. And hell, if we could, they'd fast slip out of your lame fucking frame and you and Luke'd end up indicted anyway."

Walt slowly lowered his gun and holstered it. "That's why you'll hand them over to *me*, Hawk. Let me carry the weight of cleaning up that end. I'll do the *right* thing."

"The 'right thing'?" Able spat blood. "You mean kill 'em, like all the others you've killed in your custody."

"You fucking bend to my will, Hawk," Pierce said.

"No."

"Then you kiss your ass goodbye. And your grandson's ass too. Before you take me down, I'll see you two up on them federal charges. Can you imagine what'll happen to *you* in prison for twenty, maybe thirty years if some old collar of your department's doesn't shank you first? Least you won't last long enough to see what it does to that bookworm grandson of yours."

Blinking, Able raised his gun and pointed it at Walt's head. "I shoot you now, I only kiss *my* ass goodbye."

Pierce held up his fat hands. His rings glittered in the parking lot lights. It was raining harder. "For old times, I'll give you a third option, Able," Walt Pierce said. "Stand down. Step aside."

Able blinked. *"What?"*

"You heard me," Walt said. "You stand down and I won't burn you and that boy you dote over."

FIFTY ONE

"Mr. O'Hara?"

She was in her midtwenties. Pale blond hair, Nordic good looks. Very poised. Shawn thought the stranger standing in his hospital room's doorway might constitute his new physical ideal for women. No more fucking black-haired, black-eyed Mexican cunts for him.

The woman wore a tailored cream skirt and matching jacket over a white blouse. She had her hair pulled back and was slender and tall. She clutched a leather briefcase in both hands in front of her. Shawn could imagine her nude—busty (probably implants), wasp waist and a good ass. Probably porn-star smooth down there. Shawn wondered if he was getting hard. With all the Vicodin, it was tough to tell much of anything going on with his body lately.

She said, "I'm Tracey Blair. I'm a human resources specialist for Buxton Publishing. I understand you can't talk so I'll do that and try to keep it brief, Mr. O'Hara." She scowled, taking in his condition. She was the first pretty woman to see him since his beating. The look in her eyes wasn't a good omen for the future, Shawn thought.

Tracey Blair said, "The reporter who is filling in for you is under instruction to vet all copy for the week's coming edition through an editor back at corporate. So when you sent your account of your own beating and your proposed editorial over last night, they both were passed along by her to the executive editor."

She smiled sadly, looking earnestly into Shawn's eyes. "I'm afraid that the content and statements contained in both items were of such a charged quality—and of what the executive editor regarded as extremely poor taste and poor judgment—as to cast doubt on your news judgment and continued suitability as an information gatherer for Buxton Publishing. We've therefore elected to end your term of employment, Mr. O'Hara. I'm sorry. Understanding your unfortunate situation, we'll keep you on payroll through the end of the month. We'll also extend you six weeks' severance. Your insurance will lapse ninety days after that date. So you might want to inform your doctors of that so they can push ahead with any procedures or surgeries while you still retain coverage. I should mention there were some recent revisions to our corporate dental plan. Those changes hadn't yet been announced prior to your attack. I mention this because it is possible that the dental implants I've seen ordered for you may not be covered under the new plan. We're still checking into that. We'll inform your physicians of the outcome there so you can make a decision about whether to go ahead if it's to come out of your own pocket. They're quite expensive."

Tracey placed a packet on the tray table next to Shawn's bed. "Everything is explained in there," she said. "You'll need to sign those and return them within fourteen business days if you accept terms. My e-mail address is also in there, as you can't yet speak. We'll try to rectify any concerns or details via e-mail." She took a step closer. "I'm sure everyone at Buxton joins me in wishing you a fast and full recovery, Mr. O'Hara. These things are never easy for anybody. I appreciate you taking it so well."

Shawn shrugged. What the fuck could he *say* to that? What would he say to that if he were even *capable* of *speaking*?

The human resources specialist smiled and fidgeted with the handle of her leather briefcase. "This is my first time handling a termination. I was nauseous all last night. My boyfriend cooked dinner and I wrecked it with my sour stomach. But this wasn't so bad.

I just want to personally thank you for making this so professional, Shawn. I really appreciate that."

Dumbfounded, Shawn waved her out with his right hand, confused by her sudden frown back at him. He looked at his right hand. Splinted and bandaged as it was, it looked like Shawn was perpetually flipping the bird. *Sorry, Tracey.* Well, fuck that haughty cunt sideways, anyway. He listened to her heel taps fade down the hallway.

Fuck. Unemployed. A gimp with maybe no prospect for new teeth.

Shawn was beginning to see this horrible future for himself. He'd end up living with his mother in Chicago. He'd limp on and off el-trains because his fucked-up knee would never allow him to drive again. He'd end up taking low-tier freelance assignments while looking for some other shitty weekly newspaper gig. Only fat or plain chicks would take him to their beds and those maybe in pity.

Fuck. The doctor had told Shawn that Tuesday morning they'd maybe let him spend a few hours in a motorized wheelchair. The chair would allow Shawn to operate it with his left hand. Shawn looked over at Troy Marshall's empty bed. Troy was in his own rehab session—trying to build back up some muscle in his punctured leg.

If Shawn went mobile, he could wait for Troy to sleep or go to rehab. Then Shawn could lay hands on the deputy's gun. Shawn could blow a hole out of the shitty life those fucking Mexicans had dealt him. He felt a sudden kinship with his father. Saw now how easily a man could be driven in that direction. Shawn thought about all that some more. The more he mulled suicide, the more he leaned toward the option.

But Troy was scheduled to remain hospitalized a few more days. Shawn had time to think about it some more.

Time to weigh options; time to maybe settle some scores before.

* * *

Tell's phone was ringing. He struggled out of sleep and checked the clock: nine A.M.

God, he should have been up and at work hours ago. He lifted the receiver, said, "Lyon."

"Boss? We were worried." Billy Davis.

Tell said, "I just overslept. Too much heat and walking at that damned festival yesterday." *Too much of everything, for too long,* he might have added.

Billy said bitterly, "He goddamn quit, boss. He fucking kicked it in. Effective immediately."

Tell rubbed sleep from his eyes and sat up in bed. "Who? Who quit?"

"Able Hawk resigned as Horton County sheriff this morning. Left us with our dicks in the wind."

AGUILA DEL NORTE

FIFTY TWO

Able looked sourly at his cell phone's missed calls menu. Many, many of the calls that had gone unreturned or unanswered were from his various deputies. DeeDee had called seven times. The girl reporter who had replaced Shawn O'Hara had called several times too; he recognized her name from her by-lines in the *Recorder*.

And there had been many, many calls from Tell Lyon.

By agreement with Walt Pierce, Able couldn't contact any of them—none of his ex-deputies or sheriff's office flunkies. And particularly not Tell Lyon. His agreed-upon silence bought Able Walt Pierce's silence and suppression of the evidence he held against Amos and Able for their felonious identification scam. Combined fines would likely reach two hundred grand. Both would be hung out to dry, because of the intent to obscure the recipients' illegal statuses. Hell, that latter could be treated as a crime of aiding terrorism in the hands of the right wrong-headed legal types, just as Tell and Walt had warned. Able would die in prison, no question.

But Lyon: that betrayal ate at Able's conscience the worst. He'd let Lyon set himself up as a target and now he wouldn't have Lyon's back as he'd promised to. He couldn't even extend to Lyon his promised surveillance.

Surveillance.

That sparked Able's anger afresh. Walt, making it clear that Able was now his bitch, had informed him that the Vale County Sheriff's

Office was running an indefinite tap on Hawk's home phone. Able figured that probably extended to his cell phone.

An unmarked car had, until the last hour or so, been parked out front. Able suspected the one in the car, another of Walt's flunkies, was probably equipped with a "big ear"—one of those portable eavesdropping gizmos that allow cops to listen through walls.

The only upside to Able's morning was that Amos was in school. Amos wouldn't have heard yet that his grandfather had stepped down as Horton County sheriff. It would be a few more hours until Able had to field all of Amos's impossible-to-answer questions as to why he'd resigned his post. And there was that other dark prospect: Amos had already revealed himself ready to sacrifice himself when he thought Tell Lyon would press the case against them for the false IDs. He might try to do the same in the face of Walt's threats.

Absent Amos and any hard questions, Sofia was more than taking up the slack.

"I can't talk about it," Able told her again. He felt like he was saying that to her over and over.

He couldn't talk about it without violating his pledge of silence to Walt Pierce. But Able was looking for loopholes—to at least find some way to get even a one-way dialogue going with Tell in order to warn Lyon of his precarious position and what he knew about Walt.

Sofia pressed while he listened, half-distracted. She said, "Does this all have something to do with Thalia? Is that what it is, Able?"

"I can't talk about that," he said. He was standing at the fireplace mantel. There was a framed picture of Thalia there now, alongside those of his daughter and his dead wife.

"Then it must be so," Sofia said. "You would have simply said 'no,' otherwise."

"Sofia . . ."

"Talk to me, Able. Let me help you, *por favor*."

"I can't."

"Then talk to Tell Lyon. Let him help you. He's a good man. He cares about you."

"I can't do that, either."

"Why? Tell Lyon told me that you are allies."

"We are. We were."

"What's changed, Able? What has happened? Please trust me to tell me. I'll talk to Tell Lyon if you can't bring yourself to."

"It's not like that."

"Then help me understand how it is. Help me understand why things are the way they are."

Able looked around for his car keys. He slipped the Impala's keys in his pocket. "I've got to clear my head. I'm going for a drive."

Evelia heard the jingle of his keys and ran into the kitchen. She grabbed his leg and held tight. She said, "Pap-Paw Hawk, can I come?"

He smoothed her hair, smiling down at her, surprised at how attached to her he'd already become.

"Pap-Paw has to go out for a while," Sofia told her granddaughter.

Able considered it. He said, "I'd like to take her with me if you'd let me, Sofia."

"You're sure she won't be a distraction? Particularly now? I mean, as you are now—with all this on your mind?"

"No. She'll be no distraction. Or, rather, she *will* be. The good kind."

The child would also be excellent cover.

"Do you know where you are going?"

"The library," Able said.

* * *

348

Tell was driving to headquarters when he heard the news announcement on the radio: Walt Pierce announcing that with the assistance and cooperation of Able Hawk, he would soon assume custody of Jésus Acosta. He would do that just as soon as Shawn's attacker could be released to a prison infirmary. He was also taking custody of all the other presumed MS-13 members in Horton County's jail. The other gang members would also be charged with the rapes and murders of Thalia Ruiz, Esmeralda Marquez, Marisol Hernandez and Sonya Lorca.

"We have film of them with their vehicle, a red Isuzu pickup truck, dropping Thalia Ruiz's body where it was found by them two young Mexicans," Walt Pierce asserted in a recorded interview.

Tell slammed his fist into the dash.

Goddamn Able Hawk! Was this why Able had gone completely missing? Was it because he'd sold out those damned Mexican gangbangers, and Tell in the process?

With his throbbing hand, Tell picked up his cell phone and called the university professor who had been enhancing the baseball game footage Tell had found implicating Luke Strider.

"Just say it's fucking ready," Tell said.

"I've seen the news and anticipated your call," Dan Stack told him. "It's fucking ready."

"Is it better than what we had?"

"Much. But that's relative to next to nothing, you know."

"You can make out faces now?"

"Faces, no. But race, *yes.* They're white, Tell. And you can tell it's a Dodge Ram—can see that big friggin' grill. They don't have grills like that on Isuzus. Someone should tell that to that asshole Walt Pierce."

"You and I are fixing to do just that, Dan. Make ten or twelve copies, would you?"

"Sure. For who?"

"Media. And please say you'll be available to stand with me at noon. We're going to offer our own press conference. Let's do it at your school—right in the heart of fucking Vale County. Let's run it through those bastards, down *deep*."

Tell called Julie Dexter and asked her to alert area television and print media to his press conference. Billy Davis came on the line.

"What are you planning, skipper?"

"I'm going to show my version of that film to the media, Billy. Put it up on a big-ass screen and let the reporters see it. And I'm going to name Luke Strider as my person of interest in Thalia Ruiz's rape and murder. We may *never* make an arrest. We may never have enough for *that*. But, Billy, there's nothing's going to stop me from trying this case in the goddamn sorry media. At least we'll wreck some careers."

"Our own," Billy said sourly.

"Maybe. But Strider's and Walt Pierce's for certain. Think of it as getting the first shot off. Now that Able's off the field, Walt doesn't have much more than me and all of you close to me to focus on, right?"

* * *

Able frowned to see that his e-mail to Shawn O'Hara had bounced back with the notation, "No such user."

He checked the e-mail address he'd input against the one printed for Shawn in the New Austin newspaper. They were identical. *Strange.*

Able took Evelia by the hand and walked to the pay phone in the New Austin Library's lobby. He called Horton County General Hospital.

It sounded like Shawn's black nurse—Wendy, if he remembered right—on the line. Able said, "I know Shawn can't talk yet, but I wondered if you could just get someone to pick up the phone in his room and get it up to his ear so he can listen. It's urgent I talk with him. Talk *to* him, I mean. I need to do that right now."

"Who are you?"

"Able Hawk."

"Oh, Sheriff! We met the other day."

Able shook his head. "I remember you." She had called him sheriff. Wendy must not have heard the news. But given the long hours required of nurses, that was perhaps not surprising. Able was maybe still in the saddle when Wendy started her present shift.

"Good news," Nurse Wendy said. "We have your man, Mr. Marshall, rooming with Mr. O'Hara. For Shawn's protection, I mean. You know, since Shawn was attacked in his room the other day."

Able smiled crookedly. *Someone* was thinking. He wondered which of his former flunkies had hit on that cost-saving scheme. "Give me the number to that room, or better, can you transfer me?"

"I can transfer you."

Able thought about his pact with Walt Pierce—his promise to have no contact with his deputies. There was no such thing as being too safe or overcautious with Amos's ass on the line.

"Transfer the call to the room, if you could," Able said. "But first I need you to call in there and talk to Troy Marshall, Wendy. Have Troy pass the phone to Shawn and don't identify me to Troy as the caller, right? Just say it's official police business if he asks."

Nurse Wendy said, "Mr. O'Hara won't be talking back, remember."

"He doesn't have to," Able said. "Shawn just needs to listen."

There was some jostling of the receiver on the other end. Able said, "Shawn, it's Hawk. If you're there, and if you have an ink pen or something like that handy, just tap the mouthpiece so I know you're there."

There was a rap. Able held the receiver a little farther from his ear. Evelia looked up at him, impatient. He gave her a "one-minute" finger gesture and fished a sucker from his shirt pocket. He pulled the wrapper from the cherry flavored Dum-Dum and handed it to the little girl.

"Shawn, one tap for yes, two taps for no," Able said. "Got it?"

One tap.

"Good," Able said. "You've heard I'm out as Horton County sheriff?"

A single tap.

"Yeah," Able said. "Your work e-mail's no longer working, so am I right to assume that something's happened to your job too?"

A single click.

"Fired?"

Click.

"Yeah, well, I'm sorry, kid. I didn't want to go, either. But that's another story. I can't go into that too much, presently. I need a big favor, Shawn. A *big* favor. I've established one of those free Yahoo e-mail accounts for myself." Able gave Shawn the address.

"You got that, Shawn?"

Click.

"I want you to go to the Net now and register for one of those addresses yourself," Able said. "Won't take two minutes. Then e-mail me at that address I just gave you. I'm going to send you a short note back." Able had already composed a longer personal note and burned it to a disc he was carrying with him. "Feel free to read that note, Shawn. But here's the favor, partner: I need you to forward that e-mail to Tell Lyon. Do you have his e-mail address?"

Click click.

"Fuck." Then Able said, "What about Patricia's?"

A long pause, then a single click—lighter than the rest. Tentative. "You're hesitant," Able said. "Look, I heard about before. About your e-mail to her . . . about the picture you sent. I understand why you wouldn't want to mail her for me. But this is everything for all of us, kid. This is our last shot at getting Thalia Ruiz and them other women some justice. And it's our last shot maybe at making all this grief we've endured count for something. A way for you and me to still make a difference. I can't contact Lyon directly. Once Troy's out of that room of yours, for keeps, I mean, I promise to come by and explain why. But this is critical now, getting this message to Lyon. Will you do this thing for me, Shawn?"

More hesitation. Able was aware now of his damp palms on the plastic pay phone's receiver. Still nothing. Then:

Click.

"Great, kid. I owe you large. I'm hanging up now, Shawn. E-mail me, pronto."

* * *

Shawn stared at the screen, weighing Able's words.

Why help them? Why do it?

He hated them both now.

And those Mexicans? After the beating they'd given him, they deserved every dark thing coming their way.

If he shot himself, what could he care for the consequences of leaving Hawk and Lyon twisting in the wind?

But Shawn wasn't sure yet he had the resolve to take himself out. If he hesitated, and word got out about this letter he hadn't passed along?

His fingers were poised above the keys, hesitating. *Fuck* . . .

* * *

Tell settled back in his cruiser, feeling sweat in his armpits and flutters in his belly. God only knew how he came off on camera *this* time.

And now he had to await the return salvo from Vale County's sheriff and his stooges.

Tell turned on the police band, craving white noise to distract him from his own thoughts.

But he couldn't escape himself.

Slander. There might be grounds for a slander suit in what he had just done. But Strider likely couldn't risk engaging Tell on those grounds. Tell was fairly certain of that. Alleging Tell had slandered him would mean Strider having to go to court and parade out all of Tell's allegations before a jury. And extending the allegations into a formal setting—and across time—could result in Tell or others proving the truth of the New Austin police chief's allegations against him. Slander and libel suits were probably not in the offing, then.

Assassination. Killing Tell was a real possibility. But Tell thought taking his suspicions to the media might insulate him from that threat. At least in the near term that might be so. Strider would be dodging TV reporters and ambush interview attempts in the early going. Strider would be under too much scrutiny to engage Tell himself. But that short-term safety argued for Tell stepping up efforts to bolster his case and charge Strider sooner rather than later.

The enhanced film was an improvement over the original that Tell had uncovered. And projected on the university lecture hall's big screen, the pickup truck *popped*—it was undeniably a Dodge Ram. But the two men getting in and out of the hulking truck remained unidentifiable.

Given Tell's presumed limits of Walt Pierce's imagination, Tell fully expected Pierce to claim that Tell had conspired to have the film digitally altered to make the truck appear to be a Dodge and not the much smaller Isuzu the Vale County sheriff claimed it to be.

Character assassination. That was the strongest likelihood to Tell's mind. Pierce would try to take Tell off the field in a professional context. It was the strategy—the tactic—that Tell surmised Pierce had deployed against Able to devastating effect. How else to explain Hawk's abrupt resignation?

But Tell didn't have Able's baggage. Tell didn't play it gray like Able did. So anything that Pierce contrived to use to compromise Tell would have to be manufactured or stage-managed.

That prospect, like the others, argued for speed on Tell's part. He needed to move damned fast to buttress his lame case against Luke Strider.

His cell phone rang. Patricia said, "You need to get to a computer, now, Tell. Check your personal e-mail. I've forwarded a message to you. Shawn sent it to me to get to you."

Tell was pole-armed by that. "Damned Shawn sent you *another* damned e-mail?"

"Shawn was just the conduit," Patricia said. "The letter is really from Able Hawk."

"I'll hit the library," Tell said. "It's closest."

*   *   *

Tell found a free terminal and accessed his Web mail account. He scrolled down to reach Able's twice forwarded e-mail. It read:

T.—

You must hate me for a son of a bitch now.

But I had no choice.

Despite what's being said by W.P. in the media to the contrary, I was not going to have any part in railroading even them Mexican sons of bitches on false murder charges.

The choice I made was the only one I could make to protect mine. Long story short: Some others discovered my other little enterprise in much the same way you did. I know you'll know what I mean. This other who learned what you learned meant to use it against me like you didn't.

The sorry upshot is I can't have your back as I pledged.

And I'm foresworn against contacting you . . . of talking to you. Even this e-mail is a risk. That's why I'm writing you from the New Austin Public Library. By the time you get this, I will have already deleted this new e-mail account. Yeah, I'm that damned paranoid about W.P. getting wind of this.

I've been trying to find a safer way for us to communicate. Racking my brain, I picked up the New Austin Library's copy of your cousin's fourth novel. I didn't check it out mind you—just read it over and put it back. Read all that spooky stuff about clandestine communication and dead-drops and the like. All I can say is, "Boy howdy." Surely made for rewarding reading.

—Able

Tell half smiled and deleted Able's message. He then emptied the trash and made his way to the library's mystery section. He scanned the spines of the books, walking sideways until he reached "L." He saw a canted hardcover of his cousin's fourth novel. Tell pulled it from the shelf and flipped through the pages.

Nothing.

There was a slight bump at the back of the book, however—something protruding between the board and the plastic-covered dust jacket affixed to the book with tape. Tell opened the book at the middle, bending it back wide so the dust jacket bowed up and out. Taped to the back of the rear cover was an envelope. Tell tore it loose from the book's binding. There was a CD inside the sleeve. He returned the book to the shelf and bee-lined back to the computer terminal he had used to check his Web mail.

Tell inserted the disc and opened a file slugged "T.J.doc." He was confronted with what appeared to be an empty or blank document. Yet the vertical scrollbar indicated something was there. Tell highlighted the document and went up to the color bar and clicked on black.

A mishmash of oddball symbols and icons filled the screen. Tell frowned, staring at the crazed, hieroglyph-like soup of characters. Biting his lip, he checked to see what font had been used and saw that it was Wingdings. Tell highlighted the document again and went back up to the menu bar and changed the font to Times New Roman.

He smiled as the letter appeared:

Tell,

Thank Christ you're smart enough to have gotten this far. Take all these crazy precautions as evidence of how paranoid I am with Amos's ass on the line. I don't care about me at all anymore. But I'm not gonna see Amos's life burned down by anything I initiated.

I confronted Walt Pierce about Luke Strider the night before I announced my resignation. If you're as smart as I think you are, that'd be last night, your time.

I confronted Walt and we came to blows. I'd like to have killed him if he hadn't japped me with some mace.

You see, Tell, I think Walt beat Thalia and the others to death. I don't know about the rape stuff. About that, I don't say anything, regarding Walt. Maybe the rapes were Luke acting alone. But I'm sure Walt beat those women to death, including my Thalia. Walt wears eight rings—big, pimp-like rings—and his hands are still bruised. I have no evidence Walt did this, understand. But I'm convinced. I know you know what I mean. And his reaction when I accused him is good as an admission.

So that's the purpose of this note: Going after Luke Strider ain't enough, old son. It's Walt you have to take out too.

I wish like hell that I could help. I wish you and me could talk this out. Find a way to make it all right. But in exchange for protecting Amos and me from felony charges I promised not to have contact with you or any of my folks. I have to honor that pledge 'cause Walt's watching. I'm under surveillance and my phone is tapped. Figure cell phones and my own computer aren't safe to use, either.

It's hard, Tell. I guess that's my punishment for that other thing you caught me in. The job's my life and I saw myself another ten years, at least, in the post of sheriff.

Cocksuckers have taken away my life.

For my sake, I hope you take Walt and Luke down, hard and fast.

And if you have any ideas about insulating me from gang repri-
sals, I'd appreciate having them. I figure Walt's false claims that
I'm four-square with him on his "gang" solution to Thalia's and
the others' killings—particularly now that I'm stripped of official
status and security—is Walt's way of seeing I get my ass shot by
one of them Mexican gangsters in the near term.

But I'll do my best to protect my fat ass, Tell.

You protect yourself and yours.

Wish I could help, son. Your enemies are my own.

But they beat me.

—Able

Tell sighed and ejected the disc.

He nodded at the librarian on his way out. When he reached
the front door, he broke the disc in half and dropped it in the trash
receptacle.

Walt Pierce, murderer? Maybe serial rapist?

Holy Jesus.

THEN

The doctors had finally made them leave the room; made them leave Claudia there on that bed with a sheet over her face.

The Lyons stood outside in the hallway, holding tight to one another.

Later, Tell would remember that even Chris's eyes were damp; his cousin's chin trembling. Holding fast to his older, taller cousin, Tell managed to get out, "I want him *dead*, Chris. I want to kill this Angel with my bare hands."

"Oh, trust me, I feel the same way," Chris said.

"I mean it," Tell said. "And I mean to do it. Don't try to talk me out of it."

Chris squeezed Tell's neck, looking him in the eye. "*Never*. Hell, I'll *help* you."

Tell believed him. If any man understood revenge—and had no compunctions about acting on the impulse—it was Chris. "But you have to soldier through these next couple of days," Chris said. "You have to see to Marita and Claudia . . ." His voice trailed off, leaving *You have to see to their funerals* unsaid.

"Of course. But after—"

"*After*, I'll make some calls," Chris said. "You can't possibly do this alone, Tell. Not and succeed. But, if you still feel this way in a few days, I swear I'll help you do what you want. Some others and I will have your back. I swear there *will* be a reckoning."

Tell looked up; Chris met his gaze. "It'll be goddamn ugly, Chris. I'm warning you up front—this will be bloody. I *want* it to be bloody."

Chris said softly, "I can't imagine it any other way."

FIFTY THREE

"You seem sullen, Shawn," his doctor said. "It concerns me."

Shawn typed, *I'm fine.*

"I don't see that," his doctor said. "It's early yet, but I'm going to give you a look at your face. Most of it, anyway. I'm going to show you things are coming along. The swelling's gone. Soon the stitches will come out. We're going to look at freeing up your jaw today too. Let you talk. We've reevaluated your X-rays and determined there wasn't a break of your jaw or your palate. That's very good news—I feared you might suffer a permanent speech impediment. But that's off the table now."

Shawn typed, *You'll do all this now?*

"Yes," the doctor replied. "But understand—I'll be angling the mirror. I don't want you looking at your jawline until we get those implants in place. Good news there, parenthetically. You're covered on those. By insurance, I mean."

Shawn shot the doctor a thumbs-up.

"Understand, also, there's some scarring. We'll address that cosmetically, and quite soon. Your right eyelid will require a procedure too. To eliminate its droop, I mean. But overall, I think you'll be quite surprised to find you're in better shape than you think you are. Then, after, we'll get you in that wheelchair for a spin. You must be beyond stir crazy."

* * *

Tell sat at his desk, staring at the pictures of Thalia, Esmeralda, Marisol and Sonya he'd hung on his side of the divider wall with pushpins.

He felt snookered. His impulse was to run back before the cameras and report that he'd expanded his investigation to include Walt Pierce as a person of interest. But to do that would be to tacitly acknowledge that he'd had contact with Able Hawk.

That meant one course left him, so far as Tell could see: arresting Luke Strider and somehow getting him to flip on Walt Pierce. But Tell still needed a toe in on that front and something that would *stick*.

Billy Davis was seated at his desk across the room, sucking on a jamocha milkshake and munching on Arby's curly fries.

Tell said, "Billy, I want you to see if you can get me a meeting with your friend Tom Winch."

Billy bit the end off a knot of seasoned fries and swallowed. "He might agree to that if we can find a safe place to meet. Today is Tom's day off. You want to try and do a meeting today?"

"Today for certain," Tell said. "Soon as possible. I want to end this."

"Where could you do that? Where could you do that meeting where Tom would feel safe, I mean?"

"Let's have him meet me out at our shooting range," Tell said. "You'll follow Tom out there to be sure that he isn't followed by anyone else. You'll lock the gate behind us and stand guard. See we really have no company."

*   *   *

Able couldn't stand it any longer. The flaw with his bid to communicate with Tell—well, the whole thing had been fraught with

363

flaws—but the *big* drawback from the standpoint of granting Able some flavor of peace of mind was the one-sidedness of his means of reaching out to Tell. He just didn't know if Tell had gotten his warnings about Walt Pierce's presumed complicity in the murders. He didn't know if Tell had found the hidden disc.

He put on his shoes and called to Sofia, who was in the kitchen starting plans for dinner. "I'll be back in ten minutes or so," he said to her. "Just running a quick errand."

Evelia was right there again. "Can I go too, Pap-Paw Hawk?"

"Sorry, honey. No, I have to go alone. But I'll be back real quick. Maybe bring you a surprise."

Able drove to the New Austin Library and walked straight back to the mystery section. He took a deep breath and pulled down Chris Lyon's book. He slipped his big hand between the dust jacket and cover. He smiled. *Tell, the clever cocksucker.*

It was just too bad Tell had come along at the end—when Able was to be forced off the job. If they'd had three or four years of over-lapping service together, the things they might have accomplished . . . ?

But if Tell succeeded in taking Pierce down, and if Pierce didn't try to lighten his load by ratting out Able on a plea bargain, there was no saying Able couldn't run for sheriff again—reclaim his post. Able figured those odds for fifty-fifty. The best prospect was Walt getting himself killed resisting arrest . . . or opting for suicide by cop.

Able replaced the book on the shelf and shook his head. He shouldn't kid himself. The only way he'd ever be free to be a cop again—the only way for Amos to live out from under a shadow—would be for someone to put Walt Pierce in the ground. And Able was sorely tempted to see to that bloody chore. Not just for himself and for Amos, but for Evelia's mother and the other murdered Mexican women.

Able bit his thick mustache. He needed to talk to Tell. Tell might talk him out of his sudden strong compulsion to kill Walt Pierce. Tell might have something to share that would give Able some glimmer of hope that Walt Pierce might really yet be taken down on something that Tell might have uncovered since he and Able had last spoken. He'd watched Tell's televised interviews and press conferences, hoping Tell truly had the goods he hinted at . . . that he wasn't lying to the press now as Able had once pressed Tell to do.

Able sat down at a computer and registered for another free Yahoo e-mail account. He e-mailed Shawn again. He asked the reporter to pass along another note to Tell—this one asking Tell for a meeting at eight P.M. in the New Austin Kid's Association ball fields—site of the recent Latino Festival and the fields fronting the scrub wasteland where Thalia had been found.

If Tell had nothing on Walt Pierce, then the risk of the meeting with Tell would soon enough be moot. If Tell couldn't touch Pierce, then Able was determined to put the Vale County sheriff down himself.

Able told himself that he would kill Walt, all consequences to himself be damned.

*　*　*

Diego Ortiz flinched as the fat cop with the buzz cut got down in his face again. The cop's big hand was moving toward Diego's face—the rings on his fingers catching light. Diego could imagine those rings cutting into his flesh; breaking his bones and teeth.

Sheriff Walt Pierce grabbed hold of the red bandana tied around Diego's head and wrenched it off. He shook the red rag in the teen's face. "Fucking gang colors. You're one fuckin' sad-ass mess, you know that, Diego? You and the rest of your so-called gang are just a bunch of weak-willed pussies. *El Gavilan* and that New Austin cop, Tell Lyon, they've blown through your numbers like you was just a bunch of pussy-assed cunts. And your butt-boy buddy, Jésus? Did you hear the docs chopped his leg off? That's right, your fuckin' leader is now a cripple. Figure that sorry gimp'll be passed around to the old timers to cornhole once we get him to prison. Your other members too—the ones that don't get shipped back to Mexico to be cornholed by their own in some Juarez rat hole."

"I didn't do that shit," Diego said, surly. "They didn't murder them *chicas*. And even if they did, I wasn't there or close to it anyway. I ain't done nothin'. And I've got *real* papers, I'm American-born, just like you."

"More's the pity. Fucking American kid getting dragged into this fuckin' Mexican gang shit." Pierce spat tobacco in Diego's face. "Don't you fucking wipe that off, asswipe," Pierce said. "You're a fuckin' disgrace."

"I want a lawyer."

"You don't get no fuckin' attorney, Diego. We're kickin' you loose, 'cause, like you say, we got nothin' on you. *Yet*. But we *have* got somethin' on that cousin of yours living with you, that fucking Magdaleno. Him and his baby sister and his folks? They's all illegal. We'll be comin' for them soon as the paperwork comes through from Tell Lyon and Able Hawk. Should have it by tomorrow morning. Then we're raiding your house and shipping them all back to old *Meh-hi-co*."

"Hawk ain't sheriff anymore," Diego said. He tilted his head—trying to keep the stinking stream of chewing tobacco trailing down his cheek from reaching his own mouth.

Sheriff Pierce shook his head. "Able resigning from his post don't mean *El Gavilan* ain't still helping me on the immigration-control front. Don't believe stuff you see on the news. And Lyon's ex-Border

Patrol, so you know how he feels about your kind. Hawk still hates you Mexicans. I couldn't make half the arrests I'm making of illegals without their help. And now, your so-called gang is on Lyon's and Hawk's radar in a big way. The only hope you and yours have is that some Mexican gang with some real stones—say, MS-13 or Calle 18—snuffs Hawk and Lyon. And they'd need to do it tonight to save that family of yours. To save you. 'Cause, swear to God, Diego, I'm going to take you down, hard. What do you think your mother and sister will do for cash once your drug money's deprived them? Figure they'll both be hooking inside a week. Lots of your kind, and I guess mine too—whites, I mean—they like fuckin' tight little thirteen-year-olds. Not that I really think that sister of yours is a virgin."

Diego tried to come up out of the chair but Deputy Luke Strider, standing behind Diego, pushed him back down.

"Tonight's your last good night, Diego," Sheriff Pierce said. "That is, if tomorrow morning still finds Tell Lyon and Able Hawk drawing air. If them two make it through this night, I swear to you that you'll be toast before lunch tomorrow. But those two don't have anything to fear from the likes of you, do they, Diego? Hell, you MS-13 pussies can't kill time, much less a man."

Diego stared at Walt Pierce, uncomprehending. He said, "You *want* me to kill them? You asking me to do it, giving me fucking permission? Is that what you're asking, old man?"

Walt smiled, close down in Diego's face, the light shining on his near-shaven head. "I ain't *asking* you to do anything, Diego," the sheriff said.

*   *   *

Shawn heard his computer's drive spin and the digital voice said, "You have mail."

He'd get to that.

Now his doctor was leaning over Shawn, carefully unwrapping and cutting away gauze and bandages, prattling on about Shawn's needing to "understand" and to "modulate expectations," and "not focus on scars and stitches" but on "how much progress" he had already made in healing.

Shawn's mouth was dry with anticipation. He couldn't wait to open his mouth to speak again.

* * *

Tell and Tom Winch sat on the hood of his command cruiser. Tell had parked under the shade of a tree and brought along several bottled waters. Tom Winch—pale, pudgy-faced—sipped his Aquafina and wiped the wetness from his still-growing mustache.

"What do we do now, Chief," Winch said, "I guess that's the question, huh? If I testify to the fact that in his cups Luke confessed to helping dump them two murdered prostitutes after tag-teaming them with Sheriff Pierce, my life won't be worth spit. I'll lose my job, for sure."

Tell said, "I'm sure that could happen short-term. But your testimony would allow me to arrest the two of them. That would mean new leadership and arbitration through the FOP. You'd get your job back within a couple of days. I'm certain of that, Deputy."

"Probably true," Tom agreed. "But I'd be an outcast. The other deputies are fiercely faithful to that sadistic bastard. They'd make my life a living hell. I think there's a fair chance one or more would kill me to see my testimony suppressed. 'Specially if it's all you've got against Pierce and Strider. From where I sit, that seems to be the case."

"I can't lie and say otherwise," Tell said. "Just your testimony and the film I found."

"Well that isn't near enough. And I'm guessing that's why we're having this talk I'm already regretting."

"You're a good cop, Tom," Tell said. "I can see that. And you're a moral man. You honor the job. These others you work with are thugs hiding behind badges. In the case of Pierce and Strider, they're sadistic rapists and killers *using* those badges."

"That's all true. But I have my life to think about. My wife."

"We'll get her protection, right now," Tell said. "We'll work through the unions to see *you* remain on wages but safely off the job while the trial wraps up. When it's over, I have work for you. I've been given permission to hire two more full-time officers. I'll start you at your present pay and you can retain any accrued vacation and personal time. I'll do that when the trial's over. But this offer remains between us, and I can't do it sooner. We can't have the job you know I have waiting for you looking like some *quid pro quo*, like some reward in exchange for testimony." Tell searched the man's face. "Because we both know it isn't like that. You're driven to do the right thing."

"I don't *want* to do this," Tom Winch said. "Oh my God, I don't *want* to."

"But you know you *have* to," Tell pressed. "Thalia Ruiz and at least one of these other women those two raped and tortured and killed were citizens, Tom. Single mothers. And Pierce and Strider will do it again. You're the only one who can stop them from taking some other child's mother away. Please help me, Tom. I swear I'll see you and yours are protected."

"I need a night to think about it, Chief. Just one night."

Disappointed, Tell said, "Okay, Tom. One night. But you *know* what you have to do."

"I do," he said, looking sick. "Just need a night to edge myself into it. It's just one night. One last good night."

* * *

"Oh, God," Shawn said, his voice hoarse and brittle. "Oh, Jesus!"

"It's not as bad as you're seeing it," his doctor said urgently. "Look again—imagine those stitches out. They will be in a week. Imagine those scars gone. They will be, in a month. That eye will be fixed this time next week. Your hair? You can color that. In time, the pigment might even reassert itself, young as you are. Once that ear's a little better healed, we'll have a cosmetic surgeon come in and pull it back. Sorry about the angle of the mirror and you seeing your mouth, but I swear to you, when the implants are in, you'll look *great* . . . just like you did before. We're replicating your teeth from the ones your cop friend found. I'll defy you to tell me your teeth don't look like you remember them when we're done."

"And my nose," Shawn said, "what about my fucking nose? Is there more you're going to do there?"

"That's a little different," his doctor said reluctantly. "A nose is mostly cartilage, Shawn. We can't do much more than we have. There *are* prosthetic possibilities . . ."

Shawn surveyed his face again. He didn't recognize himself. Even his eyes looked strange to him—crazed and empty. His hair had gone *white* like one of Andy Warhol's wacky wigs.

His face was a crazy quilt of welts and scars and stitches like Christopher Lee's face in that shitty old remake of *Frankenstein*.

His right eye was drooping like Stallone's in the last reel of *Rocky*.

His right ear stuck straight out like the geek on the cover of *Mad Magazine*.

With his missing teeth, his chin thrust out like that of a cartoon witch. He had an old man's mouth. Shawn reminded himself of his grandfather the two terrible times he'd seen the old bastard with his dentures out.

The worst was his nose—some bobbed, pug-looking thing. Like something a girl with a bad plastic surgeon would end up with . . . an ugly chick's nose.

When Shawn had taken the picture of himself with his nurse's cell phone—the picture he'd sent to Patricia—the screen had been too small and his eyes too swollen to see much.

The doctor pulled the mirror away. "Next time—a week from now—you'll look again at that face and see 100 percent improvement, Shawn. I swear to you. Now let me get your nose and some of your face re-dressed and then we'll see about getting you into that wheelchair. We'll get you out for a spin, yes?"

"Sure," Shawn said. At least he could talk again, though his speech sounded funny and slurred with no teeth. Lispy. "Sure. That would be great, Doc."

From the bed next to him, Troy Marshall said, "I remember you from before, kid, from the meth raid. You'll look the same, like the doc said, once they get your teeth fixed. I mean, what's a fucking nose in the bigger scheme of things?" He pointed to his own bent and three-times-broken nose. "Think I was born with this goddamn thing?"

* * *

Diego sat in the detached garage behind the Ortiz home, checking the AK-47 he'd retrieved from the MS-13's single undiscovered cache of weapons.

"You can't do this, Diego," his cousin, Magdaleno, said. "You can't snuff a cop, Diego. They'll kill you for that."

"No, the fucking sheriff asked me—ordered me—to kill this ex-cop and the other, this Lyon. You wouldn't understand, *pendejo*." Diego looked up from his gun at his cousin and shook his head.

Magdaleno was a straight arrow, clean-cut dressed American. Magdaleno had shunned every attempt that Diego had made to connect his cousin with MS-13.

No, Diego's fucking straight-arrow cousin just wanted to hang with that other gone-American newbie Richie Huerta. "This is how things really work," Diego said. "This is how things happen. This is how the world really works."

"Bullshit," Magdaleno said. "You never killed anyone, and—"

"You don't know that!"

"You've never killed anyone," Magdaleno repeated, "and you don't want to try and kill *El Gavilan* and *El Léon*. Especially not them."

"Fucking listen to yourself, Mag," Diego snarled. "You talk like you're some fucking peasant back home and that they are Villa and Zapata. I'm being a man and protecting the family."

"Yeah, you're *muy macho*," Magdaleno sneered. "You're being used by the white man."

"Fuck you!"

"No, fuck *you*, Diego! You're being *used*. If you ever watched the news, or read a newspaper, you'd know that Lyon has accused your fucking Walt Pierce's deputy of murdering Thalia Ruiz and three other sisters. That's why Pierce wants you to kill Lyon. Diego, put away that gun before you destroy our family. If you're caught, all the attention will be on us, Diego. We'll be deported, and your mother and sister will be here alone."

Diego stood and wrapped his gun back up in the blanket he had found covered within the gang's hidden stash. "I've gotta go. Gotta do this thing. You just keep your fucking mouth shut."

Magdaleno stepped up to his cousin. "You can't do this, Diego. I can't let you."

Diego smiled and then lashed out with the butt of his AK-47. He caught his cousin in the temple. He reached out and grabbed Magdaleno's belt buckle with his right hand, pulling back just enough to cushion his cousin's fall to the concrete slab floor of the garage. Diego waited to see his cousin draw a couple of breaths, then looked again at the piece of paper with the addresses of Able Hawk and Tell Lyon written there.

THEN

The pueblo was a fireball. The flames licked high up into the night sky. Flat as it was out here, Tell thought it must be visible for miles around. Soon, someone would come to investigate.

Seven, maybe eight of Angel Valenzuela's band were already dead or well on their way to dying; nothing that happened tonight was being done under color of authority, and there would be no emergency services to treat the wounded on either side. No prisoners would be taken.

As the building burned, Chris Lyon insisted Tell stay upwind, far from the smells of any burning things that might trigger stronger, unendurable memories of the fire that had burned down his cousin's pretty world.

A man—the sole survivor from the gun battle—was on his knees in the sand. He'd been shot through both feet by Chris so he couldn't run. The man's hands were secured behind his back with plastic handcuffs.

Chris had a Ruger pressed to the back of Angel Valenzuela's head, held up tight behind the drug lord's right ear.

Tell approached slowly; didn't say anything as he closed in. Chris didn't say anything either, just searched his cousin's eyes a last time. Tell nodded and Chris passed him the handgun.

Angel was watching Tell closely too, licking his bloodied lips and testing teeth with his tongue's tip.

Would the bastard sneer at Tell? Maybe spit blood at his face or on Tell's boot toe?

Would he laugh derisively and make jokes about Marita and Claudia?

The drug lord bowed his head. In a guttural, cracking voice, Valenzuela pleaded for his life. His family, he said, needed him. His children, he said, needed a father.

"Please," Valenzuela said. "Please, don't. I'm begging you. I'll pay you both . . . *much* money. More than you two can imagine."

It was Tell who found himself sneering. He said, "After so many payoffs you've offered me through your minions these past couple of years, what makes you think I'd take your money now, after all you've taken from me?"

Stepping aside to make room for Tell behind the kneeling man, Chris said, "We don't have much time, Tell. That fire's bound to bring company, and sooner rather than later."

Tell nodded but stood his ground. He said, "Not from behind, Chris. This one's going to be face-to-face." Tell said it more for Angel Valenzuela's benefit than his cousin's.

Moving a step closer, Tell pressed the muzzle of the automatic between Angel's eyes. Angel whimpered and said, "You're no *killer*. I *know* men." His voice trembling, Angel said, "I know men and you are *not* one who can kill in cold blood. You've never killed, I can tell. You are not the kind to take a life. Not like this now."

A deep, ragged breath. Tell closed his eyes, feeling that blast-furnace wind and hearing the crackle and low roar of the fire. He saw Claudia there on her deathbed.

"I'm no killer?" Tell nodded slowly. He said, "You're right for about one more second."

* * *

Chris and the others saw to the bodies.

That duty consisted mostly of dragging them some distance to throw them into the burning building.

All but Angel—they left *him* for eventual identification or for the desert scavengers. Chris did pat down the drug lord's body before they left. He found what looked like a kind of address book. He tossed it to Tell.

Back at the hotel, showered and numb with drink but still smelling blood and cordite, smelling fire, Tell walked out a ways into the desert by himself.

He stared up at the moon and all the hard stars.

After his shower, he'd flipped through the pages of Valenzuela's book of contacts.

He'd found a name: Seth Alvin.

As it grew darker around him, Tell realized he was shaking. He tried to believe it was just the cold of the desert night.

FIFTY FOUR

"Time for rehab again?" Shawn was surprised how calm his own voice sounded. But he was at last resolved, so maybe that was why.

"Yeah, that time again," Troy Marshall said. "Be nice to get back here this time though. I mean, now that we can jaw together."

"Yeah," Shawn said evenly, "will be good to talk." The doctor had replaced only about half the bandages Shawn had previously worn. "Sorry about the view, though, Troy. Jesus, I'm an ugly son of a bitch now."

"You're fine, Shawn. Better'n you think. Given how many there were beating on you, it could have been a hell of a lot worse. I've seen plenty of guys after all kinds of beatings, so I know. And I did two tours in Iraq. Saw really nasty stuff there happen to guys. Six months later, guys a lot worse off than you looked great. Give it time, Shawn. Trust me. I've seen what the docs can do. But it takes time."

"Okay."

"I mean that, Shawn. You hear me?"

"I know. I do too . . . hear what you're saying, I mean."

"I get back, we need to compare notes on Able Hawk. Love to get your take on what happened there."

"It's a puzzler," Shawn agreed. He buzzed for the nurse. Wendy Fahy said, "Problem, Shawn sweetie?"

"My guard's headed out for rehab," Shawn said, hating the sound of his own distorted voice . . . his *s*'s sounded like *th*'s . . . like that fucking cartoon cat Sylvester. "Wondered if I could get an orderly to get me in the chair again. Had that taste of freedom and I guess it made me itchy for more."

Wendy chuckled, causing static on the intercom. She said, "Sounds like me after my first divorce. I'll get Rufus down with your chair, sweetie."

Shawn waved goodbye at Troy as the sheriff's deputy clunked his way out on a walker. A little over an hour—that was the average duration of Troy's physical rehabilitation sessions. More than enough time. As Shawn awaited the orderly to arrive with the electric wheelchair, his computer chirped up again. Its digitized female voice said, "You have mail!"

Well, the hell with that. Why answer mail now? What difference could it possibly make?

And Shawn had already decided he wasn't leaving a suicide note.

Sorry, Mom . . . And it would spare Patricia too. You lucked out on that front, Patty.

Resentment . . . anger . . . betrayal.

Well, farewell to all that. Not going to guilt you, Patty. Not going to ghost your bones. I'll be the better human and leave you to your pending newlywed bliss. Still, if you hadn't left me that one night, it would all be maybe different. We both know that's so.

"Hey, Mr. O'Hara!"

Shawn looked up, momentarily startled. It was Rufus, the Mexican orderly. The last two faces he'd see . . . the last two people he would talk to would be Mexican. *Mexicans.* Just like the ones that beat him . . . and led Shawn to this decision to kill himself.

Some irony in that—their being Mexican. Or *was* that irony? Hell, Shawn was just a reporter. He didn't last long enough to even start the novel he'd promised himself he would one day write. He had planned to write himself right out of fucking newspaper work like Chris Lyon had.

Rufus helped wrestle Shawn into the power wheelchair. "You still remember how to run this gizmo, Shawn?"

"Sure. No problem."

"Well, just watch out for the old ladies out there on walkers, Shawn."

Shawn shot Rufus a thumbs-up.

Rufus left and Shawn slapped his good leg. *Damn!* He should have let Rufus take him to the john. Shawn knew from the few murder scenes he'd observed that the kidneys and bowels release at the moment of death. He had hoped to avoid that indignity. Well, at least he'd be seated when the time came. Might help contain the worst. *If* whatever was left of Shawn afterward stayed seated in the chair.

When the loss was fresh, he'd tried to imagine what his father must have looked like after putting the gun in his mouth. After seeing a few crime scene photos in books, it was easier for Shawn to guess at the aftermath. He pictured himself that way—most of his head blown away. Having seen Thalia made it still more possible to imagine what he might look like after.

Somehow, the notion of doing that to himself—and of what it would leave behind—was less than even abstractly disturbing. It just didn't matter. *Nothing* mattered.

Shawn rolled over to Troy's bed and reached under the pillow. He felt the gun, cold and hard. He checked the door to the hallway—all clear—and pulled out the gun. No gunlock—that was lucky. And a clip was already in. That was lucky too. His luck was running *good*. Thank God that Troy, the bloodthirsty leatherneck, was cavalier about gun safety. That was probably going to cost Troy in the inquest phase. Maybe cost him his badge. Well, what was that to Shawn? What was *anything* to Shawn, for whom the world was about to cease to exist?

He slipped Troy's automatic into his robe on the right side. He'd have to handle the gun with his left hand thanks to Jésus and his buddy's breaking of Shawn's right middle finger. Shooting with his "sinister" hand might throw off his aim. That could be bad news for Jésus. Shawn thought maybe *that* was irony.

With his left hand, Shawn scooped up the phone and punched in 4-1-1. He asked to be given the patient information number for Horton County General Hospital. He asked for the room number of Jésus Acosta. To sell the notion that his was a harmless inquiry, Shawn said, "He *is* permitted delivery of flowers, isn't he?"

Shawn committed the room number to memory. Jésus was quartered almost directly over his own room, three floors up. Shawn looked at his bed a last time, then wheeled out into the hall in search of the elevator.

Nurse Wendy Fahy smiled and said, "Look at you go!" Shawn winked back.

As he rode the car up, Shawn took deep, steady breaths, trying to calm his nerves. His stomach was cramping and he felt an urgent need to piss. Well, in a minute or two more, he would do just that.

He wheeled out of the elevator and checked room numbers; he veered right.

Shawn was prepared for disappointment. If a guard was posted outside Jésus Acosta's room, then he would have to forego vengeance against the gang member. But given the way the sheriff's department and New Austin police had looked after Shawn initially . . . ?

Shawn's heart rate quickened—there was a guard posted at the door, but the sheriff's deputy looked edgy. The deputy checked his watch, then, walking urgently, bee-lined for the men's room. Poor bastard, like Shawn, needed to piss.

Shawn wheeled up to the darkened room and glanced inside. Jésus was asleep and he was alone. Shawn looked both ways down the corridor and then gunned his wheelchair through the door.

The whine of the wheelchair motor caused Jésus to stir. The sheet fell flat several inches above the place where Jésus's right knee should start. God bless Able Hawk and company for costing the vicious spic a leg.

Shawn reached over and pulled the connector cord for Jésus's handheld remote from the wall. Then he drew Troy's gun from within the folds of his bathrobe and checked the safety. He flicked it off and pumped one into the chamber. Then he wheeled closer to Jésus's bed. He whacked the gangbanger's stump with the gun.

Jésus drew himself up on his elbows, looking scared and angry. He said, "What the fuck?"

"Hey, Jésus, remember me? I used to be Shawn O'Hara."

The Mexican gangbanger smiled back at Shawn, regarding him with glassy eyes. Vikes. Maybe Percocets. Hell, maybe morphine, with that missing leg. "I did a better job on you than your cocksucker friends did on me," he said, grinning. Jésus was missing four teeth up front.

Shawn said, "Least I go out on two feet. You still feel that missing leg? Do your missing foot and toes hurt like they always say in the books and movies?"

"I've adjusted, cocksucker. How about you?"

"I'm not giving myself time to adjust. Or you, either." Shawn showed Jésus the gun.

Frowning, wide-eyed, Jésus stabbed at the nurse's call button on his remote control. Shawn smiled his gummy smile and tossed the loose end of the remote's cord across Jésus's chest. "Little trick I learned from your buddy who visited my room a few floors down and gave me this." Shawn held up his right hand, displaying his broken finger. Then he said, "This is for the kicks between the legs, Jésus."

Shawn pointed the gun at Jésus's crotch and tugged the trigger. The roar surprised Shawn—actually made him flinch. The bed sheets kicked and turned red. Jésus screamed—a high-pitched scream. "You scream just like a woman," Shawn shouted back. He shot Jésus between the eyes; saw the pillow and wall turn red. More screams were echoing down the hallway now. Shawn heard feet running his way.

Shawn had heard horror stories about would-be suicides who muffed the job with guns—put the barrel to their temple or under their chins. They ended up blowing off half their face or giving themselves various degrees of brain damage without getting the job done.

The best way was the barrel in the mouth, its end pressed tight up against the palate. Just like Dad. Fortunately for Shawn, he could go that same route, thanks to the doctors having freed his jaw. Yes, his luck was going very good today.

The pounding feet were getting closer. There was no time for Shawn to fasten on some thought or image to carry him over.

Shawn forced the gun in his mouth, wincing at the touch of metal to his tender gums. He gagged on the metal in his mouth and tugged the trigger again. He heard—no, *felt*—something crack.

FIFTY FIVE

Troy Marshall was aware of a commotion. He saw Nurse Wendy Fahy bustle in, panic-stricken. She was followed by a Mexican orderly with a wheelchair.

"Shawn's done shot that Mexican who beat him and Shawn's shot hisself!"

Instinctively, Troy knew Shawn must have done it with *his* gun. *Jesus.* Troy could already envision the shit storm that would ensue for him, leaving his gun unattended like that.

The orderly helped Troy into the wheelchair. Wendy said, "That one Shawn killed was Sheriff Walt Pierce's prisoner. Sheriff Pierce and his men are on the way, but since you're a deputy too, Dr. Thorpe thought you should be upstairs seeing to things until Sheriff Pierce gets here."

Troy said, "Is Shawn dead?"

Wendy nodded, all tears. "I hear he is, I do."

"Take me back to my room," Troy said. "*Now.* Get me there *right now.*"

* * *

Able Hawk sat alone in his bedroom, thinking about the night ahead. The window was open and the breeze through the screen was soothing, cooled by the shade of the big old trees arrayed around the house. Voices from the kitchen; soft laughter. It was good to have that sort of sound again in the house, something other than the TV or the drone of his and Amos's own lonely voices.

Able also had the scanner on softly. He heard a report about a shooting at the county hospital; thought he heard the phrase "murder-suicide." He reached to turn up the radio. They likely wouldn't use the names of victims or perpetrators on the police band. He reached for the phone. Able decided he would call the hospital and ask for Nurse Wendy. Maybe she still didn't know he was no longer Horton County sheriff and would tell him who had been shot.

Evelia burst through the door. "Pap-Paw Hawk, where's my sur-prize? You said you would get me a sur-prize."

Hell of a time for her to remember his promise to bring her something back after his library trip. But he *had* gotten her something. He had stopped at the Hallmark shop and picked up a couple of small stuffed animals—a horse and a monkey.

"Forgot and left your surprise in my car, honey," he said.

"I'll go get them," she said.

"Not by yourself," he said. "The car's locked." Amos passed by then—moving through the hall to his bedroom. Able said, "Hey, Aim—need a favor." Amos walked back and looked at him, half-assed surly. They had been avoiding each other most of the day. Amos's nose was out of joint—he was upset that his grandfather wouldn't confide more regarding his abrupt resignation as sheriff. Well, better he feel pissed off than feeling guilty or the like.

Amos said, "What do you need from me?"

"Hallmark bag on the front seat of my car. Toys for Evelia." He tossed his grandson the keys to the Impala. "Can you get it for her?"

"Sure," Amos said without enthusiasm.

Evelia raced to Amos's side. "I'm coming too."

Able heard the front screen door slam as he reached for the phone again to call the hospital.

He dropped the phone when he heard the automatic rifle fire commence—dozens of rounds going off.

Able raced to the window and saw a blue pickup truck out front.

A young Mexican wearing a red bandana around his forehead was behind the wheel. He saw the Mexican—the MS-13 member— draw the AK-47 back into the cab and then accelerate away, looking crazed and scared.

Able grabbed his own gun and screamed to Sofia, "Call 911!"

Able knocked the screen door off its top hinge as he burst through, jumping off the porch and wrenching an ankle.

He ran-limped to the Impala. Its open door was full of holes; most of the glass blown out of the windows. Two legs were visible beneath the open door of the Chevy. Able recognized his grandson's bloody shoes. He looked around, trying to find Evelia as he ran to his grandson.

Amos was covered in glass; red stains were spreading fast across his pants and shirt.

THEN

It was Thalia's first day back at work since burying the memory of her husband. That's what they put in the ground—an empty box she couldn't really afford. No trace of her husband or the others killed with him had been found.

Able Hawk had taken pains to learn where Thalia worked; then he kept tabs on her intended return to duty.

In the lull between breakfast and lunch rush, Able strode in. He looked around, then chose the booth that he'd make his own over countless visits to come. Frowning, Thalia watched the sheriff choose his booth. He sat down, pressed his palms to the tabletop and looked around like it was home. He turned and smiled at Thalia, winked.

Smiling uncertainly back, Thalia hoisted a pot of piping hot coffee. She squared her shoulders and drifted his way—her first customer since her life was turned inside out.

"Sheriff Hawk."

Another wink and a smile. "Hi there, Thalia. How are you holding up, darlin'?"

* * *

Three months later, they knew one another's family names out to parents on Thalia's side and grandchildren on Able's end of such things.

Eventually, mutual trust allowed topics to spread further, but maybe more in one direction than another. Able was already plying Thalia with ricochet freebies: coupons, discount cards and sundry vouchers for myriad perks that helped her stretch her stingy paycheck.

Thalia reciprocated the only way she knew how: she became *El Gavilan's* eyes and ears within the local Latino community. Able never sought this of Thalia—she'd volunteered it, really. But by the same token, Able didn't turn down her services to that end.

It was to the credit of their relationship's underlying foundation that Thalia didn't feel used; that Hawk didn't first solicit Thalia's cooperation as . . . as . . . Well, what other word for it than . . . *that*? "Snitching" was *such* a squalid word for what she was doing, Thalia told herself. Yet it was exactly like *that*.

The point was that Able Hawk never asked that of her. It just . . . developed. They were like that together each late morning. Unguarded, trusting, candid. Thalia knew Able was the only one she was like that around. She suspected she saw those same sides of Able in a way no other did. There were no secrets between them.

Well, that was so until she learned of Luisa's relationship with Able's grandson, Amos. When she learned that Lusia was pregnant by Amos, she was torn between keeping their secret and telling Able what was unfolding behind his back.

Each passing day—and the reality of Luisa's growing belly—made it that much harder. Thalia kept promising herself the next day would be the day she would confide to Able what was going on. With only a few weeks remaining until the baby wailed its way into the world, time was running out for Thalia.

Each morning as she stood under the shower's spray, she vowed to herself, *Today is the day I tell Hawk*. Each night that pledge was amended to *Tomorrow will be the day.* She made that same promise to herself for four consecutive nights.

As she watched Hawk sitting with the other two sheriffs that last morning, she finally found the resolve she knew would see her through it the next morning. Watching Able savor his banana cream pie—aware that short fat sheriff with the rings was watching her—Thalia promised herself that the next morning she'd at last tell Able how it was. Maybe pointing out they were becoming something like official family would make it go down easier for the proud, tough old man.

Thalia promised herself, Tomorrow for certain. Tomorrow. It will change everything between us. But tomorrow he'll learn the truth. Tomorrow he'll see. He'll see it all.

FIFTY SIX

Troy looked around the room—Shawn had left no obvious note. The deputy felt under his own pillow and confirmed that his gun was gone.

Fuck! Troy figured he'd lose his badge over that.

Cursing, he wheeled over to Shawn's bed and pulled the laptop onto his own lap and looked around the computer's desktop. No suicide note there, either. Troy opened up Microsoft Word and checked the Recent Document menu and found nothing. Apparently, Shawn must have been planning his exit for a while. No suicide note, no columns. No stories and no notes. *Nothing.* Seemed to Troy that Shawn had given up on writing along with everything else.

Troy saw the icon flashing in the corner, indicating Shawn had e-mail. He checked and found two e-mails, still unopened. One was a free offer for Cialis. The other was from Able Hawk, requesting a meeting with Tell Lyon at eight P.M.

Troy checked the wall clock—three fifteen P.M. He searched around through Shawn's Sent file and found an earlier Able Hawk e-mail had been transmitted to Tell Lyon's fiancée, Patricia. He forwarded Able's newest note to Patricia. He was about to delete the original e-mail when he heard the voice:

"Take your hands off that fucking laptop right now or so help me I'll shoot you where you sit you incompetent fucking grunt."

Sheriff Walt Pierce seized the laptop with fat, jewel-spangled fingers. He got in close to Troy's face. "I find anything in the trash of this fucking computer, I'm going to burn you down even further than I aim to for leaving your fucking sidearm where that reporter could get at it and shoot my murder suspect. Jesus, but you are a sorry fucking fuck-up."

* * *

Tell's cell phone rang. Julie Dexter: bless her, she'd finally called him on a secure line from the jump.

Tell listened, half-sick as she told him about Shawn's suicide; about Shawn's murder of Jésus Acosta.

Then Julie told him of a reported shooting at Able Hawk's house. Julie said she had no further word yet on that front. She did know emergency squads had been dispatched, but that was all Julie knew.

Tell slammed on the brakes and kicked his cruiser into a skidding U-turn.

Fuck Walt Pierce and his demands on Able Hawk. Tell couldn't avoid a crime scene in his own jurisdiction, not if someone had taken a shot at Able Hawk.

He was two miles from Able's house. He hit the siren and said to Julie, "I'm headed to Hawk's now. Get Rick over to County General to see what he can do around the Horton and Vale County sheriffs already there. Then get Billy to meet me at Able's."

Tell made good time reaching Able's house. He was a block away when he passed an ambulance tearing off in the other direction.

Christ—that meant a transport. *Someone* had been hit.

A second ambulance followed closely behind; it was going fast too. *Two casualties.*

Tell skidded to a stop in front of the Hawk house. Two Horton County sheriff's squad cars were already there, securing the scene. As he climbed out of his cruiser, Tell saw some empty cartridge casings lying in the street. He called to a female deputy and pointed them out to her. "Don't let any kids take these as damned souvenirs. Could be prints on them."

Tell ran up to the house. Sofia was sitting on the porch step, crying. There was blood on the driveway, on the open door panel of Able's bullet-riddled Impala. The rear of the Chevy was pocked with bullet holes. So was the garage door and front of the house. Tell saw more holes in the trunk of an old pin oak.

It had to have been an automatic weapon.

"Sofia," Tell said, trotting up next to her, pointing behind himself, "who was in those ambulances?"

Between sobs, she told Tell that Able was riding in the ambulance with his grandson, Amos. Able had been inside the house and was unharmed. Amos had been hit "several times." Amos had been alive when the ambulance pulled out, Sofia said, but his wounds were severe.

Tell said, "Was Amos out here alone when the shots were fired?"

Sofia shook her head. "Evelia was with him. She was inside the car when the shooting started. She said Amos told her to get on the floor. She's scared . . . so scared. But she wasn't hurt. She's next door, with neighbors."

"Who was in the second ambulance, Sofia?"

"My niece," Sofia said. "The shock—well, she's gone into labor. I need to get there. I need to get there, *Jefe*."

Tell looked around the crime scene. The street was swarming with Horton County sheriff's deputies. Seven more deputies had arrived since Tell had made the scene.

He was arguably redundant here. Tell took her arm and helped her to her feet. "Come on, Sofia, Able's people will see to this. You come with me. I'll take you to the hospital."

He took her arm and helped her up. She was shaking and bent over; a mess. His cell phone rang. Julie Dexter again.

Julie said, "Chief, I have a woman on the line who says she knows who attacked Sheriff Hawk's house."

What? Tell said, "Put her through, would you, Julie?"

He saw Billy and waved him over. He said, "Bill, take Sofia here to County General. Able Hawk's grandson has been shot and Sofia's niece is in emergency labor. See Sofia gets anything she needs there and don't let anyone put her off, yeah? You're with her until I say otherwise."

Sofia said, "Evelia? I want her to come with me."

Billy said to Sofia, "Just point me—I'll fetch her."

Tell clapped Billy's back in farewell and said into his cell phone, "We connected?"

"*Jefe* Léon?" The voice was female, Latina. Older. And vaguely familiar to Tell.

"I know you, I think," Tell said.

"We met at the Latino Festival, *Jefe*. You helped my grandson, Richie."

"I remember now," Tell said. "You know something about who tried to kill Able Hawk?"

There was a long pause; labored breathing. Finally, the woman said, "I feel wrong doing this, *Jefe*."

"Well, put that aside," Tell said. "This person used an automatic rifle and turned Hawk's neighborhood into a war zone. Hawk's grandson has been badly wounded. A little girl was almost killed here. Hawk's granddaughter-in-law has gone into labor from the shock of seeing her man shot."

"I call because Able Hawk's wrath could be so terrible for my community," she said. "*El Gavilan* might burn down the whole West Side, looking for the one who shot that boy. And I call because the one who did this has said he means to kill not just Able Hawk, but to kill you too, *Jefe*."

"Who did this, *señora?*"

"Richie has a friend—you picked him up the night you picked up Richie. His name is Magdaleno Ortiz. The one who did this is Magdaleno's cousin, a boy named Diego Ortiz. Diego, he is a member of MS-13. He told Magdaleno what he was going to do to you and to *El Gavilan*. When Richie's friend tried to stop him, Diego beat him with his gun. He knocked Magdaleno unconscious. When Magdaleno came to, he told Richie. Then Richie told me."

"Thank you, *señora*," Tell said. "Thank you. You've done the right thing."

"I trust you, *Jefe*. That's why I tell you. But you shouldn't go yourself to arrest him. Diego is sworn to kill you too."

"I'll be fine," Tell said. "Where does this Diego Ortiz live?"

"I'll tell you, but understand, *Jefe*, there are children in that house too. Women and children."

"I'm not going to let this turn into a slaughter, *señora*. Please believe me."

She gave him the address and a last warning not to go himself.

Tell said, "*Gracias, señora*, but it's my job."

Tell closed his phone. Shouting above the noise of the deputies, he said, "Which of you is in charge here?"

A husky man in his middle forties said, "I'm senior badge here, so I'm saying me." Tell checked the deputy's nametag: Russell Kane. Tell assumed the man must be attempting to fill the void left by Able. Maybe he was loyal to his old chief; maybe he was a politician, eyeing promotion. Either way, he was the man Tell had to deal with.

Tell said, "Russ, I'm short-staffed at the moment. And I think you have a SWAT team at your disposal. Up front, you agree that it's my show."

"What? What's your show?"

"Our imminent raid. But there's a family at the scene—I don't want to turn this into the Alamo."

"What? What the hell are you talking about, Chief?"

"I know who shot Amos Sharp," Tell said. "I know who tried to kill your former boss. And I know where to find the little bastard."

* * *

Walt Pierce listened to his deputy's account of the shooting at Able Hawk's house. At the same time, he fiddled with Shawn O'Hara's laptop.

Pierce was staring at Able's letter to Shawn—Able's note asking Tell Lyon for a meeting at eight P.M. He saw that the e-mail had been forwarded to Lyon's fiancée's e-mail account.

Well, so be it.

He'd have Hawk watched. If Hawk stayed at the hospital, Walt would bide his time.

If Able kept his appointment—and if Tell Lyon got word and showed up? Then Pierce and Strider would be there too.

The two of them would take Lyon and Hawk out while they were isolated and while Hawk was well off his footing.

And hell, maybe Lyon *wouldn't* get word.

Maybe Hawk would be out in that ball field alone—the perfect solitary target.

Pierce said, "Them ambulances get here yet?"

"Five minutes ago," Luke Strider said. "They've got the boy in the emergency room—hear he took at least eight slugs. They don't figure he'll make it."

"What about Diego? He get away?"

"Appears so. For now anyway."

"Any chatter about Diego on the radio—any indication they've identified him as shooter yet?"

Strider shook his head.

Sheriff Pierce nodded. "Good. Go over and kill Diego, won't you, Luke? Shut his mouth for him while there's time."

* * *

The storm was getting worse—it had rained for the last hour and now there were tornado and severe thunderstorm warnings posted for Pickaway County. Patricia was about to shut down her computer when she noticed the flashing icon at the top of her laptop indicating she had e-mail.

She clicked it open, hoping for something from Tell.

She saw it was another e-mail from Shawn.

Salome was curled up on the couch, reading a magazine. Patricia said to her, "Shawn's sent another forwarded note."

Salome stood and said, "Let's have a look."

There was a flash of light and a loud thunder crack above the cabin rattled the windows. The lights flickered, then went off. Patricia's computer screen went black. She'd just plugged the thing in a few minutes before to recharge its spent battery. "Oh, damn it," Patricia said.

Salome said, "Better start scrounging up some candles and opening windows. Power's usually never off less than several hours around these parts."

FIFTY SEVEN

The emergency room doctors turned their attention to Able Hawk—his shirt was soaked through with blood. His pants were stained with blood too. Able's hands were bloodied from pressing on his grandson's gunshot wounds.

One of the doctors said, "Sit down, sir. Where are *you* hit?"

Able pushed the doctor away. "I'm not fuckin' hit! You see to my boy—you see to Amos. This is *his* blood on me. You get my Amos through this, Doc. And you see to that girl there," he said, pointing to Luisa. She was just being rolled in on the gurney. Her brown skin was bathed in sweat; tears in her eyes. "That's my great-grandchild she's having! You see to them two too. You do it now!"

Able felt hands on him again. He cocked back a fist, then saw Deputy Linda Rhodes. Linda said, "Boss, please—take it easy, boss. They're all here now, getting help. Let's get you in the men's room. Deputy Nelson's here to help. We brought you a change of clothes. We'll see they take good care of Amos and your family. TV crews are already outside. Come on, boss, let us get you cleaned up. You can't be seen looking like this."

* * *

Luke Strider was parked two blocks from Diego Ortiz's house. He walked toward the house, his gun in his waistband, hidden by the tails of his untucked shirt.

Luke saw the sheriff's cruisers and the SWAT van parked in front of the Ortiz house and slammed his hand into a tree trunk. He watched as Ortiz was led out in cuffs, surrounded by a dozen armored Horton County deputy sheriffs and SWAT team members. And Tell Lyon was there with them, holding Ortiz by one arm.

* * *

It had taken hours for them to break their suspect down; to get him talking. It was half past six now.

Unbelieving, Tell said, "What did you just fucking say?"

Tell was down close in to Diego Ortiz's face. Diego was cuffed to a chair bolted to the floor. His legs were chained to the chair too. The interrogation room reeked with the sweat of all the deputies crowded in behind Tell and Russell Kane. There were fifteen in all; probably a sixth of Horton County's full complement.

"It was Walt Pierce," Diego said. "He was the one who put me up to killing Able Hawk. To killing *you*. Now, you going to take care of my mother, right? You gonna take care of my sister and see they have help, right? I don't want them turning into *putas*."

"You sign a statement, and I'll see they have all the help they need," Tell said. He looked over at Russell Kane and shook his head. "Do you fucking believe this?"

"Only because I heard it," Kane said. He gestured at a fellow deputy. "Get the paperwork going. Get this cocksucker's statement signed. Then get a judge. Figure me and the chief got us some arrest warrants to obtain." Kane said that last with some relish.

Tell shook his head and said, "You do that, Russ. And tell this crew of yours to keep their mouths zipped on what we've got now. Let's do this pristinely and not tip our hand. I've just got word from an officer of mine that one of Pierce's own men is ready to flip. Ready to testify that one of his fellow deputies confided to him that the deputy raped and killed those women with the assistance of Walt Pierce. We've got that bastard nailed down good and tight now."

Russell Kane said, "Agreed. And my people will keep the secret. All I'm saying is we better go in with an army, it comes time to arrest these two. They don't strike me as surrender material."

"That's why we keep our mouths shut and take them down at a time and place of our choosing," Tell said. "We'll do it when they're off duty, and do it simultaneously, if we can swing it. And we do it far from their fucking headquarters. We don't want to spark a range war."

"Agreed," Russell said.

"Good." Tell waved, backing away.

Kane frowned. "Where you headed, Chief? We've got a shitload of work ahead of us."

"You see to it, would you, Russell? I'll be there for the big bad end, when we take those two down, but right now, I'm overdue at the hospital. I want to check in on Hawk."

* * *

It was a few minutes past seven when Tell found Sofia. She was sitting in a waiting room chair. Evelia was cuddled up asleep on her lap. The little girl was holding a stuffed horse and monkey in her arms. Sofia nodded at Tell.

Tell sat down next to her, said softly, "Any news, Sofia?"

"Luisa's baby is a girl. Luisa's mostly fine, although her blood pressure is still quite high."

"And Amos?"

"Still in critical condition. He was shot in one lung, one kidney and in the stomach. Those are the worst wounds. Many of his ribs are broken. They think the bullets that hit him, most of them, anyway, probably first deflected off the car and the pavement, or else it would have been worse. He's also shot in the arms and legs and hips. But those aren't life threatening."

"Able," Tell said, "is he with Amos?"

She blinked. "Able left an hour ago . . . he said he had an important meeting. He was going to have to try and borrow one of his former deputy's cruisers to keep the appointment, he said."

Tell narrowed his eyes. "Appointment where? With whom?"

"I don't know. He just said he was going to stop in and see how his deputy, Mr. Marshall, was doing. Then he had to be somewhere at eight. He said he would try to be back by ten."

"I can't believe he left Amos like this," Tell said.

Sofia nodded sadly. "Able said he felt useless. He said that sitting here, he was doing nothing, but out there, with his skills, he might at least accomplish something."

"We already caught the one who did this," Tell said. "He's already under arrest. I came to tell Able that."

"Then I really wish that I knew where he is. I know he would want to know."

Tell patted her arm and walked to the nurses' station. A bleary-eyed black nurse looked up at him, then at his nameplate, and frowned. Tell said, "I need to know which room Troy Marshall is in."

The nurse told him, her tone grudging.

Tell checked his watch as he walked fast down the hall: a bit past seven thirty.

Troy Marshall looked up sharply and frowned. "Hey, Chief," he said. "You're cutting it close aren't you?"

"Come again?"

"You're supposed to be meeting with Able at the ballpark at eight." He frowned suddenly. "Jesus, you didn't get the e-mail?"

"What e-mail?"

He told Tell about the note sent to Shawn that Troy had found and forwarded to Tell's wife, Patricia.

"I never got that note."

Troy Marshall cursed. "*Fuck*," he said.

Tell said, "Where's Shawn's laptop? I'd like to see the original note Able sent me."

Troy cursed again. "Fucking Walt Pierce confiscated that computer about one minute after I forwarded the e-mail to your wife."

Tell said, "What are you saying? You saying that Pierce has access to that note?"

"Yeah, he—"

Troy Marshall looked on, confused, as Tell Lyon sprinted from his room.

* * *

Able checked his dash clock—7:42 P.M. His cell phone's alert light was flashing red. He punched in the password to access his voicemail.

It was Russ:

"We've got the fucker who shot your grandson, boss. Got him in custody. Tell Lyon somehow had identification on the little cocksucker. Lyon went along for the arrest and got a confession. I shouldn't do this, but I wanted you to hear it from me, first. Boss, the kid, one of these Mexican gangbangers, said he was sent after you on orders from Walt Pierce. We're working on getting a warrant for Pierce and his deputy, Luke Strider, now."

Able closed his phone. He'd hug Tell Lyon when he saw him. Then he might shoot him.

No way was he letting Pierce or his stooge see jail time.

So Able would go find Walt Pierce and kill him.

Walt would almost certainly burn Able down just out of spite—for not dying to plan.

And if Amos pulled through, he couldn't leave the hospital just to go to a jail cell on forgery charges once Walt ratted them both out. Able *couldn't* let that happen. And Walt had gotten Amos shot; almost gotten Evelia killed. God only knew what living through what she had—and what she had *seen* happen to Amos—would do to Evelia.

Hawk palmed into the lot of the ballpark, tires crunching gravel. The lot was empty and dark.

Able turned off his engine and slipped his gun into his waistband—a precaution born of routine. Hands in pockets, he walked slowly out to the center ball diamond.

In the dark, from the other end of the parking lot, Able could again hear the crunch of tires on gravel. Something very heavy was pulling in.

Able figured Tell must have driven his big old SUV to their appointment.

THEN

The lights were all off at Seth's place as Tell rolled curbside across the street and doused the headlights on his SUV. He slid out quietly, his gun in hand and pressed to his leg to obscure its view. The house looked abandoned. But then Tell smelled wood burning. He saw a flicker coming from the backyard.

Creeping around the edge of the house, he saw Seth sitting in a chair on his back porch next to a small fire set up in a patio stove. Empty beer bottles were littered around his feet. Seth had another longneck in his hand. Drunk as he was, Seth still seemed fairly alert. "That you, Tell?"

Tell stepped out, his gun pointed at Seth's head. "How did you know it would be me?"

"You're the only one who ever visits me." Seth's voice cracked and he said, "I'm sorry, Tell. When you told me your family was leaving ahead of you for the holidays . . ." A long, deep sigh and a shrug. "Anyhow, I figured it was Marita's grief my conscience would have to cope with. Your daughter's grief for losing *you*. Them changing travel plans? I couldn't foresee that. You know?"

Tell stepped into the firelight. "How *could* you?"

"The money was unreal, Tell. It's been going on a long time. I was just smarter than some others. Didn't flaunt it. Didn't rush out to buy the swanky new pad or some goddamn Escalade or Naviga-tor. How'd you figure it out?"

"Nothing brilliant," Tell said. "Your boss, Angel, he kept copious notes."

"Christ, I'm surprised he could construct a sentence," Seth said. Another long pause. "You've come to kill me?"

"I want to. But I suppose I mean to arrest you. Put you on trial for what you've done. Given your day job, we both know what's waiting for you inside. Maybe I can kid myself that's even sweeter than putting you down myself."

Seth smiled sadly. "I owe you, Tell. Seems right I do at least a little something right."

It happened fast: Seth's hand moved to his lap.

From under untucked shirttails, Seth pulled out his service weapon.

Firelight on that matte finish; Tell saw it was a gun.

Tell hesitated firing just an instant—stunned that Seth pressed the gun under his own chin. Tell held his fire the extra half-second Seth required to pull the trigger on himself.

FIFTY EIGHT

Tell slowed as he neared the park. Springsteen's "My Father's House" was playing low on the radio. Tell saw the silhouette of a big pickup truck idling next to a white house that backed up to the ball fields. Only Dodge Rams were built to that over-the-top scale. Tell saw the glow of a cigarette butt jitter once on its way from a mouth to an ashtray and back to a mouth again.

He turned left onto a side street, away from the ball diamonds. He could see the lights from the fields' parking lot, but not much else.

He parked curbside, doused the lights and took out his riot gun. He tossed his white hat onto the front seat and looked down at his tan uniform, cursing Patricia for having talked him out of the black one now that stealth was required. Tell closed the door to his cruiser as quietly as he could and then walked behind the open yards of three houses so he could double back to where the pickup was parked.

Tell crossed the street and walked back in the direction of the entranceway of the ballpark. He slid up close to a darkened, white house. He crept around behind an ornamental shrub planted at the corner of the house. Tell peered around the edge of the evergreen at the pickup truck. It *was* a Dodge Ram, and it was red. The license plate was the same as the one issued to Luke Strider.

Tell figured if Strider was watching the perimeter, Walt might already be lurking on the diamonds somewhere.

A dog barked a few backyards due west. Tell hoped the neighbors and Luke would take it for harmless yammering. The moon was in quarter phase; not much ambient light. A row of pines still obscured the ball fields' parking lot from view.

Tell looked at his sidearm, weighing it. Then he looked at his riot gun. Both were too much. He didn't necessarily want to kill Luke Strider in cold blood. He wanted to arrest him. Make Strider face jail in some institution where he'd receive all the special treatment accorded a bent ex-cop. He also had to assume Walt Pierce was close by, so he couldn't be too noisy. Tell wanted to retain some element of surprise before confronting Pierce.

The concrete porch of the house whose shrub he was hiding behind caught Tell's eye. It was partly demolished—some home-owner's ill-advised attempt at a do-it-yourself improvement project. A big sledgehammer was propped next to the porch. Tell tucked his riot gun between the tree and the house and picked up the sledge, hefted it. Fucking heavy.

He stooped low and ran back to the shrub, lugging the hammer. The house had a four-foot hedge running across the front lawn and down the side to the backyard. There was a gap in the hedge about four feet from the tailgate of where the Ram sat with its lights off and engine on—a gap wide enough for a riding mower to pass through.

Tell crept along the interior edge of the hedge and down the side to the gap. He was stooped low and pressed up tight to the foliage. Tell watched the silhouette of Luke Strider's head and when it was looking west, in the direction of the barking dog, Tell ran low and fast and stopped at the tailgate of the Dodge. He walked slowly on his knees around the back and along the passenger side of the Ram, staying down low under the reach of the passenger side's mirror.

Tell reached the front of the truck. Staying down, he positioned himself in front of the driver's side front bumper. He hefted the sledgehammer, positioned it, then stood up just enough to help his swing.

The sledgehammer hit the front bumper and Tell heard a curse. Then there was the hiss of the driver's side airbag deploying. Tell hefted the sledgehammer for another swing and ran around to the driver's side door. Strider was pinned to his seat by the airbag, struggling to draw his gun.

Tell again swung the hammer.

He realized his mistake too late to check his swing.

Tell had swung in anticipation of breaking tempered glass to get at the driver. But the window was down.

Too late to check the momentum of his swing, Tell winced as he heard Luke Strider's skull crack. Tell nearly gagged. The entire side of the deputy's head was caved in. A dead man, *like that.*

Sickened, Tell pulled out a handkerchief and wiped down the sledgehammer's handle. He walked quickly back to the shrub where he'd left his riot gun and exchanged the hammer for the shotgun.

Tell took a last look at Luke Strider's caved-in head and then sprinted off toward the ball diamonds. He saw a Horton County cruiser and a Vale County cruiser parked alongside.

When Tell reached the main diamond, he saw something glittering close to a dugout. He crept closer and saw it was a handgun. With his handkerchief, he picked up the gun and shoved it down his waistband. He looked around—saw no sign of Able, and no sign of Walt Pierce.

He walked back toward the more remote ball diamonds. He heard angry voices, coming from the direction of the field where Thalia Ruiz's body had been found.

Cautiously, Tell crept toward the voices, moving slowly but steadily through the high weeds.

The rasp of Walt Pierce's voice: "You going to shoot me, just fucking do it, but it'll be your fucking ruin, Hawk."

Tell heard Able say, "Only thing staying my hand for the moment is I don't want to make it that *fast* for you, Pierce."

Tell was close enough to see them both now. Able stood by the tree where Thalia had been found, pointing his gun at Walt's head. Crime scene tape remnants still dangled from the tree.

Pierce was on his knees in the ivy, his hands thrust into the front pockets of his pants. Tell put down his shotgun and holstered his own weapon. Hands in the air he said, "Don't shoot Able, it's Tell Lyon."

Startled, Able looked his way; Walt Pierce too.

"It's okay now, Able," Tell said. "Strider's dead."

"You killed him?"

"Not intentionally."

"Good he's dead," Able said. "I'll do this one, and we'll be all done."

"We can arrest this one," Tell said. "We've got him tight. I've got the MS-13 gang member he sent out to kill you and me. I've got the one who shot Amos, and I've got a signed statement from him, admitting he was sent out by this one to kill us both. But it's even *better*. I've got one of Pierce's own deputies who will testify Strider confided to him that Pierce raped and killed all those women. That Walt and Strider were a team in raping and killing those women. We've got him, all the way up, Able."

"In custody, he'd burn me and Amos down anyway," Able said. That reminded him. "Any more word on Amos?"

"You should be there at the hospital," Tell said.

Able scowled. "Amos fading?"

"No," Tell said. "When I left, there was no change. But you've got a great-granddaughter waiting to meet you."

Walt Pierce grinned meanly. "Fuckin' touching. You two are *amusing*. Lyon, Able's right—I *will* burn him and his grandson down for that license scam. They'll both rot in jail and Able will die in there. But you're too straight-arrow to let Able kill me in cold blood. You said yourself Strider's death was an accident. A fucking Boy Scout—that's how I read you, Lyon. Figure I stay here on my knees long enough, I'll see you two come to blows over what to do with me."

"You've misjudged me," Tell said. "I've concluded you don't read men well."

Pierce shook his head. "Like hell I have misread you."

Tell thought about it—assessed all the angles.

He made up his mind. Again.

But first, he wanted to know how it had been. "What was the arrangement, Pierce? Did Luke rape them and you beat them?"

"I got me some action too," Walt said. "They's just Mexican cunts." He grinned. "You know how good they are. Hell, you're going to marry one."

And I buried one.

But Walt maybe didn't know that. And he couldn't know that Tell had already crossed that bloody borderline to secure justice for his own.

If Pierce knew that, then he would know that Tell was the last man on earth to be expected to deprive Able Hawk having his own private "reckoning" for what had been done to his grandson and for his friend, Thalia.

Tell said, "So how was it? When Thalia left that apartment where she slept with Shawn O'Hara she had no car. Did you pull up in your cruiser and offer her a ride? Called your buddy Luke for a bloody rendezvous?"

"That's close enough," the Vale County sheriff said.

"That's all I want to hear of this," Able said. "You want any more from this cocksucker, Tell, you best get it fast, because I aim to put him down now."

"No," Tell said.

Walt Pierce smiled, misreading Tell's answer. Then the Vale County sheriff frowned as he watched Tell walk over to Able.

"There's a better way to do it," Tell said. "You use this, instead." He reached carefully behind his back and pulled out the sidearm he'd found near the dugout. "This is Walt's gun, I'm guessing."

Able smiled now—a frightening smile. "It is his gun. And it is better. You were running late, Tell. I got antsy. Hid in the dugout and waited to make sure it was you. About halfway across the field, it was obvious from the silhouette it was this short, fat cocksucker. I got the drop on him. Figured this was the right place to put him down." Tell almost smiled at that. Walt's shape was *so* distinctive that Tell had made tentative logical leaps regarding identity based solely on the husky Lego man inadvertently captured by the sport photographer's camera.

Tell said softly, "It'll do. If it was me, I'd do it up close, to the right temple."

"Make it look like a suicide, you mean," Able said. "That works."

"Particularly since I'll be the one finding the body when I come to investigate this murderous bastard's abandoned cruiser come first light," Tell said. "We'll get Doc Parks here and truck his corpse to a Horton County freezer before Pierce's own even know he's missing."

"This ain't fuckin' funny," Walt said, tobacco juice dribbling down his chin now. "You ain't gonna let this bastard shoot me in cold blood, Lyon. We both know that. That's a fucking bad joke's what that is." His stained chin was trembling.

"It's no joke," Tell said, pointing his gun at Walt Pierce's head. "Try to stay still. Take it like a man, Walter. At least you know it'll be quick, like it wasn't for Thalia. Try and be the tough guy now. Might go easier on you in some way. Though I honestly can't see how."

Then Tell hesitated. He said, "Thalia's body was left over there, Able."

Able Hawk nodded. "I know, and yonder would make it perfect, Tell. But this spot where Walt's kneeling? It's *my* ground. It's smack in Horton County, I mean."

Walt was startled to feel the barrel of his own gun suddenly up tight to his temple. His eyes darted sideways toward Able Hawk. "Jesus, Able, stop kidding! This ain't fucking funny!" He wetted his lips. "I swear, I won't say nothing to hurt you and Amos. I swear to God."

"Yeah." Able said, "Keep swearin'. Now close your eyes, Walt. Think of Mexico."

* * *

Walt Pierce lay face down in the bloodied grass. Able pulled Walt's hands from his pockets. Then Able wiped down the Vale County sheriff's gun, pressed it into Walt's dead right hand, and fired another shot into the ground. He plugged the hole with some sod. Able said, "Think that'll fool you come morning, Tell?"

Tell was in no mood for jokes—gallows humor or otherwise. He said, "It'll do fine." He picked up his riot gun. "We best get out of here, Able. Just in case anyone heard the shots."

"They'll think it was kids with firecrackers," Able said. "But I've got to get back to the hospital."

He hesitated, said, "You weren't lying to try and talk me out of shooting this bastard? I mean, you saying that Amos is still hanging on?"

"No, I wasn't lying, Able. But you should get back there. Sofia needs you . . . Evelia too."

"You coming too, Tell? Meet me there?"

"Not right away. I've got a sledgehammer to dispose of."

Able looked confused. Then he said, "There aren't words enough to tell you how grateful I am for you lettin' me do this, Tell." He nodded at Sheriff Pierce's corpse. "With him alive, Amos and I would never have a future. You were right enough on that score."

"Just hope it doesn't cost you later," Tell said. "I mean your conscience."

"Fat chance," Able said. "I'm just pleasantly surprised you let me go ahead with it."

Tell frowned at "pleasantly surprised."

What a ghastly way to put it.

Tell said, "You read about my family. There were never any arrests, never any trials."

"I know," Able said softly. "Sorry you didn't get your closure."

"I got my fucking so-called closure, Able," Tell said. "Though there was nothing like closure in doing what I did to the ones who killed mine. And God evidently didn't care for Walt, so why should I? But there is one big loose end here that can fuck us both up. Troy Marshall saw that e-mail you sent me, asking me to meet you here. And he knows I was headed here to try and keep that meeting. Troy's the one who tipped me to where I was supposed to be. He tipped me to that a few minutes to eight. If he ever talks . . . ?"

Able slapped Tell's arm. "No sweat. Troy won't talk. I'll go see him now, in fact."

"Good," Tell said without enthusiasm. "That's good."

Tell walked alone across the field, back toward the baseball diamonds, his shotgun heavy in his hand.

*   *   *

Tell walked back across the field with something heavier: the sledgehammer he'd used to kill Luke Strider. He wiped off his own prints again. Frowning, he positioned the grip of the hammer in Walt's fat, still warm hands and forced them closed.

He used a blanket to carry the hammer back to the Ram. He dropped it curbside.

Fighting off a shiver, Tell started his car and got her rolling with the headlights off. He drove three blocks in the dark before turning them on.

He checked the clock on the dashboard: ten minutes after nine. Tell called his cousin's house. Chris Lyon answered. Chris said, "What are the damages?"

Tell said, "It's over now, Chris. It's *all* over. If you can handle the drive, I'd like to meet you again in Morton Springs come tomorrow afternoon. Get my lady."

Chris said, "Nah, Tell. Figure tomorrow's same as forever. How about tonight instead?"

"Can't put you out like that, Chris."

"You're not. I hear it in your voice, Tell. I've been there, more than once, where I think you are now. Power's been off, but I have a battery-operated radio and caught some newscasts. I also have cop sources out your way from old days. You need Patricia back with you tonight. But before then, I expect you've got places you should be rather than driving out to Morton Springs. Keep your cell phone on, Tell. Patricia or I will call you when we reach Horton County. All that said, I wouldn't say no to your couch tonight."

Suddenly a shade hoarse, Tell said, "Thank you, Chris."

His cousin said, "You really want to thank me, then tell me while it's still early enough for me to call him that you'll take Roy Atchity's job. Let me get a crew started digging a foundation for your place, pronto."

"Do it," Tell said. "Between the two of us, two weeks from now, I don't ever want to step foot in this godforsaken county again."

ACROSS THE BORDERLINE

Extracts from the *New Austin Recorder*:

Vale County Sheriff's Death Ruled a Suicide

By Barbara Ruskin
New Austin Recorder
Staff Writer

Horton County coroner Casey Parks has found in favor of suicide in the death of Vale County sheriff Walter Pierce.

Shortly before taking his life with a single shot to the head with his own service weapon, Pierce had become a suspect in the rape-murder of Thalia Ruiz, 35, a New Austin single mother. Ruiz's body was found in a field adjacent to the New Austin Kid's Association ball diamonds . . .

. . . New Austin police chief Tell Lyon, citing inadvertently filmed footage of the dumping of Thalia Ruiz's body—footage that he uncovered—confirmed Vale County sheriff's deputy Luke Strider and Pierce as his primary persons of interest in the rapes and deaths of Ruiz and three other area women . . .

. . . Strider's body was found in his red Dodge Ram pickup truck—a truck seen in the film found by Chief Lyon. The Ram was found alongside an access road to the New Austin Kid's Association's ball diamonds' parking lot.

. . . According to Coroner Parks, Strider was killed with a single blow to the head with a sledge hammer found at the scene. "Death would have been instantaneous," Parks told the *Recorder.*

. . . Chief Lyon told the *Recorder*, "The pressure was on the two of them—Strider and Pierce—and they apparently cracked . . . had some kind of falling out.

"We had secured evidence against Pierce and in fact had one of his own deputies lined up to testify against him in the rape and murder of Ms. Ruiz," the chief continued. "We're forced to conclude there was some sort of argument and Pierce evidently killed Strider. Then Pierce walked out to that field where the two of them had dumped Thalia Ruiz's body. On nearly the same spot where Thalia Ruiz was found, Walt Pierce took his own life."

FIFTY NINE

The service was over and the mourners were dispersing. It was stifling heat in which to be wearing black, so consequently everyone was fanning themselves and wiping or swiping sweat from their foreheads with black sleeves or gloves.

Patricia inclined her head in the direction of Shawn O'Hara's mother, a thin, crying woman who lingered over her son's fresh grave.

"I should say something to her," Patricia said to Tell.

"Really don't think so," Tell said. "My instincts are all against it, Patricia. You know how Shawn was after his beating. What he tried to blame you for. If he talked to his mother, and if she meets you face-to-face, now, in this place, and with emotions running so high? I have some bitter experience with that kind of thing at a funeral. All I'll say is that Shawn's note and e-mail to you will look tame by comparison. Please let it be, Patricia. You've both endured enough. Just leave the woman to her grief."

Patricia's eyes briefly flared. Then she said, "You're probably too damned right. She'd likely tear into me."

A voice behind them: "Sadly, she probably would at that." Able Hawk patted Patricia's arm. She offered a cheek and the old lawman kissed it.

Patricia said, "How's your great-granddaughter?"

"Already husky, healthy," Able said. "Built like a Hawk. She's doing just fine."

Tell said, "And Amos?"

"They're 'guardedly optimistic,' whatever the fuck that means. Amos lost a kidney, but I hear that's no obstacle to a life. He's going to be a long while getting his stomach back in order. And he lost muscle in one leg. May have a limp. But they tell me Amos should be able to have a career in law enforcement. If he still wants one when he gets back in the pink."

Tell said, evenly, "That's good—good he can hold on to that dream if he still wants it after all this."

Able said, "Puts him one up on his old grandpa."

Tell said, "Yeah, about that . . ." He pulled an envelope from his pocket and held it up for Able to see.

Hawk looked at the envelope, narrowing his light gray eyes. "What's that?"

"My letter of resignation," Tell said. "I've accepted a post as chief of police of Cedartown, Ohio. In about a minute, I'm going to walk over to the mayor there and quit my job. You should follow me over, Able. I'll recommend you to Rice as my replacement as chief of police."

Able grinned. "You serious?"

Patricia took Tell's arm and inclined her head against his shoulder. "Damn right he is. Lickety-split, you aren't gonna see the two of us for our dust."

Able bit his lip. "Cedartown, that's where your cousin lives, isn't it?"

"That's right," Tell said.

"Then I may just have found my retirement community," Able said. "Two of you living there, place should be like a blissful garrison." Able took Tell's arm and steered him a little ways away from Patricia. He said softly, "You really want me to put in for that job? After Pierce and all?"

"I told you what I did for my family," Tell said. "So I'm in no position to judge you, Able. But I've seen you at work. I've seen the way you do the job when it's not too personal. When you're playing it straight, you're a natural. Nobody better." Tell smiled and nodded as he saw Sofia Gómez approaching, holding Evelia's hand. "And I think you're the right man at the right time for this town. So yeah, Able, *you* should take up my badge."

Able smiled at Sofia and took her arm.

Tell and Able shook hands a last time and Tell held his hand out to Patricia.

Holding hands, they walked toward Mayor Ernest Rice. Patricia said, "Did you see that look between Hawk and Mrs. Gómez? You think they . . . ?"

"I truly couldn't care less," Tell said.

Tell handed the mayor his letter of resignation. The mayor immediately tried to talk Tell out of quitting.

Shaking his head, resisting all the mayor's arguments against leaving, Tell looked over his shoulder and saw Able Hawk approaching.

SIXTY

The Ryder truck filled with their combined possessions pulled out first. Tell backed up his SUV and followed.

Freddy Fender on the radio, singing "Across the Borderline." Patricia sang softly along.

As they pulled out of the apartment complex's parking lot, Patricia turned down the radio. She reached across the seat and took Tell's hand and held it between hers, resting them on her lap.

"Two weeks, and you haven't confided in me yet," Patricia said.

Tell scowled. "Confided what?"

"Confided what really happened that night that Pierce and Strider died."

Tell shot her a glance. "*What?*"

Patricia said, "It was that e-mail that Able sent you asking for a meeting. Able wanted to meet you in the ball diamonds the same night that Pierce and Strider died there. That's a pretty big coincidence, Tell, even to someone like me. There was an electrical storm that kept me from getting that e-mail in time—I mean, in time to alert you to Able's request. But I got access to it the next morning, after news came of Strider's and Pierce's deaths. It ate at me, Tell. So I made a phone call . . . Tell, please don't blame Chris, because I pressed him. I . . . well, I begged Chris to tell me what *he* thought had happened based on what was in the papers. After a lot of pushing on my part, he grudgingly said he was convinced the crime scenes were staged. Chris said that Hawk likely killed Strider, and then killed

Pierce too. Chris said that Pierce's death struck him as a badly staged suicide."

Fucking Chris. What tipped that spooky bastard? And had he sensed Tell's hand in events? Probably.

Tell gave her a longer look. He withdrew his hand. "Why? What made Chris think that?"

Patricia stared at her engagement ring. "Kind of gory, but when Chris explained it, it made sense to me. Chris said that cops see enough suicides with handguns—failed and successful—that they all know to do it what Chris called 'the right way.' He said that cops always do what Shawn did—put the gun in their mouth and shoot through the roof of the mouth. Chris said no cop would ever shoot himself in the temple. He said there was too much danger of brain damage or self-mutilation, but not death."

"It was a big gun, Patricia," Tell said, looking straight ahead. "Enough to get the job done so long as Pierce hit his own head."

"Okay." Patricia hesitated, then said, "But if Able *did* do it, it wouldn't bother me. It's like what you did for Marita . . . for Claudia."

"Playing God, you mean?"

"Getting justice where and when the law can't."

Tell had nothing useful to say back to that. Technically, the law *could* have done the job for Thalia—but the price for achieving it was one Able Hawk wasn't willing to personally pay . . . a cost too high for Able and his grandson. Tell couldn't quibble with that.

They drove in silence for a while, nearing the eastern Horton County line.

Patricia pointed to a billboard that read: "*El Gavilan* is watching."

Able Hawk's icy gray eyes looked down on them.

Patricia said, "He'll update those to reflect his new position, don't you think?"

Tell shrugged and half smiled. He reached back across the seat and took Patricia's hand as they crossed the border.

THEN

It was midnight. Thalia lay in bed, listening, trying to figure out what had awakened her.

After a time, the traffic noise and the creaking of the old walls fell away.

Thalia realized it was the sound of crying that woke her up. She cast off the covers and crept on tiptoe down the hall. She listened outside her daughter's door: Evelia was snoring softly.

She moved a bit farther down the darkened hallway. Standing by her mother's room, Thalia heard her mother sobbing. Thalia raised her hand to knock . . . hesitated. She remembered then it was the anniversary of her father's death.

Thalia started to knock again; hesitated again. She heard her mother say, "Never should have come here . . . *never*. We never should have made that crossing. We were *such* fools."

A sigh. Thalia took another deep breath, centering herself.

She walked down the long, dark hallway and closed the door behind her.

NOW

A young man and his pregnant wife, sitting in the lowest-rung cantina in Tubutama.

The Coyote looks them both over. The young man can't be much more than twenty. He earlier said that he was originally from Sonora. He wears raggedy Levi's, worn boots and a too-small T-shirt promoting the film *Once Upon a Time in Mexico*.

The Coyote figures if these two ever reach the other side, the kid will spend at least the next five years of his life working for chump change hanging drywall for new, shittily constructed gringo houses.

And the young woman—hardly more than a girl, really? The Coyote figures her for eighteen, or less. She is already running to pudgy, the unwanted pregnancy like some spur to her waiting fat cells.

Mexican women rarely lose their baby weight. Well, hardly any of them living in Mexico ever do.

The girl has dyed her hair some J-Lo bogus shade of honey brown—some hue no Latina was ever born with. But the girl is smart enough to know she shouldn't color her hair while carrying a kid: her roots are growing in black. There is a black stripe about three inches wide at her part. The Coyote guesses her for five, maybe six months pregnant.

She stands and excuses herself. Her man—husband? boyfriend?—waits until she is gone and says, "With the baby, she drinks anything, well, you know, her kidneys . . ."

"I have many sisters," the Coyote says. He smiles, revealing gold front teeth. "They get big with child, it's constant pissing, I know, brother."

"I'm not sure we should even be thinking about this," the young man says. "I mean, with her like this now. Maybe it is better if we wait."

The Coyote waves a hand. "Be *harder* then. Then you have *three* bellies to carry water for." The Coyote is overdue on a payment for his new Hummer. He needs the money, so he says, "No, you go *now*. Now, every drink she takes, it's a drink the *niño* gets, *sí?* And you're young, strong. You'll carry your woman, it comes to that, yes?"

"Well, sure, but—"

"A baby, out there, crossing in August? Early September? Even October? You'd lose the child. Better to go now, while she still is a few months out and when you both have two arms to carry the water. When you're not weighed down with a baby. You go *now*. Before the Minute Men increase their numbers. Before fucking Bush puts more National Guard on the border. Before they build more of that goddamn wall."

"You take many across," the young man says, almost decided. "Where do they all go?"

The Coyote smiles again, flashing his gold teeth. He says, "I hear very good things about a place called O-hi-o."

The End